The Third Gate to Hell

A Novel

[signature: Donald Reichardt]

By Donald Reichardt

Based on a True Story

Published by Waldorf Publishing
2140 Hall Johnson Road
#102-345
Grapevine, Texas 76051
www.WaldorfPublishing.com

The Third Gate to Hell

ISBN: 978-1-63684-840-2

Library of Congress Control Number: 2020948826

Copyright © 2020

Disclaimer: This is a work of fiction. Although based on true events, many a matter of public record—widely reported in news media, non-fiction books, courtroom records and U.S. Congressional testimony—the names, characters, locations, businesses, events and incidents in this book are products of the author's imagination. There may be individuals who participated in events similar to those represented in this book, but the characters in The Third Gate to Hell are fictional creations of the author, and any resemblance to actual persons, living or dead, is coincidental.

Cover design: William David, www.WilliamDavidCreative.com
Interior Design: Baris Celik

Table of Contents

Hell has three gates,

Lust, anger and greed.

- Bhagavad Gita

PROLOGUE

We grew up in Wichita, Will Martin and I. He was younger, and we didn't run together. No self-respecting senior would be seen hanging with a ninth grader. So, we observed the social distance high-schoolers and middle-schoolers have practiced since one-room schools disappeared. Yet years later, as adults, twists of fate brought us together in a perplexing dichotomy of success and tragedy.

Wichita was the largest city in Kansas, though it always felt like a small town. Nestled at the confluence of the Arkansas and Little Arkansas Rivers, where the Quivira tribe dwelled on their banks, the settlement was a stopover for adventurers on the Chisolm Trail. My hometown fell on a line between the vast prairie wheat fields to the west, the rolling Flint Hills north of us and roughneck oil fields extending south to Oklahoma and Texas. It was a true crossroads, part of the Louisiana Purchase. If it were not for Jefferson, Monroe and Livingston, I would have grown up speaking French.

To me, Wichita was nothing so complex as its history; it was simply a safe place to grow up in the virtual cocoon of the Fifties.

There were truths we didn't know those days. What we now understand as racism merely meant black people sat in their own theater section. What they called the era of peace and prosperity came on the heels of the Korean conflict claiming thousands of our youngest and brightest. We only knew a scourge that kept us from public swimming pools as a mystery taking a schoolmate's life and confining a member of our church to something called an iron lung.

Years later, we would tell our contemporaries with true nostalgia how much we longed for the good old days.

In high school, all I really cared much about was a set of constants. Preparing with my fellow South Wichita Cougars for a basketball war with Hamilton County. Nurturing a friendship with Sarah Madigan so pure it didn't occur to me I might consider other girls. Making the Dean's List and aspiring to a university business degree.

Taking care never to embarrass my parents. Montgomery and Juanita Johnson's reputation, I think, grounded me and shaped my respect—perhaps fear—of authority more than anything else could have. Being a banker's son, it wouldn't do to have people say, "Those poor people, to have a wild kid like Monty Johnson as a son."

As for Will Martin, his goals and dreams might easily have been nearly identical to mine. Except somewhere in the timeline of his life, when none of us saw it coming, a bright and admirable young man went off the rails.

PART I: The Go-Go Years

1985-1986

CHAPTER ONE

The old Broadview Hotel was an iconic resting spot for the rich and famous passing through Houston. Major entertainers stayed there. Campaigning politicians. Astronauts. Foreign dignitaries.

When the owners commissioned New York architect Felix Moreno to renovate the circa 1930s structure in 1984, he said to the owners, "You shouldn't change much on the outside. Its historic integrity should be preserved. But inside, the sleepy old place needs rejuvenation. It should call out to all who arrive, 'Come stay, and you'll be pampered. Attend an event here, and you'll have the time of your life.'"

True to his vision, Moreno did little to change the Greek Revival exterior—added some decorative embellishments around entrances and windows and installed colorful lighting on the pillared portico and rooftop, which glowed in the night.

Inside, however, he created a wonderland of gold and maroon tapestries, massive icicle-shaped chandeliers, social areas of cushy, colorful seating flanked by twin full-sized, gold-leafed grand pianos. He installed deep carpeting in the corridors which led to bright event spaces featuring modern-art wall designs, decorative pillars and large vertical windows to provide views of the city skyline.

This was the setting for a corporate party on a January evening in 1985. Moreno's renovated Renaissance Ballroom was a perfect place for a celebration, and Quivira Savings Bank had good reason to revel in this elegant space. A player in the high-flying savings and loan industry, Quivira marked its phenomenal recent growth by reaching $1 billion in assets. Employees, shareholders, family members and community leaders congregated in a happy observation of the accomplishment.

A bar was set up at each end of the room, well-stocked with liquor, beer and wine. Two bartenders at each location poured as fast as they could while thirsty partygoers streamed in, tipping generously. White-aproned chefs attended food stations in all four corners with hot hors d'oeuvres. A jazz quartet played upbeat music, competing with the growing crowd noise.

Laughter and loud conversation reached a peak and then slowly abated as the company's leader stepped onto a platform at the front of the hall.

Immaculately dressed in a navy blue suit and matching necktie, the suave and articulate chief executive officer, Will Martin, signaled for the music to stop and waited for silence. As the din finally subsided, he removed his glasses and began to speak, his voice uncharacteristically cracking with emotion.

"This is a great moment for Quivira and a personally happy and proud one for me. When you entered, I hope you picked up a memento of the occasion. Each one has a big 'thank you' message from me and the other officers and directors of your company. That comes from the heart. We couldn't be prouder of the job you've done to help us reach this milestone. But let me assure you, this is only the beginning. We intend to become the biggest player in the history of the thrift industry."

Raucous applause and cheers broke out.

Martin waited a few beats and then held up his hand. "This is not a night for speeches. This is a party to enjoy success. But I'd be remiss if I didn't recognize one man. We owe a lot to him, because he rescued this company from the ashes nine years ago. And, of course, had the good sense to bring me in to run it." Martin flashed a quick smile, and laughter rang throughout the ballroom. "Ladies and gentlemen, show your love for Max Davis."

The sixty-year-old, graying majority owner of Quivira stepped onto the platform and shook Martin's hand as the group cheered again. Davis turned toward the crowd, his cheeks flushed, a grin of pride washing across his face. In a distinct South Texas drawl, he said, "When Will joined us seven years ago, he brought a vision. I knew we had a winner, but I never dreamed we would reach these lofty heights. A billion dollars is a lot of goldarned cheese, y'all."

Again, laughter ran through the attendees.

"But it's also a lot of blood, sweat and tears, and y'all are the ones who made it happen. My personal thanks to each and every one of you."

The applause was almost deafening.

Martin signaled the band to resume playing. The two stepped off the platform and a group gathered around them, shaking hands, patting backs. It was an unparalleled moment of pride and excitement in the meteoric history of the Quivira Savings Bank.

As he walked around working the room, Martin spotted two of his biggest customers talking together, and the CEO stopped to chat. Greg Jacobson was a residential developer headquartered in Arizona but with considerable land and home-building interests in the Houston area. Walker Bannister was one of Houston's most high-profile businessmen, president of the Sugar Hills bank, commercial real estate speculator and current president of the Houston Chamber of Commerce.

"Hey guys. Glad you could come," Will greeted

them with a friendly, warm smile.

"Wouldn't have missed it," said Bannister, shaking Martin's hand and taking a sip of his long-neck beer. He was tall and rangy, about forty. His wavy blond hair was neatly cut and styled, and his Armani suit and hand-crafted Hardy Harrison cowboy boots evidenced his personal tastes. His deep voice was clearly that of a native Texan. "Don't forget, we're preferred shareholders of your budding enterprise. We're keeping an eye on how much you spend on a shindig like this." He laughed heartily.

"Seriously, congratulations, Will," Jacobson chimed in. He was older than the other two, mid-fifties, balding and neatly bearded. What he lacked in handsome good looks compared with his two friends, he made up for with an abundance of radiant charm. "Quivira has been good to us, Will. Just keep those lines of credit open, okay? We're going to ride this Houston wave as long as the surf's up."

Will turned serious for a moment. "The surf is oil, my friend. And right now, the tide looks like it's starting to ebb."

Walker Bannister scoffed. "Bullshit. It's only temporary. The whole damned world runs on oil. As soon as the Arabs quit playing around with production, you can stop worrying."

"I hope you're right. Now, guys, if you'll excuse me, I need to make the rounds. Talk to you both soon." He disappeared into a crowd of noisy well-wishers.

Bannister turned to his Arizona friend. "Will's really got this company in high gear. Let's hope he's doing the right things."

"What do you mean?" Jacobson asked.

"It seems to me he's getting pretty—what you might

call—creative with how he's raising assets. You know, mortgage loan pools, land swaps, subordinated debentures, preferred stock deals, all of that kind of shit."

Jacobson leaned back and chuckled. "I've noticed you haven't been too shy to take advantage of some of those deals."

The Houston businessman grinned. "I'm not ungrateful for the opportunities to make a little money. I hope he's not over-heating the thing. He needs to be sure it's good capital he's raising, not investment watering down their asset base."

Greg Jacobson laid a hand on the taller man's shoulder. "Walker, you worry more than my eighty-year-old mother. You know all Quivira has to do if their loan losses get too heavy is run up to Dallas with their hat in their hand. Those regulators at the Home Loan Bank will say, "Here, Will, we'll loan you another fifty million dollars. Have a nice day."

The two real estate speculators roared together.

CHAPTER TWO

Will retreated from the soirée while many of the partygoers remained, eating, drinking and dancing drunken-
ly to the band's music. Lawson Jeffries, Quivira's newest
employee and friend from his hometown in Kansas, left
with him.

"I've got a suite rented upstairs," Will said to Lawson as they approached the elevators. "Let's go have a
nightcap and get caught up. I haven't had a chance to say
ten words to you since you joined us here in Houston."

Jeffries was a big man, six foot six, with broad shoulders and a thick shock of wavy black hair. A graduate of
the University of Kansas City, he was four years Will's
junior. He followed his boss onto the elevator. "You've
been as busy as a one-armed bandit. I don't see how you
do it, Will."

Unlocking the door, Will motioned Lawson in. The
600-square-foot executive suite greeted them with subtle
earth tones and maroon and gold accents. The parlor's
marble floor was partially covered with a stunning, deep-
red Persian rug. The room featured a long, plush, cushioned sofa, several matching accent chairs and a highly
polished cherry-wood coffee table. A desk in one corner provided workspace without being obtrusive, and a
well-stocked bar beneath a gold-framed mirror lined the
opposite wall.

"Now this is what I call living," Lawson said, whistling.

"What're you drinking?" Will asked.

"A beer for me, thanks," Lawson answered.

Will went to the bar for the drinks while Lawson
stood staring out the wall-length, floor-to-ceiling win-

dow, admiring the glow of the downtown lights below. "You've come a long way from Wichita, Mr. William Randolph Martin."

Handing Lawson a beer, Will smiled and sank into a deep-cushioned chair. He loosened his tie and took a sip of his scotch. "As have you, Lawson. I just realized we're celebrating your first year at Quivira. Cheers." He raised his glass in toast.

Lawson tipped the neck of his beer bottle toward Will and nodded acknowledgement. "I really appreciate your giving me the job."

"No regrets? Leaving your home state, I mean? Cutting ties with the good old Wichita Savings and Loan?"

Lawson flopped into the sofa opposite his boss. "I miss the people."

Will took another drink and frowned. "I mean, everything's so slow there. So damned conservative. I couldn't wait to get away from the old-fashioned way of doing things. I'll never forget trying to push the city into a downtown renovation project. Remember? When I was president of the Chamber of Commerce?"

"Everyone said you came up with a great plan. And impressive presentation."

"And they turned it down flat, when they saw the price tag," Will groused. "Backward thinking. When I got down here, everything changed. I realized how great it is to live in a high-class neighborhood. Drive a car I didn't ever dream I could afford. Order custom-tailored suits and not have to ask what they cost. Lawson, I'm convinced you did the right thing, answering my call to come to Houston. I rescued you. Meanwhile…"

"Meanwhile…" Lawson repeated.

"We're going to keep growing this baby, Lawson.

You're going to get crazy rich. All of us are."

"I'm curious, how'd you come up with this idea to use your major borrowers to grow your capital?"

"The *quid pro quo*?" Will laughed. "Actually, we copied the idea from our federal regulators, the Home Loan Bank."

"You're joking."

"I'm not. When they lend us funds, we have to pay them a fee up front, and of course a yield on the money. But they also require us to purchase stock in the bank. So, I'm thinking, why not do the same thing. A developer comes to us and wants to borrow, say, ten million dollars for a project. We tell him we need something extra. We determine the fees, the yield, and what more would be required. The borrower might buy a junior piece of our loan pool or a parcel of troubled real estate from our portfolio. In many cases, they purchase preferred stock in Quivira."

Lawson's mouth hung open as he listened. "I think it's ingenious," he said. "But doesn't the land have to be appraised?"

"Sure. You've been here long enough to see how fast Texas real estate values are accelerating. A property goes on the market and its's gone the next day, at its estimated value or higher. Getting higher appraisals to meet our purpose is no problem."

"And this *quid pro quo*. It's perfectly legal?"

"Right, my old friend. It's perfect, and it's legal. Like I said, we got the idea from our regulatory agency. Speaking of which," he took a swallow of the drink, thinking, "I'm going up to Dallas next week to meet with those guys. Why don't you come along and see how we work with them?"

"Hell, yeah. Count me in."

"You'll be amazed. They treat me like a rock star. Have me picked up at the airport in a limo. Take me out to a club for lunch. More examples of the many perks coming with success."

Lawson finished his beer and stood, his hulking frame seeming to fill the room. He chuckled. "Sounds as if you've gotten used to living large."

Will looked up at him and raised his glass again. "Lawson, you do get used to it. It's a far cry from our humble beginnings in little old Wichita damned Kansas, my friend."

CHAPTER THREE

A man pushed through the revolving doors of the new office building in downtown Houston, walked into the lobby and continued past the entry door of Quivira Savings Bank. On his way by, he peered into the bank's large windows. The interior made it clear the staid, drab banks of the past, with marble columns, straight-back wooden chairs and barred teller windows were giving way to low-top, wicket-less customer counters and cushioned seating bathed in warm colors.

He continued ahead to the elevators, stepped into a car and within seconds exited on the twentieth floor, home to Quivira's executive offices.

"Hello, Bernard. Welcome. I'm Will Martin."

The son of powerful Texas Senator Travis Franklin returned the firm handshake of his host who greeted him in the foyer and flashed a wide smile.

"Call me Bernie. Never liked Bernard." The senator's son was the exact image of his father when he was thirty-five, with wavy dark-blond hair and a smooth face that seemed set in a permanent grin. Bernie's tinge of lone star state accent made him sound like some crossover country singer.

Will pushed his monogrammed French cuff back, and a ten-thousand-dollar designer watch gleamed in the light. "You're right on time. Come join me in the boardroom. I had some coffee brought in."

Franklin followed Will down a corridor and into a well-lighted room. Its long chrome and glass table and posh high-back chairs were befitting of an aggressive, go-go investment institution. Large abstract paintings, originals by Texas artist Dorothy Hood, lined the walls and added splashes of bright colors to the eye-popping, dazzling meeting space.

The CEO of Quivira Savings Bank stood at the end of the table and motioned his guest into a chair next to him. Will was slim and handsome, his thick hair showing hints of gray. He carried his body erect, exuding an air of confidence and control as he spoke. There was no small talk. As he settled into his seat, he got immediately to the point of the meeting. "Bernie, as I told you on the phone, I thought we should get acquainted. I'm interested in nominating you to our board of directors."

Will poured two cups of coffee and slid one in front of Bernie. "Cream? Sweetener?"

Bernie Franklin shook his head and took a sip of the hot brew. "I have to admit I'm intrigued. And hell, if you want me on your board, I'd be so inclined. But why me? I don't have a background in banking, and certainly not savings associations. I'd probably be as worthless as tits on a silverback gorilla." He grinned like a schoolboy keeping a secret.

For the first time, Will laughed. "That's why. You'd keep things loose around here."

They both paused to enjoy the moment.

"Seriously, Bernie, I talked to one of your business partners about you. Greg Jacobson's a good friend and stockholder of Quivira. He vouched for you. Look, most of our directors have been around here a long time, and they're good people. But they're either lawyers, old-time bankers or real estate people. We're opening up our business to a whole new way of thinking—to more commercial ventures and development deals. With your background in oil exploration, and with your contacts, I think you'd be a great asset. You could help us expand our business interests and bring in new and exciting kinds of borrowers. And investors. Not the least of which is the energy sector, which I think will know no limits."

"No limits? Are you sure? Will, you have to have seen what's been going on with crude prices?"

Will answered, "Yes. I have to follow them. We're in Texas, right? Oil is what we're all about. I'm aware the industry has slipped some the past few years. But Bernie, it looks to me like—and you tell me if I'm wrong—the slide has started to level off this year. Spikes come after dips, right? Reagan's in the White House now; he's not going to let the damned Arabs drive the prices down. I know a lot of banks and savings and loans have struggled the past several years, but with friends in Washington, we're going to put those days in our rearview mirror."

"Makes sense to me. I hope you're right."

Martin continued, "I wanted you to come in so I could show you around, familiarize you with our operation and our progress since I came in as CEO. And of course, be sure there are no conflicts of interest, and agree you'd be a comfortable fit. Are you familiar with the Garn-St. Germain Act?"

"Sort of. I didn't pay much attention to it when it passed Congress, actually. The Depository Institutions Act, right?"

Martin nodded.

Bernie continued, "It's the law they passed to turn you dogs loose, if I understand it. You got deregulated, opening up all kinds of options for you to do a lot more than little old mom and pop home loans."

"Free at last, free at last," Will quipped. "When I was an officer of a little savings and loan in Kansas, I got restless thinking about all the great investments we could get into. But we were held back by our charters. I tried and tried to get management to take us to the limits of the law—you know, real estate development, high-end business deals—but they wouldn't listen." He frowned. "They thought it was a big deal when the feds let them start offering checking accounts. I think they were afraid of pushing the envelope."

"My impression is most of the thrifts were run that way."

"True, even this one here in Houston before I showed up. About the time the government started talking about relaxing the rules, Max Davis offered me the top job here. This was a little thrift called Pasadena Savings and Loan. When I arrived, the first thing I did was change the name, and the second was to develop an aggressive business plan. As soon as we were free to do it, we got very creative about issuing preferred stock and investing in a more diversified portfolio."

"Is he still involved in the business?"

"Max owns eighty-five percent of the common stock, but it's a much larger pie now. And the deal was, when he brought me in, I would run the show. That's the only way I'd agree to come. When I took over in 1978, we had assets of barely $60 million. When our business plan started taking off, we increased assets from $216 million in 1982 to pushing well over one billion today, three short years later."

Bernie whistled. "Wow, you've had pretty phenomenal growth."

"We're not done yet. With savvy board members like you, we can trigger investment deals no one could have imagined five years ago. The stratosphere's the limit. We're going to become the biggest player in the industry. What do you say?"

"You mentioned conflicts of interest," Bernie said, "so I'll tell you up front, I had a significant loan from one of your borrowers."

Will leaned forward, listening intently.

"The developer from Arizona who you said vouched for me, Greg Jacobson. It was a—what you might call—an unusual arrangement. He gave me a sizeable loan, but he controlled the money and invested it. If it made money, I'd get the profit; if it lost, he'd forgive the loan."

"My God!" Will exclaimed. "What kind of deal is that?"

"A good one," Bernie grinned.

"I'll say. How does it stand?"

"It lost money, and it's all a thing of the past. I don't owe anything. It's been forgiven. So, I wouldn't consider it an existing conflict. Greg and I have done business deals in the past, but we don't have anything going at the moment."

"I'll run it by legal counsel. But I think they'll see it your way. And so will I. What do you think, Bernie?"

"Hell fire, Will, I say let's do it," Bernie Franklin answered, laughing. "Where do I sign?"

Will stood and walked to the window, looking out over an elegantly landscaped pond and waterfall. He turned back and asked, "One question, Bernie. Your father. Do you think your being on our board would create any problems for the senator?"

Bernie shook his head no. "We've always had a clear understanding. He runs his business and I run mine. Hell, he's not even up for re-election for two more years. As long as neither of us does anything against the law, we'll keep out of each other's way and won't worry about what people think."

"Oh, well, wait a minute. I didn't say you wouldn't be asked to do anything illegal," Will said with a stoic gaze.

There was a brief moment of confused silence, then Bernie broke into robust laughter. "Well, all right then," he said, "as long as you show me how not to get caught."

It wasn't usually his style, but Will leaned back and guffawed loudly in unison with the senator's son.

CHAPTER FOUR

The glass and chrome conference table of the Quivira Savings Bank glowed like fireworks as mid-morning rays streamed through the enormous windows and produced a rainbow of neon colors. The visual brilliance of the space was accompanied by the board members' animated conversation and hearty laughter, producing a pleasant symphony of sight and sound. This was the boardroom where Chairman Max Davis got to be the head honcho once a month. He was among those arriving, greeting other directors, shaking hands and pouring coffee at the long, transparent credenza lining the side of the room. The atmosphere bordered on joviality, in contrast to many corporate board meetings where solemnity and stiffness are the unwritten rule.

As Quivira's leaders slowly settled into their usual places around the glistening table, the two newest members stood waiting and then took the remaining open chairs. Davis sat at the head of the table. He wore a western-style sports jacket, bolo tie and cowboy boots. His Stetson hat rested near the coffee urn on the credenza. Next to Davis, at his right, sat the stylish CEO, dressed in his usual navy blue suit and tie.

"Good morning, everyone," Davis drawled and grinned widely as the jocular din ebbed. "Thank you for coming. The December meeting of the Quivira Savings Bank Board of Directors will now come to order. You all should have received the agenda a week ago. But go ahead and scan through it and we'll get started."

Office staffers had laid a binder at each place with an itinerary clipped to the top.

As the group perused the material, Davis continued,

"First order of business, I want to welcome our two newest board members. You all know who they are, because you voted them in..."

Muted chuckles echoed around the room.

"...But this is our official welcome. First, Mr. Bernard Franklin. He prefers to be called Bernie."

Max led the applause as the senator's son half-rose from his seat and nodded around the room, acknowledging their welcome.

"And Stanley Russell, our new chief financial officer."

Again, a round of applause, and Russell gave them a wave.

"As y'all know, Stanley comes to us from the auditing company of West & Eberhart. So, he'll be paramount in making us toe the line, as he always did when he was on the other side grousing about our numbers."

More laughter rippled through the boardroom.

"Being that this is Christmastime," Max continued, "and our annual party is scheduled to start in one hour over at the Broadview, we have an abbreviated meeting plan. I don't want to delay getting started on the eggnog any more than necessary."

Again, the room rang with laughter.

Max continued, "I assume each of you will introduce yourself to Bernie and Stan if you haven't already done so. Meanwhile, I'm going to turn the meeting over to Will, who will walk us through today's business."

The CEO picked up his folder and flipped open the cover, all business. "If you'll take a look at page one, we'll begin. There's a list here of the loans we want to cover today. You received this information in advance, and I'm aware most of you have discussed them with the lawyers. But let's take as much time as you need to express your opinions."

Will went through the proposals one by one, and several prompted a robust discussion about their appraised value, the economic prospects for the areas of Houston involved, the thoroughness of the underwriting and the financial viability of the applying developer. The board approved every application by unanimous vote.

They finally came to the last proposal, a loan requested by real estate developer Greg Jacobson. "As you know," Will began, "Greg has an outstanding loan from us for a development in Florida totaling a bit over $10 million. This new loan, which both the investment and executive committees have approved, is for a new Arizona project he's involved in amounting to $14.6 million. The details are outlined in your books. On the basis of the appraisal, and Mr. Jacobson's security of undeveloped land located in the Houston metropolitan area, the committee recommends approval."

"Will, you said his project is valued at $14.6 million," said Max Davis. "But the bottom line on the loan is $17 million."

"That's right," the CEO responded. "As part of the deal, Jacobson has agreed to buy $2.4 million of Quivira preferred stock."

CFO Russell added, "So he gets his $14.6 million for the development and invests the rest in Quivira stock, to help us grow our assets. *Quid pro quo.*"

A recent addition to the board, real estate broker Amanda Whitfield, spoke up. "Will, did we get an appraisal for the $17 million?"

"We did," Martin assured.

Amanda nodded. "Also, I don't see anything here

about the location of the collateral property."

"Good question, Amanda. It's up north of Houston Intercontinental Airport. Greg hopes in the near future to explore the feasibility of a residential community there, similar to The Woodlands."

Amanda asked, "Will, not to get off track, and admittedly I'm new to Quivira's *modus operandi*, but this list seems pretty short, even for December. Are things slowing down?"

"Not at all. The fact is we don't bring you every transaction that crosses Quivira's desk. Our loan officers approve all the residential mortgage applications. And since we wanted a short meeting today, we agreed the investment committee could approve some commercial projects that might otherwise come before the full board. The list here represents those totaling a significant amount. So, let's get back to the Jacobson application. This one involves Bernie Franklin."

He turned toward the new board member. "Bernie, you have something you'd like to say?"

Franklin rose. "Will, if I may, before you take a vote, I'd like to let you know Greg Jacobson is not only a friend of mine, but he has also been a business partner of mine at certain times. Not too long ago, he floated me a $100,000 loan. I won't go into details except to say it's no longer outstanding. Still, to avoid even the slightest appearance of a conflict of interest, I think it would be best if the board review and vote on it, except I'll abstain from voting."

Several directors nodded in agreement, and Will stated, "We all agree, Bernie. As for you other directors, as you know outside counsel has reviewed this one and recommends passage. Now let's take a vote. All in favor of granting this loan in the amount of $17 million, a show of hands, please."

The approval was unanimous.

"The loan is approved," Will said. "We have one more item of business— the executive compensation plan. As you know, since our current officers took over operation of Quivira seven years ago, we've experienced what I hope you agree is pretty impressive growth. Under tab two of your binders, you'll find a proposal as we go into 1986 outlining bonuses for reaching certain growth targets. They are aggressive goals, but ladies and gentlemen, we intend not only to hit them, but to exceed them. Our consultants think what is proposed for the bonuses would be fair compensation if we can significantly increase the value of the company."

"I move we accept the compensation plan as proposed," said Amanda.

"I'll second it," Bernie Franklin agreed.

Will said, "All in favor, hands please? The plan is adopted."

Following the meeting, Will retreated to his office. It was four times the size of the small cracker box he worked out of as treasurer of the Wichita Savings and Loan. In a show of respect for Max Davis, Will had agreed to transport the office furniture from the Pasadena offices when he moved the firm into this classy new building. So, his desk and chair, and the side chairs as well, were modest oak pieces from the previous Pasadena Savings building. But the appointments were new; Will personally picked them out for his office as well as for Max Davis'. Muted sea green Jerome Baxter grass cloth lined the walls. The chair rails were African mahogany, and the floor was Argentine walnut, partially covered by a floral blue Persian area rug with cream accents. His wall displayed three Marco Gillman western paintings depicting cowboys on horseback.

Sliding open a desk drawer, Will pulled out a fresh white shirt, neatly folded by the cleaners, to change into for the party. As he began to tear away the paper band, CFO Stanley Russell appeared in his doorway. Stanley had a paunchy physique and almost comically round face to match. His dark mustache seemed to droop a bit on one side, a feature made more noticeable by a slight lisp in his speech.

"Will, before you leave, can we have a word?"

"Of course, Stanley. By the way, thanks for putting together the bonus proposal."

The financial man drew his mustache up into a smile. "Well, I had some help from the compensation consultants. But I never dreamed one of my first tasks on the job would be to put together a plan to pay you nearly half a million extra next year."

Will's smile was barely perceptible. "You know as well as I do those goals are going to be hard to hit. I'll need to have my boots and spurs on to get the money. Besides, you put a little sweetener in there for the new chief financial officer, am I right?"

"Of course," Russell said. "It was a joke, Will."

"So, what'd you want to see me about that can't wait? We have a party to go to."

"I was wondering if you've seen the new audit report yet?"

"I have. I only had a chance to glance through it." Will finished pulling the paper band away and unfolded the shirt, examining it.

"Did you notice the advisory for us to restate the

financials?"

"I skimmed through it. Why?"

"If we restate the numbers, it'll result in loss reserves large enough to prevent us from paying dividends to our preferred stockholders."

The CEO was pulling off his necktie, but he stopped dead-still, absorbing the information. He turned to Stanley. "Prevent us from paying dividends for four consecutive quarters?" he inquired.

Stanley nodded yes.

Will stood motionless, in thought. "That could be disastrous."

"Not could, would! More than disastrous," Stanley confirmed. "You and Max together hold more than 95 percent of the company's common stock. Max alone has nearly 85 percent. If you fail to make those dividend payments, you'll give it all up. You'd lose control of Quivira."

Will stared into his finance officer's eyes. He never exhibited panic, and rarely did his expression register concern. He was a classic stoic. But this time, he looked as if a missile was whistling right at him. He froze for only an instant, then rallied. "Those sons-of-bitches. Look, there has to be a way around this. Can we fire the auditors and hire new ones?"

"Of course, but there's no guarantee another firm would play ball."

"Tell you what, Stanley. Let's you and I go to the party and get good and drunk. Tomorrow we'll start thinking about this problem and what the solutions are. I said solutions, plural, because every problem has more than one. In fact, I think we should meet with our outside counsel. Jason Bernstein is one of the most creative damned attorneys I've ever known. Let's see what he can dream up. And Stanley?"

"Yeah, Will?"

"No one else needs to know about this."

CHAPTER FIVE

Houston was a chilly forty-five degrees at nine o'clock in the morning on the second day of January 1986. Will scrunched down into his jacket as he filled the tank of his Mercedes less than a mile from his house in the stylish River Oaks subdivision. Unlike two periods in the 1970s, gas was plentiful.

Twice in his adult life he experienced long gas station lines as Middle East countries manipulated oil production. He lived in his native Kansas during the first, in 1970. Wichita had a history of oil production and refinery and the gas-glut price wars typical of oil towns. But during the shortage, cars waited in long lines to fill up.

The second episode would be easy for him to remember—the so-called 1979 Carter shortage. First, because it occurred about one year after Will moved to Houston and assumed his position with Pasadena Savings, now Quivira. But also, that year marked his divorce from his wife, Prudence.

As he drove back home, he passed houses valued between ten and fifteen million dollars. Most locals considered the neighborhood one of Houston's most exclusive. The sons of the Texas governor developed it in the 1920s, and it was historically home to a number of local celebrities and politicians.

Will's English Tudor two streets away was more modest. But still, his elegant five-bedroom abode was priced at nearly $1.5 million when he bought it.

A realtor showed him the house his first week in Houston, before Prudence flew in to join him. When she arrived, Prudence expressed strong concern about being able to afford it. After all, Will was leaving a position in

Wichita with a small savings association paying modest salaries. The two had been married more than ten years, but the expenses of raising a daughter and the high cost of living in the early Seventies dictated living in a modest four-bedroom home in a middle-class Wichita neighborhood.

River Oaks was a different world. That became evident the moment they entered the neighborhood and drove the long, circular drive toward the house, empty and ready for a buyer to move in. A dense grove of Texas pecans, the state tree, separated the driveway from a sweeping lawn of thick, carpet-like Saint Augustine grass. The house stood out as one of the few Tudor structures in the area. It was typical of that unique architecture. Its design of brick, accented with decorative timbering and stucco between the boards, was reminiscent of an English country estate.

"This style was really popular before we were born," Will told Prudence as he unlocked the lock box with the key the agent had entrusted to him. "It's not what we're used to seeing, but Pru, wait until you see the inside."

As they entered, it was immediately apparent the interior complemented the appearance of the exterior. It featured wall paneling and ceiling beams of dark wood. Because of the steep-pitched roof and front-facing gables, the home's multi-paned windows were tall, narrow and grouped to permit ample light inside.

"Wait until you see the kitchen," Will enthused, motioning Prudence to follow him. She gasped at the size of the large room, obviously recently remodeled with new, gleaming appliances and red, blue and yellow Mexican tile wall accents.

"I love the house, Will. But it's way out of our

reach," Prudence protested. "I know we have some cash saved up, but we have to keep saving for Hannah's college."

"We can't live here like we did in Wichita," Will argued. "I'm a CEO now, with a great salary and stock in the company. We'll be entertaining important people, and we have to step up our lifestyle. Besides, when Max offered me the job, he gave me this advice: 'When you buy a house, bite off more than you can chew.' He said with salary increases and bonuses, we would very quickly grow into a house like this."

Federal rules forbade him from getting a loan from his own savings and loan. So, Will got a mortgage from Sugar Hills Bank, whose president he was pursuing as a Quivira customer, and he and Prudence moved in.

* * *

A CEO title was what Will had dreamed of. He was able to put his gregarious style and persuasive ability to work in landing new business. An upscale standard of living, far more stylish than any he could previously afford, went with it.

But his marriage fell apart. Prudence had balked at the idea of moving from their hometown. But Will had a way of convincing people, his wife included, he was right.

"Honey, just go down there with me," he said many times, in various ways, "and I promise you won't regret it. We'll have a lifestyle you've never begun to dream of."

Yet barely a year after they settled in, Prudence and their daughter moved back to Kansas. It wasn't a sudden decision. On several occasions, she warned Will of her dissatisfaction. One evening before she left, with Hannah in bed for the night, she poured them each a glass of beer and turned off the TV.

"I was watching the news," Will complained.

"We need to talk," Prudence said, sitting down next to him on the couch. "I knew this move wouldn't work out. I don't like Texas, and I don't like Houston." She took a sip of beer and drew in a deep breath. "And Will, you're becoming someone I don't think I like anymore, either. You obsess with work. Our only friends are the people you schmooze for business. I think you fit in with this city, and with your business crowd, perfectly. But I don't. This isn't the life I want for me and Hannah."

Will gave her a perfunctory hug. "Give it time, Pru. You'll grow to love it."

He turned the television back on, paying no attention to her tears welling up.

A week later, when she flew to Wichita, ostensibly for Hannah to see her grandparents, she simply never returned to Houston.

"I'm staying here," she said on the phone. "I'm going to file for divorce."

Distraught, he implored her to reconsider in the long and tortuous call. "We can work this out. I've given you a wonderful home here. Hannah needs us both."

"I'm tired of playing second chair to your career." Her tone was flat and dispassionate. "Will, what happened to you? You used to be kind and thoughtful and considerate. Now it seems all you care about is money. Having expensive things. Being somebody important."

"I want us to have a great life. What's wrong with that?"

"Money won't do that, Will. We could have been happy in Wichita," Prudence lamented.

"Maybe you could have," he argued. "I wanted more than Kansas had to offer."

After a moment's hesitation, Prudence responded, "I didn't need a big, high-priced house to be happy. But you had to have it. We could easily have gotten by with our station wagon. Yet you had to have a luxury car that cost twice as much. I don't need to dress up and eat out four nights a week at posh restaurants, but you always insist. The baby-sitting costs alone are staggering."

There was a long, agonizing silence, and then Will gave it one last try. "Please, Pru, I can change."

"No, you can't," she responded tersely. "I'm sorry, Will. But I don't love you anymore. I've talked to a lawyer. We will both be better off going our separate ways."

* * *

Will turned into the wide driveway and remotely opened one of four garage doors. He noted Max Davis' Porsche parked at the curb. Max was a laid-back sort as he grew older and loosened the reins on the business, but he was still a stickler for punctuality.

"You said nine, right?" Max muttered as Will parked and motioned him into the garage.

"Sorry," Will said sheepishly. "I had to run over and gas my car up. Let's go inside. It's colder than Kansas out here. "

Inside, Max asked, "Where's your family?"

"Leslie took the kids out to Corky's Pancake House for breakfast," Will explained. "She doesn't like to be underfoot when I'm working."

Davis nodded. "Well, I have to say, I didn't really get to know your first wife before she took off. But I think this one's a real peach."

"Sunflower."

"What?"

"The sunflower is Kansas' state flower. Leslie grew up in Kansas, so she's a sunflower. Peaches come from Georgia."

Max cackled. "Peach. Sunflower. Whatever, she's a real humdinger."

"Now, there's an expression I haven't heard since I was a kid," Will grinned. He motioned for Max to sit at the kitchen table. "Want some coffee? I started the pot before I left."

Davis nodded yes as he settled into a chair. "And while you're at it, Will, got anything to spice it up a little?"

Will grinned and went to the bar. "Amaretto okay?"

"Perfect," Max answered.

Will poured coffee for the two of them, added generous amounts of the liqueur and sat down beside Davis.

Max said, "So Jason has an idea for getting out of this mess, huh?"

"He says so," Will responded. "Whatever he's proposing, I don't think we're going to need a permanent fix. The economy's gone through such a rough patch, it seems like everyone is gun shy. I think this will be a good year for us."

Max frowned. "Damn, I hope you're right. But I was looking at some of the numbers, and they're downright scary so far in this decade. All savings associations' aggregate net income was $781 million in 1980, and two short years later it had turned negative. You know, we rarely had failures in the past. Now, in the first three years of the Eighties, we had over one hundred savings and loan closures. All told, they represented over $40 billion in assets. Forty damned big ones right down the tubes. And that doesn't include all the mergers which technically were belly-ups, too. You know as well as I do a lot of our colleagues are running busted companies based on the book value of their net worth. They should be closed, but the regulators don't have the funds to settle their accounts. So, they limp along, broke, but they don't shut down."

"I know, Max. I'm aware of all of that. Everybody's struggling with what happened to real estate values during the recession. But damn it, we're going to be all right. We're getting into the kind of ventures offering much higher interest rates and giving us opportunities for equity positions. So, when these projects we're investing in catch a trade wind and make some money, we'll be there to cash in."

He continued, "Meanwhile, this *quid pro quo* program I started is working like magic. By jacking up appraisals of the developers' projects, they can use the excess of the loan to buy our preferred stock. We don't have to run to Dallas all the time, begging the regulators for money. Max, we'll be fine. As soon as Jason figures us out of this current dilemma."

"My God, I hope you're right,"

The doorbell rang.

"That'll be Jason." As he rose and left the room, Will said over his shoulder, "You worry too much, Max. I'll bet you a hundred our lawyer has a fix for us."

CHAPTER SIX

Jason Bernstein was considered a top corporate lawyer in Houston circles. Will met him at a Sugar Hills Country Club dinner-dance only months after moving to Houston. It only took two weeks for the Quivira CEO to bring the young, brainy attorney into the association's legal circle.

Bernstein was fortyish and portly. Rimless reading-style glasses perched on his wide nose and emphasized the large size of his nearly bald head. He moved quickly and decisively, as if he had only one minute to address the judge. The lawyer was all business as he hurried into the kitchen and sat with them at the table, setting his briefcase on the floor. He had no charts or handouts; this would be a tell, not a show and tell.

Will wasted no time with small talk. He asked, "Jason, what do you have for us?"

"It's simple and straightforward," the lawyer answered. "The immediate problem is the disparity between your financial reports and the auditors' notion of what they should be. I can't fix your books. But what I'm going to propose is an end run, a way to reorganize your company and avoid having to worry about the auditors. It might sound devious, but there's nothing illegal about it.

"I suggest you create a holding company to own Quivira Savings Bank and its subsidiaries. You two own a majority of common stock in Quivira. If you don't pay dividends, you surrender your stock to the preferred stockholders. So, you create Quivira Financial Corporation—a holding company to own everything. You exchange your common stock in Quivira Savings Bank for one hundred percent of the new holding company stock."

Max finished off his coffee and motioned to Will for another cup.

Will refilled his coffee and amaretto, slid it in front of Max, and poured another for himself. He glanced at Jason who held up a hand as if to say, "No thanks."

"Go on," Will said to the lawyer.

"The Quivira preferred stockholders would give up their shares in exchange for non-voting stock of the new holding company."

Max said, "Non-voting? Will and I would have the only voting shares? Total control?"

"Right."

Will said, "We keep control of Quivira by owning the new holding company. I like it. But wouldn't it need financing?"

Jason grinned. "That's where this idea can really help you two out. Quivira owns part interest in Rifle Village, Walker Bannister's undeveloped property near the airport. So, you buy an additional interest in the property. As part of the deal, Bannister is required to purchase $7 million of the new Quivira holding company preferred shares. I've written out the details of how the proceeds would be used to everyone's advantage."

He retrieved a file folder from his briefcase and laid a set of papers in front of each of them.

"Max, the holding company would lend you $2.5 million. Will, you'd get a loan of $1.5 million. You guys could call in your outstanding home mortgages and refinance at much better terms."

"Can't do it," Will snapped. "We're prohibited from getting loans from Quivira, you should know that, Jason."

The attorney laid a hand on Will's arm. "This is not Quivira Savings Bank lending you the money, Will, it's Quivira Financial, the new holding company—a completely different animal. Because you two will be the Board of Directors of the holding company, you can name your own loan conditions." He chuckled. "It's not as if you're some poor schmucks from Kokomo. You guys are driving this train. You deserve some perks."

"What happens to the rest of the seven million dollars we'd raise from Bannister?" Max asked.

"Pay Bannister $1.5 million in pre-paid dividends. And another $1.5 million in pre-paids to the other stockholders."

"You think Walker Bannister will go for this?"

"I'd bet on it," Jason answered. "The Rifle Village property could be a dog, or it might be a gold mine. It depends on whether the airport expansion plan goes through. Walker would like to have somebody to share the risk. You need the funding. Everybody wins."

"So, it would be in the best interests of our preferred stockholders to support this," Max observed. "They get their quarterly dividends up front. Meanwhile, Will and I keep control of the company."

Will responded with enthusiasm bordering on glee, "We can tell the auditors to shove it."

Bernstein shrugged his shoulders and concluded, "That's about the size of it. If you want to do this, I can have it drawn up and executed in a few months' time. I'm not sure what requirements there would be for running it by the regulators. I can do a little research and get back."

"Don't worry about Dallas," Will assured confidently. "I was on the Home Loan Bank Board for two years. I know those guys very well. Besides, they take their cues from the feds in Washington, who are up to their necks dealing with bank failures. They won't even be looking in our direction. The Home Loan Bank won't be a problem."

The three sat for a moment in silence. Jason waited patiently.

Finally, Will asked, "This deal. It's air-tight? Nothing illegal about it?"

"I'm your lawyer, Will. What else would I bring you?"

The CEO was deep in thought. He had a reputation for seeing complex issues immediately. Quick decisions were among his notable attributes. But this was huge, and he took his time to deliberate. Then he said, "I'm going to have Stan Russell make one more run at the auditors to see if they'll approve our numbers. He's their former partner. They should listen. But if they don't, I'm going to pull the trigger on this baby."

* * *

After Jason Bernstein left, Will and Max retreated to the study with the bottle of amaretto, no coffee. Will snapped on the television and tuned into the re-run of a previous day's bowl game, then muted the sound.

"What do you think?" he asked Max as he poured each a drink.

Max Davis heaved a belabored sigh. "God, Will, this is getting way beyond me. I'm a real estate broker, not a banker. I bought this little conservative thrift when all it did was make safe home loans."

"And was failing," Will reminded.

"Yep," Max agreed. "But then along came deregulation and complex new business opportunities. Now, you hot-shot wheeler-dealers come in and show me a whole new way of doing business. Makes me a little dizzy."

"I haven't heard you complain when the dividend checks were passed out," Will admonished.

"Oh, hell, I wasn't complaining. I brought you down here for this very reason. And I trust Jason Bernstein to help us maneuver through the mine fields. Even so, it's hard to believe how far we've come in so short a time."

"Well, fasten your seat belt," Will said. "We're just now going up the on-ramp."

"So long as we don't go to jail over any of it."

"Don't worry, Max," Will responded, un-muting the television and listening to the roar of a crowd. "Nobody's going to jail."

PART II: The Innocents

1959-1979

CHAPTER SEVEN

When I was in the seventh grade, I learned I was pretty decent at basketball. Playing on both my middle school team and one of the squads at the YMCA, I figured out what I lacked in height I could make up for in speed and court sense. I dribbled a basketball to and from school every day, and when my dad put up a goal in our driveway, I spent countless hours practicing my shots. My love and acumen for the game carried right into high school.

Our South Wichita Cougars had a powerhouse team in the late 1950s. Paul Sarkesian was our coach, and in the final year of the decade, 1959, our win-loss record was seventeen and two going into the final regular season game. With a win, we would claim a third straight conference championship and get to play in post-season tournaments for the fourth consecutive year.

Coach Sarkesian caught me in the hall before classes early in the afternoon. "Monty, ready to go tonight?" He was pudgy, jowly, husky-voiced.

"Yes, sir," I answered.

He was carrying a clipboard with our stats from a loss earlier in the season to our bitter rivals, the Hamilton County Raiders. "You scored eight points against them that night," he said, pointing to his notes. "And four assists. Monty, I need you to score in double figures tonight, and at least six assists. Can you do it?"

"I'll try, Coach," I assured him.

"Sumner Davidson only had five rebounds that game. I'm challenging him to double it tonight. I need you two to step up, Johnson."

"There's the class bell, Mr. Sarkesian."

"Go ahead then," he said.

As I hurried toward the classroom, it occurred to me how odd a motivational style the conversation was, and how nervous his challenge might have made some players. But he had to know I never got excited before a game. From the opening tipoff, basketball was all business to me. Yet that night, as the game wore down to the final minutes, I could feel my emotions building. We trailed the Raiders by three points. The clock showed only two minutes remaining. Hamilton County had the ball, and we were desperate to stop them.

Their shooting guard drove the ball up-court and, instead of taking time and looking for an open man, he handed us a bow-wrapped present with an ill-advised, off-balanced shot clanking off the rim. My heart pumped a little faster as I thought we might now have a chance. I saw our star center, Sumner Davidson, position himself to snag the rebound. But his taller Hamilton counterpart, a six-foot-eight thorn in our side all night, somehow muscled around Sumner and came down with the ball.

The problem for the big Hamilton County all-stater was that he came down at all—too far down. Dropping the ball to waist level and looking over his shoulder for an outlet pass, he failed to see me sneaking around behind him, barely inside the baseline. Before the big galoot could react, I managed to snatch the ball and hit a teammate streaking down the court with a perfect pass.

Two points for the Cougars, and we were down by only one.

Anyone within earshot could hear the Hamilton County coach scream, "Hostettler, this is the third damned time their little shrimp's stolen your rebound. Keep it high. Keep it high." I would have laughed except for the shrimp comment. "Small in stature, big at heart," my dad always told me.

We had less than a minute remaining, but Hamilton possessed the ball. Again, they challenged our defense with a screen-and-go play. It cut me off from defending the perimeter, but their shooting guard fired and, miraculously, missed.

Not only did I have hope, but a strange kind of calm swept over me, a confidence we were going to win. Yet once again, the Raiders' big center out-maneuvered Sumner and grabbed another authoritative offensive rebound.

Coach Sarkesian said during half-time, "Their big boy keeps dropping the ball down low. It's a gift. Take it."

I'd made him pay several times, so you'd think he would have learned. But bad habits don't die quickly, and with the game in the balance, his big meaty hands dropped low with the ball. I was waiting. I streaked around him and stole the ball away as he pawed at thin air.

This time, my teammate speeding down-court was covered, so instinctively I took control. I dribbled the length of the floor, and only then, as I reached the free-throw line, did anyone pick me up. The defender was their point guard, about my size but slower, so I knew I had a chance. Driving hard to the basket, I put up a challenged lay-up.

I don't really remember much about taking the shot, only that I landed hard and watched the ball spin on the rim and fall through seconds before the final buzzer sounded.

Pandemonium gripped the home team gym as our

Cougar fans rushed onto the court, hugging us players, jumping up and down, screaming, "We're number one. We're number one."

Only then did it strike me we had won the conference championship.

Getting mobbed by my teammates and then the swarming crowd felt as if a tsunami of joy would carry me away. But the best part was feeling two arms wrap around my shoulders, widening my grin. My steady girlfriend for the past two years, Sarah Madison, had me locked in an ecstatic embrace. I remember everything— the smell of her hair, the thrill of dancing around the floor in lockstep, the hysterical music in her voice as she shrieked over the din, "You're my hero!"

It couldn't get much better.

* * *

I slept late the next morning, rising at nine. Downstairs, my father, Montgomery Johnson, sat in the living room reading the paper. As usual, he was dressed in a white shirt and necktie. He looked up at me and crowed, "What a great game last night, Monty. I can't tell you how proud I am."

There's no praise quite like words of approval from your father. "Thanks, Dad. Where's Mom? I'm starved."

"She went shopping, but she left some bacon and eggs warming on the stove. Go have some breakfast and then get dressed. I want you to go downtown with me."

I nodded and headed to the kitchen for some much-needed sustenance.

My father, president of the Wichita Savings and Loan Association, occasionally took me with him on Saturdays. The institution was closed, but there always seemed to be a little work left over from the week.

"I like for you to go with me sometimes," he explained early in my senior year, "because after you get your degree you might want to come work with me. If that becomes the case, you should know what you're in for. Besides, we don't get to spend much time together, what with my business schedule and your schoolwork and basketball practice."

Wichita was always windy, and this particular March morning it whipped down the streets in an icy blast. We both had on heavy overcoats and scarves, and my dad wore a felt winter hat as well. As we entered the building, anyone passing by could easily tell I was Montgomery Johnson's son—we were both small in stature, but solid, molded from hardy Midwestern stock. I had inherited my father's square jaw and thick shock of hair. More importantly, everyone who knew us said I had Dad's warm personality and ability to command attention with a steady, sincere gaze into another's eyes. What they didn't know is I worked hard to learn his characteristics.

Dad sat down at his desk and busied himself while I wandered around the place, opening and closing drawers behind the teller windows, reading government notices on a bulletin board. I enjoyed acquainting myself with the feel of the place, could imagine the energy of people streaming in and out, investing money, borrowing money. Eventually I drifted back to my father's desk and watched over his shoulder, fingering the little plaque on his desk with the words, "Montgomery Johnson, President."

Finally, he closed the folder he was working on. "The board approved these loans yesterday," he told me. "I'm going through them to be sure all the paperwork is in order. Monday morning, I'll be calling four families and telling them they've been approved to buy homes."

I said, "It must be a great feeling, Dad."

I remember my dad turning and looking up at me, his face brimming with pride. "There's none better. Helping people live out their dreams, that's what it's all about."

"Why don't they go down to the bank and get a loan?"

"Good question. I'll be finished in a few minutes and we'll go get some lunch. I'll answer it then."

* * *

Less than half an hour later, we sat in a booth at Graham's, a busy lunch spot on a side street off of Douglas Boulevard. It was a typical hamburger-and-shake café so popular in that era. Two rows of red leatherette booths ran through the middle of the space, flanked by a window counter with chrome-edged stools on one side, and a curved, laminate sit-down counter on the other. In the small, open kitchen space, two fry cooks wearing aprons and paper hats tended to a long griddle which sizzled and popped when they flipped the meat.

After we ordered, my dad said, "This place is a great reminder of why I'm in the business. You know Mr. Graham, right?"

"I know who he is, sure."

"Several years ago, when he got out of the Navy, he came to us and applied for a home loan. He had started up a little ice cream factory over on the east side. It wasn't a big deal—not yet, anyway—but he worked hard and made a decent living. Our board thought he might be stretching a bit, but we liked the cut of his jib, you know? The property appraised right, and he wasn't really a risk. So, we okayed the loan. Now, five years later, his ice cream plant employs forty-five people and he has opened up three of these sandwich shops. When you come in here and order a malt or shake, guess where the ice cream comes from?"

I laughed with my father. "Okay, I get it," I said. "But what about my question?"

"You mean, why a savings association and not a bank? Well, after the Great Depression the government thought it would be a good idea to establish institutions to focus only on home loans. Commercial banks put a lot of their effort and assets on business customers, lending to big corporations, supporting real estate developers with money for construction projects, those kinds of activities. The banks also make car loans and personal loans, and now some of them are beginning to issue credit cards.

"When the thrifts were set up, the laws prohibited us from doing a lot of those activities. We can't even offer checking accounts. So, recognizing we had to have some kind of competitive edge against the big boys, the feds permitted us to pay slightly higher interest rates when people invest their savings with us. That means if you want to keep all your banking in one place, you might want to come get your mortgage here since you can earn more on your savings account."

I took an over-sized bite of my cheeseburger, started chewing and said, "It seems to me big banks would be a better bet. I mean, they have so much more money in their hands, if something goes wrong it might be easier for them to stay in business."

"It's a good point, and one the government thought about when they allowed savings and loans to operate. They created the Federal Home Loan Bank Board to govern our activities—mostly to be sure we followed the rules and regulations. In turn, the Home Loan Bank created an insurance corporation to insure depositors' accounts. Not many savings and loans go out of business, but if one does, its savers are protected. So, not only do we manage the business very carefully, some say too much so, but our customers have some added peace of mind in case we blow it."

My father sat back and laughed. "There I go again, boring you all the way to the north forty about the business."

"No, Dad, I asked the question," I countered. "You know I like math, and I'm good at it. I'm going to major in business, and I think this would be a great place to work. Except…"

"Except?"

"I've heard you talk about having to foreclose on people's property. I remember one summer when we had a bad drought—I think I was in sixth grade or something—and you had to call in several farmers' loans."

"That was really perceptive of you, Monty, to take note of it at so young an age. First of all, I think President Eisenhower has us smack dab in the middle of a good place. We're enjoying peace and prosperity, something we haven't had a lot of in my lifetime. You're becoming a man at exactly the right time. So, I don't think there are going to be a lot of failures or defaults on loans. It happens sometimes, and it hurts. A man loses his job and can't make his payments. A family has a major health problem and their funds get depleted. And you're right, it's a hard thing to face, for them and for us. But every business has its downside. You have to look at how much good you can do for people and take as many positive steps to minimize the risks. God knows, it's not a perfect world."

"Oh, I think it's pretty perfect," I said.

"What do you mean?"

"Did you forget? The South Wichita Cougars have qualified to go to the post-season tournament."

CHAPTER EIGHT

The early Sixties were not kind to the basketball fortunes of the South Wichita Cougars. After point guard Monty Johnson and star center Sumner Davidson graduated, things went downhill. Coach Paul Sarkesian's squads were inexperienced and less talented, and they won less than half their games in each of the next two seasons.

Near the end of the 1961 school year, in May, Sarkesian stopped by the office of head football coach and athletic director, Wally French. The two had worked together for many years and had a friendly relationship. But French called the meeting after making his disappointment clear about the Cougar's decline in basketball success.

French's office was barely larger than the janitor's closet down the hall. A metal desk and padded office chair took most of the space, and two smaller wooden side chairs across from him nearly backed into the opposite wall. There was no artwork, only copies of his degrees from Oklahoma State hanging behind him. A small trove of mementos from his playing and coaching days cluttered his desktop.

Sarkesian appeared in his doorway and French motioned him in. The basketball coach squeezed between Wally's desk and one of the chairs and eased his overweight frame into it. "I got your message saying you wanted to talk, Wally. I know what it's about. The program has hit a rough patch."

The Cougar AD was an ex-marine and looked the part. He had the solid, muscular physique of an interior lineman, and his tanned, lined face and grim expression seemed to shout, "I've been there and done that, so get out of my face."

"Paul, you're a good basketball coach."

French tried to smile, without success.

"And I realize the talent hasn't been there the past couple seasons. But I want to know what it'll take to get back on a winning track."

Sarkesian's chubby face flushed a bit. In a whisky-thick voice he responded, "I've decided I'm going to hang it up. I can't take the stress anymore."

"What?" French nearly shouted. "Damn it, Paul, I'm not asking you to resign. I merely want to work with you to get the program turned around. You're over-reacting."

The basketball coach shook his head. "No, Wally. I've given this a lot of thought. And I've talked it over with Alice. My health is not what it used to be. I'm diabetic and overweight. I have high blood pressure. I know when it's time, and the time is now. The truth is, with the pressure and the travel, and the extra hours, coaching basketball isn't fun anymore."

"You're too young to retire. What'll you do?"

"I enjoy the classroom, and of course I have tenure. I can handle some phys ed classes. And I'm not a bad math teacher—still know my way around solving for X. I'm going to teach full time."

It was settled. South Wichita would search for a new basketball coach. Paul Sarkesian would move to the classroom.

Except fate interfered. Four days after Sarkesian revealed his plans to Wally French, his wife Alice found him face up on the kitchen floor, dead from a heart attack. His hand was still grasping at the knot of his necktie, as if attempting to pull it off.

All of the South Wichita faculty and students, and it seemed like half of the city, turned out for the service at the United Presbyterian Church. Afterward, the crowd dispersed, and the procession pulled away from the church parking lot. Many of the cars lined up and headed for the cemetery burial.

In the parking lot, AD Wally French paused next to his pickup as his boss, Beatrice McMillan, reached her sedan parked two spaces away. French approached her, shaking his head slowly. "I'm going to miss Paul," he said.

"Such a sad day," South Wichita's first female principal moaned. "He was a good man."

"He was, for sure," said French. "I didn't see this coming. But Bea, thinking back to my last meeting with him, I think maybe he did. You're not going out to the burial?"

She shook her head no. "I'll stop by the house to see Alice afterward," she answered. "Wally, this might not be a good time to discuss it, and I don't mean to be irreverent. But I know you've already been going through a candidate list."

French nodded. "We have a couple of inside candidates, of course, Bea. But I want to go outside and bring some new blood to the program."

"Any possibilities?"

"I'd like you to meet a young assistant coach from El Dorado Junior College. He has excellent credentials and about a thousand very positive referrals. If he's available, can you meet him next week?"

"Of course."

They watched the last car pull out of the lot. A uniformed policeman who had stopped traffic to let the funeral procession through, climbed onto his motorcycle and drove away.

French said, "I guess I should get out to the cemetery. Bea, the candidate's name is Ron Slay. He was a hotshot point guard at Kansas City University. Made all-conference three consecutive years, and his head coach over at El Dorado recommends him highly. If you agree, I'll put the *vita* in your in-box. Let me know your schedule, and I'll give him a call."

"If he's as good as you say, we might have our man," she replied.

* * *

After one week of practice during the basketball season in late 1961, head coach Ron Slay knocked on Wally French's office door.

"Wally, got a minute?"

Slay could easily be spotted as a point guard. He had the thin, wiry frame of a toreador. His light brown hair was Princeton-cut, and he focused his clear brown eyes on his listener like lasers, as if he were surveying the court to determine the best way to pick apart a defense.

The AD motioned him in and pointed toward a chair. "Sure, Ron, come on in and have a seat. I've been curious to know how things are going so far. What's up?"

"I'm about to get us both in trouble." Slay didn't smile.

Caught off-guard, French laughed, then squinted across his desk, waiting for the bad news. "And?" he asked.

"We've had a terrific turnout of kids already, and I'm getting ready to make some cuts. Wally, ten seniors came out for the team, guys who've been in the program since their freshman year."

"That's good," French noted. "So, we'll have an experienced ball club."

"Not necessarily," Ron squirmed uncomfortably for a moment in the chair. "I'm only going to keep two of them."

Wally French's mouth dropped open for a few seconds. "Only two? Jesus Mary."

"I know. I'm going to be very unpopular."

"What the hell," was all French could stammer out.

"It'll be painful for everyone. But if I'm going to turn the program around, it has to be done."

Coach Slay's prediction was right. His decision to go with youth was immediately unpopular. Calls flooded the principal's and athletic director's offices. The new coach was snubbed at church and in the grocery store. But Wally French and Beatrice McMillan took the heat and backed their new head roundball coach.

One of the two seniors Slay kept on the team was Will Martin.

"Will's a good player, but not great," Slay said at his meeting with Wally French. "But besides helping us on the court, I think he'll set a good example for the younger players. He's well-dressed, polite, poised and articulate. I've talked to some of his teachers, and everyone agrees he's a leader waiting to happen. One of his brothers, Terry, is a freshman and promises to be a much better player. I think Will can be a good influence on him."

Wally nodded. "Let's hope he helps us win some ball games," he said.

CHAPTER NINE

I was fortunate to be pretty well-known to the South Wichita faithful. Not only did I play point guard for the Cougars during my last two years, but we won the regionals my senior season. And even though I went away to college, I was still the son of a highly respected businessman in the Wichita community. Whenever I went home, people at the bank or a store or church treated me cordially because I was Montgomery Johnson's son.

And so, on rare occasions when I returned to the Cougar's auditorium for a game, I could feel the positive attention from folks in the stands.

On the final night of the 1961-62 season, Ron Slay's first as head coach, we happened to be home visiting, so I was there. Sarah spent the evening at her parents' house and listened to the game broadcast.

Hundreds of spectators packed the wooden fold-out bleachers, and several dozen more fans stood lining the walls, single-file. I marveled at how little the gymnasium had changed. A large performance stage at one end, displaying the American and Kansas flags, took me back to Sarah's starring roles in student musicals. Huge inverted-cone light fixtures hanging from the rafters evoked memories of nights when I stared up into them, fighting for Sumner Davidson's tip-offs. The swell of crowd noise echoed off the hard surfaces of the cavernous space, just as it had so many times in our championship season.

The game was surprisingly close. South Wichita put up a fight, but as the clock counted down the final seconds, the Cougars succumbed to rival Hamilton County by three points.

As the disappointed home crowd filed out, several people stopped to say hello. Then I quickly climbed down the steps to the auditorium floor where Coach Slay was holding court with a group of parents. I didn't know Ron well. But on one occasion the previous summer, shortly before the school year, we had a nice, long talk—mostly about our favorite subject, basketball. I felt I should say hello, at least.

As the group of parents dispersed, I approached him and said, "Coach Slay, do you remember me? Monty Johnson."

"Of course, Monty." He gave me a solid handshake. "We met at your dad's bank last summer. How are you?"

"I'm good. Your boys put up a heck of a fight."

The coach shook his head. "I feel really bad for them. We've been overmatched most of our games. Six and fourteen my first year?" He laughed and shook his head in disbelief. "I thought I was God's answer to the coaching profession. Wrong!"

"Don't be too hard on yourself," I encouraged. "It might take a couple of years."

"Look, do me a favor," Slay said. "I imagine there are some pretty dejected young men in the locker room. How about coming with me and offering them a word of encouragement?"

I was flattered. "Sure, Coach. I'd be glad to do that."

As we walked off the court, Slay said, "I'm glad you came. How is everything going with you, Monty?"

"Great. School's going well. I'll get my degree in two years, get my military obligation out of the way and then come back home."

"So, you're coming back to your dad's bank?" Slay asked.

"I'm hoping it'll work out. It's all Sarah and I want

to do, come back to Wichita. There's no better place to raise a family."

"Oh, right," the coach remembered. "You got married last year, didn't you? And to a South Wichita girl, I heard. You're missing the whole college dating thing, you know."

"She's worth it," I countered, feeling my face flush. "We fell in love right here in high school. After she graduated, there was no reason to wait."

As we entered the Cougars locker room, a thousand sounds and smells invaded my memory. The strong scents of liniment, sweat and wet towels. The clatter of basketballs against metal as the trainers loaded them into lockers. The pat-pat of bare feet pointed toward the showers. Yet it seemed to me something was missing. I recall even when we lost, the atmosphere of gloom and doom lasted about ten seconds. Then it was on to the next thing—hamburgers or girlfriends or home to sleep.

On this night, Cougar players emerged from the showers wearing woefully glum expressions. They dried off silently and dressed without any of the usual after-game jokes and banter. I understood, because not only was the season over, but it ended in another loss to the hated Raiders of Hamilton County. Yet they needed to know the world hadn't ended.

"Guys, listen up," Coach Slay said, his arm on my shoulder. "Some of you know who this man is. Monty Johnson played on the last Cougar team to win a regional championship. Monty holds the school's scoring record for a single season. He has a few words he wants to say."

I scanned the scene and all the old emotions flooded back. I was pulling on my Cougar letter jacket. Thinking about my girl, Sarah. Heading out to Graham's Café with my teammates. Everything was the same. Only the faces were different.

Having no clue what to say, I simply opened my mouth and let the words spill out. "Well men," I started, "all I want to say is you played hard against a very good team. You didn't give up, and you should be proud of yourselves. I know you've had a tough year, but don't forget those words when you get out in life. Don't ever give up. Eventually you'll come out a winner. That's it."

Strangely, and there's no way to understand it, I could feel the mood of the room turn immediately up-beat. I was astounded when the players applauded my comments. Within seconds, as I started to leave, they turned to their more normal post-game joshing. As I said goodbye to Coach Ron Slay and left, one player finished dressing and hurried out behind me.

"Monty, do you remember me?"

"Sure I do, Will," I greeted him. "You're a part of the Martin clan who lived up the street from me growing up. Whenever I'd walk home from practice or a game, you were always out on the porch waving and speaking to me."

His wide grin seemed to say he was happy I remembered.

I went on, "Do you know what you said to me the day after we won the regionals?"

The good-looking, affable high school senior stared, appearing surprised I would recall something so trivial. "No, what?"

I laughed. "You said you were going to break my scoring record."

"Wow," Will exclaimed, "I did?"

"How did that work out for you?" I kidded, and we

laughed together.

"Basketball's not my strong suit," Will admitted. "I'm headed for business school next year. Maybe I'll beat you in the world of finance."

"I hope you do," I responded. "I'll tell you what, Will. You go get that business degree, and by then I'll probably be back in Wichita at the savings and loan. I'm not making any promises, but if you want to learn the banking business, come talk to me and we'll see what we can do."

CHAPTER TEN

"We're home, honey. How's it feel?"

My wife Sarah gazed around as we drove our four-year-old Bel Air through the city where we both grew up. Our two toddlers slept in the back seat. I was ecstatic the Chevy made it all the way from Philadelphia to Wichita without moaning and groaning. After overnight stops in Columbus, Ohio and St. Louis, we were completing the third leg of the journey. I regarded the trip as a resounding success with no flat tires, only two fights in the back seat and no more than a half-dozen emergency restroom stops.

"It seems like we've been gone for a century," Sarah responded to my question. "Monty, time's really flying by. It's 1967 already—can you believe it's been six years since you met me at the altar right over there at Trinity Church," she pointed northward, "three blocks from here, and said 'I do?'"

I steered the car across the Kellogg Avenue bridge and drove toward the Wichita Heights subdivision and my parents' house. I had traveled this route so many times, I could do it with my eyes closed.

I reached out and took her hand. "I'm really glad I said those two little words."

She turned those bright blue eyes in my direction and agreed, "Me too."

I smiled at Sarah. "You know, I remember talking to my dad about coming back some day to work in his business. That was years ago, when I was still in high school. It's hard to believe it's about to become a reality."

There was no question in my mind I had it made. Armed with a master's degree in business, a military discharge and a wife who'd been my high school sweetheart, I was returning home to what I expected would be a bright future. Eight years had zipped by since the sit-down lunch in Graham's Café with my dad.

So much had happened in America since then, unprecedented events running the gamut from positive to tragic. A war ramped up in Vietnam and drew protests in America. President John F. Kennedy was assassinated. Congress created Medicare. The Beatles appeared on U.S. television. Dr. Martin Luther King, Jr. stood in front of the Lincoln Memorial and delivered his most famous speech, "I have a dream."

Sarah and I had already witnessed and lived a lot of life since our marriage. But my admiration for bank president Montgomery Johnson and his principles of service to his customers couldn't be denied. I wanted nothing more than to live in Wichita and work in my father's savings and loan association. And perhaps one day, earn that same kind of respect in the community.

I felt well-qualified to move right into the business—could probably run it one day soon, given my education and military experience. It took some overachieving, but I finished my undergrad degree with highest honors in the school of business at Northwestern University. After three years as a Naval officer, working in the Pentagon, I moved on to Wharton and completed my MBA.

Sarah was my steady rock through all of this. She earned her teaching degree, gave birth to two beautiful babies and provided support and encouragement to me.

As I said to her when we made the decision to return, "We could go to New York or someplace and chase the big money. You've certainly earned the right to choose such a life for us. But all I really want to do is go back to Wichita and work in Dad's savings and loan. Our sons would grow up around two sets of grandparents."

"That suits me fine, Monty," she responded. "I love it there, and we want the same things."

So, as we approached my parents' house, talking about our future, I reminded her, "You made a promise, right? It's okay to get a teaching job. But until the boys start school, you agreed to be a stay-at-home mom."

Sarah nodded. "I know. It's what I want, too, Monty." She looked around the neighborhood. "It's good to be back. So many of our old friends are still here. And our families. It will be new times seeming like old times. You know what I mean?"

"I do," I answered.

"There you go again," Sarah joked. "I never tire of hearing you say those words." We laughed together.

We pulled up Center Street and into the driveway of my parents' neat, conservative ranch-style home in the upper-middle-class area. It wasn't the more modest place I had grown up in; like the others on our street, that house was what I call poor-folks' craftsman. It was constructed of wood siding, with a large, railed front porch and five wide wooden steps down to the front walk. Inside, the wall-papered rooms were small and dark.

The structures in this neighborhood were sprawling ranches with brick and stone facades and deep vertical windows anchored with flower boxes. The interior of my parents' house was spacious, with tons of light streaming through the rooms, highlighting pleasant, pastel-painted walls. Except for the kitchen and bathrooms, their home had deep-piled, wall-to-wall carpeting.

This wasn't the place of my growing up, but it was home.

"Let's go in and say hello to Mom and Dad, drop by your folks' house for a bit and then go have dinner at the hotel. You and the boys can apartment-hunt all day tomorrow while I start my new job."

Our sons began to stir as we brought the car to a stop. The front door to their grandparents' house opened. My folks, Montgomery and Juanita Johnson, greeted us with broad smiles and outstretched arms. It's funny, I never noticed them changing as I grew up. But on returning after being away for several years, I immediately saw the encroaching gray in my mother's hair and my dad's spreading midsection.

At least, we would be around them as they—and we—aged.

* * *

The day after arriving in Wichita, I showed up at Wichita Savings and Loan before it opened. Dad had given me a key, but I discovered he was already inside getting ready for business.

As the other employees trickled in, tellers, loan processors and accountants, each greeted me warmly. I knew many of them from the days I hung around there as a boy. They treated me with the same warmth and regard they showed my father.

It was an exhilarating first day on the job. But it soon became a near-nightmare.

The morning started with my dad on the phone contacting applicants whose loans were approved. The association treasurer, a thirty-year veteran, took me under his wing. He showed me the company books, reviewed and explained correspondence from regulators and introduced me to staff I didn't know. I could hear occasional outbursts of laughter from Dad's office as he delivered good news to loan applicants.

At about nine-thirty, though, the world of the Wichita Savings and Loan turned grim, almost tragic.

Sometime after the incident, my dad shared the whole back story with me. Harley Lemkin was a middle-aged black man nearly everyone around town knew about. A native of Wichita, he was an all-conference halfback in the Fifties for the University of Kansas. He received second team all-American honors and played two seasons for the San Francisco Forty-Niners. After being cut before his third season, Harley returned to Wichita with a wife and child. They had three more, and now there was another on the way.

But ever since returning, he had difficulty finding employment. Harley had a degree in sociology but no true job training and no encouraging prospects. He worked in Nathan Graham's ice cream factory for several years and then found a job at the Beach Aircraft company cleaning new models as they came off the assembly line. Yet there didn't seem to be a path for advancement.

Weeks after this frightful day, my first on the job, when I met his wife Mary Mae, she described the man's anguish. "He told me, 'I'm trying to get ahead,'" she recalled him saying one Friday when he brought home his paycheck and wrote checks to pay bills. "But he felt with all these mouths to feed and the low pay he was making, we couldn't get anything saved up. He said, 'Every damned thing I make goes right out the window the next day.'"

Mary Mae told me she was a native Californian whom Harley met while playing ball out there. She came from a middle-class family who fell on hard times because of her father's bout with obesity and diabetes. Her marriage to Harley and their move to Kansas was an escape from a deteriorating family situation.

She told me, "I complained to him we had to get a bigger place. With these kids growing up, three bedrooms isn't enough. Harley said maybe if I got a job, we could buy a house. So, I asked him, 'Who's going to do the wash every Monday and ironing on Tuesday? Get them ready to go to school, pack their lunch boxes, see they've got their homework done? Who's going to go buy the groceries and cook the meals? And who's going to have this baby in four months?' He didn't have an answer for those questions, just shook his head and kept writing checks."

This morning Harley didn't go to work. He showed up at our Wichita Savings and Loan. The barrel of a four-ten shotgun rested on his forearm as he entered and pulled the door closed behind him. I watched with incredulity as he stood in the lobby, motionless, with his eyes scanning the space. He looked like a frightened man to me.

Several early customers had already come and gone. Only two remained when Harley came in—one making a deposit at a teller window, the other seated at the desk of a loan officer, filling out paperwork. It took a few seconds before anyone could comprehend what was happening, a sort of stunned silence. But then I heard several peopled gasping loudly in disbelief. As if an alarm went off, everyone dropped to the floor, crouched behind desks or fled to the back room from a man holding a weapon in the usually calm and sedate institution.

"Mr. Johnson!" Lemkin's deep, booming voice echoed through the place. "Mr. Johnson!"

I was occupied with the treasurer at his desk when

the incident began. I felt the adrenaline pump through my body as others scrambled for someplace to hide. I didn't think about it, merely reacted instinctively as I had so many times on the basketball court. I took a deep breath and hurried toward the lobby, facing the gunman.

"Sir, sir, put down the gun." I tried to say it as calmly as possible. "What's this all about?"

I could hear my dad's footsteps emerging from his office, making a rapid *tap-tap-tap* on the marble floor. Within seconds, he scurried to the front and shouldered in front of me.

"Harley, what in God's name are you doing? You're scaring these people half to death. Are you holding us up, or what?"

I wanted to interfere, to re-engage and protect my father. But there was something about the way their eyes locked that held me back.

"No, sir, Mr. Johnson. Ain't holding you up. Just want you to approve my damned home loan like you said you would."

I stood stock-still as Dad took another step toward the distressed man. "Now, Harley, I didn't make you any promises, and you know it. When you came in looking for a loan, I said you might not qualify. Do you remember? I told you your income and expenses would make a mortgage a real stretch. And the house you want is way over your head, Harley. You can't afford it. Now, put the gun down and let's discuss this in my office. There's no need to frighten all of these people."

Lemkin appeared to sag. The barrel of the shotgun lowered toward the floor, and tears rolled down the big man's face. "Got to get ahead somehow, Mr. Johnson. Can't live in a two-by-four apartment with a big family.

Need some space. Need a house."

That was my cue. I stepped past my father, eased forward and gently grasped the stock of the four-ten. "Please let me have the gun, sir. Go to Mr. Johnson's office and talk it out, okay?"

A surge of relief flooded through me as Harley Lemkin nodded and loosened his grip on the gun. I carried it back gingerly and laid it on the desk of a loan officer who, I later learned, retreated to an office and called the police. My father motioned for me to follow them into his office. He sat down behind his desk and motioned us into the chairs across from him. Harley sank heavily into one of them, distraught and still sobbing. But with my heartbeat still pounding away at workout pace, I remained standing, looking down curiously at the former ball player.

"Harley, this is my son, Monty. This is his first day on the job—you gave him a helluva scare. Monty, this man used to be one of Kansas' best football players."

That turned on the light switch for me. "Oh, sure, I remember seeing you play when I was a kid."

"The board denied his loan application last Friday," Dad explained.

Two police officers suddenly appeared in Dad's office. "We had a call, Mr. Johnson. Is this the guy who brought the gun in?"

"Now, everything's under control, officers," my father assured.

I looked out and could see two other policemen in the outer office, picking up the shotgun from the loan officer's desk and examining it.

"I don't think Mr. Lemkin here intended to hurt anybody," Dad continued. "If he did, we'd all be dead by now, right Harley? He was merely trying to get our attention."

"I don't care if he was trying to pick daisies," the cop said. "It's against the law to brandish a weapon in a threatening manner. Sir, stand up. We're going to have to arrest you."

"Are you sure it's necessary?" my father asked, his voice straining a bit with incredulity.

"Damned right it is, Mr. Johnson," the other officer answered.

Exhaling heavily, Harley stood and shook his head as the policeman pulled his arms behind him and put the handcuffs on. The big man's face was streaked from tears, and I could see his lower lip tremble.

My dad tried to calm him. "Now look, Harley, do what they tell you. I'm going to call a lawyer I know, and he'll come down and help you. Monty here is smart as a whip and has a business degree to prove it. As soon as we get this all cleared up, he's going to sit down with you and your wife and see if he can help you get out of this financial hole you're in."

Harley nodded silently as the two policemen led him away. The other two officers followed with the shotgun.

My dad stepped to his office door and called out, "Everyone all right out there?" He turned to me and said, "Son, go out there and try to calm everyone down. Make sure nobody's having a breakdown or anything. I see a reporter from *The Wichita Gazette* coming through the front door, and I'm going to have to deal with her."

I nodded and began to make the rounds, speaking to employees. I'd worked in the Pentagon. Achieved a certain amount of academic success. Yet I'd probably never felt as important as at that moment, when my father sent me out to calm down the troops.

Several customers arrived, not appearing to realize what had transpired, forcing the firm to resume business as usual. Then, suddenly, a news reporter and cameraman from WOTE-TV burst in the front door. They stared around frantically, seeming flabbergasted at the calm atmosphere in the lobby.

"You're too late," I said to the reporter. "It's all over."

"Well, what happened?" the newsman demanded.

"Let's step outside, and you can talk to me there," I said. "Let these people get their business done."

I managed to get through a brief interview without stammering. After the newspaper and television reporters were gone, I walked into my father's office. "Are you all right, Dad?" I asked.

He sat behind his desk and took a long, deep breath. "I think so. Still a little shook up, I guess. My God, what if something much worse had happened? Someone got shot, maybe killed. I couldn't have lived with it."

"Years ago," I said, "when I was still in high school, I remember you telling me there were times when not everything in this business comes up roses."

I watched him take another deep breath and try to smile. "Well, son, this morning you got your first big dose of that lesson. Plus, you're going to be a TV star your first day on the job." He paused, as if deep in thought. "Listen, I want you to take Harley Lemkin on as a personal project, will you? He might have to go to trial, but the lawyer I called could possibly get him off. We can testify he never pointed the shotgun at any of us, so we weren't actually threatened. It would be the truth. Even if Harley has to go to trial, I can't imagine he'll be convicted on a felony charge. You'll have time to look over their financial situation, talk to his wife, see what kind of house they might be able to afford. At least explore whether there is anything we can do to stabilize their lives. It might be possible to help them get what they need."

"Sure, Dad," I said without hesitating.

"It's days like this I'm glad you decided to come back," my father said. "I'm getting too old for turmoil like this. I might retire a lot earlier than you thought."

I grinned inwardly. There was only one word to summarize my regard for Montgomery Johnson that day—admiration.

CHAPTER ELEVEN

My father arrived at the office late on a soft spring Wednesday morning in April 1968. He was out of town for two days and, exhausted the morning after returning, slept late. I think I could count on one hand the number of times he did such a thing. But I was secretly glad; it gave me a chance to open the office and get the savings and loan up and running on my own, for a change. On most days I had to hustle to meet him walking into the building.

At mid-morning he stopped by my office.

"So, you finally decided to come earn your big salary?" I teased.

Dad shook his head, grinning. "I can't take those long conferences anymore," he said, plopping down in one of my side chairs.

"Come on, Dad," I protested. "You're still a young man."

"The national association meetings are making me older, fast. It seems every issue we're dealing with spells doom and gloom for the industry."

I waved the thought away. "The pendulum always swings. You taught me that."

Dad haw-hawed at that. "The pendulum is going to swing more your direction in the future, I promise." He paused in thought. "By the way, we haven't talked recently about Harley and Mary Mae Lemkin. Have you been able to help them?"

I nodded, feeling a wash of pride. "I have, Dad. We sat down and worked them through a budget they can live with, including a savings plan for a down payment on a house. But even better, I managed to get Harley some technical training. When he completes it, he'll be able to make more money." I felt a little anxious as I continued. "Dad, I used some of our discretionary funds to finance it. I hope that was okay."

His response was a huge relief to me. "Of course it was," he assured. "I'm proud of the way you stepped up to the plate. A nice couple is going to have a better life because of you." He rose and started out, then turned back. "Your responsibilities here are increasing gradually. Realizing how nice it was to sleep late this morning, I might start cutting my hours back."

"That'll be the day," I joked. "Saying and doing are two separate things."

He smiled and said, "You and Sarah and the boys come over for steaks tonight. I'm serious. We'll talk about this some more."

* * *

We were grilling Kansas City strips on my parents' back deck at six that evening. Mom and Sarah were inside busily putting together side dishes of pasta and vegetables.

Our two boys, Dwight and Truman, were playing tag in the back of the yard, jumping in and out of the elaborate gazebo Dad had built. It was a large lot and a great place for them to play.

When they moved in, Mom and Dad spent a lot of time making it a special place. They installed a winding brick walkway all the way back to the shelter and hung a porch swing inside, where they could sit on cool nights and enjoy a cocktail. They lined the picket fence around the perimeter with a mix of hostas and spirea bushes. Breaks in the shrubbery featured rock-ringed beds of peonies, cornflowers and marigolds. Two huge red maple trees anchored the corners of the sweeping lawn of Kentucky bluegrass.

"Be careful out there," I shouted.

True to form, my sons ignored me.

As the steaks seared, Dad reprised the conversation from that morning. "I've thought about what I was telling you—reducing my hours," he said.

"Yeah, I know, Dad," I ribbed. "You talk a good game, and then you panic and start working even harder."

"I'm serious about it. You already know the business better than I do, and my workload in the industry association is increasing by the day."

"How did everything go at the conference?" I asked. I demonstrated my dexterity by sipping from my beer bottle with one hand and flipping a steak over with the other. The meat sizzled in protest. "The post they've been talking to you about—did you accept it?"

"I did," Dad answered. "You're looking at the new vice chairman of the savings association's lobbying arm, the U.S. League."

"Congratulations, Dad. I think it's a great way to start closing out your career. They couldn't have a better man to represent them in Washington."

My father waved the comment away. "You're biased, of course. You could do it standing on your head. In fact, very soon I want to get you involved in the League. There are several committees you'd be well-suited to serve on, maybe even chair one."

"Say the word, Dad. You know I like that kind of action."

My mother appeared at the deck doorway. "Are you two going to stand out here and yack forever?" she chuckled. "How much longer do we have?"

"Five more minutes, maximum," Dad responded.

"Then we'll go ahead and toss the salad," she said. "Oh, and Monty, don't forget to bring my grandbabies in with you." She giggled and disappeared back into the kitchen.

"One thing before we go in, Dad," I said. "I don't know if you remember Will Martin or not."

"Sure, the kid who went to South Wichita. His family lived down the street from us before we moved out here to Wichita Heights. What about him?"

"He called me yesterday, and we had a long talk. You know, he graduated a couple of years ago in business at Topeka University. Very charming young guy. Everyone says he's smart as a whip. He wants to come in to talk about a job."

"Isn't he working for Dave Carlson's office supply company across town?"

"He married Mr. Carlson's daughter Prudence when he graduated. I'm told he's pretty much running the place now. But Dad, he wants to get into banking."

"Would he be a good fit for us?"

I answered, "All I know is he was president of the student activities association his junior year, treasurer of the student council as a senior, and finished with top honors from the university's school of business. I've crossed paths with him a few times since he got back. He has the polish and panache of a true leader. When he married Prudence, everyone assumed he would inherit the business. But I don't think it's what he wants."

My father nodded understanding. "So, he's looking for a way to ease out his new father-in-law's company, am I getting it right?"

"It's not just that. He really believes finance is his true calling. He's restless selling office supplies. If Will wants to come work for us, maybe you could talk to Mr. Carlson, leave him the impression it's our idea."

I watched my father grimace in his fake, joking way. "Ouch. You always try to stick me with the nasty jobs, don't you?"

"You're a better diplomat than I am," I grinned. "Seriously, I think Will could really help us grow the business, if he wants to come."

I held the platter, and Dad forked the steaks onto it. "Bring him in and talk to him," he responded. "I said we'd start increasing your job description." He laughed. "You are hereby appointed personnel director. If you think Will is right for Wichita Savings and Loan, go ahead. He'll be your first new hire."

"What about his father-in-law?"

My dad gave me a "thanks a lot" look. "Okay, I can make peace with Dave," he conceded. "But you'll owe me one."

* * *

The summer months zipped by. Autumn slipped in and brought mild and magical sunny days lingering on into evenings of soft breezes and long shadows. Midwesterners for decades referred to the near-mystical time as "Indian Summer."

With my dad out of town on League business, I was left to close the building on a Friday afternoon. I was about to lock up when Will Martin surprised me by scooting out the door behind me.

"Will, you startled me," I said to Wichita Savings' newest employee. "I thought everyone had left. You're the last man out."

"Right. I was on a call with a good prospect," Will said as I locked the door. We stopped to talk on the nearly deserted sidewalk. "A nice couple over at Rose Hill are making an offer on a twenty-acre farm, and their agent is helping them shop a loan. She's coming in Monday to talk about it."

I shot him a grateful smile. "Rose Hill. It would be a good community to get a foothold in. You know, my father and I really like the way you've taken to the business. In a very short period of time we can tell how much you're helping grow our deposit base. You have a rare talent, Will."

"I've been thinking about it, Monty. It seems to me there's so much more we can do."

"Like what?"

He answered, "More business loans, for instance. For construction and development. And more competitive interest rates on deposits."

"You're aware our charter has limitations. We're governed by federally mandated rules we have to follow. I appreciate your aggressive thinking, but until and unless the laws and regulations change, we're simply going to have to keep doing what we're doing."

Will grinned. "I think the laws will change, and when they do, we need to be ready to seize the moment. I've been reading the white papers coming out of the U.S. League. Washington doesn't want us to go under, so they have to listen to us. We can't stay boxed into a corner forever."

"Dad's been getting me started in some of the League's activities," I said. "Tell you what, after I get better positioned with them, and you have a little more experience under your belt, maybe we can get you involved."

"Do you think so? That would be terrific," Will enthused. "I have a lot of ideas for turning this industry on its head."

I grinned and slapped my protégé on the shoulder. "Well, hang onto them for now. Your time will come, Will. Until then, you could do a lot worse than plying your trade at Wichita Savings and Loan."

CHAPTER TWELVE

Downtown Wichita in the Seventies was dotted with only a few tall structures—the Maytag Hotel, the new Bell Telephone building, the Kansas State Bank and a recently completed office tower. Most of the city was spread out horizontally, with rows of one- and two-story, non-descript retail establishments lining its grid of streets.

One such shop on a side street off of Kellogg Avenue featured Native American jewelry, art and crafts. Inside the tiny retail space, cases were crammed with Zuni, Cherokee and Hopi jewelry made of silver, copper, turquoise, coral and abalone shell. Shelves were lined with colorful pottery from the Pueblo, Iroquois, Cheyenne and Shoshoni. A profusion of blankets, basketry and paintings from multiple tribes covered the walls from ceiling to floor.

"Blackbear Bosin?"

"Yes," the Native American behind the counter was a large man, his lined face deeply bronzed. His coal-black hair was pulled back and tied in a short ponytail, and he had on a white western-style shirt and bolo tie secured with a beaded clip. There were silver and turquoise rings on two fingers of each hand. He smiled broadly at his visitor. "You're Will Martin."

"I am." Will approached the store owner and extended his hand, the other clutching a leather briefcase. He was thin and smooth-faced. He wore a custom-made navy suit, white shirt with monogrammed French cuffs and a striped navy and white necktie. His black wing tips were highly polished. His wire-rimmed glasses gave him a serious and studious look. "Thanks for seeing me,

Blackbear."

"Call me Chief. Everybody does."

"Are you? A real chief, I mean."

"My grandfather was a Kiowa chief in Oklahoma. My background is Kiowa and Comanche. But most of my people are gone now."

Will glanced around at the shop. "I've never been in here. You have a lot of stuff."

Blackbear laughed. "This 'stuff,' as you call it, is all authentic Native American craftwork. Art, weaving, basketry, jewelry, the works. My goal is to have products representative of every tribe in North America. I'm about halfway there at the moment. Come on back to my studio." He turned and pulled away the hand-woven blanket covering the door behind him.

As Will followed him, they entered a space more than four times larger than the storefront. Artwork, some life-sized, was scattered around the studio.

"These paintings are amazing," Martin exclaimed. "Really complex and dramatic. Is this all your work?"

"It is," Chief nodded. "I was self-taught, but I've been doing it a long time. I paint for art's sake. I do the commercial work you called about so I can eat."

"Then let's get to it," Will said.

Blackbear pointed toward two wooden straight chairs and they sat.

"As I told you on the phone, I'm treasurer of Wichita Savings and Loan. But I'm also president of the Wichita Chamber of Commerce. In a week, I'm going to present a proposal for a downtown revitalization to the Chamber Board and Wichita City Council. A beautification of downtown Wichita."

"Sounds interesting."

"If I'm successful, you won't recognize your city. It'll attract a lot of attention, and small businesses like yours will benefit from the increased activity here in the heart of town."

"I like it already. How can I help?"

Will opened his briefcase and extracted some papers. "Chief, I've sketched out some drawings to illustrate what things should look like, but I'm no artist. I need to have these translated into professional drawings that will dazzle the folks in the audience. Can you do it?"

Blackbear rifled through the pages, running ideas through his head. "Yeah, I can draw it for you. But I have another idea you might like."

He rose and motioned Will toward the back of his studio. He switched on a set of over-head fluorescent lights to illuminate the entire section of the room. "See this half-finished billboard over here?" Blackbear said. "I'm doing it for a local radio station. They're going to put it up outside their studio to advertise their newscasters. What's unique about it is I have a projection system which can take the original photo montage of their news personalities and blow it up on the large board so I can paint it. I do a lot of this work for companies like Boeing Aircraft and Cessna. I was thinking, maybe I could do a rendering of your proposed project and then paint it on a large board. Instead of handing out eight-by-eleven images, you'd unveil a billboard-sized rendering of the new and improved Wichita, Kansas. The city hall boys'd be overwhelmed."

Will remained motionless for a moment, considering. Then, the normally understated man burst out, "My God, Chief. That's a fantastic idea. And you can do all of this in a week?" The native American nodded and smiled.

"I'm not even going to ask how much it'll cost," Will said. He shook Blackbear's hand and they had a deal.

Will turned back as the Native American walked him through the front door. "I'm told the huge statue of an American Indian chief standing at the confluence of the two rivers west of here is your creation."

Blackbear stood a little more erect and said proudly, "Yes, it is. It's called 'Keeper of the Plains.'"

"Whenever we're trying to attract new business, I always take our visitors past it," Martin said. "It's such an impressive piece of work."

"'Keeper' is my only sculpture so far, forty-four feet high. I made it from steel and then chemically treated it to turn all of those beautiful autumn colors."

"It's pretty spectacular."

Blackbear grinned. "There's a humorous story about it. You probably know Orleans, France is Wichita's sister city."

Will nodded.

"Some of their city fathers were here on a visit and saw my sculpture. They wanted me to sculpt one for their city, so I did. I made it, used a cutting torch to slice it into sections, crated it up and shipped it along with instructions on how to reassemble and weld it back together. Three months ago, they flew me over there for the unveiling. After all the speeches and pageantry were over, I pulled the cord on the drape covering it and got the surprise of my life." He watched his listener with a glint in his eye, then, "They saw the colors from the oxidation treatment and thought it had rusted in transit. Are you ready for this?"

Will's face reflected total fascination. "And?"

"And they had painted it battle-ship gray."

After a silent moment, both men erupted into laughter.

"I hadn't heard that story," Will confessed. "I don't think there was anything in the newspaper."

"They covered it up. They were too embarrassed," Chief chortled. "And so, Mr. Martin, I will render your downtown Wichita project. And I will convert it to a billboard. But do not—I repeat, do not paint it battleship gray."

* * *

Will was a presenter extraordinaire. From oral reports in his college classes, to presentations at the savings and loan board meetings, to speeches at association audiences, he was always unflappable, articulate, poised. On the morning of his appearance before the business and political leaders of Wichita, he walked into the room exuding confidence. The City Council chambers were too small to host a large gathering for the presentation, so they commandeered the auditorium of the recently finished telephone company building.

The hall featured theater-type seating for two hundred people. It sloped down gradually from two back entrances to a wide stage at the front, providing a good view from anyplace in the room. Dimmable overhead lighting was set at half-brightness for the meeting. Blackbear's covered billboard and a podium from which Will would present were illuminated by a spotlight.

"Ladies. Gentlemen," Will began. "We have all ruminated for nearly a year about the future of Wichita's downtown, and how we can bring it back from its current tired deterioration. There are plenty of ideas floating around about what we should do. And how much we can spend. We, at the Chamber, have listened to all of the opinions and suggestions, and we've debated a good bit about it. But we've come to a consensus, and today I'm pleased to say I have the answers for you."

He spoke for nearly an hour, describing various aspects of the plan—street and sidewalk improvements, modern lighting, bold new landscaping. He passed out packets of material listing each aspect of the project and estimated costs. And then, as they rifled through the material, Will stopped. He waited several beats, watching for the majority of his audience to look up, ready with the closing argument.

Then he said, "I give you 'The Wichita Renaissance.'"

He pulled the cord and Blackbear's drapes dropped to the floor, revealing a spectacular mural. Renovated buildings. Walking spaces replacing streets. Imaginative landscapes. Drawings of people wandering in parks and mingling in gathering spots—fountains, gazebos, seating areas, waterfalls. Blackbear Bosin's artwork and billboard demonstrated the beauty and immensity of the project.

There was an audible gasp, then applause. Nearly half of the crowd rose in response. Some walked forward to get a closer look, pointing, chatting back and forth about various aspects of the scene. The mayor, Raymond Hall, stepped to the podium and shook Will's hand. "Mr. Martin," he said, "you've given us all a fantastic vision to discuss. Thank you for your hard work, and for this incredibly professional presentation. Now, members of the council, we have work to do. Each of you, go back through Will's proposal and we'll review it in detail at our next executive session."

Will laughed. "Heck, Mayor Hall. I think you could take a vote right now." He winked and the entire group broke into laughter and another round of applause.

* * *

Will looked uncharacteristically tired—disheveled, even— as he entered the Westside Sports Bar on Kellogg Avenue. Though dusk was falling outside, he still had to pause for a moment for his eyes to adjust to the darkened establishment. A hand waved from a booth near the back and he squinted, then waved back at Lawson Jeffries. A television set perched on a high shelf near the end of the bar piped in an old football game featuring Wichita State University. Several groups of Shocker fans strained to watch it from booths nearby.

"I got us a pitcher," Jeffries said, filling an empty glass and pushing it across the table to Will as he sat down. "Your favorite brand. Hey, I heard you did a great job today."

Will loosened his tie and took a long swallow of the cold brew. "Man, it has been a long day. This is really good beer. Lawson, I don't think it could have gone better. The city council won't have any choice. They're going to have to adopt my idea. And when they do, Wichita Savings and Loan will be right in the middle of the biggest growth project in its history."

Lawson was a big bear of a man, six foot six. He sat up straight and towered over his friend and colleague, looking down at him with surprise. "Whoa, you mean we'd be able to get in on this somehow? Will, we can't do that. You know the laws won't let us make commercial loans."

"I'm not talking about lending them money," Will

explained, "although as you know we're working on Congress to loosen up the restrictions on what we can and can't do, who we can and can't make loans to. But Lawson, this improvement deal is too good for us not to get involved somehow, and I'm going to figure it out. If it's approved, there'll be development bonds issued and contracts let, and somehow I'm going to get us a piece of the action."

The crowd roared on the TV screen as Jeffries ran a meaty hand through his thick thatch of dark, wavy hair. "Man, I hope you're right." They both sat quietly for a minute, in thought, sipping their suds. "Will, whatever happens, today was probably a landmark day for you. It's no secret some folks have been talking about you running for office. From what I heard, that discussion heated up today after your appearance."

"Hell, I don't want to be a politician. I want to run my own S&L."

The big man frowned. "You'll never have the opportunity here. Monty Johnson's dad has run our company for years, and when he steps down Monty will simply take over."

"I know, I know," Will said. "But Lawson, I've been looking around. I'm keeping my eye on some opportunities. And making a lot of friends in the industry. When the right deal comes along, I'm going to step in and grab it."

"What about Prudence? Would she be up for a move? Seems to me, growing up here in Wichita, all her old friends being here, and having an old man who's owned a business here for years and years, she would have a hard time tearing away."

"Pru and I had an understanding when we got married," Will told him. "Wherever my career takes me, there she'll go."

As Wichita scored, the noisy, half-drunk patrons cheered raucously at the monitor, nearly drowning out his words.

"Man, what a dump this is," Will continued. "Why are we having drinks here?"

"I like the place," Lawson said. "I come here and watch games a lot."

"That's because you're a jock," Will joked. "You were born in a football uniform and played like a champ. No one was surprised when the Chiefs drafted you, even though you came from a small college. I thought you would make a career of it instead of hanging it up after a few years."

"The money was good," Lawson acknowledged. "But it's not an easy way to make a living—tough on the body, you know? Besides, I got stung by the banking bug. I've never said anything to you, Will, but I appreciate everything you did to help me get in at Wichita Savings."

Will replied, "It's only the beginning. When I find my spot, when I take over as the head tin lizard, you can come with me, if you want."

Lawson nodded and emptied his glass.

"We should be drinking martinis at the Wichita Country Club," Will said. "A place like this is okay for the college crowd. But Lawson, remember, we deserve the very best of everything when we've got it made."

CHAPTER THIRTEEN

My dad got me involved in national association activities not long after I started working at Wichita Savings. He didn't say it at the time, but I knew he wanted to begin a long, gradual withdrawal from the spotlight and one day, when he was ready, let me have the reins. He wanted me to take an industry role for my own sake, but it was also part of a grander scheme to groom me for his ultimate retirement. In other words, an unofficial succession plan, although I knew that event was years away.

In the early Seventies, I joined the legislative committee of the U.S. League of Savings Institutions, the savings and loans' representation in Washington. It was a period of tumult in our nation's history. We experienced a slow and messy end to our involvement in Vietnam. Skyrocketing gas prices were leading us into recession. The Watergate scandal resulted in President Nixon's resignation as he faced articles of impeachment.

Against this background, in 1976, the committee chose me to be its chair.

We decided to push Congress and the regulators to recognize the harsh realities of a disastrous economy. The high interest rates we had to pay on deposits, and the shackles on our ability to provide mortgages at profitable rates, had us caught in the middle. We were making low interest home loans and paying high interest to our investors. The rules had us set up to fail. I knew this dilemma would be a hot topic at all association meetings.

I always enjoyed the national conventions. They gave us a chance to catch up with some old friends and meet newcomers to our business. Dad usually led the charge. But at the U.S. League's annual conclave the first year I headed up the legislative effort, he stayed behind. It gave me a chance to take Will Martin with me and get him some exposure on the national stage.

As we walked toward The Arlington Room of the President Hotel in Chicago, a block from the headquarters of the League, I remember thinking we must have posed an interesting juxtaposition. Will was thin and rangy. I was shorter but more solidly built. Yet despite our obvious difference in appearance, I knew there was a similarity in how we carried ourselves—confident, congenial.

To me, striding into a room with purpose was a learned trait, because I'd observed and emulated my father ever since joining him at Wichita Savings. Will's extra gear of charisma and poise seemed to be natural-born. As I watched him interact, it reminded me of when he was a boy greeting a high school student passing his house with a self-assured kind of ease you rarely saw in someone so young.

Many of the conference-goers were already congregating in the hallway near the ballroom entrance. Registration envelopes including nametags and other conference materials were fanned out alphabetically on long tables with crisp white tablecloths. Coffee service was available on several others. We found our packets and walked together toward the caffeine where other attendees poured cups and exchanged greetings and handshakes.

Will held back and watched as I mingled in the crowd. He only stepped in when I introduced him to someone I knew. At some point when I became distracted, he drifted away, poured himself a cup of decaf and melted into the gathering.

After fifteen minutes or so, the lights flickered a signal to begin filing into the Arlington Ballroom, where rounds of eight would greet us.

I found Will and grasped his shoulder, steering him into the room. "We'll be at one of the front reserved tables since I'm going to be a presenter," I told him.

We found our places at a table closest to the podium.

After several long presentations, interrupted by a twenty-minute break, we reached my spot on the agenda. The League chairman, a Virginia thrift owner who served as interlocutor for the meeting, announced from the rostrum, "Most of you know Monty Johnson, vice president of Wichita Savings and Loan. As chairman of the legislative committee, we've asked him to update you on where things stand with our friends in the U.S. Capital."

Though I took notes with me, I knew my remarks by heart. As always, when I had to make a speech, I practiced for about a week with my most critical audience, my wife Sarah. After she grilled and coached me, no audience of industry executives or government regulators could throw me off.

"Good morning," I opened. "A friend of mine, a professional speaker, once told me, 'The worst time you can get yourself scheduled for the agenda is just before quitting time. The second worst is right before lunch. If you draw either of those short straws, quick, tell a joke.'

"So, there was a woman who went to the doctor," I paused as the laughter ran through the crowd, then subsided. I continued, "'What's the problem?' the doctor asked. 'I'm not sure,' the woman answered. 'I seem to be off my feed.' So, the doctor asked her, 'Do you wake up grumpy in the morning?' 'No,' the woman told him.

'He wakes up on his own.'"

Hilarity erupted in the audience, and I was ecstatic my little story didn't bomb. In one of our practice sessions, Sarah insisted it would not.

I went on, "That's the difficulty many of us have these days—the growing problems in our industry wake us up grumpy. But I'm here to assure you, the legislative committee of the U.S. League is working hard to find the cure.

"If you've been around our industry for the past ten years or so, I don't need to tell you what new challenges have emerged. I joined Wichita Savings a year after Congress slapped limits on savings rates for both banks and savings and loans. Ever since then, you and I have struggled to hold onto depositors and, at the same time, deal with a slow-growth economy and attract new borrowers who could increase our income. Elected officials and regulators nod sympathetically when we say we can't survive when we're forced to make low-interest, long-term mortgages and pay depositors high interest on investments. But so far, they've done little to level the playing field. Many of you have instituted alternative mortgage types and begun to offer interest-bearing checking accounts. At least, they've allowed us to go that far.

"Yet those are baby steps. With increased bank competition and the poor economic conditions, we've lost more than one thousand associations in the past decade. It's a trend we have to stop. Your legislative committee has developed an aggressive agenda, and we are going to Washington, D.C. to promote it."

For the next forty-five minutes, I went through the measures we would promote to give our business a chance to survive. Phase-out of maximum interest rates on savings accounts. Approval to issue credit cards. Removal of restrictions on commercial and real estate loans.

"We had heated arguments in committee meetings about how far we should push into these previously prohibited areas of operation," I said. "But in the end, we agreed the League's position should be to loosen the reins, deregulate to a certain degree and trust we won't abuse the privilege."

As I reached the conclusion of my remarks, I could sense a restlessness, due more to hunger than boredom from my talk. At least, it's what I told myself. Whichever, I knew it was time to wrap up.

"My time is up," I concluded. "Our committee is open to your ideas and reactions. Meanwhile, we will promote our platform aggressively in hopes that, when your spouses get up in the morning, they won't have to wake up grumpy."

I chose to take the laughter and applause as a genuinely favorable response to my talk, not relief we'd reached lunchtime.

The chairman announced from the podium, "Ladies and gentlemen, we are set up in the adjacent Beeson Room with a buffet. Please enjoy yourselves. We'll re-convene here for afternoon business at one-thirty."

I found Will in the swarm heading for the exit and said, "You're on your own during break. The legislative committee is holding a private session in a room down the hall."

"No problem," Will said, nodding. "I think I can handle lunch without you." I laughed and drifted out of the ballroom with several of my fellow committee members.

In other times, the legislative committee get-together might have been a congenial affair. But as we sat down in a conference room and the plates were served, I could feel an atmosphere of heat in the air. Like the industry itself, the committee was split between doves and hawks. Many of us clung steadfastly to the pure mission of residential mortgages. Even as difficult as conditions had become, we searched for ways to achieve our objective.

Meanwhile, the leaders of struggling or failing savings and loan institutions—and the number was climbing—were sounding a little desperate. Too, I knew some new players were coming in and didn't like the hand they were dealt.

"Monty, I heard what you said in there, and I don't disagree with the direction," said the owner of a California thrift barely seconds after the food was served.

I remembered him being combative and bombastic at some of the committee meeting debates when we were hammering out the legislative wish-list.

He continued, "But damn it, we have to take the gloves off. We're all sitting on a pile of long-term mortgages with interest rates that are killing us." His voice began to rise.

I thought he would come up out of his chair at one point.

"I need to be able to get into the trenches with these commercial developers," he argued.

"George, calm down," said an owner named Phil from Massachusetts. "You had your vote when we put together our plan. Not everyone thinks we should abruptly shift gears. Jimmy Carter's leading Ford in the polls. He was a farmer and small businessman before being elected governor down in Georgia. Supporting the average person is his mantra. If he's elected in November, the populist Dems are going to take over the White House. Because of our mission, we'll get a fair hearing."

"I disagree, Phil," half-shouted Rodney, a sun-bronzed Texas thrift CEO. "I don't care if Ford beats Carter or vice versa. Unless one of them comes in with both guns blazing for deregulation, we've got to get a better grip on Congress. The laws have to be changed, pure and simple. One more thing…"

George, the boisterous Californian interrupted, "Rodney's right. Hell, the White House didn't create this problem. The Federal Reserve caused all of this grief in the first place. When they shrunk the money supply by raising banks' reserve requirements, interest rates skyrocketed. They drove my investors—and yours, Phil—straight into the arms of the securities markets we can't compete with. We've all had people lined up outside our front doors, wanting to withdraw their savings to go get a better deal."

Sensing the discussion going nowhere, except perhaps out of hand, I decided to intercede. "Let's step back for a minute. We had this argument earlier this year, and nothing has changed, except we're in the middle of a national election. The same regulators are in place, and we need to get even closer to them than in the past. And folks, the agenda I reported out there in the Arlington room is the one we all finally approved."

I continued, "Here's my biggest concern. If we work all the parties—White House, Congress, regulatory agencies—and get anything close to what we want, we have to be vigilant. Some of you, like our California friend George here, want us completely free from the shackles of long-term mortgages. I understand that might help us dig out of our hole. But I also worry we might lose sight of why our industry was first created. Financial access to affordable housing."

The Massachusetts owner, Phil, took the cue. "Right. If the government turns us loose to street brawl with banks and other forms of investment, it could be an invitation to a wild west cowboy kind of freedom. We have to earn a profit, but we need to be careful about the industry being snapped up by speculators, real estate developers, construction contractors, anyone with a little cash to invest. We're talking about a recipe for corruption. Look, people, some of you want to rebel against the system that's been working for decades." He turned and addressed George and Rodney directly. "Just because you hail from California or Texas doesn't mean you're not in the U.S. of A. We don't have any room in our industry for Fidel Castro."

"Why, you supercilious son-of-a-bitch," George shrieked, rising and lurching backward. I felt my heart skip a beat as his chair toppled and banged heavily against the wall. The Californian strode around the table and confronted Phil as I and several others grabbed and tried to restrain him. A few dishes crashed to the floor. George broke our hold and grabbed Phil's lapels, seething. Someone, I'm not sure who, yanked Phil back in time to prevent disaster. Meanwhile, several of us steered George away from the Massachusetts man.

I was stupefied when George continued on out the door.

"Come on, George," I implored. "Come back in and let's discuss this amicably."

The Californian continued his exit, and to my surprise, Rodney, the Texan, followed, scowling at the rest of us as if we were enemies. "You sumbitches are living in the past," he barked at us before disappearing behind his friend.

Several waiters hustled around to pick up the spilled dishes. We all sank glumly back into our chairs, astonished at the outburst.

"Sorry, everyone," I offered limply. "I guess I can't keep control of the troops."

"Don't be silly, Monty," said a long-time committee member who'd stayed out of the fray. "Except for George's bad behavior, I'm not surprised by the argument. We can expect this debate to go on for years to come."

I said, "What I worry about is, if attitudes like George's rule the day—high-risk investing and speculative loans—what's to keep some mortgage broker in Milwaukee or, heck, a barber from Alabama, from getting a state charter and starting his own thrift? I'm not a big fan of the regulators. But if they ever take the handcuffs completely off, the last thing we should want is for this industry to lose our compass."

I watched as several others nodded in agreement. Thankfully, the dessert plates were being served, lifting my spirits a bit. "Let's have some cheesecake." I tried hard to sound enthusiastic.

CHAPTER FOURTEEN

The luncheon in the Beeson Room was served buffet style. Always unfazed by meeting new people, Will engaged two of his fellow line-mates in casual conversation. "Looks good enough to eat," he joked as they began filling their plates. "I hope that's not mystery meat up ahead."

"Don't see any Tex Mex here," said the man moving along the opposite side of the serving table.

"Or 'cue either," chimed in the small, bespectacled man behind Will. "How can it be lunch without barbecued ribs?"

"You two must be from Texas," Will offered.

"I'm Max Davis," responded the first. "In case you can't tell from my New York accent," he chuckled at his own joke, "I'm from Houston, owner of Pasadena Savings and Loan." He ladled a big helping. "Well, guess I'll have to settle for goldarned baked chicken."

Spooning some vegetables onto his plate, Will turned to the barbecue lover behind him. "You're from Texas, too?"

The man nodded. "Fred Katzen. I'm director of the Federal Home Loan Bank in Dallas."

As they moved from the steam table and surveyed the room, Will joshed, "Wow, the regulator and the regulated. And you two are speaking to each other?" They all laughed. "I'm Will Martin, Wichita Savings. Mind if I sit with you?"

"Come on, Will," Max Davis urged. "I see three spots open over there."

Will set his plate down next to his new friends and introduced himself to the table's other occupants.

They appeared to know each other; all were engaged in seemingly private conversations.

"Hi, everyone. I'm Will Martin. It looks like we were late to the party. Most of you are almost finished."

They each acknowledged him with a wave or half-rose and reached a handshake across the table.

A woman whose name tag said, "*Hello, I'm Ruth*," snickered. "Some of us cut out early so we could get to the head of the line."

Will smiled. "Then you missed my boss' presentation."

Ruth chuckled and said, "Sorry. Maybe you can tell us what we missed," but immediately returned to her discussion with the woman sitting next to her.

"So, you're with Wichita Savings and Loan," said the Texan, Max Davis. "You work with Monty Johnson? The guy who made the last speech?"

"Yes. Do you know him?" Will asked.

"No, but I wouldn't mind meeting him, since he heads up the legislative committee. I'm interested in how we can get those do-nothing politicians to cut us a little slack."

"Max is new to our industry," Fred Katzen explained to Will. "He's not used to how slowly the wheels of government turn."

Davis said, "I bought the place a year or so ago. I'm a mortgage broker by background. This little thrift down there was teetering on the brink, so I like to think I rescued it."

Will nodded. "Good luck making a go of it. You're getting in at the right time."

Max said, "Hell, I'm running into the same problems my predecessors were having. Maybe they got out at the right time."

"Max, I'm betting you didn't buy into your business because you thought there was no way to make some money. Like I said, we've been through a rough patch, but I think the climate's going to get a lot better soon."

"What makes you think so?" the regulator, Katzen, interjected.

"Several reasons. For one thing, I think we're going to emerge from the horrible rate controls they put on the entire banking industry ten years ago. Fed policies mandated limits on what we could charge for mortgages. Then they let the rest of the financial world offer higher yields than we were allowed, picking off our depositors by the boatload. I'll bet the savings and loan Max bought was struggling because of slow growth from losing investors."

Davis now turned toward his articulate new friend, listening intently. "Slow business growth and inflation—high prices, yes. The bean counters call it stagflation. Those yahoos always have to make up a name for some bag of crap they created."

Now Will's engine was running. "Right. The laws for too long have put a cap on the rates we can pay on savings. And now with interest rates going astronomically high, depositors are bailing out right and left to find better returns on their investment."

"That's right," Max shook his head. "Like high interest CDs we're not permitted to offer. I've hired a money guy as director to try and figure our way out of it. But we're still not generating enough income. Will, we're getting smaller. Between the high rates we pay on money, and this sluggish economy, it's like slogging through frigging quicksand. So, you said it's a good time to get in. Again, like Fred here, I ask, why do you say so?"

By now the others at the table finished eating and began to drift away. Will and the two Texans sat alone, deep in their discussion. Will put down his fork and turned his full attention on Max and Fred. "We can innovate our way out of this mess. Find alternative mortgage instruments. Push the government to let us invest directly in construction projects, make commercial loans, sell competitively priced CDs. We have an army of community leaders in this industry, and every one of them has standing with their local politicians. I'll bet you know a few good old boys down there in Texas who wield a lot of clout on the Hill."

"That's true," Davis responded. "Got a fraternity brother from Baylor sitting on the House Banking Committee."

Will reached out and grasped Max's arm. "There you go. You've hit on why we're going to turn this ship around. We're emerging from a tough operating environment. But with a little brain power and some help from our friends, I predict in the next few years you won't even recognize the industry you've gotten yourself into. And now, I have to go find a bathroom."

Finished eating, they rose to leave. Max Davis grasped Will's handshake firmly. "Wichita Savings and Loan, huh? Are you guys all in with this innovation idea?"

"Well, I'm treasurer of the institution, but I'm working for a pretty conservative father and son management. I mean, you heard Monty Johnson this morning—he's my boss. He wants what's best for the industry, and he'll do a great job of advocating for change. But I'm not sure Wichita Savings is going to be on the leading edge."

Davis said, "Will, like I told you, I've hired a director, but I'm not sure he's got the stuff. Plus, I recently found out he's got a couple of things in his background the feds might be looking into. Maybe he's not the right guy, know what I mean?" He handed Will a business card. "I'd like to hear more of your ideas, if we get the chance. Okay if I keep in touch? There could come a time when we might be able to help each other."

The two Texans, Max Davis and Fred Katzen, watched Will walk down the corridor toward the men's room. "I like that young man," Max told the regulator. "He seems real sharp."

Katzen nodded agreement. "I'll tell you one thing. He talks a good game. If he's as adept at managing as he is expressing his opinions, you could do worse than getting him down to Houston to help you run your place."

Davis regarded Katzen with mild surprise. "Fred, I wouldn't expect to hear such words from you. As a regulator, the last thing I'd think you want to deal with is a young buck with game-changing ideas. Think what a headache he would be for you and your folks up there in Dallas."

The regulator smiled. "I've told you ever since you bought Pasadena Savings, I'm on your side. Max, this crunch the industry's been in the past few years is as bad for us regulators as it is for you. We're the ones floating you the loans. We need for you to succeed. I admire the young blood like Martin coming in and looking for ways to fix the problem. Anyone as intelligent as he is working in my jurisdiction will have my ear, I promise you."

Max Davis patted Katzen's shoulder. "That's what I like about you, Freddy boy. You don't consider yourself the enemy. Maybe we'll get rich together."

He squinted down the hallway. "As for young Will Martin, I'm fixing to talk to him again, sooner rather than later."

* * *

It was eight at night when Prudence picked Will up. Despite being a center for aircraft manufacturing, Wichita did not have robust commercial air traffic. The airport was small compared with others in the Midwest, such as Kansas City and Tulsa, and at that hour, only a few travelers straggled through the baggage claim and out the doors toward transportation. Unlike larger terminals, the lack of activity permitted Prudence and several others to park curbside and wait for their passengers.

Will tossed his suitcase into the trunk of their four-door sedan and kissed his wife briefly as they switched sides so he could drive. Climbing in behind the wheel, he glanced back and smiled at their tiny daughter Hannah sleeping soundly in the back seat.

"How was it?" Prudence asked as they crossed the Kellogg bridge toward their house.

"I learned a lot," he answered. "Monty made a great presentation. Oh, and I met a very interesting guy. He bought a savings and loan down in Houston. I think he's going to offer me a job."

"In Houston? Eeeeuw! What kind of job?"

"Well, he didn't say. Just told me he wanted to stay in touch. I don't think he's exactly in love with the guy running his company."

They drove in silence the rest of the way. Arriving at the house, Will pulled the car into their driveway and went back to get the suitcase while his wife woke Hannah. Prudence carried her into the house, the slumbering tot's arms and legs wrapped around her mother.

"I wouldn't want to go to Houston," Prudence complained as she started up the stairs with her sleepy load. "There's nothing down there but heat and humidity. And oil refineries."

Will set down the luggage at the foot of the staircase and went toward the kitchen. "Do you want a beer?"

"I'll get Hannah down and join you in the den," she answered.

Will was already settled on the couch, his jacket and shoes off and tie loosened, when Prudence returned. He handed her the beer as she settled beside him, and they shared a long kiss. "I missed you, Sweetheart," he said.

"Me too," she responded. Taking a long sip of the beer, she said, "Will, you're so ambitious. First you quit Daddy's company, and now you're talking about going to Houston. You have a great job here with Monty Johnson, and everyone around here loves you. You're the president of the Wichita Chamber of Commerce, for God's sake."

"Right, and when I spoon-fed them a great plan for the future of the city, what did they do?" He waited.

She didn't respond.

"You're damned right, they turned it down. Too expensive, they said."

"Everyone told you it was a fantastic plan and presentation. Daddy told me it's not the direction the City Council felt they should go, that's all."

Prudence paused, fixing her gaze directly on her husband. "I want Hannah to grow up in Wichita where our friends and families are," she scrunched up her face, "not hot old muggy Houston, Texas."

"Look, Pru, this guy hasn't even offered me anything. We talked. That's all. But honey, my future is someplace where I can be the top dog. It's different if you're the CEO of a company You call the shots. There's no committee meeting to knock your ideas down. And you have a lifestyle to match the responsibility. We can be rich if we play the right cards. You told me when we got married, you'd go where I go. If I'm offered this job, we'll see if you live up to your word."

CHAPTER FIFTEEN

Texas during the oil boom years was a natural home for the go-go spirit of free-wheeling businessmen and women. Inhabitants of the lone star state embraced a universe reflecting their history. The Republic of Texas sprang out of a desire by American settlers and Texas-dwelling Mexicans for a break from laws they didn't accept. Because of such rebellious defiance, the Republic of Texas fought for and won its independence in 1836.

When Texas not long afterward became one of the United States of America, the rebel mindset of its citizens didn't change. Or of others flocking to a place where they could express their independence. They clung to the fierce self-rule determination that colored their past. They viewed the federal government with wariness, even after it bailed them out of debt. When their opinions clashed with Washington's views, some even insisted they could legally secede if they chose to.

Houston was the epicenter of the stand-alone attitude. The go-for-broke energy business made its engines hum. A cowboy culture oozed from its pores. Because it had no zoning laws, rather a mishmash of local ordinances, neighborhood plans and confusing policies, it was possible to see a forty-story high-rise office building next to a neighborhood church, traffic jams notwithstanding.

When Will Martin moved to Houston, his embrace of a wildcat approach to the savings and loan business seemed to be a good fit. Yet his polished personal style, punctuated by his sartorial excellence, set him apart from most of the rough-and-tumble Texans he was about to do business with.

Nothing brought this contrast home more quickly than his meeting with Max Davis the first night Will arrived.

Gilley's was a wildly popular country and western bar. It was located in Pasadena, a town a few miles south of Houston and the home of Will's new company, the little Pasadena Savings and Loan. Men and women clad in western garb gathered there to eat, drink, dance and ride the iconic mechanical bull. The only patrons there who wore a suit had just left work, and even then, they lost their neckties and donned cowboy hats and boots.

When Will arrived in his customary tailor-made suit and tie, he seemed oddly out of place. It was six o'clock. Still too early for the regulars who came to drink, dance and party. But an after-work crowd filed in to hang at the bar to meet and greet.

Will stood in the doorway looking around for someone to rescue him. Max Davis did.

"There you are," Davis said, approaching from the bar with a longneck beer in tow. "Welcome to Texas, Will. Did you have a good flight?"

"It was a little rough," Will shook his hand. "I could use a drink, for sure."

"Let's go get you one. Scotch, right?" Will nodded and followed Davis as his new colleague wended his way through the gathering throng. Max emerged with the drink and led Will to an open booth. "This is my hangout. They always take good care of me at the bar, because I run up a pretty good tab every month."

"You do business here?" Will asked, looking around at the cowboy décor.

"Sometimes," Davis answered. "Depends on who I'm dealing with, but I'm at Gilley's several nights a week. Hell, I grew up in the area, and I guess I'm a cowboy at heart. The chili and barbecue suit my appetite, and I like Texas and Mexican beers. My wife likes it here, too."

A loud whoop echoed across the massive dance floor from the far end of the room. A young woman dressed in western garb was giving the bull a challenge, although the operator was letting her have an easy ride. She waved her hat in the air as her friends cheered her on.

Max laughed. "I'm too old to ride that mechanical bull over there, but it's still fun to hang around and watch the young crazies get thrown off the danged thing."

Will watched the action around him. A live band had taken the stage and started their version of "Honky-tonk Woman." A dozen or so couples converged on the dance floor and two-stepped around the floor. Some beer-drinking couples were throwing punches at the boxing machines near the entrance, laughing and laying bets. The crowd was growing, and so was the noise. Will studied Max, who appeared to be taking it all in as if he owned it, proud to be a part.

A waitress approached, smiling widely.

Max motioned for another round of drinks.

"I was put off when I walked up outside," Will said. "I've seen better looking pool halls in small-town Kansas. But inside, the place is amazing—fantastic dance floor, first-class performance stage, and that enormous bar is impressive."

Max smiled, seeming pleased his favorite haunt made a good impression. Over the rising din, he asked, "Your wife and kid stayed behind?".

"I'm going to do a little house hunting the next few days," Will told him. "Prudence and our daughter will come down next week sometime."

"She's taking the idea of moving here okay?"

"Prudence isn't overjoyed, I'll tell you frankly," Will said. "She's lived in Wichita all her life. This will be a big change for her. But Max, once she gets down here, sees what kind of nice place we can live in and gets accustomed to a much bigger city, I think she'll be fine."

"I assume you plan to find something here in Pasadena," Max said, "so you'll be close to the office."

Their drinks came, and Will took a long swallow. "I thought I'd look in Houston, Max. I've heard River Oaks is a great area, with good schools. I need to live where I can get to know the city's business and political leaders."

Max frowned. "Will, I'm planning on you growing this goldarned company, so such a high-toned neighborhood won't be out of your price range for very long. But it's a lot more of a commute than you might want to make."

Will finished his drink and leaned in toward Max. "That's what I want to talk to you about. I don't plan to spend a lot of time down here in Pasadena." He watched Davis's face scrunch up quizzically and continued, "I'll drive down here a day or two a week to go over things with the group, check out the books, get a report on new business. But Max, I've put a lot of thought into this. Pasadena Savings isn't going to grow like you and I want it to unless we get in the middle of things. Houston is the key. We'll reel in much bigger fish than we can down here. I plan to advertise aggressively in the Houston media. There's nothing wrong with Pasadena. Hell, you've got Gilley's right here. And it's famous, I know. But downtown Houston is where our company needs to be. I don't have a timetable for it, but we need to move up there as soon as it makes sense."

The waitress approached again, and Max turned to Will. "Are you hungry? They've got great ribs here."

"Sure, I could eat some ribs," Will answered as the server made a note on her pad. He held up his glass. "And another one of these."

"You've kind of caught me off guard with all of this," Davis said when she left. "Tell me more about what you're thinking."

Will responded, "I'm going to lease an office downtown. Get to know the movers and doers in the city. When it's time, we'll move the whole operation up there. Nothing against Pasadena, but unless you're talking about dancing the Texas two-step and riding that bull over there, this isn't where the action is."

"We've got a lease on our office space," Max argued. "We'd have to wait until late next year, at least."

Will grinned. "You're a real estate man, Max. You know leases can be broken. All it takes is money. If we can make a lot more of it up there than we can down here, well…"

Max went on, "And hell, you know I live down here. If we move to Houston, then I'll be the one getting a shitty commute."

"Max, I don't expect you to come in the office every day. You're chairman of the board, not the CEO. You've got better things to do with your time, including running your real estate business. You have me to run the show now. You can come up to board meetings or when the regulators come to call, other similar events. But I'm in charge. You relax and enjoy the ride."

"Jeez Louise," Max exhaled. "Don't get me wrong, I hired you to come down here and shake up this little operation I bought. It sure hasn't been pulling its weight the past couple of years. But you're moving pretty goldarned fast."

The server laid large platefuls of ribs in front of them, and another round of drinks.

"Max, there's no such thing as too fast. You wait, you miss the gate. You sleep, you weep." He laughed. "When you hired me, you agreed to let me run the show. Did you mean it?"

"Hell yes, I did," Max stiffened a bit. "Did you think it was a line of crap?"

"No, I simply want to be sure we see it the same way," Will responded. "Tomorrow we're going to start building up the assets of Pasadena Savings. I've gone over the reports you sent, and I don't need to tell you the company's basically broke. Max, we're going to breathe new life in this dead puppy. I'll probably even pitch my real estate agent for some investment, who knows? And we're going to dog Washington until they give us some slack. I intend to let Houston know we mean business."

He turned and watched as a young cowboy catapulted off the bull with his arms and legs flailing, his hat flying, and landed hard on his tailbone. Will tapped Max's shoulder and pointed out the rider as he picked himself up, rubbed his backside, smoothed his hair before putting his hat back on and glanced around with an embarrassed grin.

"We're not going to be like some clumsy yahoo picking himself up off the floor, Max. We're going to get on that bull and ride it."

They laughed and dug into their ribs.

CHAPTER SIXTEEN

Pasadena Savings and Loan's new headquarters encompassed nearly a full floor of a recently constructed office tower, one of many being planned or built in Downtown Houston. Post-modern architecture was beginning to get its footing. The boring, rectangular, functional style of the so-called modern era was becoming eclipsed by architects' desire to create more colorful, whimsical features and lavish use of materials. The design of this granite and glass structure, aptly named the Houston Eclipse, featured a sweeping, curved façade near the roofline reminiscent of the great Gateway Arch in St. Louis. On the street level, the two-story entryway seemed unsupported by anything. As one passed through it, a shimmering waterfall cascaded into a pool and fountain on both sides of the glittering steel revolving doors. Inside, three retail floors were connected in an enormous atrium by two sets of escalators.

The upper seventeen stories were designed for offices, including Pasadena Savings' in the top floor. Situated in the southwest corner, Will's workspace provided a perfect vantage point to watch the aggressive growth spring up in Houston's central business district.

Max Davis, chairman of the company, was making his first visit to the newly acquired location. Workers were still completing the buildout, attempting not to trip over movers hauling in furniture and boxes of company records.

"Jeez, what a nice space," Max marveled. "Now, this is what I call first class."

Will said, "We're right where we need to be. This city is on fire—the Astrodome baseball stadium, the

Galleria mixed-use mall, the Summit Concert Hall. Who knows what else is on the horizon?" He walked to the huge window over-looking downtown, tugging Max with him, and pointed toward Louisiana Street. "Look over there at the fifty-story Shell building. Fantastic. And right over there, on Travis, they're going to start work on the Texas Commerce Tower. Seventy-five stories, Max. It'll be the tallest building in Texas, one of the biggest in the world. We couldn't be in a better spot to grow this business."

Davis looked out at the booming city and nodded. "I know I approved the lease, but I choked a little bit on the price tag."

"It's a good deal," Will answered. "Compared with what others are paying for square footage around here, we got off pretty cheap. Houston might be a little over-built, but not for long. With all the national firms bring-ing their headquarters, subsidiaries and divisions here, you won't be able to get office space like this much lon-ger. Don't forget, I took out an option for two additional floors at the same rate. In a few months, we'll move the banking operation into the first floor, giving our custom-ers easy access at street level. And if we need expansion space for headquarters, we can have the floor below this one. Max, if we're going to operate like a big-time com-pany, it's going to take some investment."

"I agree. But given Pasadena Saving's recent finan-cial history, you can understand why I'm a little con-cerned."

"Yes, I can. But let me worry about a return on our investment." Will walked to his desk and pulled a large folder from a drawer. "And speaking of Pasadena Sav-ings," he hesitated, studying Max's eyes, "I want to talk to you about my plan for a name change."

Max pulled a chair closer and sat down, waiting.

Will continued, "We need to ditch the Pasadena Savings and Loan identity. It doesn't reflect Houston, and it's reminiscent of an old-time thrift that nearly went belly up."

"What would we call it?" Max asked.

Will opened the portfolio, extracted some documents and unfolded them, revealing an artist's rendering of graphics. The first was the bold image of a sign, striking in bright green and blue colors and a modern, forward-leaning font, with the words, "Quivira Savings Bank."

Max stared. "What is that? Quiv—what?"

"Quivira," answered Will. "This name and design will go on every piece of company literature, any appropriate office space, everything the company touches."

"Okay," Max acknowledged. "But what in hell is Quivira?"

"I don't want to bore you with this, but I'll give you the brief notes version of the story," Will said. "In the sixteenth century, the Spanish explorer Francisco Coronado and his troops travelled north from Mexico searching for gold. He kept striking out, but when he reached New Mexico, he heard about a wealthy civilization called Quivira. A guide steered him southeast to Texas. But when he got to the panhandle, the natives there told him he was going the wrong direction. They said the real Quivira was north in the great plains, where gold hung from trees.

"He ended up in Kansas, where he actually encountered a tribe called the Quivira, later known as the Wichita. But he never found gold. The moral is he should have kept going south when he got to Texas. If he had gotten down here, where Houston is today, he might have struck it rich, like we're going to. That's what I have planned for us, Max, to make a pile of money. And we're going to call it Quivira, where gold hangs from trees."

He waited. Max's eyebrows were raised as he scanned the various drawings depicting the new name and graphics. "Hell, Will, I don't care about the history. I like the name. Let's do it." He shook Will's hand enthusiastically. "Now, take me around and show me my new office. And the boardroom where I get to be the big cheese once a month."

* * *

They spent thirty minutes walking through the corridors, reviewing plans, discussing features of the building. Will pointed out where and how various aspects of the company's operations would be performed.

As they reached the new boardroom space, Will told Max, "I'm going to manage this company like a big business should be run. We're going to have a strategic plan to steer by. All of our loan personnel, our lawyers and accountants—everybody will know what our goals and projections are. Every presentation to the board will be thoroughly developed, detail by detail. No deal will be made without input from the executive committee and the outside lawyers. Max, I'm going to put my business degree to work. You'll be proud of this company when we get it rolling properly."

"This all sounds good to me, Will," Max enthused.

They ended up in Will's office, and Davis prepared to leave. "I'll see you at the next board meeting," he slapped Will on the shoulder. "In our fancy new digs." He started out the door and then stopped and turned back. "Oh, what about your wife, Prudence? Cute gal. And your little daughter. Are they getting to like Houston okay?"

Will hesitated for a long moment. "Prudence has gone back to Wichita," he said finally.

"What, to see her folks?"

Will squirmed a bit, as if searching for words. "No, Max, she's gone back for good. We're getting a divorce."

Davis' jaw dropped, and he leaned back as if someone had shot him. "Holy tarnation. When did all this come about?"

"Pru left several months ago," Will answered. "She never should have come."

Davis came back in and sat down, staring up at Will. His blank expression was one of confusion and disbelief. "Good God, Will. You haven't mentioned a word about it."

"I don't talk much about my personal life, Max. Never have. I stick pretty much to business."

"But...jeez, she wasn't even here long enough to try the barbecue. I've only had a chance to be around her twice. The time when the two of you came down to Pasadena for dinner at our place. And the dinner we had up here at the Travis Club to introduce you to the board. I'm just flabbergasted."

"Pru wasn't happy here. She wanted to go home."

"What about your little girl?"

"Pru's getting custody. To be honest, it's a little contentious. We're still talking to lawyers about visitation rights and all the legal nonsense." He sat back, a sad frown washing across his face. "That's really all I want to say about it. It's for the best. Right now, I have my hands full getting Quivira off the ground."

Max nodded and smiled. "Quivira Savings Bank. I like it. It's got a nice ring to it."

CHAPTER SEVENTEEN

For several years, before the demands of success and the lure of luxurious living stole his heart, Will kept in constant touch with several high school pals. He exchanged weekly phone calls with Anthony Redman and Bill Dickerson, basketball buddies from his South Wichita days. None of his college relationships produced such promise of lifelong friendship.

So, it came as no surprise when Anthony called him with an invitation in October of the same year Prudence left Will and divorced him.

"Bill and I and maybe a couple of others hope to come down to Dallas for the Cotton Bowl," he said. "Notre Dame's playing the University of Houston. It's the Fighting Irish, Will! I may have a line on some tickets, and if they come through, we'll have an extra. Why don't you come up and join us? You can even root for Houston if you want, since that's your stomping grounds now. Besides, their mascot is the Cougars, just like South Wichita."

"Oh, sure, Tony," Will answered. "Root against Notre Dame? My dad would kill me. He's mad enough I'm not a practicing Catholic anymore. I appreciate the invitation. But this business has me running a lot of different directions at once. If I'm not chasing prospects with millions of dollars to invest, I'm flying somewhere to an association meeting. Sorry, but I don't see how I can get away."

* * *

Two days later, however, Will called Redman back. "Tony, I was wondering if you still have an extra Cotton Bowl ticket?"

"I have a few feelers out for a taker, but if you want it, it's yours," Tony answered.

"I've given it some thought. Pru's been gone for months, and I haven't done anything fun since. And after all, it's New Year's. Where will you be staying?"

"The Candlelight Suites, not far from the stadium."

"All right," Will said. "I can fly up and meet you at the hotel. Who's coming with you?"

"It's me, Bill Dickerson, and his sister Leslie. She's gone through a messy divorce, and he thought it would do her good to get away. You might remember her."

"Of course. Really cute, a freshman when we were seniors," Will said. "She would hang around Bill and me, and I used to tease her unmercifully. She would flirt right back. I remember wishing she was a year or two older. Sorry to hear about her marriage. At least, we'll be in the same sad boat. Tony, I'll see you on New Year's. Call me the week before with the details."

None of the planning for the day factored in the un-expected; one of the worst ice storms Dallas experienced in several decades struck the day before. Yet according to news media reports, the game was still on.

When Will's driver pulled onto the tarmac at Hooks Memorial, a large private Houston airfield catering to business flights, the Cessna Citation was fueled and ready to go. The Quivira charter's regular pilot, Hollister, greeted Will as he climbed into the craft. "Mr. Martin, this is Jeannine, our co-pilot for today."

Will reacted with mild surprise; Jeannine was the first female pilot he had flown with on the Citation.

She offered a business-like handshake. She was freckle-faced and red-headed, her hair pulled back in a bun beneath her cap. Her manner was sternly professional. "Mr. Martin, the weather looks nice and clear all the way to Dallas. It's still very cold up there, and we're going to fight a bit of a headwind, but nothing to worry about."

"Glad to have you flying for Quivira," Will said. He retreated to his favorite seat over the wing and extracted reading material from his bag.

Shortly after the crew went through their checks, and before taxiing out, Jeannine left the cockpit and approached him. "Anything I can get you before we take off, Mr. Martin?"

"I'm fine, thanks, Jeannine." He grinned. "I know where the booze is kept."

She laughed.

He asked, "Did you know this plane was made in my hometown?"

"You're from Wichita then," she answered.

"Right," he grinned, as if surprised she knew. "Jeannine, I hope you weren't insulted if I looked a little astonished when I came aboard. I'm not used to seeing a woman pilot."

"I'm not offended," she said. "I've gotten used to it. But I'll tell you what, Mr. Martin, there are a lot more like me coming."

"I hope you're right," he smiled. "I'm working toward getting more women in my boardroom."

Jeannine gave a polite nod and returned to the cockpit. Ten minutes later, they lifted off.

It was a short, but extremely turbulent flight to Big Prairie Muni Airport, four miles from the stadium. Will heaved a heavy sigh of relief as Hollister taxied off the runway and brought the Citation to a stop. He could see the limo outside waiting for him as he pulled on the overcoat he had carried with him. He would need it. The limo driver standing outside the car, and the workers hustling around the facility, exhaled frosty clouds as they breathed the frigid air.

"Bundle up tight out there, Mr. Martin," Hollister cautioned. "It's about twenty-four degrees Fahrenheit, winds gusting at thirty. It'll be chilly at the stadium."

Will pulled the camel hair coat snugly around his neck as he started down the steps. "I thought we were in Texas, not Minnesota. See you after the game."

Will knew the driver. He had called the same service the Home Loan Bank used to pick him up when he came to Dallas to meet with the regulators. "Morning, Ruben."

The driver tipped his hat and opened the door. "Mr. Martin. If you need more heat back there, let me know."

The streets were still iced over. The sand mixed with salt made grinding sounds under the all-weather tires of the stretch limo. Within minutes, they were pulling under the portico of the Candlelight. It was a low-rise building with no striking features, unlike the newer, more spectacular hotels where he usually stayed in Dallas. No staff emerged to greet him, as they did at the Park Two Hotel or Empire Plaza downtown.

"Wait right here in front," Will told Ruben as the driver held the car door for him. "We're picking up three other people, then right on to the stadium."

Anthony, Bill and Leslie were in the lobby. Will greeted his old pals with handshakes and shoulder slaps and Happy New Year's Day greetings. He gave Leslie an awkward hug. She was togged out in a heavy coat, scarf and fashionable knitted cap. Her smooth face and bright green eyes were stunning.

"Are you sure you want to do this?" Will joked. "It's

friggin' freezing out there. I assume the game's on television."

"You wimp," Anthony shot back. "You grew up in Wichita, for God's sake. I don't remember you whining about winter in Kansas when we ran around in shirtsleeves, blasting each other with snowballs."

Will laughed at the memory.

"Besides," his friend continued, "we saw the monster stretch you climbed out of. We have to ride in that baby. Let's do this."

As the driver dropped them in the limo area, Will left him with instructions. "If you need to gas up so you can run your heater while you wait, do it right away and then come back. This game could be a blowout, so we might need you available early."

"No way," Bill Dickerson protested. "We're not missing one minute of it. I assume they'll have something in the stadium to warm us up."

Notre Dame took the first lead of the game, but Houston soon came roaring back. By halftime, the Irish trailed by a 20-12 score.

"What's the matter with Joe Montana?" Bill lamented. "He doesn't look like the quarterback we're used to seeing."

The four headed toward the concession stand with thousands of other half-frozen fans. As they walked, Leslie fell in lockstep with Will behind her brother Bill and his friend Tony. She hugged tightly against Will for warmth. Her nose and ears were lobster-red, and she was shaking almost uncontrollably.

"I've never been so cold, not even in Kansas," Will said to her. "You look miserable. If you want, we can go back to the hotel and watch the rest of it on television."

Her eyes brightened. "You wouldn't mind?"

"Of course not. I'm shivering harder than you are."

"Tony. Bill. Do you want to go back and watch it on TV?" Leslie appealed.

They both turned back in disbelief. "Are you crazy? It's Notre Dame," Tony shouted with incredulity. "Let's get some brewskis and tough it out. The Irish have to make a comeback."

"Actually, I'm as miserable as Leslie," Will told them. "We're going back."

"Suit yourself," Tony said, and he and Bill hot-footed it toward the beer line.

In the car en route to the hotel, Leslie continued to cling to Will's arm. "I might never thaw out," she laughed musically, then focused her dazzling green eyes on Will's face. "You know I had a crush on you, right? When we were in school?" She watched his surprised expression. "Remember how I used to hang around and watch basketball practice, when you and Bill were seniors? You don't think I was there to watch my brother play, do you?"

Will replied, "I was so full of myself. And you were so young."

"I'm grown up now," she said. "Are you staying at the same hotel?"

"No, I'm flying back tonight. I have business in Houston tomorrow."

Her bright, smooth face wrinkled into a frown. "Oh, no, Will. We're just getting re-acquainted. I hoped we could have some time to talk more."

Will failed to respond for several minutes, then said, "Why don't you fly back with me?"

"What? To Houston?"

"Why not?" he persisted. "I'd like for you to see where I live. We could get caught up."

Leslie stammered, astonished, "But...but what about the guys? I have a plane reservation home tomorrow."

"It's no problem. We'll get the ticket changed, or I'll pay for a new one out of Houston. Look, we haven't seen each other in years. Leslie, you are a beautiful woman, and we should get to know each other better. This way we can."

Her shoulders lifted slowly in a shrugging motion. "Well, since it's you, I don't think Bill and Tony would mind. We'll have to get in touch with them, somehow. And I have to pick up my bag; I haven't unpacked, we just checked in and met you."

"Then it's settled. We'll stop by, pick up your suitcase, and I'll call the pilot to see if he can get us in the air ahead of schedule. It's usually not a problem. Ruben can drop us off, then wait for Tony and Bill and give them the message. In fact, I'll write one out. I promise it'll be okay."

As they approached the hotel, Will instinctively cupped his hand under Leslie's chin and kissed her, slowly.

"Oh, wow. This is really too much," she bubbled. "Will, don't you think this is moving a little too fast?"

Will smiled and kissed her again, his hand remaining on her face. "Look at it this way. We've known each other literally for years. Maybe we're behind schedule."

She giggled at the thought. "I can't believe we're doing this," she said, her voice shaking with excitement. "But Will, I want to."

CHAPTER EIGHTEEN

Will hadn't had sex in many months. Not only had his marriage to Prudence deteriorated quickly after their move to Houston, but so also did their love life. Ever since the break, Will stayed at the office for long hours most nights, rather than rattle around the spacious house they bought together.

When Leslie returned with him from Dallas, it would be the first time since Prudence left anyone except Will had crossed the threshold. Leslie wandered from room to room, "oohing" and "aahing" over the place. "Will, I had no idea you lived in such a mansion," she gushed. "You could get three of the houses I grew up in into this wonderful home."

"You really like it?" he grinned widely.

"More than like," she told him. "I absolutely love it. It's beautiful."

He put her suitcase down beside the stairway and hung their coats in the hall closet. "I never understood why Pru was so unhappy living here."

Ignoring the comment, Leslie said, "I'd like to freshen up. Could we get something to drink? After all, it's still New Year's Day, at least until midnight."

Will laughed. "Of course. I make a pretty good margarita."

"Sounds yummy," she said and disappeared into the powder room.

When she returned, smelling of fresh perfume, they sat in the great room in front of a roaring fire and sipped their drinks. "I have something to tell you, Will," Leslie said. "You might not like hearing it. Tony told me last week Prudence and some doctor have paired up. He left his wife and three kids before she went back to Wichita. Tony knows someone who knows someone who heard as soon as your divorce goes through, they're going to get married." She waited a tick and watched his face.

Will showed no emotion.

"I'm sorry to be the one to break the news," she said, on the verge of tears.

After waiting quietly for a moment, Will stood up and paced across the room, carrying his drink with him. "I don't get it. Why didn't Tony tell me? Or your brother?"

"They didn't think it would be right to have such a conversation over the phone, so they were going talk to you in person, today. Except we sort of changed the plan."

Will went to the bar and fixed them another drink. When he returned, she asked him, "Do you hate me for telling you?"

He shook his head no. "Leslie, it's okay, really. I've accepted the fact we're through. I don't understand why she came out here with me in the first place."

"I don't know. But I'm sure of one thing. She was crazy to leave." Leslie took his drink and put it on the coffee table next to hers. She unbuttoned her blouse, then his shirt, and kissed him as she pushed him back into the sofa. They kissed heatedly while articles of clothing fell to the floor one by one. Finally, naked, Will groaned, "I've never done it on this sofa before. Think we should we go find a bed?"

"This is the perfect place," she whispered. They stretched out with their nude bodies folded together. Their lovemaking was hot, noisy and passionate.

Afterward, they lay together for a long time, catching their breath. Will finally said, "Good God. That was fantastic. It's been a long time for me."

"Same here," she admitted. "But I don't think we forgot how."

He chuckled at her dry humor. "Leslie, I have an idea," he said.

She answered, "So far, I've liked all of your ideas. Tell me."

"Let's go take a shower together. If we feel like it, we can do it again right there."

She half-shrieked, "Will Martin. I've never made love in the shower before."

"I think you'll like it," he told her. "Leave your clothes here. I have robes upstairs. We can come back down for a nightcap. He put on his shorts, and she her panties, and they walked together to the stairs. He picked up her suitcase. "I'll put this in the guest room," he offered.

"No," she countered. "Put it in the master."

* * *

They ate breakfast at Houston Intercontinental. It was ten-thirty, and her flight would board several minutes before noon.

"I can't believe we did it so many times last night," she gasped. "I'm embarrassed."

"Don't be." He toasted her with his orange juice. "Happy New Year," he said. They laughed lustily together.

"Will, is this the start of something?" Leslie asked, her voice quavering a bit.

"Of course, it is," he replied. "The second I walked into the hotel lobby in Dallas, I was attracted to you. I couldn't believe you were the skinny little girl with a ponytail I used to tease all the time in Wichita. But then, after last night, well…"

She looked into his eyes, hers growing misty. "How could we possibly make it work? With you down here and me up there?"

"Let's take it a step at a time. I'm coming to Wichita in three months. There's some business with the divorce and custody, and my parents have an anniversary. Let's plan on spending as much time together as possible. Meanwhile, we have phones. We can talk every day. Are you okay with that?"

"Am I?" she responded to the preposterous query. "I can hardly wait."

CHAPTER NINETEEN

It had been some time since I had talked to Will Martin. We attended many of the same association meetings, especially those of the U.S. League, but it seems we always served on different committees or had responsibilities that didn't cross paths. One time, I remember we passed each other in the lobby of the hotel where a League meeting was taking place.

Will paused for a moment, smiled wryly, and said, "Didn't you used to be Monty Johnson?" Then he grinned and walked off to another meeting. I regarded that brief encounter as one of friendship.

On another occasion, I saw him during lunch break. We were at a League meeting in Baltimore. Will was in the hotel lobby engaged in a spirited conversation with several people.

Trying to top his previous performance, I walked up behind him and said, "I recognize the face, but the name escapes me."

Will looked back at me, and without smiling said, "Hello, Monty. It's good to see you," then turned and resumed his conversation.

It threw me off a bit, knowing I must have interrupted something important with a lame joke. Still, I was disappointed he barely acknowledged me.

But then, in March of 1979, Will came by Wichita Savings to see me. He called ahead, to my surprise, and told me he had something important to discuss. "Of course, Will," I replied. "I have the morning free."

He had hardly changed. A few gray hairs were creeping in, and his new glasses made him appear a tad more distinguished, if that was possible. But he had the same youthful smoothness to his face, the familiar steadiness in his dark eyes exuding intelligence and control.

And as always, he wore the finest clothes on the planet. He could have stepped right off the pages of *Gentlemen's Life* magazine.

"Monty, thanks for making time for me," he said, oozing politeness.

"Nonsense," I replied. "It's always great to see you. I wish we had time to sit and chat when we're running around like crazy at League meetings."

"As do I, Monty," he said. Will leaned back and glanced around my office. "The business is going well?"

I shrugged, non-committal. "You know. We're all slogging through it. How about Quivira? Are you still growing the asset base like crazy?

"It's coming along. I have a few new ideas I'm going to try next year."

"You're never short on ideas, Will. Never have been. I wish you all the success down there."

"No hard feelings about my leaving, then?"

"Are you kidding? What makes you ask such a thing? You had a terrific opportunity in Houston. Right on the ground floor. I would have had you bottled up here forever. You always wanted to be the top gun."

Will hesitated, as if something heavy was on his mind. "Monty," he said, "I've been up here for a week, and I'm going back tomorrow. The reason I wanted to see you is to invite you to my wedding."

You could have knocked me over with a feather duster. I'd heard about his breakup with Prudence and her new pending marriage. Nothing happens in Wichita without word getting around pretty fast. But as for Will's plans, I had no idea.

"That's wonderful, Will," I said. "Who's the lucky lady?"

"You probably know her family, the Dickersons. Her name is Leslie. Her brother Bill was in my class at South Wichita. She's coming out of a divorce like I am, and we really hit it off. Will you come?"

"Of course I will. When and where?"

"It's going to be very small. Only family and a few good friends. You were my mentor here, you and Mr. Johnson, and I hope he and your mother will come, too. It'll be sometime in July. I'll call you with the date and the place, as soon as we have reserved a hall."

I asked, "You're not getting married in the church?"

He responded a little sheepishly, "My marriage hasn't been annulled, and Leslie left the church anyway, during her marriage. My parents don't like the idea, of course, but we're going to have Reverend Walter Steinkooler do the vows. Leslie attends his church, and he's agreed to do it."

"Let me know the details. I'll be there in my Sunday suit," I said cheerfully.

The next week, it brought me a huge amount of pleasure to call Will in Houston. "I talked to my mom and dad about your wedding plans," I said. "My father says he'll be there on one condition."

"Which is?" Will asked.

"You have it at my folks house in Wichita Heights. Will, they have a fantastic back yard, and you can have a tent put up. Their deck is a perfect place to set up a bar for a reception. All you'd need to do is find a caterer, and you'll be in business. What do you say?"

"I don't understand." I could hear genuine wonder in his voice. "Why would your parents want to extend such a nice gesture to me?"

"They always liked you, Will. And you did a lot for our company while you worked here. And for the city of Wichita. Besides, it's my dad. His life is one big nice gesture."

"That's an extraordinary offer," Will said. "Of course. I'll pay for everything. And Leslie is right there, so she'll take care of the arrangements. I'll have her call your mother. Please tell them how much I appreciate them."

I felt oddly ecstatic after we hung up. Will and I hadn't seen eye-to-eye on business matters when he worked for us in Wichita. For my family to be able to do something noteworthy in his life brought me inexplicably immense joy.

CHAPTER TWENTY

"What a wonderful time, sweetheart. I couldn't have had a more beautiful, happier wedding if we'd been at St. Patrick's Cathedral." Leslie leaned across the car seat and kissed Will's cheek.

He beamed.

She continued, "The Johnsons were so great about everything. And Will, honey, you ordered perfect weather."

"Of course. That was my one job." He flashed her a quick smile. "Did you get to meet everyone?"

"I knew nearly everybody already. Except Lawson—what was his last name?"

"Jeffries. Lawson and I go back to our days together here at Wichita Savings. He was a terrific football player who went pro after he graduated from Kansas City University. But he eventually decided to go into business. Actually…"

"What?"

"I wasn't going to tell you this, because you might think my mind was on business instead of our wedding. But…"

"But what?"

"I had a few minutes of private conversation with Lawson and asked him if he wanted to come to Houston. He's a talented man, and I hate to see him waste his time stuck in such a conservative work environment."

"What did he say?"

"He's going to think about it. You're not angry?"

"Of course not. Will, we're married. Married! What's there to be angry about? And Paris. I can't wait to get our honeymoon started."

"You're fantastic, you know it? Leslie, do you mind if we take a short detour on the way to the airport? We have some extra time until our flight."

"Where are we going?"

"You'll see," Will said.

He swung the car around a sweeping curve and onto a side road starting as blacktop and eventually becoming gravel. Passing under an archway with the words "Holy Redeemer" in intricate metalwork, Will steered through several turns and pulled off to one side.

"What are we doing at the cemetery?" Leslie asked, puzzled.

Will turned toward her with a somber expression. "I haven't told you about this yet. But I don't know how long it'll be before we get back here, to Wichita. My parents came today, and I'm happy about that. But they were distant, and I know it's because I'm no longer the devout young Will Martin I used to be. Leslie, when I and my siblings were children, my mother carried three more babies to full term. But each one died, one after a day, the other two at birth."

He turned off the car's engine and looked around, getting his bearings. "They're buried here, and I think I can find them. I wanted to pay my respects before we leave for France. It could be the last time I'll be out here for a long time—until my parents…" His voice quavered.

She wrapped her arms around him and said, "Of course, Will. Would it be okay if I go with you?"

"Sure," he said and stepped out of the car.

Leslie retrieved some of the flowers she had brought from the wedding, and they tip-toed between headstones until, after a fifteen-minute search, they found the three tiny gravesites.

"Thomas Christian Martin," Leslie read on the first. Then, "Margaret Adrianne Martin, and Priscilla Victoria Martin. 1953, 1954 and 1955. They were each conceived and passed away a year apart, Will."

He stood staring, not speaking.

"You were just a boy. It must have been so traumatic for you."

"Maybe. I don't think I'll ever forget it," he confessed softly. "I was the oldest, nine or ten, but we weren't told much about what was going on. Just that my mother was in the hospital, and we weren't allowed to go see her. The only vivid memory I have of the time is once, when I was at home alone for some reason, I went outside in the backyard and cried and cried. I've never talked to them about it since then."

His voice trailed off, and again he stood staring at the little graves in silence. Leslie knelt and placed a single rose on each headstone, then turned back toward him with tears streaming down her face. She wrapped her arms around Will, sobbing quietly, and they stood there for several long minutes, not speaking.

Finally, Will drew in a breath loudly and said, "Let's go to Paris."

* * *

The taxi ride to the Balzac Hotel near the *Champs Elysees* in Paris was a wild experience. The driver of the little taxi stuffed to the gills with Will's and Leslie's luggage wove in and out of traffic, speeding through roundabouts with little regard for human life, least of all the Americans'. The Frenchman spoke a little broken English, about the same amount as Leslie knew of French from her school days. Somehow, they communicated well enough to get to the destination.

Will watched Leslie's astonished expression with amusement as the driver pulled in front of the hotel.

"It's beautiful," she exclaimed.

The five-star mansion, once the home of French writer *Honoré de Balzac,* was a picture of opulence. A recent renovation, rather than imposing a more modern façade, preserved the 19th century style employed by architect Paul Dechard when he was designing the original townhouse for the director of the Paris Opera. They climbed out of the car and followed the bellman inside, staring at the edifice, which fit in ideally with the historic feel of Paris.

As they entered their expansive suite, Leslie paused to admire the neo-classical furnishings featuring richly colored, luxurious fabrics. She then flew to the corner window, gazing out at the Paris skyline.

She turned to her new husband and exclaimed, "Look, Will, there's the Eiffel Tower. And the *Arc de Triomphe.*"

He joined her at the window, staring out over the city.

"Are we in heaven?" she asked dreamily, her green eyes shining.

Will wrapped his arm around her waist. "As close to it as we can get," he responded.

* * *

The newlyweds spent five days drifting around the city, riding the *Bateaux Mouches* down the Seine River, strolling through museums, lunching *al fresco* at little brasseries. They spent half a day at the *Musée d'Orsay* and most of another at the *Louvre.* The July weather was on the hot side, but not unbearable, and they walked miles each day.

"This is the finest restaurant I've ever been in," Leslie said the third evening as they dined at *L'Astrance*, with its rich, gold-hued décor and its menu specialty, buttermilk and burnt toast crumb soup. "But it seems so expensive."

"Honey, we're on our honeymoon," he admonished. "Relax and enjoy. Tomorrow I'm taking you shopping."

"Will, I don't need to buy anything in France," she said.

"You should have something from Paris. It's an absolute requirement," he grinned.

* * *

The next morning, shortly after breakfast, they headed out. "I heard about this boutique on *Avenue Montaigne*," Will said. "Let's see if there's something there you'd like."

After a ten-minute stroll, Will steered her into *Belle Femme*, a charming place with stunning displays of women's dresses and gowns. "We'll be going to a lot of fashionable events in Houston," he said. "Let's start right here building your new wardrobe."

Leslie spent the next two hours trying on gowns, finally finding one fitting her trim figure perfectly, showing a bit of cleavage. Its jade hue complemented her eyes. "I love this one, Will," she said. "But it looks really, really pricey."

She started to turn toward the sales lady, but Will stopped her. "Don't," he said. "This gown looks incredible on you. I'll have her ship it to Houston."

"But you haven't asked her the price," Leslie said.

Will shook his head, a smug grin displaying his pride. "I don't have to ask the price. I know I can afford it."

She gave him a curious look, her green-eyed gaze wide. "Will, how much do you make? I've never asked."

He pulled her close to him and whispered, "About a million."

"Dollars? A year?" she squealed.

"Sssh," he shushed her. "Sometimes more. Depends on the annual bonus. And stock dividends in any given year."

Leslie stood silently for a moment, absorbing the information. Then she turned to the salesperson. "*Je vais acheter*. I'll buy it."

PART III: Downfall

1986-1988

CHAPTER TWENTY-ONE

In Texas, deer hunting is not a sport; it's a religion. When Bernie Franklin was a small boy, he traveled with his family from Houston to San Antonio on the first day of the general deer hunting season. As they tooled along Interstate Ten, they encountered a steady stream of pickup trucks headed east from the hunting leases in the Austin and San Antonio areas. With few exceptions, each pickup they passed had a dead deer strapped across its hood. The nine-year-old boy stared in wonder at this surreal parade of fur and antlers, stretching for miles.

Several years later, Travis Franklin, then a United States Congressman from Houston's eighth district, took teenager Bernard with him on his first deer hunt. "Your brothers have both been hunting several times," Travis said. "Now that you've learned to shoot and handle a gun safely, it's time you and I went out and found you a live target."

Bernie shot his first buck when he was fourteen. Excitement radiated from his face as they climbed from the blind and he ran to examine his quarry.

Over the next three decades, Bernie continued to hunt once a year with his father.

On a chilly 1986 January morning, the two drove northeast out of Houston to the 200-acre Rocky Road deer lease in Nacogdoches County. Travis Franklin, now a United States Senator, paid for their exclusive use of the lease for the entire day. Bernie drove his Ford four-by-four while his father snoozed. The two wore heavy sweaters and hunting jackets with bright vests. The elder Franklin sported a wide-brimmed cowboy hat; his son wore a Houston Astros baseball cap.

After the two-hour drive, Bernie jostled his father's shoulder. "We're here, Dad," He pulled onto the property and steered the truck down a rutted path toward the hideout they always used. It was still dark, but their prey would soon be out foraging for food.

Emerging quietly from the vehicle, they shouldered their rifles and climbed up the metal ladder into the tiny hut, Bernie dragging a small duffel bag behind him. They settled in quickly, speaking softly. It was late in the season, and although this property still had plenty of game, a constant stream of bow and gun hunters in the weeks before them likely made the animals more skittish. Deer were always sensitive to the smell and sounds of humans anyway. And when one bolted, they all did.

Yet the daily need for the white tails to emerge from their beds to eat worked in the two hunters' favor. Plus, the owner seeded the area with supplemental feed to lure the animals for his customers.

Bernie pulled two sets of binoculars from the duffel and handed one to his father. It was beginning to get light and time to begin their watch.

"When your brother and I came out here on opening day, we spotted a fantastic old boy,"

Travis whispered. "He was mature, had to be past his prime so ready to be taken out. But he had to be pretty damned smart, too, to live so long. If he's still around, I'm sure we'll see him."

"Why didn't you shoot him then?"

"I let your brother have the shot, but the old codger disappeared on us. He had to settle for a smaller buck."

"What are the odds we'll see him again?" Bernie asked.

Travis grinned. "Mature bucks are like old men.

They roam far and wide when they're young and rambunctious, but they don't stray far from home in their senior years. They prefer to stay around the neighborhood." He chuckled at his own bit of wisdom.

"Just so they're not wearing sandals and black socks," Bernie grinned at his father.

"Look," his dad suddenly whispered, a tinge of eagerness in his voice. "Here come some of the rascals now."

Bernie joshed again, "Yup. Out for the early bird special."

"Those are all does and young males," his father peered through the glasses. "Let's wait it out and see if the big daddies come calling."

They sat patiently, frequently scanning the area with the binoculars. The sky was brightening, and within an hour the area would be bathed in full January sunshine.

After a thirty-minute wait, Travis Franklin sat up more alert. "Look at those two bucks," he said.

Bernie gazed through his glasses to see the large whitetails emerging from the underbrush, heads down, muzzles on the ground, foraging for their breakfast. Occasionally one would lurch upright, head high, responding to some sound in the distance, then return to his eating.

"The one on the right, I'm sure it's him," the senator said. "Look at his rack."

"Why don't you take him, Dad?"

The senator looked at his youngest son in surprise. "Don't you want a shot?"

Bernie smiled back. "He's your find, and you haven't gotten to shoot one yet this year. I'm giving him to you."

The elder Franklin nodded, raised his rifle into the blind opening, and stared into the rifle sight. "Come on, big boy, let me have a clean look."

The second deer ambled in front and spoiled the shot.

"Get out of the way, you damned scalawag. Okay, okay, he's moving into the bushes now. Our big target is all alone."

At that moment, the older and larger buck jerked his head up, listening intently to some sound drifting in the cold wind. He stared directly in the direction of the blind. The dark colors on his face evidenced his advanced years. Travis' finger slipped slowly, deftly onto the trigger and squeezed. *Crack*! The shot was off, and the hunters could hear the bullet's impact as it hit the whitetail.

Like the violent flush of a quail covey, the deer lunged and bolted, kicking as he sped across the rock and brush terrain. "He's running, he's running," Bernie shouted. "I know you got him."

"Come on, big boy, get down, get down," the senator exclaimed as he followed the animal's wild dash across the field and into the underbrush.

"There. He's given up, Dad," Bernie said. "Let's go."

Travis led the way as they clamored down the ladder. He took his rifle with him. "I'm certain he's gone," he told Bernie, "but I'll bring it along to make sure, in case I need to take another shot."

"Hell, Dad," Bernie said as he stuffed the binoculars into the duffel and pulled it along with him down the steps. "You won't need another. He's gone, no question."

The sun was full ablaze now. As they approached the buck sprawled on the ground, Travis unloaded and leaned the rifle against a tree. He was trembling slightly; even veteran hunters' adrenalin pumps through them like an oil gusher when they make a kill. "My God, Bernie, look at that." He grasped one side of the antlers, pulled the deer's head up and latched onto the other side. "Look how wide his damned rack is, and ten points, too. I can't wait to get him on my wall."

He laid the buck's head back down and took a deep breath. "I could sure use a snort of something right now. The excitement takes the breath right out of you."

"It just so happens…" Bernie began, and let his action finish the statement. Unzipping the duffel, he pulled out a bottle and two plastic cups. Travis sat down on a nearby tree stump and accepted the drink with a nod. "Twelve-year-old single malt," he proclaimed as he examined the bottle. "You're coming up in the world, son. There's hope for you yet."

They sipped silently for a moment. Then, "Speaking of coming up in the world, how's your oil venture doing?"

Bernie shook his head in disgust. "We were doing okay, managed to bring two wells in. But damn it, Dad, with oil prices dropping like they are, it's going to start costing more to operate the things than we can make off of them. If the business keeps heading south, we'll have to shut them down."

"The old boy who bought out part of your company, the developer from Arizona, he's still involved?"

"Greg Jacobson? So far, but we can't continue to work as partners. He's borrowed a lot of money from Quivira Savings in Houston, and they put me on their board."

"Quivira? That's a savings and loan. What the hell

are you doing on their board?"

"Young hot shot named Will Martin is running it, and he's building their assets like crazy. I've never seen such incredible growth. This guy's really smart. He called me in and invited me onto the Quivira Board. He's making bets on a lot of new kinds of investments and thinks oil and gas might be good for their future."

"You need to tell it like it is. I'm not sure oil prices are through dropping. The damned Iranians are seeing to it. Might be in for some rough weather since we're so dependent on foreign oil. The only thing keeping us in the game is oil being based on U.S. dollars. If that ever changes, look out."

"Not going to happen," Bernie said, adding, "You don't have any problems with this board deal, Dad?"

"We decided a long time ago to stay out of each other's business. I don't have a problem with it, except savings associations are biting the dust right and left. Are you sure this one's solvent?"

"They seem to be."

Travis held his cup out and his son poured another shot into it. "So, like I said, we agreed to operate our business at arm's length. But when we get into an election year, I don't want to have to field a lot of questions about my son's involvement with a failing bank."

"You're not going to need any help. President Reagan's got your back."

"Maybe. Sure, we're good friends. But don't forget his numbers were in the toilet until he tax-cut our way out of the recession. If the pendulum swings, and I'm running a campaign, I don't want any negative factors to deal with." The senator finished his drink and said, "Make me a promise."

"Of course, Dad. Anything."

Travis stood and picked up his rifle. "If things are solid going into election year, do whatever you want. But if the Reagan numbers start to go back in the dumper, and the savings and loan you're tied up with begins to go down the same sad road as all the others…" he raised the weapon toward the horizon and squinted through the sight, "…you get your ass out of their boardroom."

"No problem," Bernie agreed.

"Now let's go fetch the truck and call the old boys to come help load this big guy up. I want to get home and start bragging."

Father and son walked side-by-side through the field toward the deer blind and their truck.

"And Bernie, thanks for letting me have the shot. I won't forget it next time."

"Sure thing. Anyway, when I go home and tell Marlene I didn't take a shot, she'll be ecstatic. She rags on me all the time about going out to shoot Bambi."

Travis Franklin roared with laughter. "Son, that's what you get for not marrying a Texas woman."

CHAPTER TWENTY-TWO

Stanley Russell was intimately familiar with the audit firm, West & Eberhart. He worked there for eleven years before jumping ship to join Quivira Savings Bank as its chief financial officer. As Quivira's finances became increasingly entangled in complex real estate investments, Will recognized the need for a higher level of accounting expertise on his staff. Further, Stanley was already familiar with the thrift's complicated transactions, having been responsible for its previous audits. All it took to lure Stanley to the other side was the promise of higher compensation, potential bonuses and preferred Quivira stock.

Several days after Will's meeting with Max Davis and Jason Bernstein, when they conceived the idea for a Quivira holding company, the CEO summoned Russell to his office.

"Stan," Will said, "I think Jason came up with a silver bullet to solve the predicament you and I discussed—the West & Eberhart auditors' insistence that we restate our earnings."

"I can't wait to hear it," Russell responded.

Will described the plan for incorporating the new entity and raising capital from developer Walker Bannister, thus circumventing the audit dilemma.

Stanley whistled. "It's ingenious, if it's legal."

"Jason assured us it is."

"When do you plan to pull the trigger?" asked the chief financial officer. "I assume we'd have to notify the audit firm."

Will leaned forward. "We're not going to tell them anything until we have to. Stan, we'll only take this step if we can't get West & Eberhart to bend a little. Guess why you're here talking to me."

Russell shook his head in resignation and grinned uneasily. "Of course. You want me to put on my persuasion clothes and go see them. Convince them to change their minds."

"You worked with those guys. You know how their minds work. Why not take a crack at it?" He stood and walked to the window, peering out at the Houston skyline. "Stanley, we're building a great thing. Quivira will be the model other savings associations will emulate." He turned back and smiled at his CFO. "I came here to create something great and get rich doing it. I know you took this job for the same reason. We can't let some penny-ante auditors who haven't kept up with the times wreck our business."

The CFO shifted in his chair and tugged at his collar. "It won't be pleasant. They might not consider me the enemy, but we don't get along like colleagues anymore." He shrugged his shoulders. "But I'll give it a go."

* * *

Later that week, on a crisp January morning, Stanley drove into a parking garage and walked half a block toward his former place of employment. West & Eberhart occupied two floors of the Great United Insurance Company building, a thirty-story downtown bronze-glass structure. Russell entered the firm's offices and paused briefly to speak to former colleagues as they got their workday started. The Quivira CFO carried a briefcase heavy-laden with files and papers representing a year's-worth of financial data.

The meeting was scheduled in one of the company's small conference rooms. As Stanley arrived, one of its partners waited there with stacks of papers in front of him. Winston Hillschlager was the auditing firm's engagement partner assigned to the Quivira Savings Bank account. Although the firm's policy was to assign a second, concurring partner to large and complex clients such as Quivira, Hillschlager was alone for this discussion.

The auditor rose as Stanley Russell entered the room.

"Good morning, Stan. How are you, old friend?" Winston extended his hand.

The portly CFO appeared uncomfortable as he accepted the handshake.

"Want some coffee?" asked Hillschlager.

"I'm good," Stanley set his briefcase on the table and began to extract papers.

Hillschlager squinted briefly at Russell, as if puzzled by the lack of cordiality on the part of his former partner. "All right then," he said, "we'll get down to business. You have some concerns about our 1985 audit findings, so let's put them on the table."

Stanley Russell sat down and shuffled through the pages. "I went over your material weakness letter. I have several differences of opinion with you guys, but I'll start with the biggest—your insistence that we increase our loan loss provision by $32 million before you'll issue a clean audit opinion. It's not acceptable."

Winston Hillschlager responded, "Stanley, we think it's more than justified. The previous year Quivira increased the provision for loan losses six-fold, an incredible difference from one year to the next. It defies sound accounting principles, and we think it's a dangerous precedent. As a result, we asked your management to improve your procedures and controls. But it doesn't appear you did. Instead, you continue making huge construction loans without detailed plans from the borrowers. You fail to conduct site inspections ensuring the developments you funded were progressing on schedule. You make some loans without proper appraisals.

"Even worse, Quivira's asset base gets weaker every year. You lend money to shaky investors and finance developments near toxic waste dumps. Stan, you don't need to look any further than the multi-million-dollar loans you're making to your own preferred stockholders to see the quality of your investment portfolio has eroded."

Stanley ran a hand across his droopy moustache. "You're aware of the ominous consequences of restating our earnings, right?"

"We are," Hillschlager agreed, "but we don't think it would be the end of the world."

"We'd end up with a $20 million loss instead of the $12 million profit we're stating."

"Yes, I know."

Stanley's tone grew more strident. "Then you also must realize we wouldn't meet our minimum net worth requirements under the Federal Home Loan Bank regulations?"

"Yes, I do," Winston acknowledged.

The CFO rose and began to pace the room, becoming more agitated. "Winston, you're putting us in a hell of a bind. If we do this, we'd be so strapped we couldn't even pay management bonuses."

"Stanley!" said an incredulous Hillschlager. "Are bonuses what you're worried about, for God's sake?"

The auditor sat quietly and watched Russell become more heated.

"Of course not, I'm simply saying you're trying to handcuff us," Stanley scoffed. "That's not the worst of it, not at all." His voice's decibel level grew to a high pitch, and he pointed a finger at his adversary. "The worst of it is we'd have to cancel dividend payments to our preferred stockholders. And as a result, Max and Will would have to give up all of their frigging common stock." By now, Russell's comments were growing loud and strident.

"Stan, calm down," Winston pled. "We know it puts you in a tight spot. But we have our own reputation as auditors to uphold."

"I'm not going to calm down, Goddamn it," Stanley's pudgy face was a deep crimson. "Your reputation, horse shit. We have a great management team trying to work our way out of a dilemma the government put us in. They said we had to grow our way out of the mudslide caused by insanely high interest rates. Winston, can't you see? That's all we're doing here. You need to recognize our new way of doing business for what it is—creating a new high growth pattern so we can keep the business from sinking. If this management team is forced to give up its common stock, there's no way to lead Quivira out of hell."

The auditor shook his head. "Losing control of the stock doesn't mean Quivira's board would have to replace the leadership team. If Will is so indispensable, they can keep him on, Stanley."

"Jesus, man. We need a break here."

"What you need, Stanley, is to restate your financials, earn a clean ruling from us, and get on with turning your savings and loan around."

Russell sank down in his chair, but the color in his

face showed he was still steaming. He stared lasers at his former colleague, as if he was betraying him. "We're old friends. I worked side by side with you."

Hillschlager smiled. "And you did a terrific job for us, Stanley. Heck, when you were here, you came down pretty hard on Quivira. Remember the material weakness letter you issued in 1983? You didn't seem to have a problem at the time calling attention to their deteriorating loan portfolio. I thought Quivira's move to hire you would strengthen their financial management. Frankly, Stanley, I'm disappointed you've signed off on such questionable lending practices."

The meeting came to a screeching halt as Will Martin appeared suddenly in the doorway. Winston's and Stanley's faces registered surprise.

"Sorry to interrupt, gentlemen, but I was in the neighborhood," Will said quietly and politely. "So, I thought I'd check in to see if you're making any progress."

"I'm afraid not, Will," Hillschlager said. "Have a seat. Would you like coffee?"

"I'd love a cup." He spied the pot on a side credenza. "You guys sit. I'll get my own." He continued as he poured. "What seems to be the problem?"

The auditor said, "You're familiar with the challenges. You've read our letter."

The CEO sat down. "We can't do what you're asking, Winston. Max Davis and I would lose control."

"Yes, we know that," Hillschlager acknowledged. "Stan and I were just discussing the point. But Will, we've been telling you for some time now the quality and worth of your investment portfolio was going downhill. With the rapid growth you've had in construction loans, you don't track them like you should. Your internal audit and closing functions need to improve dramatically. And your files for monitoring loans should be standardized. It looks to us like you're sort of shooting from the hip."

"Okay. We can work on our processes and procedures, right Stanley? But we need West & Eberhart to recognize the changing nature of our business. Can you do that? If you're so concerned about our loan losses, let's fix it."

"And how do you propose doing that?" Winston asked.

"Simple. We'll restructure any troubled loans—extend the terms to give our borrowers more time to pay, minimize our risk of losses. Wouldn't that strengthen the loan portfolio?"

Hillschlager shook his head no. "You can go ahead and restructure your loans all day long, Will, but it won't solve the underlying problem. And the fact you've begun pooling your weak loans and selling pieces off like junk bonds doesn't help. You still need to acknowledge the weakness of your portfolio and accept the loan loss numbers we've recommended."

Will sat contemplating for a moment. "Look, this isn't the old savings and loan business you've audited in the past. My God, you're aware of what problems we're all having with the real estate market and the regulators' attitudes that we have to fund our own way out of the mess. If we're going to survive, we need you people to understand our business. We're in a higher risk environment than even two or three years ago."

He waited to let the thought soak in. "Winston, I promise, if you'll cooperate with us, we're going to work our way through this problem. This is what Congress basically told us to do. This loan loss situation you're stuck on is a temporary distraction. A year from now, we won't even remember it." He took a sip of coffee and leaned forward. "We pay you a lot of money in fees every year, and up to now it's been a decent relationship. What are the odds of West & Eberhart seeing this our way?"

"Slim to none." Winston Hillschlager responded. "No, not even slim," he added.

"Does your concurring partner agree with you?" Stanley Russell asked.

"Absolutely," the auditor said.

Stanley rose halfway out of his chair and started to respond, but his boss' hand on the CFO's arm stopped him.

Will's voice remained calm and clear, as if offering a benediction. "All right then," he said, "I'd like to request a meeting with your national office. They have the benefit of the larger picture of what it's going to take to restore the health of an entire industry. Will you agree to set it up?"

Hillschlager stared at Will, open-mouthed. "Are you sure? They'll simply back us up, Will. You'd be wasting your time. And ours."

Will stood, and Stanley followed his lead.

"Call them," Will said. "Let me know when and where we can meet."

The two Quivira officers turned and left. The West & Eberhart partner watched them go, his eyebrows raised in disbelief. As Will and Stanley walked silently through the audit company offices, Russell nodded politely to several of his former colleagues.

Downstairs, as they disembarked from the elevator and walked outside to the parking garage, Stanley commented, "God, that was pretty brutal."

"They don't understand our business anymore," Will said. "They're stuck in the Seventies. Their national office will have more of an Eighties mentality. I'll make them understand." As he reached his car, he smiled at his fellow officer. "Auditors are like lawyers. They issue an opinion based on what you've told them. Hillschlager doesn't get it. Look, Stan, I once had a college prof who told me I could sell a wet tee shirt contest at a convent. Don't worry. I'll talk to their national office, and we'll win this battle."

Stanley laughed. "I sure hope so. I don't doubt your debating skills. I've seen you in action. But I know those people at their national headquarters. They are likely to get stubborn and back up their Houston group. Then what?"

"We have a fallback option. Jason Bernstein's holding company idea."

Russell said, "When the regulators get a whiff of that, they'll do more than hold their nose."

"I don't think so," Will answered. "By the time they smell it, it'll be flushed down the pipes—*fait accompli*. Sin of commission, not omission. We'll bow our heads and say '*mea culpa*.'" He flashed a grin, headed for his car and said over his shoulder, "See you back at the ranch."

CHAPTER TWENTY-THREE

The *Houston Business Press* was a highly respected weekly newspaper read cover-to-cover by most of the captains of enterprise in the metro area. It was one of a sixty-publication syndicate, the United Business Consortium headquartered in Chicago.

Dontrell Porter was the first African American hired by the publication in the early Seventies, initially as a sales associate right out of the University of Texas. He was subsequently promoted to account executive and then to the top sales job, advertising director.

In 1982, when their long-time publisher retired, no one seemed surprised the syndicate tapped Dontrell for the position. He made friends easily and helped grow the paper's revenues and prestige. Married to the daughter of a prominent insurance executive, he held memberships in the Sugar Hills Country Club, the Move Houston Forward initiative and two civic service organizations. A year after he was named publisher, the city's daily newspaper, *The Houston Ledger*, took the unusual step of including the leader of a rival publication, Dontrell Porter, in its list of "Future Leaders of Houston."

But Porter had problems keeping the ship afloat. The waning business climate so dependent on oil and real estate didn't bode well for a business newspaper. Advertising pages began to slip, and thus so did total pages. Faced with having to cut back, Porter looked for low-hanging fruit.

The publication's editors took pride in its special sections. Each Friday, it focused on one of a key group of industries, full of energetic reporting and targeted advertising from the specific business sector. In the first week of the month, a special report on the hospitality and tourism industry appeared. The second week, the paper featured manufacturing. In the third week, energy. Then in the fourth week, real estate.

The editors worked in a rhythmic routine. Every Monday morning, they met to review the week's story log and discuss questions or problems. On this particular Monday in February 1986, Publisher Dontrell Porter surprised his editorial staff by appearing with them in the conference room.

"Folks, I'm sorry to horn in on your meeting," he told them, "but I need to apprise you of a difficult decision I've made. You all know we had to discontinue the tourism and manufacturing special sections. As I said at the time, the ad revenues didn't justify the news space we were giving those industries any longer."

He hesitated and cleared his throat. "As painful as it is, we're going to stop publishing the energy and real estate special reports as well."

A collective, muffled groan buzzed through the room.

Porter continued, "If you haven't been living in a cave, it should be obvious those industries are both in a world of hurt. The oil business hasn't gone away—I mean, it's what Houston and Texas live on, for heaven's sake. But the trend is drifting in the wrong direction, and you've all seen predictions it'll get worse instead of better. That means Houston's refineries won't handle the volumes of crude we're used to seeing.

"As for real estate, look around you. The market is drying up. Savings and loans are falling like dead leaves in October. Banks, too. I don't know where it will all lead, but I do know this: We can't sustain the status quo at the *Houston Business Press*. Talk to our sales reps and you'll know what I mean. The ad revenues simply aren't there to support business as usual."

"Dontrell," interrupted Real Estate Editor Garrison Shack. "Is this a temporary move until the economy improves, or are the special sections a thing of the past?"

The publisher smiled. "I wish I could give you an answer. But I can't. Unless you can tell me what the future looks like. All I can say is if, and when, this cloud above us dissipates, I'll be on your side. Still, no promises the sections will return." He sighed. "That's it. Sorry to be the bearer of bad tidings. The good news is, nobody's losing their job."

"At least, not yet, right?" Shack offered.

"Not a joking matter, Garrison," Porter answered softly.

"I wasn't joking," the editor answered.

* * *

Porter and Shack ate lunch at *Mi Casa* every Monday after editorial meeting. They were fellow graduates of the University of Texas school of journalism. Two years ahead of Garrison, Dontrell recommended his fellow Longhorn to his predecessor as a reporter when the younger man graduated. Then, shortly after becoming publisher, Porter promoted Garrison to editor.

The two still held season tickets to the 'Horns' football games, leaving their wives behind to fend for themselves while they traveled to Austin or wherever Texas was playing on a given Saturday.

Their moods were not upbeat after the meeting.

"Let me have a Number Four with flour tortillas," Dontrell said to the waitress unenthusiastically.

"Same for me," Garrison echoed.

"Oh, and bring two *Tres Amigos* beers," the publisher called after her. He smiled wanly at his friend. "Sorry I had to deliver such crappy news to you editors."

"Jesus, what a blow," Shack exhaled. "I have a good line-up of articles for the next installment. What am I supposed to do?"

"Spread them out into the next few weeks' editions," the publisher advised. "Hold back the ones with no time sensitivity."

Garrison said, "I'm going to make a good group of contributing writers unhappy this afternoon. This has been a pretty decent freelance gig for some of them. With the cutback, I'll have a lot fewer assignments for them now."

Porter nodded acknowledgement. "Meantime, there's something else up this clever sleeve of mine."

The waitress brought their beers, and the real estate editor looked impatient as he waited.

Dontrell went on, "I think since we're being victimized by a lousy business climate, our esteemed publication should earn its chops exploring the underlying causes of the decay."

"What in hell are you talking about?" Garrison asked, taking a drink from the longneck.

"Investigative reporting. We've been doing a lot of articles about high interest rates, stagflation, surging unemployment, gas shortages and all that bull hockey. But what about some of the villains who got us in this bind? Shouldn't we expose the frauds?"

"Such as?"

The meals came. The publisher poured a generous amount of salsa over his food. He took a bite and continued as he chewed. "Such as, the real estate market. We know the economy started going downhill when Johnson spent a fortune on Vietnam and poverty programs at the same time—remember, guns and butter? Nixon took us off the gold standard and triggered high inflation and unemployment. Carter mismanaged economic growth and let Iran paralyze his administration, so there was no way in hell he could lead us out of recession. I could go on and on."

He took a sip of beer. "But here's my point."

"I was hoping there might be one," Garrison chided mischievously.

"Shut up. I'm getting to it. Maybe monetary policy, supported by wrong-thinking political leaders, led us down a path to business decline. But there were also a helluva lot of self-serving businesspeople and greedy labor unions reaching out to grab what they could. Instead of helping solve the problem, they acted like the bandits they were and made it worse."

"Jesus, Dontrell, you sound like some consumer advocate. What are you driving at?"

"We can't write about one side of the problem and not the other. Your industry, real estate, is one of the worst. All of those savings and loans that are collapsing? I don't think it's all the government's doing. I don't mean to tar everyone with the same brush. We should be fair. But there are greedy people running some of those thrifts. If we're going to be honest in reporting about business, we should expose them."

The editor sat back and stared at his boss. "Okay, so?"

"I picked up something interesting last week. My wife and I were having drinks with a couple we know. He's an accountant over at West & Eberhart. This guy drinks too much, and he really got into his cups. Started talking about a big brouhaha some of the audit partners got into with Quivira Savings."

"Quivira. The high-flyer guys?"

"That's right. Apparently, they had a blowout over how Quivira stated their earnings. Now, they're a private company so I don't know if we can get hold of their financial statement or not…"

Garrison broke in, "What about your friend? Can't he get a copy of their audit?"

"I can't push that. Telling me what he did was a breach of client confidentiality. He's a friend, and I don't want to get him in legal hot water. He's loose-tongued when he's drunk, but otherwise he's a straight-up sort. No way can I ask him to leak it to us. However, I did some more snooping around on Saturday, called in a marker or two, and here's something we can start with."

Porter took a paper from his pocket, unfolded it and slid it across the table.

Picking it up, Garrison Shack read in a low voice, "Dallas Home Loan Bank, 1984, $100 million, 1985, $82 million." Looking up at his boss, he said, "I know what this is. Those are loans the Federal Bank makes to savings associations. Are you saying these went to Quivira?"

Dontrell nodded. "So my source tells me."

"Putting two and two together, if the Dallas bank is pushing so much cash at a company they're supposed to regulate, and yet the auditors say they're not buying the thrift's reported numbers, something smells like fish in Denmark."

"Seems so, doesn't it?"

"Guess I need to go call on the boys over at Quivira

Savings," said the real estate editor.

"I don't think I'd play it that way, Garrison. I'd start out in Dallas. The regulators get copies of the audit reports. Maybe you can catch them off guard."

* * *

The Solar-Carras Federal Building in Dallas' government district loomed over Commerce Street, its stark white vertical columns giving it the appearance of a giant jail cell. It was a fitting architectural design, since the structure was once a Federal Courthouse. After the courts were relocated, it was downgraded to a Level II facility, meaning it had fewer than 450 tenants, a moderate level of public contact and routine functions similar to commercial activities.

At this lower level—absent law enforcement or court-related functions—building security was not rigid. Recommendations to tighten access in federal buildings circulated following an incident at a New York corporate headquarters when a gunman rode the elevator to the executive floor and threatened the company secretary. Still, the government was moving slowly on lower-level facilities.

Garrison Shack appeared in its lobby the morning after his lunch with Publisher Dontrell Porter. A pudgy, middle-aged security guard seated at the information desk greeted him as the editor approached.

"Help you?" The guard's flat voice was rivaled only by his bored demeanor.

"I have an appointment with Fred Katzen, president and supervising director of the Federal Home Loan Bank." Shack fought back a snicker at his fib.

"Yes sir, show me some ID and sign in." The greeter pushed a book toward him and watched with little apparent interest as Garrison signed it and flashed his driver's license. "Fifth floor," the man said, waggling his head in the direction of the elevators.

As Shack walked through the entrance displaying a sign, *Federal Home Loan Bank*, staffers sat working at their desks or in cubicles without acknowledging his presence. The editor kept walking until he reached a row of offices appearing official. The largest, in the corner, seemed to be a good bet, so he approached a clerk sitting at a desk outside the doorway.

"Good morning. Is the director in?"

"Mr. Katzen? Yes, he's in there. Is he expecting you?"

"I'm with the *Houston Business Press*. I'll only take a minute of his time."

The clerk motioned for him to wait and disappeared into the office. Re-emerging, she asked, "What did you say your name was?"

Garrison smiled. "I didn't."

She appeared flustered. "Well, may I tell him what this is about?"

"Quivira Savings Bank."

Again, she disappeared.

When she returned, a head poked out behind her.

"Sir, who are you with?" Katzen's high-pitched, piercing voice echoed through the room. He had a beak-shaped nose some might describe as hawkish. Dark, beady eyes peered through large wire-rimmed spectacles, and the director's graying, thinning hair swept across the top of his head in an unruly comb-over.

Garrison walked to the door and offered his hand. "*Houston Business Press*. I have a question or two about a savings association you regulate."

Katzen smiled. "Oh, so you're a business journalist. You're one of the good guys. Come on in, I'll help you if I can."

Settling behind his desk in a black leather chair that enveloped him, Fred Katzen appeared smaller than he really was. He sat with his elbows propped in front of him, his fingers touching together as if waiting for some-one to serve a meal. "What can I do to help you get a good story?"

"You're the bank president, correct?" Shack began taking notes on a small pad.

"President and supervising director," Katzen watched intently as Garrison wrote it down.

"I'm writing an article about Quivira Savings," Shack said. "I thought I might get their regulator's per-spective."

"I'm happy to do it. Go ahead, shoot."

"First of all, I'm sure you're familiar with their go-getter chief executive, Will Martin?"

"Absolutely. Will's a smart man. Aggressive. I actu-ally recommended that Max Davis hire him. He's really growing the company. And he's becoming a leader in the industry. You can quote me."

"Speaking of how Quivira is growing, I've un-earthed some numbers of capital infusions your agen-cy has provided in the past couple of years. Let's see," he scanned his notes, "I'm showing a hundred million in 1984 and another eighty-two million last year. How much do you intend to send over there this year?"

Katzen fidgeted, "It...it's not how it works. See, they have to come over and make application, then we review it and grant the loan."

"So that's all there is to it? They just ask for the

money, and you send it over?"

The director fixed a cold stare at his visitor, appearing annoyed. "No, I'm trying to explain. They have to present solid collateral. Good appraisals. They have to justify it."

"How much do you think they'll need this year?"

"I don't have a way to predict…"

"But Mr. Katzen, you're their regulator. Surely you have some idea of what their need…"

The director interrupted, "Look, Mr. whatever your name is. You didn't tell me your name, did you? Listen here, we have a whole list of savings associations we regulate, not only Quivira. They're all going through a trying time. If they bring us solid collateralized loans, we justify making them the loans they need to keep operating."

"What about appraisals? Do you review them to be sure they're accurate?"

"All of our associations present a list of appraisers for approval. We review those, and if they pass muster then the association can use any of them to evaluate a real estate deal."

"But you don't review their individual appraisals, do I have it right? You know, to be sure the loans they make are supportable?"

Katzen glared at the editor. "That would be micro-managing. I'm not going to appraise them out of existence."

The newsman said, "Here's my question about Quivira. Making those millions of dollars available to them, how can you tell you're not throwing good money after bad? I mean, word around Houston is Quivira is in some kind of trouble, making risky bets on huge real estate developments. Have you seen their 1985 audit yet?"

"What is this? I thought we were going to have a friendly interview. You said you were writing a nice piece about one of your good companies down there."

"You regulate those guys, and my sources say they're fighting with their auditors. Are you propping up a failing company, Mr. Katzen? Are they covering up poor financial results?"

Beginning to tremble with anger, Katzen stood and strode around the desk. "Okay, the damned interview is over. You're supposed to be a business newspaper. You should be supportive of your Houston enterprises. You're acting like some kind of liberal, left-wing, smart-ass investigative reporter."

Garrison stood as Katzen approached him. The director grasped Shack's arm and yanked him around.

"Mr. Katzen, I wouldn't do that." Garrison stiffened in resistance.

Several office workers appeared outside the doorway, attracted by the noise of the fracas.

"We're not going any further," Katzen was nearly shouting now. "Interview over, see, smart guy? I don't even know if you are who you say you are. Get out of my office. Get out of my building." The director tugged again at the resisting editor. "I said out."

"Look, sir, settle down. What you're doing is assault."

"If you want more, you'll get it. I've got a whole army standing there in the doorway at my disposal, mister troublemaker. Now get your ass out my office and stay out."

He gave a last shove and Garrison hurtled toward the door. The editor gathered himself, nodded, and left through the gathering crowd of curious workers.

One of Katzen's minions went into the office. "Mr. Katzen, are you all right?"

The president removed his glasses, inspected them, put them back on and smoothed his hair. "I'm fine. I'm going to talk to building security about tightening up access. The man waltzed in here like he owned the place. He was a reporter on the wrong side of a story. I'd had enough."

"Reporter?" said the employee. "That's not good. If he writes about this, you'll come off as some kind of belligerent, hard-nosed type."

Katzen shrugged his shoulders. "I hope so. When you're a regulator, a tough reputation is a good thing."

CHAPTER TWENTY-FOUR

In the spring of 1986, Will attended his first Houston Chamber of Commerce Board meeting. Businessman Walker Bannister, chairman of the Chamber Board, invited him several days earlier as the two had lunch to discuss a business transaction.

"Quivira has been a member for years, and you haven't been to one damned meeting," the developer complained. "We need to have you involved."

Will stirred his soup and responded, "Bannister, that's Max Davis' territory. He likes networking over there and enjoys sitting on the marketing committee. Besides, I'm heavily involved in the U.S. League. It takes a good bit of my time."

Bannister bit into his Reuben and chewed aggressively, washing the bite down with a swallow of sweet tea. "You're going to start coming, Will. Two reasons. First, I need you on the airport expansion committee. I don't need to tell you how important it is to both of us. And second, I want to nominate you to the board so you can eventually succeed me. We can make you treasurer right away. I know you're involved in the savings and loan national scene, but I'll tell you from experience this position gives you a hell of a lot of political clout, locally. It'll come in handy. Join me at our meeting next Tuesday and I'll show you what I mean. You're familiar with some of the players, but I want the entire team to meet you."

The Chamber meeting was about what Will expected. Committee reports. Reviews by the organization's executive director of certain new developments in the metro area business community. Discussion about task forces either in progress or needing formation. Only after the meeting did Bannister make it clear why he wanted Will there.

"Come take a ride with me," the developer said as they left the building and walked to the parking garage. "There's something important we need to discuss."

After a brief wait, they watched the valet bring Walker's brand-new Jaguar XJ-S convertible to a screeching halt. Bannister laughed as Will surveyed the sleek sports car with eyebrows raised.

"When did you get this beauty?" Martin asked as they climbed in.

"Last week," Bannister beamed. "Jaguar doesn't have their own convertible out yet. This baby is a modification built under contract by a company up in Ohio." He sped out onto the street, whipped around several corners and ramped onto U.S. Highway 59, headed north. "You geezers driving around in your old man cars don't know what you're missing." He gunned the Jag and it lurched onto the highway doing eighty.

"And this is why you invited me to your board meeting, Bannister—so you could show off your new toy?"

"Not guilty, your honor. You'll see why we're out here in a few minutes."

Soon they were speeding past Houston Intercontinental Airport. Will learned after moving to Texas the airport opened in the late Sixties to supplant the outdated Hobby Airport not far from downtown. Besides being an early butt of jokes about its distance from the city, the new facility went through construction delays and millions of dollars of cost over-runs before finally opening. In 1981, three years after Will's move to take the Quivira helm, the airport's third terminal opened. Annual passenger traffic grew to about fifteen million.

Walker wheeled the car onto a side road and within minutes coasted to a stop on the shoulder. He climbed out of the car and walked toward the adjoining field with Will scrambling to follow.

Bannister pointed toward a wide-open area dotted here and there with thorny shrubs, blackbrush trees and an occasional Texas longhorn steer grubbing for grass. "Right over there are the eighty-nine acres you guys funded for me. I agreed to let the seller graze his cattle to keep the growth short, but that's temporary. Your investment committee negotiated the loan with me, so you've never had a look at the property. All you saw was the paperwork when you and the board signed off."

Will grinned. "The paperwork was about as attractive as this piece of scrub brush."

Walker laughed. "I wanted you to see it for real, Will, because you know what's coming. Right?"

"Sure. The airport expansion. If it gets final approval, they're going to build an international terminal."

"This is the acreage your company bought a chunk of in exchange for funding your new holding company. Remember? The $7 million you squeezed out of me. But Will, this is only the beginning. I'm on a buying spree, and I want you to take the ride with me. When the expansion goes through, if Quivira and Bannister Holdings put together the right package, we'll end up filthy rich."

"I know the mayor's pushing hard to get the expansion started, but it's not a done deal," Will said. "There'll have to be several votes, bonds to be sold, federal government approvals and involvement. We're talking about a long list of maybes and what-ifs."

Bannister fixed his dark brown eyes firmly on his

business associate. "It's going through. I've had some long discussions with the mayor's chief of staff. They've been promoting the project like crazy out here with the county leadership and surrounding communities. They have friends in Washington who'll help them, not the least of which is one named U.S. Senator Travis Franklin. I'm sure you've heard of him." Walker grinned, then turned serious. "Will, I need to know if Quivira is getting on board with me."

Martin nodded. "We said we're prepared to support the expansion. And we know when it happens, this area is going to explode with development. My guys have already identified some parcels we can buy, but the price tag's pretty high."

Walker said, "It's all going to keep going up, especially with some help from you and me. A lot of these good old boys out here have been sitting on acreage for years, hoping when the day comes, the expansion will move in this direction. I'm ready to close on some deals that will drop hundreds more acres on my lap. If Quivira will finance me on it, you and I can have some flipping fun."

"As in, flipping the property back-and-forth to each other, right? Drive up the assessed value."

"Damn, you're smart. You understand appraisal heaven," Walker said.

"Bannister, let's get in your shiny new sports car and go back to Quivira Savings Bank. I want to pull a couple of my loan committee guys together and have a talk about the future of Houston Intercontinental Airport."

* * *

That evening Will and Leslie drove to the Sugar Hills Country Club. It was one of the oldest and most prestigious private clubs in Houston. Longtime member Bannister Walker had provided their membership recommendation.

The clubhouse was stunning upon approach; it featured a wide white portico supported by eight massive pillars. The building was fronted by a circle drive richly landscaped with Texas lantana, autumn sage, cast iron plant and hummingbird bush. Broad sweeps of deep green Bermuda grass connected the shrubbery and several small parsley hawthorn trees.

Will stepped out of his silver luxury sedan and handed the valet the key while a second attendant opened the door for Leslie. She wore a light cotton brightly flowered sundress with a three-strand pearl necklace and matching earrings. Will was dressed in his customary navy suit.

Inside, the club carried out a western motif, starting with several Gib Singleton bronze horse sculptures in the lobby. Dale Rayburn cowboy etchings hung throughout the main dining room. The greeter nodded pleasantly and immediately escorted them to a table set for four next to a window overlooking the golf course, awash with long, darkening shadows.

"Bring us a bottle of Dom Perignon," Will said to the waitress.

She nodded and left as the Martins' guests arrived. Will and Leslie stood to greet them.

"Welcome to Sugar Hills," Will said to the couple. "Meet my wife, Leslie."

The dinner was not for pleasure. Will was recruiting investors. Attracting new customers for Quivira's growing portfolio was his forte. As the four sipped champagne and perused the menu, Will eased into the subject.

"When we spoke last week, you seemed open to

some new investment ideas," he said. "My firm is growing like bull thistle and making money for a lot of people. Oh, you can get a decent return in the stock market if you guess right. And CD rates will bring you something in the sixes—we offer one in that range. But that's a far cry from where they were five years ago, when they were paying interest in the teens."

Will leaned forward, his clear, soft voice oozing charm and confidence. His dark eyes penetrated. His entire manner seemed to summon credibility. "We have designed a new product you might want to consider. We are grouping together large numbers of the mortgages we own and offering shares. Purchasers of these certificates have been earning up to sixteen percent on their investments."

The prospect said, "Isn't that what junk bonds are?"

Will smiled politely. "Junk bonds are exactly what they are called. By contrast, our products consist of well-collateralized loans simply bundled in such a way that, even if some of the loans go bad, they're tied in with so many good mortgages the investments can't fail."

* * *

As they drove home, Leslie let out a sigh. "It was a wonderful meal, Will. And I thought those people were nice."

"So did I," he said. "Especially since he committed fifty thousand to my loan pool."

"You're such a smooth salesman," she observed, her praise sounding dreamy. "The man seemed to be eating right out of your hand. You could have sold him the moon tonight."

Will laughed. "I don't think of it as selling. I love to entertain, especially in an elegant setting such as Sugar Hills. As for the investment pitch, it comes naturally. I believe in Quivira and what we can accomplish. That makes it all right to ask people for their money." He glanced over at his wife. "And honey, thanks for not drinking too much."

Leslie sat up straighter, appearing miffed. "What a thing to say. What do you mean?"

"You know," he replied. "We've talked about it before. Sometimes you pour it down a little too fast. That's been happening with increasing frequency. I appreciate you respected where we were tonight, and why we were there. We do a lot of entertaining, and very often with people in a position to make us richer.

"I need my beautiful wife by my side. Sober."

CHAPTER TWENTY-FIVE

The Quivira Board at its July 1986 meeting spent three hours discussing and approving the company's loan applications, investment plans and opportunities. They were down to the final two loan requests.

"The next one is a line of credit application by developer Greg Jacobson," Will said. "You all know him, of course. He has outstanding construction loans with us already, and by way of the *quid pro quo* program, he is also a preferred stockholder of Quivira. This one's a little unusual. Greg is part of a consortium hoping to partner with Bernie here on a copper mine venture in Chile. He needs to show his prospective South American interests a valid funding connection, if it's needed. You've all had the information in advance, and the executive committee approved it last week in the amount of nine hundred thousand. What questions do you have?"

Amanda Whitfield turned to Franklin. "Bernie, I assume since your company is involved in the venture you'll refrain from voting?"

"That's right," the senator's son replied. "As y'all know, this isn't the first project I've done with Greg, and anytime we do something with him I abstain, to remove the appearance of a conflict of interest. The fact is, Jacobson doesn't intend to activate the LOC, but he needs to make a showing to those boys that he has a good banking relationship."

"So, you're saying if we approve this, no cash will flow?" asked Max Davis.

Will answered, "That's correct, Max, not unless the funds become needed, in which case it would come before the board again for a vote. It's a paper transaction to get them to do business with him."

"Will," Amanda added, "The outside directors ran this through counsel, and we don't have a huge problem with it as long as Bernie doesn't vote."

Will nodded. "Then if there are no more questions, show of hands voting yes on this application?" He turned toward a secretary taking notes. "Let the record show the vote was unanimous in the affirmative."

The secretary nodded and jotted down the result.

"And finally," Will said, "there's a loan application from developer Walker Bannister. As you're aware, he is also a holder of Quivira preferred shares. This covers his proposed purchase of seven hundred forty acres of farmland northeast of the Houston Intercontinental Airport. Our underwriters spent a good bit of time on this one. The land is adjacent to eighty-nine acres he bought previously which we financed and later bought into when we created the Quivira holding company. You all approved those transactions. Again, this loan application was negotiated with our senior loan officers and agreed to by the investment and executive committees. We would appreciate the board's full approval so we can move this transaction forward."

"Will, the outside lawyers had what you might call a mild concern about this one," Amanda said. "Looking at the size of the deal and the previous outstanding obligations Walker has with Quivira, our involvement with this one developer is getting stretched pretty high. This loan would push his outstanding Quivira debt to $105 million."

"Amanda," said CFO Stanley Russell, "you're aware Walker is considered one of the premier builders in the state, right? His mixed-use development over in

San Antonio, *Vista Ciudad*, was named a Gold Award winner by the American Builders Association last year. And let's face it, when the airport's international terminal is completed up north, that property is going to go off the charts in value—hotels, supply chain businesses, luxury homesites, the works. So, we want to be in the game with a direct investment because of the high-stakes payoff."

Whitfield squirmed a bit. "Oh, I get the importance of the area, Stanley. But the question I have is, since Walker owns the Sugar Hills Bank, why isn't he investing in it with his own capital?"

"I can answer that," Will broke in. "First of all, Sugar Hill's pretty tapped out, capital-wise, from some of the other major deals they're involved in. Quivira has the funds available to do this. Second—and I'd appreciate everybody's keeping this in confidence—but Walker's in early discussions with a possible buyer for Sugar Hills Bank. He can't make this kind of aggressive play with his own bank's funds while those negotiations are going on. So, do we have your agreement? All in favor?"

Everyone's hand went up and the secretary recorded the vote in her notes. She didn't add Amanda Whitfield's hand was the last to be raised, and slowly.

* * *

Later the same afternoon, Amanda Whitfield returned to her office. Compared with the extravagant board room in which she had spent the morning, this setting was austere and unimpressive. Her real estate company occupied less than one thousand square feet in a small strip mall off the Southwest Freeway halfway between downtown and suburban Sugar Land. Like all the other businesses surrounding it, the facility had a plain brick front with two large windows. A small sign over the door read "*Whitfield Real Estate*" in block letters. Inside, two rows of five old wooden desks each were assigned to the firm's agents. In the back of the space were two offices—Amanda's, and that of a minority partner she had taken into her business four years previous to help her venture into commercial sales.

Despite the spartan workspace, Amanda's firm had a successful track record of sales for the past twenty years.

She sat down in her partner's office. "Being on Quivira's board is one real challenge," she said. "I've been in this business a long time, served on a lot of national boards and panels. I know my way around the block. Yet this company's managers are super-slick. The deals they present are so complex, so unique, I can hardly untangle them well enough to be certain I cast the right vote." She laughed. "I'm not sure it's all worth nine grand a year plus five hundred a meeting. Especially when we're voting those guys multi-millions in salaries, bonuses and perks."

CHAPTER TWENTY-SIX

An overcast Houston sky seemed to hover like a bad mood on a Monday in March 1987 as Quivira's Board of Directors prepared to meet. The boardroom lacked its usual glitter; the colors normally streaming through the wall-to-wall windows to illuminate the glass and chrome conference table and spark lively conversation were instead muted and dull. Dreary, would be an apt description of the morning's sights and sounds.

The meetings were typically orderly, good-natured and remarkedly positive. They were half business session and half pep rally. Information behind loan proposals put before the directors was well-documented, thorough in explanation, enthusiastically recommended by management and endorsed by outside counsel.

"We don't vote on anything until we have the lawyers' review in hand," board member Amanda Whitfield remarked to her real estate company partner after attending her second session. "Will Martin and the other officers run a very professional ship. When he invited me to join the board, I was worried we would be figureheads, you know? But we have thorough discussions about transactions, and they answer all of our questions."

Smooth and efficiently managed would be the best way to describe the monthly conclaves.

Yet on this day, the board meeting had a markedly different, more contentious atmosphere. At certain points it became noisy and riddled with angst. The day's chaotic nature was created by a visit from three of the institution's regulators.

Seated around the long conference table, cluttered with folders and papers, board members were bunched more closely together than usual to make room for the guests. Leaders of the Federal Home Loan Bank of Dallas were there to discuss preliminary findings of their 1986 review of Quivira's financial health. Fred Katzen, president of the federal agency, and McCormick Baxter, the Home Loan Bank's general counsel, were present. But the person leading the show was Victoria Del Rio, the agency's senior examiner. She was about forty, five feet, two inches tall and stoutly built. Her smooth, mahogany-toned face was framed by shoulder-length, midnight-black hair. Large-framed glasses partly obscured her large, dark brown, shiny eyes. As she addressed the group, she delivered her report with authority, her firm voice sounding a hint of Spanish accent.

"Good morning. I'm here to discuss our examination of Quivira's asset quality which, as you know, is still in progress," Del Rio said. "I'll review highlights of interim reports indicating concerns about many of your transactions. Our study involves twenty examiners from all five states in the district. Before we're finished, we'll have racked up more than five thousand hours and generated a report that promises to be several hundred pages long. The primary focus is on asset quality because of our concerns about Quivira's underwriting and appraisals.

"The issues piling up amount to serious concerns. Let me give you some details."

Del Rio cleared her throat, glanced at her notes and continued, "First, we have identified many of your borrowers who are struggling to pay off loans they've received from other institutions. That's a concern. Second, you have loan losses you haven't recognized in your financial statements, another troubling development."

Stanley Russell nearly exploded. "Hold on. Ms. Del Rio, I need to remind you our financial statements are audited. We received a clean audit on our 1986 financials."

She appeared reluctant to comment, but finally said, "I'm aware you did, Mr. Russell. But you also had to revise your 1985 statement, did you not, after your auditors wouldn't approve…"

The treasurer interrupted, "Not true."

She continued, "…and then you replaced them with a more—shall we say—agreeable firm?"

"Victoria, your statement not only insults Quivira's integrity, but it also disparages one of the most prestigious auditing companies in the U.S.," Russell barked.

Will Martin held up a hand. "Let's move on, shall we?"

"All right," Victoria said, "let's talk about the holding company you've formed, Quivira Financial Corporation."

Will nodded. "We did that to raise capital more efficiently, plain and simple."

"You funded it with a questionable transaction involving one of your biggest borrowers who's also a holder of Quivira preferred stock. It has the appearance, at least, of a conflict of interest. Then the holding company's first order of business was to loan you, Mr. Martin, one-and-a-half million dollars, and you, Mr. Davis, two-and-a-half million. We were surprised, to say the least."

"Why so?" Max Davis roared.

She answered, "Making a loan to a director is a violation of regulations which say directors can't use the institution to fund their own personal interests."

Jason Bernstein spoke up. "Come on, Ms. Del Rio.

That's a stretch. It's true Quivira Savings Bank can't loan its directors money. But these loans came from the holding company. Perfectly proper."

Del Rio said, "I disagree. And I think my opinion will be upheld."

"Victoria," Max Davis interjected, "Y'all are as wrong as mismatched socks."

She ignored him and continued, "The second thing your new holding company did was pre-pay dividends to your preferred stockholders, many of whom are sitting in this room."

Bernstein continued the argument. "The holding company has a right to declare a dividend to its owners."

"Not when a major auditing firm says Quivira should have reported negative earnings," Victoria responded. She paused, as if to let the friction die down. "I can cite other major improprieties we're concerned about. For example, the mortgage pool you sell slices of so you can off-load your riskiest loans to third parties. Modifications on struggling commercial loans which lower your income. And poor safeguards in place for appraisals."

Max Davis said, "What do you mean, poor safeguards?"

"Sometimes you buy property without appraisals. Other times you use inflated appraisals so your borrowers will buy preferred Quivira stock with the excess."

Russell abruptly sprang from his chair. "Your own agency approves our list of appraisers. Don't forget to put that in your report."

Victoria Del Rio took a deep breath. She appeared to be fighting off being shaken from the attacks. Her voice quavering, she said, "We didn't want this to be contentious. I'm trying in good faith to tell you what the final document will look like. What you do to fix some of these problems is up to you."

Finally, Will spoke up. "Victoria, the problem is Congress de-regulated us because of the terrible market conditions and in effect said, 'You find your way out of this until the economy improves.' Then when we get creative in doing so, you regulators rule against us. We can't do business the old savings and loan way. Is it possible you don't understand the nature of our transactions? Could your criticisms of our underwriting and appraisals possibly be wrong?"

She shook her head. "No. Circumventing regulations and ignoring sound financial management go beyond mere creativity, Mr. Martin. We don't think the real estate market will get better any time soon. If it doesn't, the taxpayers will get stuck with a very large bill for all of this high-risk activity you are carrying out. We're prepared to recommend corrective action."

Will rose and said in a smooth and polite tone, "I think we all need a break. Let's let the temperature of the room cool down for about fifteen minutes and reconvene to discuss your proposed remedies. And ours."

As board members filed out, the regulators remained.

"Fred," Victoria Del Rio said to Katzen, "based on their improper business practices—some I believe to be illegal—we came here determined to issue a cease and desist order. I've heard nothing to change my mind."

"Neither have I," said the Federal Bank's attorney, McCormick Baxter.

Katzen sat silent for a moment. He removed his glasses and wiped them with a handkerchief. "No, I'm not willing to endorse a cease and desist. That's too severe."

"You can't be serious," Victoria argued. "This association is stuck in bad loan hell, and if we don't stop them, the fallout will be enormous. We've already contacted the enforcement office of the federal insurance agency in Washington about this. They're totally on board with a cease and desist action."

"No," said the president. "I won't agree to it."

"Fred," said Baxter, the lawyer, "what is it with you and this company? You sound like a Quivira stockholder rather than their regulator."

Katzen's shrill voice pierced the room. "Watch yourself, McCormick. Have you forgotten who you report to? I resent what you're implying. There are other ways to get Quivira to behave. I'm not going to regulate them into oblivion." He stood. "And now, if you'll excuse me, I'm going to make a trip to the restroom."

As Katzen stomped out, Del Rio and McCormick gazed wide-eyed and open-mouthed at each other. "What's our Plan B?" asked Victoria.

The lawyer responded, "We have to put a stop to this—the *quid pro quo* program, real estate for stock deals—all the wild west things these cowboys are doing. So, we can issue a supervisory directive. They would be permitted no self-funding activities from this day forward."

Victoria nodded in agreement as meeting attendees trickled back in.

When the meeting reconvened, Stanley Russell resumed the argument. "Victoria, you're looking at this like all we do here is fraudulent activities, and I resent it," the burly treasurer intoned, his voice filling the room. "You say the *quid pro quo* is unsound financing. Well then, Fred, what you do at the Home Loan Bank is every bit as questionable. You lend us money, take a fee and then we're required to buy stock in your bank. That's all we're doing here with some of our own borrowers. We got the idea from you."

Fred Katzen sat silently, listening.

"And the Quivira Financial Corporation loans to Mr. Martin and Mr. Davis are not illegal. What I'm saying is you may have regulatory concerns, but damn it, we have regulated company concerns. Like someone once said, after you issue your report, where do we go to get our reputation back?"

Without hesitating, Baxter, the fed counsel, took over the meeting. "None of your arguments are going to hold water when the full report is issued. You're going to have to respond, because we've got the full force of the State of Texas and the Federal Savings and Loan Insurance Corporation behind us. And that means the taxpayers of America. In your heart of hearts, you can't deny the quality of your loan portfolio is in trouble."

He continued, "What do we do about it? There are three options: option one, a supervisory directive would require you to stop the risky activities. It's voluntary; option two, a supervisory agreement is a more formal enforcement where you directors promise to fix violations or unsound practices; option three, a consent agreement. This is executed by the board if the institution becomes insolvent. We've decided the best course of action is option one, a supervisory directive. You'd agree to no more self-funding activities such as the *quid pro quo*."

Will shot a glance at the lawyer, Jason Bernstein, who gave a subtle nod.

The CEO responded in a calm and cordial manner,

continuing to sail against the headwinds of the brewing animus in the room. "Since as you say, we can no longer self-fund, then any capital we need will come directly as loans from your bank. Right?"

"Correct," said Katzen.

"And that would require us to purchase stock in the Federal Bank, right, Fred?"

"Also correct," the president acknowledged.

"*Quid pro quo*?" Will gave him a sly grin.

Muffled chuckles rippled among the directors. The bank president sat mute with his lips shut tight in annoyance.

"Okay," Will said. "Send the agreement over, and we'll approve it."

Baxter McCormick fixed a cold stare at the Quivira CEO. "And you'll comply?"

For the first time all morning, Will's voice took on a hard edge. "Now you're insulting us. This meeting is adjourned."

* * *

Immediately following the session, three of the key Quivira attendees gathered in Will's office. Treasurer Stanley Russell, majority owner Max Davis, and outside lawyer Bernstein comprised the post-mortem team.

"I thought they'd come in prepared to issue a cease and desist order," Bernstein said. "What in the hell happened?"

"Katzen wasn't about to take drastic action against us," Will answered. "Don't forget, I was on his board. I know Fred's mindset as well as I know my own. He likes us—likes me. Considers himself my mentor. He's not the attack dog his staff members would like to have running their office. It seems to me this gives us a little time to restructure our outstanding loans and get our balance sheet in better shape. Then maybe we can get them off our backs."

Stanley Russell, the treasurer, smiled agreement. "That's what I like about you, Will. You always have a plan in the face of the hurricane. It won't be business as usual, but we can continue to get things done under this arrangement."

Will added, "You're right. Men, all we got was a slap on the wrist. Keep your foot on the gas. This bump in the road is not going to be the beginning of the end for Quivira."

CHAPTER TWENTY-SEVEN

I remember once at a family gathering, my uncle asked me how I enjoyed fatherhood. I told him it was great, then I gave him a wry smile and added, "…except when I have to break up fights, or call them down for making too much noise, or give time out for sassing their mom or dad." And I added, "I'm really looking forward to the teenage years—I'm sure they'll be much easier to deal with."

My uncle had a booming, hearty laugh, and he leaned back and gave me an earful. "You'll find out the hard way if it's true or not. But remember this, Monty. After they fly the coop, those are the things you'll miss the most."

He was right. When Sarah and I became empty-nesters, our weekday evening activity changed dramatically. Our two boys were off to college. There were no more after-work basketball practices to drop by and watch. No more games of catch, homework reviews or board games until dinnertime.

We abandoned parents created a new pre-meal routine—a glass of wine while watching the television news. Otherwise, things would be so quiet around the house we'd be listening to our own hearts beating.

Not that we minded the change. Sarah and I always relished our quiet time together. We simply had to become accustomed to such a luxury becoming the routine.

I usually listened to the news with one ear and thumbed through my golf magazine at the same time. But on this particular evening, a breaking business news story had my full attention.

"In the world of business today, a Reagan appointee to the board that insures savings and loan institutions resigned amid allegations he owes huge sweetheart loans to Lincoln Savings, an association he is supposed to regulate. Lee H. Henkel Jr. is reportedly a friend and ally of Charles Keating, the top executive of Lincoln Savings, which provided the loans in question. Keating, a former lawyer, real estate financier and anti-pornography activist, has been involved in GOP politics for a number of years. He took over at Lincoln in 1984, and it grew from a break-even proposition to a firm with reported assets of some five-and-one-half billion dollars. Federal regulators in San Francisco are investigating Lincoln's risky investment practices and reports Keating might be using the company for improper personal uses."

Sarah looked at me with alarm. "Are those things true, Monty? What did she mean by 'improper personal uses?'"

I held my hands out in an "I don't know" gesture. "Hard to say. I remember back in the Seventies, when he became involved with American Financial Corporation, the Securities and Exchange Commission accused him of some fraudulent financial dealings. There've been rumors for years Keating was doing questionable things at Lincoln Savings like selling his customers worthless bonds and living a rich lifestyle at their expense—huge mansions, yachts, private jets. I think the truth will come out in the investigations. All I know is Lincoln went down a similar road as Will Martin's company, Quivira.

Everyone at League meetings talks about their questionable tactics—making high-risk real estate investments and iffy loans to people who can't pay them back."

Sarah stood up and stretched. "I'd better get dinner on the table or you'll divorce me."

I laughed. "Fat chance. You'd take all my yachts and luxury cars."

She bent down and gave me a hug. Then, as she started to leave the room, she stopped. "Monty, what do you think gets into people like Charles Keating? Or Will Martin? How can they treat people who trust them with their money so cavalierly?"

"I'm not sure, honey. Maybe a taste of the good life makes them a little greedy. Hearing things like this news story makes me wonder if anyone embodies the ideals of our profession anymore. And I know the answer immediately. My dad. If I learned anything from him, it was to keep a true sense of community and be a good citizen. It was a principle he followed right up until retirement—in fact, Sarah, he still does. I can remember, more than once, hearing him say, 'Sorry, but we don't do that at Wichita Savings.'"

Sarah turned and hugged me again, tighter, longer. "I love you, my basketball hero."

I chuckled, surprised. It was an endearment I hadn't heard since high school. "That was a long, long time ago," I said.

"No," she said. "It's now."

* * *

It rained the next day. In Kansas, precipitation comes in two sizes. One is what the farmers like to call "not enough to settle the dust." It slips in, unexpected and unannounced, douses a small area for about five minutes and moves on, scarcely wetting the pavement. The second is the polar opposite. Dark, roiling clouds warn of its coming, sometimes for an hour before it arrives, and then a gully-washer unleashes its fury.

This particular morning's downpour was the second variety, accompanied by gusts of wind, because it was Wichita.

Promptly at eight, as always, I parked behind the Wichita Savings building and entered through the rear door, shaking my umbrella as I stomped into the back hallway. I was the first to arrive. It smelled damp and musty in the back of the building, and I scanned the ceiling for leaks. Seeing none, I walked toward my office. Glancing out toward the street, I could see a figure standing by the front window under a large golf umbrella. We wouldn't normally unlock until nine, but there was no way I could let the poor soul stand there for an hour.

I opened the door and shouted, "Come on in out of the deluge," then realized I knew the visitor. "Oh, my gosh, Lawson. You're way early."

The big man, my old friend Lawson Jeffries, struck an imposing figure standing under the huge umbrella. As he approached, he angled it against the storm and held a cardboard folder high under its protection.

"Hello, Monty." He entered and shook the water from the umbrella onto the rug placed in the entrance for that purpose. "I knew you came in early. And I hoped maybe we could get our business out of the way before you got too busy. I have a full day of work ahead."

"Of course," I said. "Come on back. It's good to see you."

"You, too," Jeffries replied and followed me into my office. He settled his big frame into a chair and said,

"You're doing well since taking over from your dad?"

I shrugged. "He was more than ready to retire. I don't need to tell you how the business has changed—how much harder it is. It's been a tough last few years. We've been buying up a number of small, struggling institutions in the surrounding area, and I hope to make a go of it. But you're aware of all the consolidation going on, for survival. It wouldn't surprise me if we get invited to some merger talks in the near future."

I took a deep breath, wanting to change the subject. "But Lawson, I want to know about you. It was good to get your call on Friday. I had already heard you were coming back, but general manager of the public broadcasting outlet here? What do you know about running a television station?"

Lawson smiled. "It's public broadcasting, Monty. The job is pretty much sales and fund-raising. It's all I've done since I hung up my spikes. I'm as grateful as I can be they're giving me this opportunity. I learned a lot while I was in Houston, and I don't think Will's critics are giving him a fair shake. He's done some great things for the city. Worked hard for the Chamber of Commerce to attract new business. Organized an effort to help push through the airport expansion. Now the only thing anyone talks about is the corner he and his board of directors painted Quivira into. I guess I got out at the right time."

"I'd think so, Lawson. You were on a sinking ship down there. So, tell me, how's Will doing, anyway?"

The big man said, "Oh, I don't need to tell you about Will. They keep shooting missiles at him, and he goes on deflecting them. Every time the regulators tell him there's no hope, he cranks his creative brain up another gear and produces a brilliant plan to save the day."

I shook my head, feeling a sharp pang of sadness. "Will ran into the same hornet's nest we all did. Knowing him and his grandiose view of things, it didn't surprise me he'd go at the problem with guns blazing."

I decided it was time to change the subject, so I sat up as if someone had flipped my switch. "Now, let's talk business. You're moving back to Wichita. You've found a house and you're shopping for a mortgage. Lawson Jeffries, old friend, you've come to the right place."

CHAPTER TWENTY-EIGHT

In addition to my national leadership in savings association activities, I also took over where my retired father left off with Wichita civic activities. It was an unspoken expectation, and I was glad to do it. I was active in the Greater Wichita Chamber of Commerce and several civic organizations, including one of my favorites, Wichita Forward. My keen interest in that one came from an encounter I had shortly after joining my father at Wichita Savings and Loan. At Dad's urging, I took an African-American family under my guidance and helped them develop a plan to get them through a financially difficult period. I drew heavily on my business degree to advise them.

Former star University of Kansas football player Harley Lemkin was a hard-working employee of one of the city's aircraft manufacturers. But the lack of job skills and the financial burden of a large family dragged his finances down. I worked with a technical school in the area to get Harley additional training, which Wichita Savings and Loan paid for.

After a regular monthly meeting of the small organization's volunteer board in late 1987, I asked the Wichita Forward director, LaTasha Wright, for a private meeting. We sat in her office and spoke amiably about our families for a short time, and then I cut to the subject. "Wichita Forward does a good job of finding students part-time employment so they can finish school," I said. "But it seems to me we could be doing so much more."

"What are you getting at?" LaTasha was a former high school business teacher hired two years ago to lead the non-profit. She was highly respected around Wichita and worked hard to build the organization's budget. But her only staff was a full-time clerk and part-time bookkeeper. To accomplish delivery of any significant program, she had to rely on volunteers, so adding new elements was a stretch.

"If you're thinking about scholarships," she speculated, "it's an idea I've been turning over in my head. But I don't have the people to pull it off."

"Scholarships aren't a bad idea," I acknowledged. "But I'm thinking of how many low-income people we have in the Wichita area who might otherwise succeed if there were better job training programs in the area. You're familiar with the employment problems in the minority community. The opportunities aren't there. We have all of this aircraft industry here, oil and wheat business as well. I think we could make real progress."

I told her the story of my earlier success in finding Harley technical training and helping him launch his own appliance repair business.

"Now," I said, "a former aircraft cleaner in a dead-end job has more business than he can do on his own. Not only that, but the higher income qualified him and his wife Mary Mae to get a mortgage. They were able to move their growing family into a much-needed house."

"It's a super idea, Monty," LaTasha said, "but I don't have the resources to create such a big program."

"Sure, you do," I argued, smiling at her mystified expression. I held out my hands as if to say, "I'm one of many."

"I stepped in to help Harley out when his employer should have been doing it," I said. "We can recruit a lot of companies to volunteer their up-and-coming managers to a few volunteer hours every week. They can pound the pavement, identifying the right prospects for training. Twist some educators' arms to open their doors for classes. Most importantly, knock on the doors of the Wichita business community to open their purse-strings and help fund the thing.

"We have a well-meaning board, but they come to meetings and do little else. I'll help you light a fire under them. You have the non-profit status and bank account which can accept donations. I'll find you a business-oriented volunteer to manage the financials. All you'd need to do is put a public face on the effort, cheerlead and trouble-shoot. What do you say?"

"I say, I'll support it if you'll chair the jobs program committee," she challenged, coming as no surprise to me.

I squinted at her and thought for a moment. "I'll tell you what I'll do, LaTasha. I will chair it for a year, and I'll find you someone to handle the program finances. And I'll identify a successor for myself after that. Deal?"

"Deal," she answered with a huge grin.

It took me less than a week to find not only the businessman to manage the new program's finances, but also to succeed me as chair of the committee—both in one person. I had already planned it sitting in LaTasha's office.

I decided on the regular meeting of the Wichita Chamber of Commerce to make my move.

"Hey, Lawson, great to see you here," I said as I encountered my former employee coming into the conference room.

"Hello, Monty," Lawson Jeffries shook my hand enthusiastically. He had a knack for making you feel as if you were the one person in the world he most wanted to see. With some people, such an encounter might have been contrived. Not with Lawson. You could tell his sociable greeting was genuine.

Entering the room, with other members streaming in behind us, I pulled him aside. "Lawson, after the business program, let's skip the Chamber lunch today and go over to Graham's Café. There's something I'd like to discuss."

"Why do I think I should decline?" he asked, his dark eyes twinkling.

"Great!" I enthused, ignoring his reluctance. "I'll meet you there."

* * *

I always felt a surge of nostalgia whenever I stopped in at Graham's. This was the restaurant where, as a senior in high school, I promised myself I would one day return to Wichita and my father's business. As Lawson and I slid into a booth, I swear I could almost hear Dad's voice.

"This place never changes," I remarked.

"Not even the menu," Lawson confirmed. "It's a real shame they closed down the ice cream plant."

I said, "It became too much of a burden as Mr. Graham got older. He didn't have kids who wanted to take it over, and the truth is he couldn't compete with the big companies anymore. But the restaurants have really caught on. He has seven of them now, and a general manager to run them. That's more than any national chain has here in Wichita."

I paused and changed the subject. "Lawson, I don't know if you've heard the latest about Quivira Savings."

He responded, "Maybe not. I haven't talked to any of those guys in almost a month. I've been too busy sinking my teeth into this new job."

"It's bad," I told him. "I hear the regulators have put them under a consent agreement. It's one step away from cease and desist."

"So, they have to shut down all the activities they've been doing to build their asset base? The *quid pro quo*? Stock for loan swaps? All of those fund-raising schemes are gone?"

"Right," I confirmed. "The only way they can capitalize is to borrow from the Home Loan Bank. And the feds won't lend them any money until they get their loan deficiencies straightened out. It's a catch twenty-two. They're in a complete bind. It sounds to me like a death sentence."

"I can't say I'm surprised," Jeffries said, "but still…" His voice drifted off, the thought left unfinished.

"I tried to warn Will over and over again," I said. "When he was here at Wichita Savings, he did a wonderful job. He found new borrowers and went after deposits aggressively. I admired how hard he worked, and the way he represented us in the community. But he hammered at me and Dad to push back against the rules. We had long discussions about it. I told him it wasn't our style to walk that tightrope, but he had a hard time accepting it.

"After he went to Houston, I talked to him at U.S. League meetings about rumors he was taking a lot of risks. Obviously, I didn't see the books or audits, but everyone said his loan portfolio was deteriorating. Whenever I'd ask him about it, he would shrug it off. I don't know if Quivira Savings would have survived anyway, but I don't think he gave the company much of a chance."

I stopped momentarily, in thought, then said, "Why am I telling you this? You were there on the scene. You surely could see it coming."

"I was a hired gun, Monty. The big-money trans-actions with the developers, and with Bernard Franklin and majority owner Max Davis, went on in the executive offices, in the boardroom and at the Federal Home Loan Bank in Dallas. Even so, I feel bad Will's dug himself such a deep hole."

"It's possible he was leaning on some poor advice," I said. "But he's a survivor. If he hasn't done anything illegal—and I'm told he says he hasn't—he'll figure out his next move. You know, with so many associations failing, I'm lucky Wichita Savings and Loan isn't in the same boat."

"Monty, it's not luck," Lawson remarked. "There's a reason you're buying up all of those insolvent sav-ings banks rather than the other way around. Promise me something. I talk to a few of my friends down there occasionally. But everyone's gotten a bit spooked and close-mouthed, know what I mean? Will is still a good friend. When you hear anything new, and I'm sure you will through your industry contacts, keep me informed."

"I will," I promised. "And now, enough about the savings and loan business," I said. "I brought you here to talk you into something else. It's important, and it's right in your wheel-house."

Jeffries grinned and nodded. I could tell there would be no way for him to say no.

CHAPTER TWENTY-NINE

The Dallas-Fort Worth airport, or DFW, opened for commercial service in 1974. Its initial four terminals were served by a number of major and regional airlines. By 1988, plans were under discussion to rebuild the existing terminals and add more runways.

When Will Martin arrived at DFW late that year, his use of commercial travel represented a stark contrast with the many times he had arrived in style, on the Citation charter, with a limo waiting for him. On this occasion he deplaned and carried only a briefcase as he entered the terminal and walked briskly to the area where Home Loan Bank President Fred Katzen waited in a small business room.

"Hello, Will," Katzen said, shaking the Quivira CEO's hand vigorously.

Will returned the handshake and glanced around the room. It was utilitarian, with a small table, six chairs and no amenities.

"Do you want me to order some coffee?" the regulator asked.

"Not for me, Fred. My turn-around time is two hours, so maybe we should get right to it."

"I agree. Will, I hate that we're having this conversation. You and I have had a good relationship. Seeing Quivira so close to the end cuts deep. I tried to support you guys, but I can only go so far. When your auditing firm calls you out, I have to listen."

"What do you see as the most pressing issues?" Martin asked.

Katzen took off his glasses and stared at Will, seeming surprised by the question. "You know what they are.

Your auditing firm and my staff insisted a number of your loans be re-appraised. For years we held off from looking over your shoulder at the valuations. But there are too many you can't justify. The new appraisals are forcing Quivira to recognize an additional $197 million in loan losses you previously failed—or, I should say— refused to report. That's the tipping point. Your company is underwater."

"I can bring it back. I've done it before."

Katzen stood and paced toward the window looking out toward passengers streaming by.

"My God, this isn't easy, Will," the regulator said.

"You think it is for me?"

"Of course not. But you're aware we asked your directors to remove you and the other officers. You know the board said no. That refusal triggers very lucrative golden parachutes for you and the other executives." He returned and leaned down toward Will with his clenched fists resting on the table. "My God, man, think about how that appears. It makes the financial situation even worse."

Will motioned for Katzen to sit. "Listen to me, Fred. There's a reason I didn't step down. When you called and asked me to come over, I said I wanted a chance to describe the plan I have to get us out of this mess."

He opened his briefcase and started to pull out papers.

Katzen waved him off. "Don't bother. My staff and I reviewed the executive summary you sent over. You're proposing to recapitalize through an acquisition by a New York group, headed by the Goldberg Kaplan Investment Bank. Problem is, it involves capital infusions of real estate and very little cash."

"I can make this work, Fred. They're a respected firm with solid assets. If we can get my plan approved, I'll step aside if I have to." Will's clear, dark eyes seemed to plead with the regulator.

The director shook his head. "I'm sorry, I truly am. I thought we could have one last discussion, maybe come up with something nobody's thought of. It's not going to happen. Too many on my staff think I've been easy on you. Damn it, man, when you guys set up that holding company and voted yourselves loans, you made things worse. You stated in the paperwork the loan was for business purposes. When our examiners dug into it, they found out you used it to pay down your mortgage and re-model the house. What in hell were you thinking?"

Will smiled. "I was going to pay it all back, based on the salary and bonuses I received the previous years. But the business went south."

Katzen heaved a massive sigh. "You're an intelligent man, Will. But that wasn't smart. It was wrong and dishonest."

They sat without speaking for minutes. Finally, Katzen concluded, "I can't save your company. Neither can you."

* * *

In the forty-five years prior to the 1980s, only 143 savings and loans failed, costing the regulatory insurance agency—and thus America's taxpayers—a little more than $300 million to resolve. By contrast, in the first three years of the Eighties, 118 insolvent thrifts cost $3.5 billion to settle.

As the decade wore on and interest rates continued to spiral, the picture grew worse. Faltering savings associations presented a massive problem for a government agency with too few resources to close them. Despite facing a no-win situation, savings and loans that had enough cash to operate were allowed to struggle on.

Until regulators determined they couldn't.

For Quivira, that conclusion was reached in a somber meeting at the Federal Home Loan Bank Board's offices in Dallas, several days after Katzen met with Will Martin. The president presided over a discussion with two of his key staff members, Victoria Del Rio, district examiner, and McCormick Baxter, the general counsel.

"We're all aware of the dire straits Quivira has reached," Katzen said with resignation in his voice. "We've tried to get both management and the board to turn their situation around."

Del Rio and Baxter nodded agreement.

Katzen said, "The loan re-appraisals make their situation untenable."

"More than untenable," Victoria confirmed. "Plus, the officers' golden parachutes make their financial credibility impossible."

Katzen continued, "We forced them to cut off dividend payments. We rejected a 1988 audit showing only $40 million in loan losses. Certain they were actually much higher, I obtained a consent agreement from the board acknowledging grounds for appointment of a receiver."

"That's a dagger through the heart," said Baxter.

"So, there's nothing more to be done," Fred Katzen concluded. "I'm prepared to recommend transferring management of Quivira Savings to the Federal Savings and Loan Insurance Corporation."

The lawyer said, "I talked to the state finance director in Austin, kept him apprised of the unfolding events regarding Quivira. I told him we were going to declare them insolvent. After he consults with the governor's office, they'll agree to move forward with closing the firm as soon as the federal agency is appointed receiver."

The room fell silent for a long moment.

"So, it's final," Katzen sighed. "I thought Quivira would make it. Martin and his team are so intelligent. Maybe that was the problem. They were too smart. It's a sad day. Let's move ahead."

* * *

What Texans call a "blue norther" blustered into the Houston area in the early morning hours on December 9, bringing a stark drop in temperatures. Except for employees arriving at work in heavier-than-normal clothes and clenching their chattering teeth as they hurried into the building, everything seemed to be business as normal at Quivira Savings Bank.

As the day's activity got started, nobody paid much attention when the CEO, Will Martin, pulled on his overcoat and hurried through the office and out the front door. It was not uncommon for him to rush off to some meeting, or to the airport for an out-of-town trip.

But within minutes, the orderly and business-like day of the firm changed dramatically to unreal chaos. The front doors burst open, and a long line of federal agents streamed in briskly. "Ladies and gentlemen," the first woman to enter announced, "we are here to close your business. Please do not remove anything from the premises. Leave all work files and other company information exactly where they are sitting."

Without another word, some of the feds swarmed around the bank's file cabinets and began loading them on hand carts. Others took the elevators to the top floor, barged into senior managers' offices, rifled through desks, confiscated files and stacked them up. Agents carried them out in boxes by the hundreds.

Several federal representatives entered the bank with a pile of paper notices and began to tape them in the windows, facing street-ward, notifying depositors of the thrift's closing. Quivira workers stared at each other with horrified expressions, obviously having no idea what to do. The din created by their stunned and frenetic outbursts took on the tenor of a robbery in progress.

When it was over and the federal agents were gone, the once neat and orderly bank resembled a war zone. Papers were strewn everywhere. Empty file drawers had been dragged out of place. The once stylish and stately Quivira Savings Bank was in complete tatters. As were its employees.

"What in blazes is happening? Where the hell did Will Martin go?" one junior loan officer rasped loudly. "Why wasn't he here talking to them?"

"Yes, and to us!" shrieked an accountant from her cubicle.

"The coward wouldn't even stay around to support us when we're getting shut down," another exclaimed. "He must have been tipped off."

"Look, guys, take it easy. This has to be the worst day of Will Martin's life."

"Yeah? Well, what about us? Can you say 'unemployment'?"

PART IV: Life After Death

1989-1995

CHAPTER THIRTY

Seven years had passed since Sarah and I attended a South Wichita high all-class school reunion. "We went to them regularly for a while," I said to an alumnus who was going down a list, phoning to encourage attendance in one of the early 1980 years. "But we started seeing fewer and fewer of our old gang, and consequently tons of people we didn't know. There were more children of people we knew than alums we went to school with. We decided to leave those get-togethers for the younger folks."

However, this year was different.

"I had a call today from someone urging us to come to the South Wichita reunion," I said to Sarah as we finished dinner one early evening two months before the May event.

"My goodness, they never give up, do they?" she exclaimed. "We've told them every year for the past five or six we aren't going anymore. Do you want some dessert?"

"I'll pass. I'm trying to get these extra five pounds off. Let's go outside and have coffee," I said. We retreated to our favorite spot on the screened-in porch. Our golden retriever puppy Ella jumped from her dinner on a mat in the corner and scurried out the door as I held it for her. She was always afraid she might miss something. Sarah and I settled on a love seat and pulled on the sweaters we kept there for frosty evenings. Ella sat staring until finally deciding she could jump up and make a pillow of Sarah's lap.

"I know we agreed we'd been to our last reunion." I sipped my coffee and continued the discussion. "But this one's different. They're planning a special observance of the class of 1959. Lord, it's hard to believe it's been thirty years."

"I believe it, old man," she kidded and gave me a playful hug.

"So," I went on, "as part of the class recognition, there's to be a special tribute in honor of the basketball team, because we won the regional finals that year. Honey, I think we'd be hard-pressed not to go."

"Then we will," she said cheerfully.

* * *

The late spring event attracted hundreds of alums. Following a number of year-specific gatherings in the afternoon, all the classes congregated in the gymnasium that evening for a big dance and the thirty-year salute.

It was good to see my fellow members of the basketball team, with only two no-shows. One, I heard, had died in an accident, and another was waging a battle with multiple sclerosis. Sumner Davidson was there, and as we hugged hello, I was surprised at how much weight our big center had put on. It occurred to me later he was probably as shocked to see my dome covered with pure white snow.

We herded up toward the stage where we would be introduced, one by one. Only then did I realize Coach Ron Slay had joined us.

"Ron," I exclaimed. "I didn't expect you to be here."

"Hello, Monty. It's great to see you," Slay greeted me with his customary warmth. "I know Paul Sarkesian was your coach that year, but they asked me to represent him, since I was his successor. I feel a little conspicuous doing it."

"Nonsense," I said. "You're the absolute right person to be here with us. After all, you're a bigger celebrity than any of us. But promise me after all this hoopla is over, you'll come and say hello to Sarah. She is out there somewhere hunting down her old cheerleader chums."

After the player introductions, the recounting of the season and a video tribute on an overhead screen, the band began to play. It was the signal we were officially has-beens and the dance was beginning.

Ron and I weaved our way through the crowd, and after a search we found my better half. "Ron," I said, "you remember my wife Sarah?"

"Of course I do, but it's been years," the coach gave her a self-conscious hug. "It's good to see you again."

Sarah held onto his hand, as was her habit when expressing true friendship. "Ron, you've accomplished some wonderful things since we saw you last. Topeka University is lucky to have you as its head coach."

"No, Sarah, I'm the lucky one."

"Don't be silly," she went on, gushing. "Monty keeps me up to date on all of your honors. Coach of the Year, I don't know how many times. Conference Hall of Fame, National Coaches Hall of Fame. And last year, serving on the Olympic Games basketball selection committee. I'd say you're standing in tall cotton, Mr. Ron Slay."

I watched the coach's face turn slightly crimson, and he grinned mischievously. "Well, Sarah, you know what they say. When your enemies die off, people start giving you awards."

Sarah squeezed his hand, and we three laughed heartily.

"Monty," Slay said, "I try to keep in contact with as many of my old players as possible. It's hard when you're this old. Have you seen Will Martin recently? I know he worked for you before leaving Wichita. The last I heard he was down in Houston running a bank, so I thought maybe you kept in touch."

"Unfortunately, yes," I answered. "You haven't heard the bad news?"

Coach Slay scrunched up his shoulders. "I guess not."

"Will's savings association went belly up in December. They were riding high down there for a while, but things started going downhill the past few years. The government took them over."

"My God, that's awful. What's happened to Will?"

"He's going through a tough time. There's some talk the FDIC might charge him with some kind of fraud accusations. I hear he's also been threatened with other lawsuits. And of course, he's out of a job."

"I can't believe it, Monty. We all thought he'd be a huge success."

"That's not the worst of it," I added. "Part of the resolution of this whole thing is an order they're trying to get him and his top officers to sign. If they do, they would be out of the banking business for the rest of their lives."

"I had no idea, since we haven't talked in so long. But it doesn't sound anything like the Will Martin I remember."

All I could do was shake my head. Simply talking about Will's fate depressed me. "He's a great guy," I said. "Smart. Articulate. He was truly a leader in our industry before the world started to collapse all around him. It's not all his doing, but it seems to me he got a taste for the finer things of life and it sort of—I don't know—turned his head, clouded his decisions."

Ron asked, "If he signs the order, he couldn't come back home and work at your place?"

"That's right, Coach. I've heard he's considering a return to Wichita. But he'd never come work for me, even if he could. Will was down there moving in business and social circles we don't have here in little old Wichita, Kansas. No, I predict even if he comes back, he won't stay long. Will is a different person than you and I knew when you coached him. Or when he managed his father-in-law's store or worked at Wichita Savings and Loan.

"As soon as he gets on his feet, we'll see him go after something a lot bigger, there's no doubt in my mind."

CHAPTER THIRTY-ONE

The three men sitting around Will's kitchen table created a strangely familiar sight. Will, Max Davis and Jason Bernstein were the same participants in a meeting three years earlier, when they hatched a scheme to create Quivira Financial, the holding company that the Home Loan Bank examiner and lawyer objected to so strongly.

On that January morning they shook hands and agreed to fund Quivira Financial with $7 million from developer Walker Bannister. Will and Max would get loans from the new entity totaling $4 million. Holders of their new preferred stock would get pre-paid dividends.

Those actions were sharply criticized in the Bank's final report summing up Quivira's demise.

Today they were meeting again. But the purpose was wildly different. They were out. Quivira was in the hands of the federal government. Regulators were insisting they agree to leave the banking business forever. And on this meeting, the outside lawyer, Bernstein, was summarizing the fallout from the events they had been through.

"For starters, the Federal Deposit Insurance Corporation—the FDIC—is ramping up to sue you," Jason said. "There's a huge wall of resentment rising up in Congress, the regulatory agencies, the public in general, to recoup as much of the losses from this industry as possible. They keep saying, 'the taxpayers are demanding it.' Well, I don't think the average taxpayer knows beans about what went down, or how much money has been thrown at the thrift losses. It's a lot of political hay being made. The federal insurance agency says they don't have enough funds to pick up the tab for all of these thrift closures. If they can't wring the money out of the failed institutions, they're going after their leaders."

"Meaning us," Max offered.

Jason nodded. "I've been informed they're going to name all of your executive officers as well as every one of your outside board members. We're talking about quite a few million dollars."

Will squirmed in his chair. "And they'll charge us with—what?"

"The same stuff you've been hearing from the consumer advocates, the news media, the individual investors. The holding company was a subterfuge to fund your personal loans. You gamed the system to help make your friends rich, like Bernie Franklin. Quivira's officers feathered their own nest with enormous salaries, bonuses and stock perks. You mismanaged, making risky loans and writing them off, destroying the firm's assets with poor investments, colluding with the regulators—maybe making it worth their while, so you'd get away with it."

Will stood up and paced across the room, then back. "Let the FDIC sue us. We can justify everything we did. I'll go on the stand."

"No, you won't," Max Davis argued.

Will sat back down and leaned toward his former boss. "Max, I've managed to get countless investors to pull millions out of their pockets and hand it to me. Why would you think I couldn't convince a jury we're innocent?"

"I don't know," Max said, his forehead showing deep worry lines. "If we're charged, and I can negotiate a lighter deal, I won't go to trial."

Will shook his head in obvious disagreement.

Jason continued, "I've only mentioned the FDIC.

There's more. You're going to get hit with lawsuits from individual investors. Not the Walker Bannisters and Greg Jacobsons of the world. But the schmucks who bought twenty-thousand bucks worth of your CDs who got caught in the crossfire. Or loan pool investors who saw their funds go up in smoke. They're mad as hell and want someone's hide. Their lawyers will fight to get to the front of the line and create a class action."

He paused, as if mincing words. "Don't be surprised," he said slowly, "if you get death threats."

"Those investors knew the risks," Will protested.

"Did they? The basis of their case will be they didn't know. You disguised the risk. Only after the auditors and regulators picked you apart did those investors know what hit them."

"Whose side are you on, damn it?" Davis roared, the blood vessels in his face turning scarlet.

The lawyer chuckled. "I'm not taking their side, Max. I was right there with you, remember? I'm telling you what's going to happen. And don't forget, you've already seen the tip of the iceberg in the media. Columnists. Editorial writers. Financial reporters. They've already started painting you as bad actors. But when the lawsuits start, you'll be getting negative press non-stop. Dragging Quivira through the mud. Standing you up next to Charles Keating and taking pot shots."

"I need a drink," Davis looked around the room.

Will went to the bar and returned with a bottle and an ice bucket. He poured Max and himself each a drink, then looked at Jason who shook his head no.

"There's one more thing," Bernstein said. "Congress. Very soon, the House Banking Committee is going to start hearings on Quivira. You'll get letters asking you to appear."

"Bull hockey," Max yelped. "I ain't going."

"It's a set-up," Will agreed. "They've taken all of our records, and we can't get access to them to defend ourselves. We'd be sitting ducks."

"Not to mention," chimed in Max, "everything we would say in the hearing would be used some way in lawsuits. It'd be a no-win for us."

Jason said, "I agree. But if you don't go voluntary, they'll subpoena you. They'll tell everyone it's not punitive, that the hearings are meant to learn what went wrong so they can correct for the future. It's pure baloney. You'd better get personal legal counsel lined up."

"What about you?" Max asked. "Wouldn't you represent us?"

"Sorry, guys," the attorney answered. "My firm has its hands totally full handling Quivira's aftermath. We can't represent the individual officers, too." He stood and picked up his briefcase. "I wish you both the best. I'm sorry it turned out this way."

After he was gone, Max sat staring into space. "Jeez Louise. This is real bad. I'm as nervous as a cat at the dog pound. What in hell are we going to do?"

"Max, we're going to go in the den and get drunk. Then we're going to man up and fight the bastards."

* * *

The majority party chairman of the House Banking Committee was Gordy Hernandez, from Arizona. He hailed from Phoenix, coincidentally where the controversial savings and loan figure, Charles Keating, once ran the American Continental Corporation. Before aiming its sights on Quivira, Hernandez's committee raked Keating's Lincoln Savings over the proverbial coals.

Hernandez poked his head into the office of his committee's ranking minority leader, Ernesto Brunetti. The representative of a tough Italian district in St. Louis, Brunetti took pride in aggressively pursuing his populist views. At least, when they lined up with those of his political party.

"Ernie, is this a good time?" Gordy asked cordially.

"I have ten minutes for you, Gordy. Then I've got to go to a Goddamned press conference."

Hernandez entered and sat across the desk from his fellow committeeman. "I wanted to be sure our staffs communicated sufficiently about the Quivira hearings. Everything copasetic with you?"

Ernesto flashed the know-it-all, cynical smile he was known for. "I'm told we got most of the regulators and auditors to agree voluntarily," he said. "But Katzen, the federal regulator in Texas who was so cozy with Quivira's management, my people say he's not coming. Right?"

"So far," Hernandez admitted. "We'll see."

"And same goes for the main dog, that son-of-a-bitch Will Martin?"

"As of yet, he's not agreed to appear. You know the drill, Ernie. If they don't come, we'll issue a subpoena."

"Those are the two guys I want to hang out to dry. Katzen and Martin. They represent everything I resent about businessmen. Arrogance. Dishonesty. Fraud. However this savings and loan disaster plays out, the guys who bled their banks dry knew the taxpayers would have to pay the bill for their failures."

The chairman half-smiled and lowered his head in a gesture of polite discourse. "Now, Ernie, as I've pointed out many times at these hearings, we're not a judiciary body. We're an oversight committee. It's not our job to be judge and jury. We're supposed to get the facts about what went wrong so we can write responsible legislation."

"That may be so," the Missourian said. "But Gordy, I don't need to tell you who sits on our committee from my side of the aisle. You think I can control them? They're going to make a strong argument for the citizens they represent. And they're going to do it by singling out who's to blame."

"Such as?"

"They'll go after Katzen. He was soft on Quivira, let them get away with risky business practices while his staff sounded alarms every time they conducted a review or received an audit. And Will Martin, the CEO who cared more about making his big developer friends and board members—and himself—rich than running a responsible business the taxpayers didn't have to bail out."

The Congressman squinted his eyes with disdain. "And the son of a senator from Texas, a sneaky little snake named Bernard Franklin. He went on their board so he could help make multi-million-dollar loans to his builder buddies. One of whom, mind you, gave Franklin a one-hundred-thousand-dollar loan with no strings and no requirement to pay it back. And then, the guy just happened to pony up big bucks to help bail out Bernie's loser oil exploration business. Do you think he might have hoped for some political advantage in doing that for the senator's son?"

The sly grin returned. "You can say all you want to about fact-finding and no finger-pointing. But Gordy, those men were scratching each other's backs with taxpayer dollars. We're going to massacre the sonsabitches."

CHAPTER THIRTY-TWO

The trial in Houston U.S. District Court was near an end. Charged with misusing Quivira funds for his personal gain, CEO Will Martin was on the stand in his own defense. After his defense attorney, Karl Thomas, questioned him, Will was cross-examined by the lawyer for the Federal Deposit Insurance Corporation.

"Mr. Martin, you testified you would have repaid the loan from your holding company, Quivira Financial, if the firm hadn't collapsed."

"I had every intention to do so." Will was calm and composed, his clear voice exuding confidence.

"The truth is, you got the loan illegally in the first place, didn't you?"

"Object, your honor," Thomas interjected. "That point is not in contention."

"I'll allow it," the judge said.

"It was a legal loan," Will stated. "I could not receive a loan from the Quivira Savings Bank. But the holding company had no such restrictions."

"You never intended to pay the loan back, did you?" the lawyer grilled. "You were padding your own bank account."

"I had earned more than one million dollars in salary and bonuses three years running. There was no reason to think I wouldn't continue to earn at that pace and easily repay it. Unfortunately, the entire real estate market collapsed, leaving me and many others destitute."

The lawyer paused and fixed a serious glare at his interview subject. "You mis-used the funds, didn't you? You promised it was for business only, yet you diverted the money to your own personal use."

"I used it to temporarily take care of some home remodeling costs and to pay down an existing mortgage, it's true," Will admitted. Then, fixing a serious look directly on the jury, he added, "But why would I defraud the very company I built into a huge success? That would make no sense, and there was no intent to do so. Had we not encountered a disastrous market failure, I would have repaid the loan and none of us would be sitting here today."

In his closing statement, the FDIC lawyer pounded home his point again as the federal jury listened intently.

"Ladies and gentlemen, to many people, a million dollars would be a fortune. In fact, to many, half of that is more than they will make in their lifetime. But to Will Martin the huge amounts of money he borrowed from Quivira Financial and never paid back ended up costing you, the taxpayers. We proved beyond any reasonable doubt this man, this chief executive officer of a failed and disgraced savings association, illegally voted himself a business loan for one and one-half million dollars neither you nor I could obtain on such favorable terms. We further showed you he vowed in the paperwork to use the money only for business purposes. But he lied. William Martin misapplied four hundred fifty-eight thousand dollars of the loan for his personal use, to remodel a house and pay down a mortgage.

"This man was motivated by nothing more than pure, old-fashioned greed. You are left with no choice but to protect the taxpayers the defendant, Will Martin, defrauded. Do your duty and find him guilty."

Minutes later, Will's lead counsel, Karl Thomas, concluded his closing argument with an opposite appeal. "The prosecution has not satisfied their burden of proof that our client intended to mislead either Quivira Financial or the regulators. You heard Mr. Martin testify he had no intention whatsoever of fraud. Mr. Martin was no predator—he was a victim of the demise of the Texas real estate economy like everyone else. No evidence has been offered here to prove he had any devious motive. He had every right to believe Quivira would make the same kind of earnings as previous years. And if so, he would easily be able to repay the money he legally borrowed from his own holding company.

"Instead, the same factors that destroyed the entire Houston economy, including the savings and loan industry, reduced this man to financial ruin. He had to sell his house and other possessions. His only crime was believing in Quivira Savings—the company he put his heart and soul into—so strongly he had no doubt he could turn the ship around."

* * *

Jury trials of something so mundane as a savings and loan scandal rarely attracted the same attention other more sensational events might. A kidnapping? Murder? The courthouse steps would be mobbed after the verdict. Any media attention at all involving the closing of a bank? Not so much.

Yet this was Quivira Savings, a once respected institution in Houston, now fallen from its pedestal. Ever since its abrupt invasion by federal agents, the association garnered continuous news coverage of the aftermath.

And so, the news of Will's acquittal drew a gaggle of reporters.

The normally unemotional Martin emerged from the courthouse sporting a smile of relief.

The media swarmed around Will and his lawyers. Television reporters and camera crews. Radio reporters with recording packs slung over their shoulders. Newspaper writers with notepads.

"Mr. Martin," one of the TV newsmen shouted over the others. His camera crew jockeyed for a good shot. "What's your reaction to the jury's decision?"

The camera lights illuminated his face and bounced reflection off his glasses. "I'm obviously relieved," he said in a deep, calm voice. "I've maintained from the outset—even testified under oath before Congress—I've done nothing illegal. The decision today supports it. I'm deeply grateful to my attorneys here for bringing out the truth in the courtroom."

"What will you do now?" a woman from another station asked.

"I'm in the process of moving to Kansas City, Missouri," he answered. "I plan to get involved in the real estate mortgage business up there."

The first reporter pressed on, "We've been told you held the door open for the prosecutors when you entered the courtroom. Were you trying to curry favor with the enemy?"

"I have no enmity toward my accusers," he responded. "They saw things their way, and we saw it another. They were just doing their job, I suppose."

Quickly the television and radio crews dispersed, but one person remained, Garrison Shack, the real estate editor for the *Houston Business Press*. "Will, would you permit me another question or two?"

Will nodded. "Of course, Garrison."

"Will, you signed a prohibition order banning you from banking. How are you able to set up a new mortgage firm?"

"This company will be involved in real estate investments. Those activities aren't covered by the ban from banking."

"You could have easily gone to jail today. What prompted you to fight the charges, rather than plea bargain?"

"First of all," Will said, "I don't agree with your premise. It would not, in my opinion, have been easy for this jury to convict me. The facts were clearly on my side."

"They deliberated for more than four hours," the newsman countered.

"That's true. There were several points of law for them to consider. But in the end, they got it right."

"You've said for public record your finances are tapped out as a result of Quivira failing. Yet you've managed to retain top lawyers, so I imagine they're pretty expensive." He turned to the lead lawyer. "Counselor, I assume you didn't take this case pro bono."

Attorney Karl Thomas frowned and held Will's arm as if to say, "Let me take this one." He bristled a bit as he answered, "Our clients' fee arrangements are personal and private. We have an arrangement with Mr. Martin involving some personal property, and we won't divulge more. Next question?"

Shack turned back toward Will and said, "Your partner, Max Davis, didn't fare as well as you. He's doing six months in prison for his Quivira activities. Considering you were acquitted, do you think if he knew then what he knows now, he'd take a different tack?"

Will paused a few moments, as if contemplating whether to answer. Finally, he said, "Max was no more guilty than I. He chose to plea bargain. I told him I thought he should fight the charges, but he decided not to take the gamble, and I'm sorry it turned out the way it did. Now, Garrison, if you'll excuse me, I'm really tired. I'd like a little time to huddle with my attorney."

* * *

The deposed CEO and his lawyer relaxed in a back booth of the Shipyard Tavern. Will Martin nursed a scotch while Karl Thomas had a martini.

"I thought Leslie was going to be here," puzzled Thomas. "We agreed she'd be a sympathetic optic for the jury."

Will shook his head in the negative. "She wanted to come, but I decided against it. Told her to take our kids out and do something fun. I didn't want her exposed to all of the accusations, all the finger-pointing I've endured. Or the possibility of a guilty verdict."

"Ye of little faith," Thomas joked.

"It turned out fine, didn't it? I'm very grateful," Will said. "You were masterful in there."

"You were fantastic up there on the stand," the attorney said. "You should have been a lawyer."

Martin laughed. "For some reason, I've never had a problem stating my case. It comes naturally to me, and I enjoy it. But I wouldn't want to argue on someone else's behalf. You did a great job of that today."

"I had no doubt," said Thomas. "Exactly why the FDIC chose to file such narrow charges is baffling to me, but we'll take it. It wasn't a walk in the park, but they made it easier than it might have been."

Will shrugged his shoulders. "They didn't really want me. It's Bernie Franklin they'd lick their chops to get. His dad has been their adversary in the Senate—held up their funding, led the charge to deregulate. Threats to their power and existence. They couldn't figure out how to pin something on Bernie, so they settled for me. Everything in this world is political."

"So, you're going back in business, Will?" Karl asked.

"You know I'm broke. I had to put a stack of quarters together to pay you. There's an old friend up in Wichita I've kept in touch with, knew him when I worked at the savings bank there. He knows my situation and offered me an opportunity to help him with his Kansas City properties. I'll go up there and settle until I can get a new venture up and running."

They raised their glasses. "To you, Will," the lawyer offered. "You've been through hell the past few years. Here's to a brighter future in Kansas City."

CHAPTER THIRTY-THREE

The stop through Wichita, en route to Kansas City, gave Will a chance to hook up with old friends. One was Lawson Jeffries. Will was waiting for him at lunchtime in the Westside Sports Bar where they met one night several years previous, before embarking on the Houston adventure.

"I remember you liked this spot," Will said as Jeffries arrived and settled into the booth across from him. "The last time we were here, after I made a presentation to the Wichita mucky-mucks, I told you we should be eating at the country club. Do you remember?"

"Yes, I do," Lawson answered. "That was several country clubs ago," and he chuckled. "So, you're moving back?"

Martin shook his head no. "Kansas City. I'm just passing through. Leslie flew up there with the children so they could house hunt. She can't wait to get settled in, off to a new start. I wanted a chance to see you since I was driving through. And I have a dinner date with Taz Collingsworth. Do you know him?"

"I know Taz," Lawson confirmed. "The richest man in Wichita. Friend of powerful people. He donates generously to my station. I might have known you'd want to see him."

"Public television. I can't believe it."

Lawson Jeffries leaned back and guffawed. "Why? Because there are no angles to shoot? I'm happy with where I landed. I work hard, Will, but even so, I'm actually enjoying the slower pace. Everything was such a fever pitch in Houston. Hustle the next big deal. Keep the regulators off our back."

"I think you've hit on the part I liked the most. And of course, the lifestyle it all provided," Will said.

"You do enjoy living the good life." Jeffries changed the subject. "So, you're meeting Taz tonight?"

"He has some interests in Kansas City—a couple of hotels and a private golf club. He'd like to get his hands on their casino, but Missouri law says the state has to run it. Taz thought I might be able to help him with some things up there, and in turn I can earn a living while I set up my own business. Scratching backs, right?"

"You never miss a beat." Jeffries grinned at his old friend for a minute and then turned serious. "How are you, Will? I saw your testimony, yours and all the others in the Congressional hearings on Quivira."

"Saw it? How?"

"It was on public cable. You were steadfast to the end, Will. I'll give you credit. You convinced me you got the shaft when they closed Quivira."

Will frowned. "Well, I did. They should have let us keep the company and recapitalize. Instead they pawned it off like some old discarded furniture. The buyers are making out like pirates. The thing I hated most about the hearings, though, was how the bastards worked Bernie Franklin and Fred Katzen over. It pissed me off. They promised it wasn't going to be judicial, and then they hammered them like prosecuting attorneys. Those two guys are friends of mine. I resented it." He paused. "Lawson, I'm sorry I got you down there and then everything went sour. That's not what I had planned for either of us."

"I know," Jeffries said. "It's water under the bridge. We'll be fine. I have a job I enjoy, and you've got the FDIC trial behind you. There's nothing but open field in front of us."

"Ever the old football player, huh, Lawson? Yes, my friend, we're going to be all right."

* * *

One of the most exclusive neighborhoods in Kansas City, Mission Estates, was the perfect place for the Martins to settle. With a median annual income above $250,000 and many homes listed in the millions, they would get to know some of the district's elite. Nearby, the famous Country Club Plaza, the nation's first outdoor mall built in the 1920s, offered fashionable shopping and fine dining. It was a perfect setting for what Will had in mind as his next career move.

Just as important, there were older, yet fashionable, homes in certain parts of the Mission Estates area Will and Leslie were able to afford. As they had in Houston, they could live in an upper-class home, not one of the pricey mega-mansions like those of their nearby neighbors, yet close enough to enjoy the status of living in a glitzy section of town.

Their new Kansas City neighbors and friends didn't need to know they had filed for bankruptcy. It was the linchpin of a legal move Will concocted to prevent total financial disaster, and it involved his trusting parents.

Will phoned his father from Houston the day after the court's acquittal to tell him the good news. But the call had another purpose as well. "Dad, I told you how they drained my finances when they shut down Quivira, right?" he said. "And I might be able to protect some of the income I earned if I could get some help. Well, that's what I need from you."

His father was one of the most honest men Will knew. He grew up on a farm in California's San Mateo County, where Will was born. When they moved to Wichita, Will's father became involved in the grain storage industry and picked up business experience. But he never strayed from the hard-working ethic he learned from tilling the soil. Plus, he and his wife raised their children as devout Catholics, seeing to it they attended Mass and became good Christians. He taught his children those principles growing up, and he was convinced they would live by them in their adult lives.

"Son, you let those big-money schemers and crooked politicians take advantage of you," he told Will on the call. "Tell me how I can help."

"I'm going to wire some money to your bank account. I'll need the account and routing number. This is my money. I earned it, Dad, and I need to protect it from the scum-bag lawyers who're trying to take everything I own. Leslie and I have suffered enough loss without giving up everything we worked for."

"Do you swear this is legitimate, Will? There's nothing against the law about our doing it?"

"Dad, I swear. Please hold onto it until I need it, okay?"

Their new Kansas City house was every bit as posh as the Houston place in River Oaks. Whereas their previous home was typically dark, English Tudor style inside and out, their Mission Estates house was a white, classic colonial structure with large windows permitting natural light to fill the rooms. It was set well back from the street and featured a large, fenced back yard ringed by Leyland Cypress trees.

Two days after moving in, Will told Leslie about the arrangement with his father. He'd just come home from a late meeting on Taz's behalf. It was nine o'clock, and

Leslie was having a cocktail and listening to a CD of old favorites.

"And your dad agreed to do it?" she asked, her speech slightly slurred.

"He did," Will answered. "Leslie, I researched the law. If the attorneys don't serve a summons to my parents within 120 days, we're home free."

She stood and walked a little shakily to the bar. "I'm having another. Want one?"

"Sure, I could use a drink," he let out a big sigh. "How many of those have you had?"

Leslie returned with the cocktails and bent to kiss Will as she handed him his scotch. "Only two or three or four, I don't know. I'm celebrating our big, new, beautiful house. She sat and leaned into him, her head resting on his shoulder. "We're going to be okay then?" she asked. "Financially, I mean?"

"I'm making some contacts, getting a couple things going so we'll have steady money coming in. When the time's right, I'll pull the trigger on what I sent to my dad's account. We'll be fine."

"I think you're fine," she giggled, sliding an arm around his shoulder and kissing him again. "Maybe we should have a little fun, break the house in right."

He looked around. "Are the kids down for the night?"

She slid his hand inside her blouse. "Sound asleep in bed."

He left his hand there, caressing. "Then let's go get into bed."

"No bed. Let's do it right here." She pushed the pillows off the sofa and began to pull off her jeans."

He helped her with her pants, and then her panties.

"Our first time," he whispered, pressing against her body.

"First time what?" she said.

"First time we ever did it in Kansas City."

She giggled again and sank lower into the sofa.

CHAPTER THIRTY-FOUR

Early in 1991, a United States-led coalition launched Operation Desert Storm and swept Iraqi troops out of Kuwait in a little over one month. But by fall, as the Kansas City Catholic Youth Soccer League went into full swing, a war against Saddam Hussein was the last thing on anyone's mind. Sacred Heart and Saint Aquinas were locked in a scoreless battle, and parents and friends of the middle school players paced the sidelines, shouting support, urging their young charges on.

Will's son Kris, new to the Sacred Heart team, showed in practice he was the fastest player and most accurate kicker. In the second game of the season, he was in the starting line-up at center forward. The match was a see-saw battle with very few shots on goal. Suddenly, in the final minutes, the Sacred Heart winger intercepted a pass. He centered a perfect relay to Kris, who out-maneuvered a defender and nailed the upper corner of the goal with a perfect shot.

Frantic screaming from the Sacred Heart faithful split the air and went on continuously until the whistle signaled the game's end. Will and Leslie, and their other two children, Haley and Chip, rushed onto the field, trying to get to the young man being mobbed by his teammates. When they finally reached Kris, they all locked in a bear hug.

"I'm proud of you, son," Will beamed. The thirteen-year-old was red-faced, as much from the accolades as from the soccer action.

"Great game," Leslie said, planting a kiss on his forehead.

His younger brother and sister clung to him, their

personal hero.

As the Martins began the long walk to the parking lot, a father and his son, dressed in Saint Aquinas' green and gold, fell in lock step with them. "Nice game, young man," the other boy's father said. "This is Sacred Heart's first victory over Saint Aquinas in three years, did you know that?"

"No sir," Kris responded politely.

"We'll get you next year."

He extended a hand to Will. "Harman Tucker."

"I'm Will Martin. This is my wife, Leslie. We're new in K.C., so we don't know about the rivalries yet."

"New from where?"

"Texas. I ran a savings bank down there. You might remember what happened to all of us in the thrift industry. So here I am, starting over."

"Yeah, it was tough. I'm a developer, so I saw up front and ugly the squeeze the economy put on you guys. I had to fight to keep my head above water with the enormous interest rates we had to pay. What brings you to Missouri?"

"I grew up down in Wichita, so I'm very familiar with Kansas City, both the Kansas and Missouri sides of the metro area," Will said. "A friend of mine in Wichita has properties up here he doesn't have time for. I'm helping him out until I can set up my own business."

They reached Harman's car and Will stopped. Leslie hurried on to catch up as the children dashed toward their car.

"So, a savings bank, huh?" Tucker said. "Were you one of those old-fashioned thrifts or the innovative kind that sank their teeth into investments and commercial real estate?"

"The latter," said Will. "Many of the old-fashioned savings and loans fell further and further behind the curve of runaway inflation. I took on the challenge to grow us out of the problem when Congress turned us loose. We increased our assets like crazy. But the regulatory machinery was much too slow. They didn't understand the market realities, so like a lot of others, we were forced to lock the door and turn in the keys."

"Will, let me ask you something. Not meaning to butt into your work for your friend, or to interfere in your setting up a company. But I'd like to talk to you about an opportunity. I might be able to use your help on a new project, and you should be perfect for it. Would you be interested in hearing more?"

"Harman, it never hurts to talk," Will answered.

Tucker fished a business card from his wallet. "Give me a call in the next day or two. We'll have lunch and discuss it."

* * *

Overland Park, Kansas in the Sixties and Seventies was one of the fastest growing cities in the nation. The Kansas City metropolitan suburb promoted the development of residential neighborhoods, shopping malls, industrial parks and a brand-new city hall. It was boom time, with population rising from 28,000 in 1960 to more than 100,000 by the end of the Eighties.

Leading the city during much of this incredible growth was Al Atchison, a business graduate of the nearby University of Kansas. The tall, affable but business-like broker for investment firm Brooks & Whittier won a spot on the city council in the mid-Seventies. Four years later the voters elected him mayor, a position he would hold for many years.

As he helped guide Overland Park through its period of explosive growth, Mayor Atchison clung religiously to the tenets of orderly development, low taxes and excellent quality of living. No new major development came before the council for re-zoning, set-back exceptions, street access or any other issue without first passing muster with the mayor.

Kansas City commercial developer Harman Tucker was well-known on the Missouri side of State Line Road, but he had never made a foray into the burgeoning Kansas suburbs. In the late Eighties, he methodically purchased property in Overland Park through straw parties, thus keeping speculation from driving prices artificially high. By 1991, he had managed to piece together enough acreage of aging businesses and strip malls to go forward with plans for a major office complex. The time was ripe, and Tucker was ready to make his move.

The builder's meeting with Mayor Atchison and Harry Wallrafen, chair of the city council's community development committee, started right on time, ten a.m. Introductions were cordial but brief.

Tucker had more the look and demeanor of a construction hand than businessman. He was built like a prize fighter. Except for the business suit he wore, he could be mistaken for the character in cigarette ads wearing jeans, plaid shirt and cowboy hat, sporting a two-day growth of beard.

"Gentlemen," said Tucker, "if you'll follow along in your handouts, I'd like to walk you through some critical data. The first page illustrates how available space inside the Overland Park city limits is becoming tight. In other words, you're underbuilt and will lose business to surrounding communities if you don't move quickly.

"Page two is a list of companies who've indicated a desire to move into the K.C. metro area, then existing businesses looking to expand their employee base and operating capacity. The next page—and this is critically important—is a survey demonstrating demand for new business amenities is growing fast. New technologies are emerging, and forward-looking companies want to take advantage of them.

"To further expand on this chart, let me give you a prime example. If you read last month's issue of *Business Future Magazine,* you saw an article about the future of computing in this country. This year, the internet has been made available for unrestricted commercial use. Computers now operating on the net have reached more than one million. That will grow exponentially. Something called web pages are going to begin opening up. The first actually went live a month ago.

"If you're not familiar with any of this, don't worry. It's new to a lot of us. But what you do need to know are two things: first, businesses will begin using the internet to operate in new, more efficient and effective ways. They'll have computer pages their customers can access to get information, even order products or supplies; and second, the communities and developers who recognize this explosion in technology are going to come out winners.

"I plan to equip all of my new office developments with the technologies to enable businesses to stay abreast of these newer, better ways to do business." Tucker opened a large portfolio and pulled out a pile of specs and renderings. "Now let me get to the meat. Here's what I'm proposing on the project sites I've purchased."

For the next half hour, the three reviewed plans,

raised questions, discussed side issues.

As the presentation ended, Mayor Atchison said, "Harman, I think maybe your project can fly. Harry here, and his development committee, will need to go through the details you've raised—zoning requests, ingress and egress. But if you can jump those hurdles and assure us you have solid financing behind the project, so we don't get stuck with a half-built ghost town, I think we can support it."

Harman stuffed the stack of papers back into the portfolio and stood, extending a handshake. "That's great, Al. Thanks to both of you."

The mayor said, "You have several developments in progress over on the Missouri side. So, I assume you'll have a point guard, a manager to pick up where you leave off today?"

Tucker smiled. "I've got just the man. He's new to Kansas City, but he has a wealth of experience in handling complex real estate and financing issues. I'll put him in touch with you. His name is Will Martin."

CHAPTER THIRTY-FIVE

Charisma, self-assurance and an ability to grasp the big picture quickly were all traits that drew people to Will. Overland Park Mayor Al Atchison and Development Committee Chair Harry Wallrafen seemed favorably impressed as Will went through his first meeting with them, representing developer Harman Tucker. He reviewed the status of financing for a new office park in their city. He brought them up to date on construction schedules and plans, subcontractor lists and all other aspects of the project, pending city approvals. He answered every question they had with clarity and precision.

"It looks like you have everything lined up well," said Atchison. "You've got the financing available and ready to be signed. We've reviewed all the zoning and setback problems, and I think we can get approval. What's the tenant situation?"

Will smiled. His experience with Quivira, however disastrous it ended, prepared him for this meeting. As a prime source of commercial development funding at the savings bank, he had met with dozens of builders on projects as complex, many even more troublesome.

"We have a tentative commitment from a major tenant wanting to take five floors of building one, and a good list of others who want into the project as well," he answered. "If they all come in, we'd be seventy percent occupied from the outset. As soon as the council gives the go-ahead—assuming they do—this list will be ready to sign."

He handed out a roster of companies that signed tentative commitments.

Wallrafen whistled loudly. "I like this. I like it very

much. If you can bring these companies into our little city, we would be happy."

Will grinned. "There's still the matter of the tax abatements. I'd like to get an idea of where we stand."

Mayor Atchison replied, "I've reviewed your project with the county superintendent. He agrees you clear all the eligibility requirements, and he's sure he can secure everything with the county commission within the next week. As for Overland Park, the issue will be part of the presentation with the council next week. It looks like you have all your ducks in a row, so we'll put you on the Tuesday agenda."

Will stood and collected the papers he had distributed, tossed them in his briefcase and snapped it shut. "I'll look forward to it. Gentlemen, it's a pleasure working with you."

As they rose to leave, Will added, "Oh, by the way, just so you know, besides handling some of Harman's projects, I've founded a new business, Martin Capital. I'm setting up to make hard-money real estate loans using a pool of investor funds. Anyone with an investment retirement account or Keogh retirement plan can do a lot better than the current market rates with the kind of deals I will be putting together.

"Of course, I plan to keep the Martin Capital activity totally separate from anything I do with Harman's development firm, to avoid the appearance of conflict. But if you, or any of your friends or relatives, might be interested in getting in on the bottom floor of a very lucrative venture, I'd be interested in talking to them."

Atchison stared at Will for a brief moment, then curled his mouth up slightly at the corners. "I guess Harman didn't tell you what I do for a living?"

"He didn't, no."

"I've been a broker over at Brooks and Whittier since I graduated college."

"Al, this is a little embarrassing," Will said. "Sorry."

The mayor continued to glare until he couldn't hold the laughter back any longer. Then Will cackled along with him at the gaffe.

Al went on, still chuckling, "So, you can count me out. I don't think I'd be a good prospect for you. Now, if Harry here has any interest, he's free to call you. Heck, I tell all my clients they should diversify. And if you can get them a safe bet even a few points higher than the market, why would I want to hold them back? Right?"

* * *

Will had leased office space in the same building as Harman Tucker's. It was on the front row of a low-rise business park consisting of a dozen red-brick structures. Each one featured a common entrance with a hallway running past ten enterprises, five on each side.

After returning from his Overland Park meeting, he put his briefcase on the desk and walked down the hallway to Tucker's office. The builder waved him in.

"Everything's set for Tuesday," Will said. "We'll meet with the full council at ten. They should have all the abatement clearances from the county by then, and it looks like we'll be able to close the deal. All we have to do then is run over to Crystal Savings, sign the loan paperwork and you'll be in business."

"Great, Will. It's been fantastic working with you on this one. You've represented us really well in every aspect—the financing, city politics, everything. I'm happy you came on board."

"I'm not doing it for free, remember," Will said with

a subtle smile.

Harman grinned back. "Oh, I'll honor our contract. I hope we can do more projects together."

Will hesitated. "Remember we agreed I could launch this investment business I had in mind?"

Harman nodded yes.

"I've incorporated and put the word out, looking for investors. But Harman, we'll keep our lines from crossing, I promise."

"I'm fine with it, Will. Shoot fire, if you can get the thing up and running and start earning fantastic interest, I might become a client. You probably aren't aware I didn't start out as a contractor. I was an investor."

"How'd that happen?" Will asked.

"I had a little business upstate in St. Joseph handling small business loans for mom-and-pops who didn't know which end was up. I got lucky with it. Grew it like crazy. After ten years, I sold it for fifteen million. Still pretty young and didn't know what the hell to do with my money. A home builder I knew said, 'I'll take some of it off your hands, for the right terms.' So, I made him a six-month construction loan and was amazed at the interest I could earn. He put me in touch with a few other builders, and I had a real deal going.

"Funny thing is, I went out on some of those building sites and got interested in how the subcontractors got lined up, what order they had to come in at, what kinds of problems they were causing the contractors. And I told myself I could manage the process better than these guys. So, I decided to do my own development. Built two subdivisions. One thing led to another, and *voila!* I eventually went into commercial work."

"That's amazing," Will said. "Maybe if I can get the

venture going well, I'll do the same thing."

"Shit. Competition," Harman joked.

When Will returned to his office, he picked up the phone and listened to his messages. After erasing two sales calls, the third caught his full attention.

"Will, this is Harry Wallrafen, the community development chair of the Overland Park City Council. You mentioned an investment opportunity this morning. I might be interested in hearing what you have to say. I own an insurance agency, and it's set up with a retirement plan just aching for good solid investments. Call and let me know when we can get together. Oh, and if it's okay, I'd like to bring my dad along. If you can do something inside his IRA, which is sitting right at two million, he might be interested as well."

CHAPTER THIRTY-SIX

The Promenade Three was a swanky, white-table-cloth restaurant in Kansas City's Country Club Plaza. It was Will's place of choice to wine and dine affluent prospects for his real estate investment firm. His guest was Valeta Vansyckle, a wealthy widow whose ten-bedroom estate was mere minutes from Will and Leslie Martins' more modest home in the same section of Kansas City.

It was no accident Will was able to engineer this luncheon date. Valeta was on his target list of potential investors for months. Finally, he discovered one of his new investors served on several charity boards with the woman and recommended she talk to this successful investment man.

"I know your time is valuable," he said as they sipped mimosas and waited for their food. "I can't tell you how much I appreciate your meeting me here."

The woman was sixty and silver-haired, slightly overweight. Her make-up was impeccable but too heavy; her clothing and jewelry were off-the-chart expensive. "You came highly recommended by Larry and Theresa Callaway, Mr. Martin."

"Please, call me Will," he interjected.

"All right, Will. Theresa told me you made them quite a nice profit on their investment last fall. When my late husband died, nearly all of his money was tied up in a stock portfolio. I'm really pleased with the stock market right now, but I'm always willing to listen to new ideas."

"The Callaways have invited us to a prospective member event at Ward Parkway Country Club," Will said. "I think you're a member there? Larry and Theresa were my very first investors when I opened the business. Mrs. Vansykle…"

She broke in, "All right, now. If I call you Will, you have to call me Valeta." She flashed him a perfect-teeth smile.

"Okay, Valeta, I have years of experience in real estate investing, and in spite of what the stock market is earning, I think you'd find you could do much better. I looked at some charts the other day on the Standard and Poor's 500—I'm sure you already know that's the index most reflective of the overall market—and it showed from 1972 to 1982, the stock market lost half of its value."

He watched as her upraised eyebrows expressed surprise.

"Now, here we are in 1992, another ten years later," Will continued, "and the market has only gotten back to the point where it was in 1972. Twenty years and it was back where it started. Valeta, you're right, we are seeing it start to gain some momentum again. But do you want to take the chance it won't nosedive again like it did in the early Eighties?"

Valeta Vansyckle's demeanor turned deadly serious. Will had her full attention.

"You've heard the old expression, 'Don't put all your eggs in one basket?'"

Valeta nodded yes.

"The rule applies doubly to investing your money. I'm sure your husband meant well, but when he left you only stock, he didn't totally protect you from the potential downturns.

"You live in a big, beautiful house. I've driven by it, because we're practically neighbors. So, you must be aware the people who build homes like yours are not only financially sound, but they also must borrow a lot of money to carry out their projects. The way I make you money is to pool your investment with others' and lend it to the high-end contractors who build homes like yours in all the right Kansas City area neighborhoods. I make sure they're financially solid and lend them construction money. In turn they pay me—actually, you, as one of the investors—a high rate for the use of the money. No stock market declines. No risk. Just a handsome interest on your investment, guaranteed because it's all done with a contract."

"My, Will. That sounds wonderful."

Will retrieved a set of materials from his briefcase. "Valeta, here's a brochure showing how it all works." He watched for a moment as she scanned through his expensively produced, high-gloss, four-color pamphlet. "I'm not asking you for an answer today. I think you should take time to look through this, read the agreement you would sign if you should invest in Martin Capital, then perhaps talk again to the Callaways about their experience. If you'd be more comfortable, even get in touch with your stockbroker or financial advisor and see what they say."

"How much would I have to invest?" she asked.

"That would depend on how much money you'd want to earn at the interest rates you see there on the chart. But right now, there's an opportunity for a $250,000 investment. I'm putting together a fund to lend two million on a mansion about to be built over in Forest Brook. I'm sure you're familiar with it—it's a neighborhood of multi-million-dollar houses in Leawood, on the Kansas side of the metro area."

"Oh, I'm very familiar with Forest Brook," she assured him. "A friend of mine, a fellow board member on the three-county Council on Aging, bought there two years ago. And you have this builder ready to borrow?"

"I do. I need one final investor to close it out in the next few days. So as soon as you talk to your support team, if you decide to go ahead, come to the office and we'll sign the papers."

Valeta pulled the agreement out of the packet of materials. "I don't need to talk to anyone, Will. I'm a very good judge of character. And I can tell a terrific opportunity when I see it. I assume a check would be all right. Do you have a pen?"

CHAPTER THIRTY-SEVEN

Summer storms that slip up the tornado trough from Texas to Oklahoma to Kansas and Missouri can be destructive forces of nature, often laced with deadly, twisting winds and the battering assault of horizontal rain and hail. The one rampaging through the Kansas City metro area on this particular August night was such a threatening menace.

It began about ten, after their children were asleep. Will and Leslie went to bed, but then an endless roar shook the trees outside and pounded against windowpanes, making it impossible for them to rest.

"Should we get the children up and go to the basement?" she asked.

Will considered for a moment. "With all of those storms I remember from growing up in Wichita, I don't recall one time our taking shelter in the basement. Did you?"

"We had a storm cellar in the backyard, but we didn't ever go down there," Leslie answered. "My dad would stand watching out the back door, toward the southwest, looking for a sign of a funnel. If he had ever seen or heard one, I think he would have rounded us up and sent us there. It's different when you're the grown-up. And Will, we have a finished basement, not a board door opening up to a hole in the ground with a dirt floor."

"Let's do what your dad did," Will suggested, "go down to the first floor and watch, wait this thing out. If it gets any scarier, I'll go upstairs and wake them up and we can go down to the basement game room."

Leslie stretched out on the couch in the great room while Will retreated to the sun porch and watched the weather maul their row of Leyland cypress bordering the privacy fence at the back of the property. After a few minutes, he heard a racket above the coyote-like howling of the wind. But it wasn't the freight train roar associated with tornados. Rather, it was a metallic banging and rattling progressing rapidly down the street next to the house.

Will dashed through the great room toward the front hall.

"What are you doing?" Leslie squealed as he passed.

"Our garbage cans are blowing down the street," he answered with urgency. He yanked his raincoat from the hall closet and pulled it on, then the old baseball cap he wore when grilling in the back.

"Let them go, Will," she demanded. "You can retrieve them in the morning."

"They're banging around out there like a Chinese gong," he answered. "They'll wake up half the neighborhood."

The rain was still coming down, but more a steady torrent than the earlier wild squall. Will sprinted down the street, fighting against the drenching downpour. He caught the first one, puffing hard from the run, and then nabbed the second, nesting it inside the first. Farther down the street he managed to snare the lids, lodged against the sewer drain. Dragging his bounty to the house and around the back where the receptacles lived next to the garage, he stood astonished, staring at two garbage cans still in their place, lids intact. "Holy crap!" he exclaimed.

He laid the retrieved cans on their side, wedging them between two shrubs. A neighbor would be searching for them in the morning.

The wind gusts resumed, as strongly as before, and

Will could hear a *crack-crack* of something serious happening in the back of the yard, the noise starting slowly at first and then gaining intensity. He wheeled around and watched, with the monsoon battering his face. One of the forty-feet-high Leyland Cypress surrendered to the elements, its gigantic roots ripping up violently from the earth. The force of the big tree crashing down and demolishing a section of the six-foot fence spit limbs and boards into the air. The rumble echoed across the yard, followed by an eerie silence broken only by the splatter of rain on the roof above him.

Will stood gazing at the aftermath for a long time before retreating into the house. He ditched his soggy coat and cap in the laundry room and stepped out of his shoes.

"What happened?" Leslie came out to check on him. "I heard a horrible racket out there."

"One of our trees fell. I'll deal with it tomorrow You go on to bed. I'm soaked clear through. I need a hot shower."

Before going into the bathroom, Will tip-toed down the hall and checked the bedrooms of his daughter and sons.

They were all three, deep asleep.

* * *

The next morning, Will stopped by Harman Tucker's office before he got to his own.

"Some storm last night, huh?" the developer remarked.

"It brought a massive tree down in my backyard," Will acknowledged. "Harman, do you know someone who can go out and cut it up for me?"

Harman gave him an "Are you kidding?" expression. "What in God's hell do you think I do for a living?" he asked.

"Fine, give me a number. Oh, and someone who can repair a six-foot privacy fence, too?"

Tucker grinned. "I'll make you a deal. The Overland Park project has been moving along well, but it could be in jeopardy now. Developments like this can undergo all sorts of hazards—labor problems, subcontractor failures, building permit snafus, re-zoning concerns, cost over-runs—you name it. But sometimes the costliest is the damned weather. The tornado apparently touched down a few miles south of Overland Park, in Olathe, Kansas," Harman said. He wrote down the phone numbers and handed the note to Will. "Call these guys about your tree and then ride with me. I've got plumbing, electrical and HVAC headed out there to survey the damage."

"All right," Will said, "As long as I can get back by mid-afternoon. Taz Collingsworth wants me to run over to one of his hotels and meet some people on a problem."

"You're still working for that guy?" Harman asked, sounding a little miffed.

"He's a friend," Will answered, "and consulting for him helps pay the bills."

Rush hour traffic was heavy, and it took nearly an hour to arrive at the building site. The on-site project manager and an electrical subcontractor were there, picking their way through the wreckage. The streets had been paved a week earlier, but now they were littered with debris from the storm. Harman steered carefully around scattered pieces of building material and glass.

"It don't look too bad," the project manager an-nounced as they approached. He was burly and bearded, and his speech pattern said everything about his country upbringing. "I don't think there's any structural damage, but I don't want to start up 'til we're sure. I'll get the engineer out here to make sure the building is safe to go in and get this crap off the road so the boys can get in tomorrow."

The electrical subcontractor, a wiry older man, said, "If you can give me clearance by tonight, I can have my crew ready first thing in the morning."

The two followed Harman and Will as they picked their way through the scattered rubble and went inside the building.

"Looks a lot more serious than it is—only minor damage, I think," Harman said. "But let's be sure. Damn, we were sailing along without any big cost overruns. Let's try to hold this to a minimum. I don't want a six-month job to become a year of pain, okay?"

They nodded. Harman and Will climbed back into the pickup.

"Could have been a lot worse," Harman said as he eased the truck off of the property.

"I don't know how you do it," Will said. "With everything that can go wrong on one of these projects, I wonder if it would be worth the headaches."

As they drove toward the Missouri side, Harman looked over at him and grinned. "Headaches? Yeah, I guess, but man, you're talking about multi-million-dollar migraines. There's no question it's worth it. Besides, when the thing's done, standing there and looking at what you built is an aphrodisiac."

"I suppose you're right," Will said. "One of the builders I knew in Texas acted like creating a big development out of nothing was better than sex."

"For sure." Harman waited a minute or two. "What's

this business for Taz you've got to do?"

"Nothing urgent. I'm helping him restructure a couple of loans on his hotels. Busywork. But someone has to do it, and I have a lot of experience working through financial problems."

They crossed State Line Road, into Missouri. "I have to knock off early," Harman said. "My kid's got soccer practice this afternoon. Your son—Kris, is it? He's quite a player. I assume he'll be back for Sacred Heart this year?"

Will shook his head no. "Kris tested off the charts on some pre-college exams this summer. We're sending him to a special prep school in Connecticut for brainy kids like him."

"Sounds expensive."

"It is, especially when we're paying for his younger brother and sister to go to private schools." He laughed. "And I suppose they'll all want to go to pricey colleges in a few years."

"What, Harvard? Yale? Maybe I can help you out," Harman said, grinning.

"Help me out? What are you talking about?"

"One reason I asked you to come out with me is, I wanted to talk some business."

"Okay, shoot."

"I've been watching you, seeing how you're building your investment business. You appear to be making your clients some real money, and I've noticed a lot of them coming back for more. I also like the team of professionals you put together to work for you. It's a nice little company now."

"I don't have any complaints," Will commented.

The builder said, "I have a proposition. Between

selling my previous business and the success I've had in development, my net worth is getting to be, let's say, pretty respectable. I'd like to jump in and help you grow the company exponentially, provide some significant backing and make Martin Capital a big-time operation. What do you think?"

"I'd like to hear more," Will responded. "Tell me what you have in mind."

"Like I said, I'd be interested in capitalizing the thing for you. I'd have a few conditions. First, I would be chairman of the board. You'd be president and chief executive officer. Second, you'd have to quit farting around with those little projects Taz Collingsworth has you doing. I know the fees he's paying are putting some change in your pocket, but Will, I'm talking about making you rich."

"Okay, I follow. What else?"

"You'd have to close your Martin Capital bank accounts. Everything would run through the accounts we set up together."

"That's not a problem. Anything else?"

Harman hesitated a long time. As he pulled onto Ward Parkway, he finally said, "This one might piss you off a little bit. But it shouldn't, Will. It's nothing personal. I'd require it of anyone I went into a high-end financial business with."

Will laughed loudly. "Come on, Harman. Out with it."

"You'd have to take an industrial psychology test."

"A what?"

"People do it all the time. I've used it with some of my office managers to match their skills with the job. It would be as much to see if we could work together effectively as anything else."

"Oh, I know what it is, Harman. I went to business school. But I've never had to go through anything like it before." He waited a long time before saying, "Seriously, I wouldn't be offended."

The developer pulled the pickup into the parking lot. As they walked into the building, Tucker asked, "Just what in hell happened down there at Quivira, Will?"

Will looked at him, surprised. Tucker had never broached the subject. "Harman, you were around when it all hit the fan. Everyone was struggling with the economy and inability to overcome those hellacious interest rates. We were one of many."

Harman stopped at the door. "But you guys took a lot more heat than most of the others. I saw the House Banking Committee hearings. Was it because of Bernie Franklin?"

"The Dems wanted to get the senator by hanging Bernie out to dry," Will explained.

The developer said, "What I heard was Travis Franklin's campaign managers forced his son to resign from your board. And the regulators held off closing you down until one day after the election to protect the senator's re-election. Is it true?"

"I don't know all of the politics. But the God's truth is they shouldn't have shut us down at all. We had a re-capitalization plan all worked out with an investment bank in New York. It would have kept us solvent and enabled us to stay on our feet. When they refused to accept it, I was furious. They kicked us all out and sold the bank off for pennies on the dollar. The deal they made ended up costing the taxpayers a lot more money than necessary and made the purchasing company rich. Where's the justice in that?"

"I hear you," Harman agreed. "Look, don't worry about this test thing—you won't have any problems blowing right by it. But get those bank accounts closed when we are up and running."

"I didn't say 'yes' yet, Harman." Will stared at his friend.

"No, by God, I guess you didn't. What do you say?"

"Yes," Will smiled widely.

CHAPTER THIRTY-EIGHT

The membership of the Ward Parkway Country Club included some of the richest and most well-known influencers of Kansas City's business and political life. The facility itself did them proud. Elegance oozed from every aspect of the approach to the sixty-year-old establishment. The guards who greeted visitors at the massive, gated stone entrance were friendly and polite almost to the point of obsequiousness. Within the gates, the lush, immaculately groomed landscaping was impressive, even to those who lived in nearby mansions. A portico was manned by valets in jackets and ties.

Inside the building, past the coat-check and up a short flight of steps, the deep-carpeted hallway led past a mahogany and brass lounge with a long, well-stocked bar and heavily cushioned chairs and sofas, then on to several exquisitely appointed meeting rooms. Finally, the hallway forked, with each corridor leading to a large ballroom. One was extraordinarily decorated with crystal lighting, original paintings and huge framed windows overlooking the golf course. The other was decorated in a more modern, but every bit as stylish, motif.

Will and Leslie were accustomed to posh venues. Their life in Houston frequently included entertaining or being entertained in some of the city's finest clubs and restaurants. But since their move to Kansas City, this was their first invitation to such a refined setting. It was a formal evening, the semi-annual prospective member dinner-dance, and they were dressed for the occasion. Will wore his custom-fitted tuxedo with silver tie and cummerbund, and Leslie had on one of the twenty or so designer gowns hanging in her closet.

"Is that new?" Will asked as they emerged from the car and he handed his key to the valet.

"No, sweetheart, but I haven't worn it in ages. Don't you recognize it?"

"Not sure," he stared.

"It's the dress you bought me on our honeymoon. Remember?"

"Of course, to match your eyes," he answered. "I'd forgotten—the one at *Belle Femme*." As they entered the building and walked toward their waiting hosts, Larry and Theresa Galloway, he added, "After three kids, it still fits you like a glove. Ooh, la, la."

Leslie giggled.

After exuberant greetings, their hosts guided them toward a round of ten, as yet unoccupied.

"Here's our table," Larry said. "You sit there, Will, next to Theresa, and you beside me, Leslie. Boy-girl-boy-girl."

They all laughed.

"Will, you'll meet people here you probably couldn't get in to see in their offices or living rooms. Not that they're snobs—they're actually some of the finest people you'd want to be around. But the demands on their time—their business and community obligations—make them pretty inaccessible. I've arranged our table so some of my friends can meet an entrepreneur who might make them a lot of money. Like you've done for Theresa and me."

A young woman in a gold jacket arrived with a trayful of flutes. "Would you like some champagne?" she asked. "Or if you want something else, I'll be happy to get it."

They all chose champagne just as the band struck

up its first number, a soft, swingy version of "Fly Me to The Moon." Several couples glided immediately onto the floor and displayed a variety of dance steps.

The Callaways introduced Will and Leslie to a number of members and guests who were drifting in. Will could carry on a smooth conversation with anyone. For Leslie, social interaction was more difficult. They both hailed from Smalltown, USA, but it was easy to see which one had comfortably moved on.

Will tossed disapproving glances her way as Leslie drained the glass of champagne and snared another from the tray of a passing waitress. That one was half gone within a few minutes. Meantime, the Galloways drifted away into the gathering crowd, leaving the Martins to fend for themselves.

The pre-dinner dance music turned to several soft, slow numbers, and it was the kind Will could dance to. So, he led Leslie onto the floor. "You put those two glasses of bubbly away pretty fast, Leslie. Maybe you should slow down."

"Actually, it was three," she corrected a bit haughtily, her speech already slightly slurred. "You missed one. But who's counting?"

"I am. You drink a lot more than you used to. You have to stay sober. Honey, have a good time, but take it easy on the booze. We have a lot of people to meet, and we need to make an impression. We might want to join this club."

Within minutes, an elderly man dressed in a sky-blue tuxedo appeared carrying a three-note xylophone. With the flourish of a symphony player, he sounded dinner.

"Will Martin here is an investment banker." Larry

appeared to know everyone who was settling in at their table.

Will nodded and smiled.

Larry went on, "If any of you have some spare change sitting around, talk to him. He'll grow it for you."

There was a rustle of chuckles and comments of greeting.

"Hi, meet my wife, Leslie," Will said to them, gesturing. "We both look forward to chatting with you all."

The menu consisted of a salad of toasted pecan and sliced strawberries on greens, served with a sauvignon blanc; and a main course of beef wellington done in a buttery pastry, with sides of carrot mash with *crème fraiche* and shredded brussels sprouts done with slow-fried shallots. The waiter offered two red wines with the main course, a Chilean malbec and a California cabernet. Will watched and frowned as Leslie debated, then asked for a pour of one in her red glass and another in the glass of white she had emptied. Several times during the meal, the waiter returned to refill glasses, Leslie's most often.

When they brought out dessert, chocolate truffle layer cake, everyone at the table buzzed. Will ordered coffee but Leslie opted to finish off her cabernet.

Far too soon to be leaving, Will offered an apologetic excuse to Larry and Theresa, something about children at home and an early workday. He guided his wife to the exit.

Driving home, Will was livid. "Damn it, Leslie. We've talked about this before. You drink too much. I wanted to make a good impression on those people. Because you got sloshed, we had to leave."

"Don't be so dramatic," she protested, leaning back against the headrest with her eyes closed. Her words spilled out sloppily. "Everyone loved you. Don't be so pious."

He clenched his jaw and continued on without further comment. Ten minutes later, as he pulled into the driveway, she was softly snoring.

"Damn," he said. It took an exerted effort to help her out of the car and inside, up the stairs to their bedroom. Her feet and legs were moving, but she remained limber as a rag, hanging onto Will with her arm around his shoulder. He let her fall onto the bed and went to check on their children.

Kris was charged with getting his younger siblings to bed on time. Ensuring they were all asleep, Will returned and struggled to get Leslie's gown off. He left her in her underclothes, covered with a sheet, and went to spend the night in the guest room.

* * *

When Will went down for coffee in the morning dressed for work, Leslie was already there. Her hair was uncombed. She wore a robe and sat at the kitchen table, her cup in front her, head in her hands. Without looking up, she said, "Don't say it, Will. I know, and I'm sorry. If it's any consolation, I'm nursing a massive hangover."

"Have Chip and Haley already left for school?" he asked coolly.

"Yes," she said. "I told them I had a migraine." She took a long sip of coffee and shuddered. "Kris isn't up yet."

Will popped two slices of whole wheat bread in the toaster and poured his coffee in a to-go cup. "I have to go right in. I'll take the toast with me."

Finally, Leslie looked up at him. "What more can I say than 'I'm sorry'? Don't be mad."

"It's okay, Leslie. I'm not pissed," he said. "We got out of there before you puked or anything else to embarrass us."

"Ohhhh, God," she exhaled. After another sip she asked, "Did you find any prospects?"

"I gave out a few business cards. Before things got too hairy and we had to bail, Larry said they could get us moved up on the wait list if we want to join. Two of the others at our table offered to co-sponsor if we ask."

Leslie brightened at the news. "Well, it's something. It wasn't a total loss. How much do you think it costs to join?"

"Larry said, 'If you have to ask, you can't afford it,'" Will looked at her mischievously. "No, seriously, what he said was seventy thousand dollars."

"To join? Will, you're talking about twice what our club cost in Houston. What about monthly?"

"I didn't ask," he said, "but it wouldn't be cheap."

"I don't meddle in your finances. I trust you to do the right things. But you're making enough money to afford something like this if we wanted in, right?"

"We have the money sitting in my father's account, but it's too early to touch it. This roof over our heads costs us fifteen grand a month. Plus, our kids' private school tuition and now, Kris's education next year back east. But a club membership like this would be a write-off, a cost of doing business. I might charge it to the company. I'll give Larry a call next week."

He took the slices from the toaster, wrapped them in a paper napkin, picked up his coffee and started toward the door. Turning back, he said, "Just one thing, Leslie. You can't binge-drink when we're around our friends. And especially around new people, potential clients."

"I know, I know, I know," she moaned, her head back down in her hands. "I promise I'll behave. It's just—just that Kris is leaving next week." She began to cry. "He's my baby. He's only fifteen." She pulled a tissue from her robe pocket, wiped her eyes and blew her nose. "He says with the workload they pile on, he might not be able to come home for the holidays. I don't know if I can stand it, Will."

Leslie's tears continued to flow, and her entire body shook softly as she sobbed.

Will reached across and rubbed her shoulders, but his movements were stiff and forced. His narrowed eyes and gritted teeth exhibited his annoyance.

"Leslie, stop this self-pity," he said harshly, sternly. "You have to pull yourself together; you can't go on this way. Don't worry about Kris. He'll be fine. This school will be good for him."

CHAPTER THIRTY-NINE

Of all the challenges of being president of any type of company, I think the most difficult are those which require life-altering decisions about those in your employ. My company, Wichita Savings and Loan, like all savings associations, went through chaos in the Seventies and Eighties. It's a wonder any of us were still standing. Because of my position on the national board, it seemed every week I got a frantic phone call.

"Monty, when are we going to get some relief from Washington?" someone would plead. Or, "Monty, if they don't let me go through with this merger, I'll have to close my doors," another would lament.

Between 1980 and 1989, the number of our institutions fell from nearly 4,000 to just over 2,600. To me, those closures added up to a lot of people put out of work.

During that period, quite a few savings banks merged to stay afloat, some through their own volition, others through government assisted transactions. I agonized mightily over Wichita Savings' state of affairs as it became harder and harder to raise capital. We had not made an acquisition of another savings bank since 1985, and it appeared consolidation was the only way to effectively serve our customers.

Being so active on the national scene, especially after my father's retirement, I was aware of many merger discussions taking place between institutions. Which associations were safe from the chopping block? Which were not? Which were solvent? Which needed help? After careful consideration and discussions with my board, I decided we had to merge Wichita Savings and Loan with the Topeka National Savings Association. Even though their president was an old friend, and we had deep respect for each other, the negotiations were arduous and lasted for months.

Finally, with the involvement and help of the federal regulators, we arrived at an agreement.

"This is the hardest day of my life," I said to my wife after I finally shook hands over the deal on a Friday afternoon and arrived home from Topeka. We were having our usual glass of wine before dinner, but this time the TV was off. It was obvious the minute I came through the door, exhausted and sullen, I would need to talk.

"You did everything you could, Monty," Sarah assured me. "You ran Wichita Savings with honesty and integrity, and your customers will be in a good place."

I nodded. "I only wish I could say the same for our employees. Come Monday morning, right after the board meeting, I have to deliver the sad news." I took a long, slow sip of the pinot noir and let it warm my throat. "And then, of course, there's the other thing."

"What?" she asked.

"Dad. He would never say it, even think it, but I can't help feeling I've let him down. He ran the company for so many years, successfully. And it's all going away under my watch."

Sarah bristled in a way I had only seen a few times in our life together. "Monty, you stop this right now. I will not allow you to take responsibility for what has happened in your company and in our country. The politicians jerked the real estate loan business around to suit their clever notions about what's important. They made it their own little political football. You've said yourself it wasn't you who took us off the gold standard. You didn't create double-digit interest rates. It wasn't Monty Johnson who got the economy bogged down and had to leave savings and loans to dig a hole so deep they couldn't get out."

I stared at my wife in disbelief as she continued the rant.

"You did not cause inflation, recession, stagflation, and all the other 'ations' the government's lawmakers foisted on you. And on all the others in the same boat. At least, you're making your own plan. Think about how many others let the government bail them out for millions of dollars and tell them how they had to close their doors." She inhaled deeply, obviously realizing she was totally worked up. Finally, she said, "Most importantly, you didn't take personal liberties with your customers' hard-earned money. I know your father is proud of how well you've weathered the storm."

What would I do without her? I put my wine down, wrapped my arms around her and said, "Sarah, honey, you're the best thing that ever happened to me."

"I didn't happen to you, silly," she returned my hug. "You picked me out of the crowd."

Our blonde, furry golden retriever Ella poked her nose into my leg, signaling it was time for her to go outside and do her business, the real stuff of life. I grinned at Sarah and shrugged.

"Go ahead, before she pees on the floor," she chuckled. "I'll get the salad started."

Monday was hard.

"Just tell them straight, no beating around the shrubs," Dad said on the phone Sunday evening. "Those people know how hard you worked to keep the ship from sinking."

So, it's exactly what I did. After a short but sweet board meeting in which I summarized for them the final numbers, we went into the bank. Employees were getting ready to open for the day.

"Folks, if you'd gather around for a minute," I announced, "there's something I need to talk to you about."

As they approached, I could see the question in their eyes. What's the old boy up to now? I don't remember feeling as much pressure on the basketball floor.

"You know our asset base has shrunk considerably, even with the supreme efforts you all have made to get and keep customers. We've seen the lines of people waiting some mornings to get in and withdraw their deposits, because we can't compete with the other investment opportunities anymore. The bottom line is, we have agreed to a merger with Topeka National Savings, and in three months our banking operations will transfer up there."

There was a low-level buzz from the whispers back and forth.

I plowed ahead. "Each of you will receive a package telling you your options. If you choose a separation, the terms will be in the material, and I think you'll agree they're fair. If you wish to transfer to Topeka, there's a form to fill out and, if we can find a place for you there, we'll work with you on it."

I paused for a moment, gathering myself. There was a lump in my throat the size of Russia. "You have all been wonderful to work with. Many of you for a lot of years. I love each and every one of you. That's it for now."

"Monty," said one of our long-time loan processors. "What will happen to you?"

"I'm going to Topeka to help with the transition. I

promised them a year, less if they don't need me that long. There's another opportunity up there, not in a savings and loan, I'm looking into." I waited, but there were no more questions. "And now," I continued, "it's time to get those doors open and help out our fine customers."

When I returned to the office and sank into my chair, I could feel the heavy weight of the world pressing down on me. "What will happen to you?" she asked. Just like that. I almost lost it. I was telling these people their jobs were toast, and they were worried about the boss.

I thought about folks like my dad who'd built a great industry, then about some of the scoundrels who had taken advantage of it—cheaters and frauds who were now inventing ways to tear it down. Like Charles Keating, who had been found guilty of ninety counts of fraud, racketeering and conspiracy.

I looked out into the bank at business being carried out as usual. It was a true privilege to work with these rock-solid, principled people. Yet this marked the end of a wonderful era, for me and my father. Unlike anything I had faced, the future was as blurry as an August dust storm blowing in from Western Kansas. I was sailing toward uncharted waters—a consulting engagement that could end in several months. Then what?

CHAPTER FORTY

Lawson Jeffries called me. I hadn't heard from him since Sarah and I moved from Wichita. He was going to Kansas City, he said, for some kind of college reunion, and wanted to stop through Topeka and say hello. I was delighted to be able to see my old friend.

"You'll have to stay with us," I insisted.

"Monty, I can't. I'm coming up Friday afternoon and thought we'd have dinner. I need to drive on up to K.C. and stay overnight there, because the schedule of activities starts early on Saturday."

"I had planned to go see Ron Slay coach his team Friday evening, but I can cancel."

"No, don't," he insisted. "If you don't mind, I'd like to go with you."

"Fine," I agreed. "I'll get us tickets and we can have a bite afterward, if there's time."

"What about Sarah?"

"She'll be fine. One of our boys, Dwight, is finishing up his residency at Kansas Medical, so she grabs every chance she can to drive up to Kansas City and baby-sit. I grouse about her making the drive, but she counters it's less than an hour each way, and if we lived in Chicago or Atlanta, that wouldn't even be across town. So, she wins the argument and gives Dwight and his wife a rare opportunity to get away and have some 'us time'."

"Monty, one thing," Lawson said. "If we have dinner, you have to let me buy."

I laughed. "The non-profit business must be picking up. I might let you pay. I'm retired now, and on fixed income."

We met at Topeka Arena promptly at six-thirty. It

was an old stone structure showing its age. Constant traffic exhaust had soiled the exterior, and it hadn't been sand-blasted in fifteen years. Inside, however, a recent renovation produced sparkling ramps and hallways leading to a brightly lit, shiny basketball floor, ringed by four thousand nicely padded seats.

Lawson looked stronger and healthier than ever. "You never age, you son of a gun," I poked him in the ribs as we entered the building.

"Hello, Monty. You look like the world of consulting agrees with you."

I patted my middle-age belly. "Far too much. I realize the only way I stayed in shape before was to worry the pounds away. I play a lot more golf now than the business allowed when I was gainfully employed, but that doesn't do the trick. Guess I should get a real job."

The ticket-taker handed me the stubs and said, "Enjoy the game, Mr. Johnson," as we walked through the gate.

"It didn't take you long to become somebody here," Lawson seemed awed the man would know me.

"Don't be too impressed," I advised him. "It's not like Wichita. Here, the only people who recognize me are the gatekeepers at ball games and waiters where we eat once a week. Other than that, call me Monty Anonymous."

Pre-game activities were already over, and the teams had retreated to the locker rooms. We sat and watched Ron bring his Topeka University Eagles back onto the court and gather for last-minute instructions.

"Talk about someone who never changes," Lawson remarked. Slay was still trim and fit and displayed the same boyish face we'd known for years. "I haven't followed them this year," Jeffries continued. "How are they doing?"

"Oh, you know Slay. His teams are never out of the running. This one's not his best, they're so young. But he has them in a spot to challenge for the conference title. Some coaches have a magic touch, and he's definitely one of them."

"I think it's true in any walk of life," Lawson turned serious on me. "I always thought that way about you in the bank business."

His comment made me flush; I could feel the heat on my cheeks. "Lawson, don't get whimsical on me," was all I could get out.

They put up a furious late-game battle, but the Fighting Eagles lost by three, their second conference loss. Afterward, we went down the steps and crossed the court, hoping to catch Ron after he addressed his team. "I left him a message this afternoon," I informed Lawson. "His trainer called back to say he wanted to join us if he could."

Eventually he came into the corridor, those big innocent-looking eyes of his shining at the sight of old friends.

"Sorry I couldn't get you boys a win," he lamented. "We weren't able to contain that big horse of theirs."

"They played their hearts out, though," Lawson offered. "Are you up for a bite to eat?"

Ron said, "I'm starving. There's a little Italian place two blocks up the street, to the north on the right-hand side. They have unbelievable *calzones*. Let's meet up there."

"Sounds like a plan," I responded.

By the time Lawson and I retrieved our cars from

the parking garage and found the place, Ron Slay was already seated in a booth. "I ordered us a pitcher of beer, if it's all right," he said as we joined him.

"It's fine with me," I said. "Lawson is buying."

We were still laughing when the waiter came. We ordered *calzones*, and then our conversation drifted from the game, to old basketball and football memories, to business and finally, in some kind of natural progression, to our mutual friend, Will Martin.

"I'm going to see him in Kansas City while I'm up there," Lawson revealed. "Reunion activities close out on Sunday afternoon, and he wants me to have dinner in the evening with him and Leslie. I'll head back to Wichita on Monday."

"I hear Will has his own business," I prompted.

Lawson replied, "He's running a high-end real estate loan business with some other guy. Says he's pulling in millions in funds from well-heeled investors."

Ron interjected, "I'm confused. After his trouble in Houston, wasn't he banned from working in the bank business?"

"This is different," I explained. "It's not a bank *per se*. It's a private investment company making construction and bridge loans to developers and builders. I know it seems very similar to what he was doing with Quivira Savings Bank, but this kind of business operates out of the watchful eyes of government regulators."

"I don't see the difference," Slay admitted.

Lawson said, "About the only distinction is these investors aren't protected by government insurance like our savings and loan customers were. It's riskier, but if Will does his job right, he can make them a pile of money."

"And himself," I added. "He managed to beat the rap when the FDIC put him on trial for his Quivira activities. Do you think they're through, or is there more trouble in his future?"

Lawson grinned. "Oh, we're talking about Will Martin. If there's a lot of money to be made, he'll chase it, and as a result someone will be watching, waiting for him to do something wrong." He leaned back, looking philosophical. "I've never been around someone who seemed so unsatisfied with 'just enough.' You know what I mean? He always has to reach for a better this, a more expensive that. Always wanting more. I think the worst thing he did in Houston was get entangled with those high-roller developers who thought a hundred million in net worth was an invitation to work toward a billion. All of them were scratching each other's backs, making huge amounts of money with one major deal after another, many of them making no sense at all when economic reality set in."

"It sounds a lot like pure, old-fashioned greed to me," Ron said.

"Call it what you want—greed, addiction to the good life, a drive to be somebody—I'm not sure," Jeffries responded. "However you label it, Will fell in love with the upscale lifestyle when he left his humble roots in Kansas. Once he had a taste, I don't think he could ever go back."

Lawson shook his head with dismay. "When their house of cards collapsed, Will tried his best to salvage Quivira. But the feds said there wasn't enough left of value. Give the man credit, though, he keeps getting back on the horse and riding it again. All of them do. Some of his biggest customers went bust, or at least so they testified. But believe me, they didn't get rich by being dummies. They had to have ways to squirrel away some of those millions they made."

He paused when the food arrived, then continued. "Will went bankrupt, are you aware of that? But if I had to bet, I'd lay odds he knows where some of his nest egg is buried. And I have no doubt he's putting another one together right now. Maybe I'll find out this weekend."

When Lawson stopped, we all sat in silence. It seemed like the wind went right out of the conversation. Lawson's whole dissection of what happened made me deeply sad.

It was Ron Slay who broke through the gloom, like any good coach would do. He topped off our glasses from the pitcher and then raised his. "Let's drink to Will's success. And to how lucky we are we don't have to hide our nest eggs."

CHAPTER FORTY-ONE

Kris was gone, sent off to Connecticut to start his sophomore year at the new school. In the four months from then until Thanksgiving, Leslie's drinking became more intense and higher volume, supplemented by a prescription drug.

"I'm going through a very difficult time," she said during her annual physical exam in October. Her physician completed the tests and was writing out an order for blood work.

The doctor asked, "What's the problem?"

"My son. He's gone away to school, and I am torn up about it. I miss him so much, and I worry night and day about him. I've learned because of his workload he won't be home for Thanksgiving and maybe not for Christmas."

The physician laid down her pen. "How are you dealing with it?"

Leslie stared at the floor. "I'm embarrassed. I've always drunk too much. My husband nags me about it. But with Kris away, I admit it's getting worse—I rely on alcohol to help me cope. Even with several evening cocktails, I have trouble sleeping, and then I struggle to get through the day. I'm miserable."

"Can't you fly out to visit your son?"

Leslie pouted. "My husband's work schedule won't allow the time off to travel. And I can't go alone, because we have two other children at home." Her eyes pleaded. "Is there anything I can do to ease this pain?"

The doctor frowned. "I can prescribe Citalopram. It's an antidepressant. It should help you. But you'd have to make me a promise."

"Anything," Leslie's eyes brightened at the offer of help.

"That you let this medication do the job and stop reliance on alcohol." She took off her glasses and fixed a serious stare at her patient. "And you'll follow my directions for this drug to the letter."

* * *

Despite her agreement to follow doctor's orders, Leslie fell into a pattern of taking the Citalopram and also drinking in excess. This alcohol-medication combination helped her sleep better, but during the day she often appeared disoriented or distracted.

"Do one or the other," Will pleaded with her one November morning when she seemed extremely drowsy and lethargic at breakfast. "It's bad enough you've been drinking more, but this prescription you're taking makes it ten times worse."

Will had completed his now-regular responsibility of getting the children off to school. He sat at the table finishing his coffee and bagel and watched as Leslie remained motionless, unresponsive to his conversation. His ambition and ordered personality motivated him to appear at the office every morning at eight on the dot, ready to work. This new wrinkle in his life—Leslie's lack of involvement—made it difficult. It was already seven-thirty, and instead of driving to work, he was dealing with a deteriorating situation at home.

"We both agreed, this is a good thing for Kris," he went on. "You have to get yourself together, Leslie."

She made an effort to rally, rubbing her forehead and sitting up straighter. "I'm trying, Will," she mumbled. "But honey, I didn't realize I'd miss him so much. And now not coming home for Thanksgiving." Her eyes teared up.

"We knew this would be a demanding year." Will's voice sounded flat, devoid of empathy. "Kris might be able to come home for Christmas, or if not, at least in the summer. Until then, you can't go on like this. For your kids' sakes, if not for your own."

* * *

A trip to *Sint Maarten* was Will's idea, conceived to take advantage of their children's Thanksgiving vacation and possibly act as tonic for Leslie's growing sadness. But Kris' looming absence from the family event seemed to continue weighing on Leslie. She begged him to call off the trip, but Will insisted on sticking to the plan.

"We owe it to Haley and Chip to get away for a few days," he persisted. "They'll have some beach time, and the resort has resident nannies who can watch them if we want to shop or have our own private dinner. I promise, this will be good for us."

Leslie perked up during the first two days of the trip. They took the children to the beach and on driving tours. They explored the little restaurants scattered around the Dutch side of the island where they were staying. Leslie had several drinks each evening but laid off the Citalopram and seemed to sleep okay.

On their third day there, Will sprang a surprise.

"One of the ladies is coming to take the kids to the beach," he said to Leslie as they dressed. "I thought we'd go into Phillipsburg and look around."

"You're sure they'll be all right?" Leslie asked.

"The manager introduced me to the lady yesterday when I went down to make our dinner reservations. Leslie, she's great. Speaks very good English. Has kids of her own. She'll take them swimming and get their lunch.

We can be back in time for dinner. Everything'll be fine."

Phillipsburg was the shopping Mecca of the island, and the duty-free jewelry stores were plentiful. As they strolled down Front Street past the shops and art studios, Leslie paused at the storefront of each jewelry establishment to gaze at the glamorous merchandise.

Finally, when they stopped momentarily at Worldwide Diamonds, Will suggested, "Let's go inside."

"No, I'll fall in love with something in there," Leslie protested. "We can just window-shop."

"Come on," he insisted and held the door for her.

The saleswoman greeted them graciously. "Is there anything special I can show you?"

Will glanced at Leslie. "Let's look at the diamond bracelets. You've always wanted one to complement the Yurmans you wear."

"Pick out some you really like," the woman said to Leslie, "and we'll take them back to our private viewing room. There's a cruise ship scheduled to dock any minute, and it could get a little noisy and distracting in here with the tourists."

The private room was small but nicely furnished with several Queen Anne wing-back chairs, all featuring the curving shapes and cushioned seats representative of that style. A walnut table and two side chairs near the back wall provided a place for the salesperson to lay out several pieces at a time and discuss them with customers. Along one side, a full bar was stocked with refreshments.

"Can I get you a drink?" the lady asked.

Leslie glanced at Will.

"Sure, we're on vacation, aren't we?" he said. "Mimosas if you have them."

After two of the champagne drinks each and a

half-dozen bracelets, Will said, "I like this one," indicating an elegantly designed six-carat diamond and sapphire number. "How much?"

"Normally it's ten thousand five hundred," the saleswoman answered, clasping it around Leslie's wrist. "But I can let you have it today for eight-five hundred, duty free."

"American dollars, right?" Will probed.

"Correct."

"It's too much, Will," Leslie protested. "I can find something less expensive."

Will stopped her from slipping the bracelet off her wrist. "It's perfect. Christmas is coming up. Consider this an early present." He said to the salesperson, handing her his credit card, "You'd take this if your husband gave it to you, right?"

The saleswoman looked at Leslie. "You're a lucky woman. Congratulations. You'll love wearing this keepsake."

* * *

Just as the Dutch side of *Sint Maarten* is the island's commercial center, so the differently spelled French side, Saint Martin, is better known for fun life and fine restaurants.

As they crossed the border onto the *Rue de Hollande* and headed north, Leslie constantly ogled her new bracelet. "I really love it, Will," she gushed, displaying more life and energy than she had in months.

Will grinned at the prospect of getting his wife back again. "Honey, every move I have made since leaving Wichita was for moments like this. Traveling to exotic islands. Staying at grand places. Affording nice things. Seeing the smile on your face when we bought that bracelet made me a happy man. Having plenty of money means never having to say you're sorry." He roared at his own joke, and she joined him in the hilarity.

The main road toward *Grand Case* at the island's northmost reach featured a number of attractive cafés. Will picked one at random for a late lunch and pulled the little convertible into the parking lot.

They sat on the patio with the breeze from the *Baie de Grand Case* bathing their faces, shielded from the hovering sun by a large umbrella. Several more mimosas and an omelet later, Leslie pulled her chair closer to Will's and kissed him passionately.

As her breathing grew more fervent, she whispered, "Let's go find a place."

"What? Like a hotel?" he asked.

She let out an alcohol-fueled giggle. "No, baby. I saw some isolated little side roads on the way up here, over-looking the beaches. We can go park somewhere private and do it in the convertible."

"You navigate," Will instructed as they pulled from the parking lot.

Only minutes after they headed back south, Leslie pointed, "Right there. Turn in," she said with urgency. Then, "See? Take this little road." She pointed to a rutted, dirt side path appearing to lead down to a secluded beach.

They were high, looking down on the bay. No other cars were in sight.

Again, Leslie said, "Turn there."

Will followed her directions, and they steered into a little area shielded from the road by tall, dense shrubbery. "This looks perfect," Leslie enthused. She leaned across and kissed Will again as she unzipped his shorts and slipped her hand inside, all inhibitions drowned out by the liquor.

Will looked over his shoulder sheepishly. "We can't do it right here. Somebody will come along. It's a public road."

"No one can see us in this little spot," she said between kisses. She was still caressing him.

He was aroused.

"And besides, I saw the sign," Leslie said. "That's a nude beach down there, so who in the hell will care?"

Leslie slipped her shorts off, climbed over the console and mounted Will face-to-face as he pushed the driver's seat back. It had been months, and the mimosas were working their magic.

Afterward, he said breathlessly, incredulously, "Leslie, where in God's name are your panties? Didn't you wear any?"

She laughed. "We're in France, honey."

* * *

They arrived back at the resort barely before dinnertime. The nanny was waiting for them in the back where they parked. She rushed out to them with a frantic expression and urgent waving gesture.

"What's wrong?" Will asked, turning the engine off.

"Mr. Martin, there are two men, two police officers, inside. You have to talk to them. I will take the children swimming. They are already waiting at the pool with their suits on. I'll see they get something to eat."

"Wait a minute," Will insisted. "Please, stop. Tell me what's going on?"

"I don't know, Mr. Martin, but it sounded important. Go and talk to the men," she urged dramatically and disappeared around the side of the building.

Will looked at Leslie. Curiosity and confusion registered on both of their faces. Their world the past few years had been a constant series of subpoenas, accusations, lawyers and courtrooms. "What now?" Will said, annoyed at the intrusion on a family vacation.

The two uniformed local officers were waiting inside the front door.

"Mr. and Mrs. William R. Martin, of Kansas City, Missouri?" one of them asked, his facial expression and voice utterly deadpan.

"Yes." Will answered.

"Do you have a son named Kris at school in Connecticut?"

PART V: The Third Gate

1998-2009

CHAPTER FORTY-TWO

In many respects, 1998 was a down year in finance and politics. Iraq became a looming problem. The U.S. House impeached President Clinton. Prosecutors charged Eric Rudolph with six bombings, including the 1996 Olympic Games. A General Motors strike dragged through the last half of the year. A federal judge ruled dozens of brokerage houses cheated investors and approved a $1.03 billion settlement.

In contrast to all of this chaos, and more, Kaycee Holdings, the venture put together by Will and the developer, Harman Tucker, was having a good year. The office staff grew to a dozen people. Loan processors, accountants, lawyers and clerical employees kept the business humming. Will and his team were securing lucrative real estate loans and making money for their clients.

A week before Christmas, one of Kaycee's earliest investors and the Martins' membership sponsor at Ward Parkway Country Club, Larry Callaway, stopped by the firm's office. It was a frigid morning. A four-inch snow had rolled into Kansas City from the Rockies three days earlier, and although sand and salt were making the streets passable, getting around was still precarious.

Callaway trod cautiously as he emerged from his car and walked into the building. He wore a heavy coat and stocking cap. Inside, he wiped his feet and greeted the receptionist.

"Which one is Will Martin's office?" he asked.

"Mr. Martin's out of town, sir. Is there something I can help you with?"

"My name is Larry Callaway. I wanted to talk to him about an investment," he answered. "Is Mr. Tucker around?"

She rose and walked around the counter. "If you'll have a seat, I'll see if he's available." She went down the hall, but Callaway remained standing, waiting. When she returned, Harman Tucker followed behind her.

"Mr. Callaway? I'm Harman Tucker. We haven't met, but I know who you are. I'm Will's partner. Why not come on back?"

Harman gestured toward a chair in his office. It was small and efficiently furnished with industrial looking furniture. "What's on your mind?" he asked, sitting down at his desk.

"Oh, I came into a little windfall and need a place to park it," Larry said. "I thought Will might have something going on I could be interested in."

Harman smiled. "Hell yes, Larry. Let me tell you about a new project we're working on. You can get in on the ground floor. How much are you thinking of investing?"

The two men sat and discussed Kaycee's pending transaction with an apartment complex builder. Tucker ran through the details, and they reached a tentative agreement on Callaway's involvement. Then the talk turned casual and personal.

"The woman out front said Will's on a trip."

Harman nodded yes. "He took his kids for a little jaunt to the Caribbean. They wanted to get out of this miserable Kansas City weather for the holidays."

"Speaking of Christmas," Larry said, "I got Will's card a couple of days ago. I thought it a little odd."

"How so?" Tucker asked.

Larry reached into his coat pocket and retrieved the envelope. "I brought it along because I wanted to ask him about it. My wife Theresa and I became friends with him and Leslie. We live fairly close, and they joined our country club, but we haven't seen them in quite some time. Anyway, their card each year has been a picture of the two of them, but this year it only had Will's photo. Is something going on I don't know about?"

Harman Tucker sat looking flummoxed, not speaking for several moments. He stammered a bit as he said, "My God, you don't know? Leslie's dead."

The investor sat staring at Tucker, his eyes wide and his jaw hanging open. It seemed difficult for him to speak. "Dead?" he finally managed. "Dead how? When?"

"Well, my gosh…It's been some months ago," Harman told him. The developer appeared ill at ease with this awkward topic. "I don't know a lot of the details. Will didn't talk much about it. I know he had to go down to the police headquarters a couple of times to give statements." He looked down at his hands, rubbed them together. "You might want to ask him about it when he gets back."

"This is incredible," Callaway said. "We hadn't seen them in a long time. We heard from neighbors they just lost one of their sons."

"Right, right," Harman said, squirming. "Their oldest boy Kris was killed in a car accident last year. Will's family has had a real run of bad luck, for sure."

Back home, Larry gave the news to Theresa. Her hands flew up to the sides of her face. "Oh, that's awful," she said. "What in the world happened to her?"

Larry shrugged. "His partner didn't seem to know much, or at least he wasn't telling me any of the details."

Theresa said, "Let's see if Bob and Kathy Raffensburg will have dinner at the club tonight. They live right across the street from Will, and Kathy was friends with Leslie. If anyone will know what happened to her, they should."

* * *

It was trivia night at Ward Parkway Country Club, the twice-a-month runaway favorite of the membership. A buffet supper was served, after which a professional trivia emcee came in and ran the contest. Members usually teamed up with the same friends for each of these raucous nights. Alcohol flowed plentifully, and the noisy players cajoled, argued and laughed about who was right and who was wrong.

Larry and Theresa never participated, feeling the event spoiled the country club atmosphere and made conversation impossible. On this night, however, learning the Raffensburgs were up for meeting them, the four met and staked out a table in the bar some distance away from the frenetic action in the main dining room.

After cocktails and small talk and ordering food, Theresa broached the subject of Leslie's death.

"Oh, yeah," Bob Raffensburg confirmed, "one of their kids apparently found her in the bedroom. This was four or five months ago. You didn't know about it?"

"We haven't seen them in a long time, obviously," Larry Callaway acknowledged. "I have a business relationship with Will, but we haven't talked in ages. What in hell happened to her, anyway?"

Kathy waited as the waitress brought their food, then said, "It was awful. I'd gotten to know her pretty well, but things started to change a lot when their boy was in school back east and died in an accident. I stopped over to say 'hi' a few times, but she seemed distant, almost like she was medicated or something. Several of the other girls in the neighborhood said the same thing. Then one night there were police cars all over the place, an ambulance, all kinds of activity going on over there."

"So, what exactly is the story?" Larry persisted impatiently.

Kathy's voice took on a hard edge. "If you want to know what I think, I say what happened is that man, Will Martin, murdered his wife." She glanced at her husband Bob, who glared at her.

The Callaways both gasped. "No! What makes you say so?" Larry exclaimed.

"She was found with her head wedged between the bed frame and the nightstand," Kathy continued. "How does such a thing happen if you don't get some help? There are all kinds of rumors going around the neighborhood, like, he suffocated her with a pillow."

"My God. That can't be true," Larry said. He motioned for the waitress to bring another round of drinks. "Will's a stand-up guy."

"I don't like the idea of people going around making such accusations," said Bob Raffensburg, casting a quick glance at his wife, "including you, honey. But I understand where people are coming from, when you think about Will Martin's past…" He hesitated.

"What about his past?" Larry insisted.

"He was caught scarlet-handed in fraudulent business deals in Houston, with the savings and loan he ran. They kicked him out of the banking profession for life. It's possible to believe someone with so checkered a past and such blatant disregard for the law, could commit a crime like that."

"Bob, that's unadulterated horse manure!" Callaway exploded.

"Larry!" Theresa admonished, gasping at his brazen outburst.

He shrugged his shoulders in apology. "Sorry, Bob. Sorry, Kathy. But I know something about what happened at Quivira Savings. I did my homework before Theresa and I did business with him. We talked to him extensively about it, and he was very forthcoming. He got dealt a rotten hand down there and took the fall for some other people. Some unscrupulous developers who were gaming the appraisal system. And their buddy, the son of a famous senator. I don't put any of that on Will Martin."

Everyone paused, as if waiting for the heat to die down. "From what I heard," said Bob, "none of the gossip turned out to be true, according to the sheriff's office. They ruled out foul play. Said she died of asphyxiation because of how she got her head caught."

"But how in the world does anyone get their head between the bed and night table?" Theresa questioned.

Kathy said, "One thing we heard about the examiner's report was her alcohol level was off the charts. Several neighbors who talked to him while he was investigated said he stayed unemotional through the entire ordeal. As cool as a clam. All I can think of is those poor kids of theirs, Haley and Chip. They've been through a lot."

"As has Will," Larry Callaway added. "I wonder, what more can go wrong for the man?"

CHAPTER FORTY-THREE

No one could accuse Valeta Vansyckle of not being classy. She dressed in top-brand business suits, accented by silk scarves and expensive jewelry, for every
non-profit charity meeting she attended. It was on such
an occasion she steered her Mercedes into the Kaycee
Holdings parking lot on the way home from the symphony board's monthly gathering.

She entered the office with a flourish, as if expecting
the world to stand at attention in her presence. With no
one at the reception area and the other workers buried in
their work, Valeta appeared to grow angry. She tapped
her fingers noisily on the counter-top until finally a man
abandoned his desk and walked forward to greet her.

"Yes, ma'am?" he said. He was middle-aged, completely bald, with pale, blotchy skin.

"Good morning," Valeta said. "I would like to talk
to someone about my account. I've moved and want you
to make a record of my new address."

"The receptionist is at lunch, but I can help you with
that," he said, sitting down behind a computer. "I'm one
of the accountants." He slid a memo pad and pen across
the counter. "If you'll write down your name and previous address, I'll access your file and make the change."

Valeta handed him the information and waited while
he entered keystrokes on the computer. He frowned as
he stared at the screen, continuing to type. Finally, he
looked up and asked, "Is it possible your account is listed
differently than the name you wrote down here?"

"No, that's my name."

"Excuse me one moment," the accountant said and
walked to his own desk in the back of the office. He per-

formed some functions on his computer and looked up at the Valeta, shaking his head. She tapped her fingers impatiently on the counter.

"Mrs. Vansyckle," the man approached her, carrying the memo pad note she had written on. "Are you sure you have an active account with us?"

"Of course, I'm sure," she responded indignantly. "Why else would I be here, trying to perform the simple function of changing my address? What's wrong with you?"

"Well, ma'am," he said, "I found an old account of yours that's been closed out. It shows you made two investments in the past. One in 1991 of..." he caught himself and looked around nervously. "Here, I'll write it down."

"Yes, correct," she confirmed in a tone punctuated with exasperation.

"And another in ninety-two of..." and again he wrote it down. "Is this right?"

"It's correct," she chirped.

"But ma'am, that's all the records show. Both of those investments were paid in full and closed. The account is currently inactive."

"What?" she burst out. "Sir, I put in a much larger amount more recently in the form of a cashier's check. I haven't received the statement, which is why I'm here— to get my new address recorded in your files."

He pursed his lips, as if at a loss. "I'm sorry, Mrs. Vansyckle, your proceeds from the original investments were paid out in full. The account is inactive." He slid the paper and pen toward her. "How much do you think you gave us a cashier's check for?"

She shoved the pad back, bristling. The woman who

normally personified grace and style exploded. "How much do I think? I don't think, I know!" she screeched. "One million dollars."

Valeta looked around to be sure everyone in the office heard. By now the space was deathly still. All eyes were turned toward the accountant and the source of his discomfort.

"You have one million dollars of my money, sir."

"But…but we don't have any record…"

"Look again." She demanded.

She waited, tapping her foot as the shaking bookkeeper keyed frantically on the computer. He shook his head and walked to the back again, opening a metal file cabinet. His hands trembled as he thumbed through paper files, then turned and gave a shrugging motion.

Returning to the front desk, the accountant said, "Mrs. Vansyckle, do you have some paperwork I can look at?" he asked.

"I've been waiting for the confirmation," Valeta spat out. "That's why I came in, to tell you I haven't received a statement because of my change of address. Get Will Martin out here. Now."

"Mr. Martin isn't in the office today," a young woman called out meekly from her desk. "One of his kids is sick."

"Then get Harman Tucker," Vansyckle demanded even louder.

"Ma'am, he's out of the office, too," the accountant bewailed. "He had some business over in Kansas."

Valeta nearly shouted, "Then call Will Martin at home. You have one million dollars of my money, and no damned record of it? Call him. Right now." The curse word coming from Valeta Vansyckle's mouth seemed oddly out of place. It was clear she meant business.

The accountant dialed the reception desk phone hastily, listened, placed his hand over the mouthpiece and said shakily, "It's his answering machine." Then, "Mr. Martin, it's Myron. Please call me back as soon as you get this. There's a problem here at the office."

By now, everyone in the room sat on high alert, watching the disturbing proceedings. Valeta stood at the counter and roared at all of them, "The next person you people talk to will be my lawyer. Before he gets here, you'd better find my account and my million dollars, or there'll be hell to pay."

She stomped out, slamming the door behind her. A profound and deadly silence pervaded the office.

* * *

Four days after Valeta Vansyckle's dust-up in the Kaycee Holdings office, an FBI agent paid a visit to the firm's chairman, Harman Tucker. The president, Will Martin, was still absent, playing nursemaid to his daughter who was homebound with a severe case of the flu.

"Mr. Tucker, I'm assistant special agent Shirley Dresden of the Bureau's Kansas City field office. I spoke to you on the phone."

The thirtyish, attractive woman had her hair pulled back tightly into a bun, making her face appear even more slender. She had on a white uncollared top, dark suit and black low-heeled pumps.

"As I told you," the federal agent said, "We're conducting an investigation of possible irregularities in Kaycee Holding's financial transactions. We have started interviews with a number of your clients and plan to go through their monthly Kaycee and bank account statements. Today I have a warrant for Kaycee's records."

"Shirley, you can look at any damned thing you need," Harman said. "I'm as surprised as the next guy this has come up. I'd like to know what in blazes is happening."

"I have a list here of where we want to start," she told him. "But Mr. Tucker, I have one question regarding your president and CEO, Mr. Martin, who I'm told is out of the office for the week."

"Okay, shoot."

"Before the two of you created your partnership, it's our understanding Mr. Martin already had the business up and running, is that correct?"

"It is. Will founded Martin Capital about a year before I offered to bankroll a bigger operation. So, we formed Kaycee Holdings, of which I'm chairman."

She asked, "Did you get access to all of the account and bank records he had before you formed the new company?"

"His customer records became the Kaycee Holdings customer accounts, if that's what you mean. As for the bank accounts of Martin Capital, we agreed he would close those."

Agent Dresden asked, "Did you get something in writing to that effect?"

"No," Tucker responded. "It was a handshake kind of deal."

"And are you certain he closed those accounts?'

Harman sat back and took a deep breath, squinting his eyes. "If you're asking, do I have proof he closed them, no I do not. I took the man at his word."

CHAPTER FORTY-FOUR

Federal prosecutor Santiago Jackson entered a small conference room in the downtown Kansas City FBI field office where agent Shirley Dresden was waiting. She sat at the far end of a metal-and-wood-veneer table which was surrounded by six matching chairs. Two windows overlooked the parking lot four stories below. Hanging on the opposite wall was a large photograph of FBI Director MacDonald Duvenal.

Santiago looked younger than his forty-six years. His hair was close-cropped, and a thin moustache grew just above his dark upper lip. The gray suit he wore strained against the broad shoulders and deep chest of a man who could have played running back for the Chiefs and still worked out.

Dresden looked up from a pile of paperwork and rose to greet him with a hug. "How are you?" she asked.

"I'm good, Shirley. It's been a while. Still raising little rug rats?" His broad smile flashed ultra-white teeth.

"They got up off the floor," she snickered. "They're teenagers now."

"Oh, so they hate their mom, right? That's a teen's job."

The agent turned serious. "It hasn't happened, at least not yet. The three of us are best friends."

"Great," Santiago said and sat down next to her. "Where are we on this Kaycee Holdings case?"

She responded, "After weeks of investigation, we have the evidence needed to take it to a grand jury." She pulled a document from the pile. "This is the list of potential witnesses we interviewed."

Jackson took the paper and scanned through it.

"As you can see," Dresden went on, "some of the firm's accountants and lawyers talked to us, all claiming no knowledge of the scheme. Some of them expressed surprise at how long it has been going on. There was a certain degree of embarrassment at not having caught it over such a long time."

"Would it be a problem if they're called to testify—the lack of oversight, I mean?" asked Jackson.

"I don't think so," Shirley replied. "The tracks were well covered, making it difficult to pick up on. It would be hard to accuse them of laxness. And besides, it might not ever get to them. Adrienne Yarbrough hinted there could be a plea bargain in the offing."

"Yarbrough. She's handling the defense?"

The agent nodded yes. She continued, "And, of course, we spoke to a number of the firm's investors who were victimized financially." She produced another file and handed it to the attorney, pointing at the top page. "This list shows the amount each individual invested and how much their accounts were shorted over time. The most egregious case is Valeta Vansyckle, the woman who first blew the whistle. She put a cool one million dollars in the pot, and it never found its way into a Kaycee Holdings bank account."

Santiago whistled softly. "One million big ones. Now there's a major helping of trust. After seeing so many cases like this, are you ever awestruck at how much of a sucker a rich person can be?"

"Not really," responded Dresden. "The people who jump right into these things, get-rich-quick ideas, ponzi schemes and such, are usually as greedy as their perpetrators. And the perps are super salesmen. That's how they get by with it for so long."

"I know, I get it," Jackson said. "I've seen it all over the years. And yet it never ceases to amaze me they aren't a little bit more careful with their mega-millions. I would be." He ran down the list one more time and asked, "So this guy we're going to charge, Will Martin, was simply skimming off the top?"

Agent Dresden said, "It was pretty straight-forward. I did a little digging into his previous career as the CEO of one of the biggest failed savings and loans a decade ago. He ran Quivira Savings Bank down in Houston."

"I remember Quivira," said the prosecutor. "Their top dogs all got kicked out."

Shirley said, "They had a neat little scheme where a developer would come to them for a loan, they'd get it appraised for more than the loan request. Then they would tell the developer, 'You're asking for, say, a million bucks. We've got an appraisal saying we can lend you one million one hundred thousand. You take the million for your loan and pay us a hundred thou in exchange for some of our stock.' That's how they built up their assets, by lending more than the ask."

She continued, "They called it *quid pro quo*. It wasn't technically illegal unless it could be proven the appraiser was being paid off, which was pretty hard to do. The important thing for the company officers was they could bank the money and then vote themselves big bonuses and other perks for increasing the assets."

Santiago broke in, "That's why they got the ban from the banking industry?"

She nodded agreement. "And for other similar kinds of slick deals. So, Martin moves to Kansas City and is once again making real estate loans. Except this time, if an investor wants in on the loan pool, he says, 'I need one million, one hundred thousand to make the loan.' But he's lying—he's only lending the builder one million. It's like before, at Quivira, except now instead of giving the investor stock, he quietly stuffs the extra one hundred thou into his own bank account."

"Eventually building his illegal take to nearly nine million," the prosecutor said. "What about the Tucker guy, the partner? He has access to those same accounts, doesn't he?"

"It's one of the clever things about Martin's operation. These are bank accounts he had before his partner came into the scene. He promised Tucker he would close them when they formed the merger, but he never did. That's where he hid the loot. His own private stash."

The lawyer said, "According to your report, he carried this scheme out over a number of years."

"You're right," Dresden replied. "There were times when he had to use some of the skimmed funds to cover up previous transgressions. It's amazing how he was able to keep track of it all. You know what they say—you should never lie, because you have to keep making up new stories to cover up the old ones. After a while, it's hard to keep track of who you've told what. This man must have some kind of IQ to be able to pull it off for so long."

"Where in hell was all of the money going?" asked the prosecutor.

Dresden answered, "This man likes living the high life. He and his wife, until she died last year, joined a very expensive country club and lived in a pricey castle over in Mission Estates. They also had a kid going to an exclusive, astronomically priced school back east until he was killed in a car crash. And their other two kids enrolled in a twenty-thousand-a-year private school. He had no shortage of places to spend his ill-gotten gains."

Santiago Jackson shuffled through the files again, absorbing the information. He looked up at Shirley. "Your boss is on board with this?"

"One hundred percent," she answered.

Santiago heaved a heavy sigh. "I'll go ahead and send him the formal letter informing him he's the target of a grand jury investigation, to be charged with federal and state crimes. We'll see how he and Ms. Yarbrough respond."

* * *

One month later, in March 1999, Will and Adrienne Yarbrough slogged through two inches of snow and slush into the FBI building. The wind howled behind them as they pushed through the revolving door and signed in at the security desk. Arriving in the fourth-floor conference room where Prosecutor Jackson and Agent Dresden met earlier, Will shook their hands, helped his lawyer off with her coat, and removed his own. He folded it carefully on the back of a chair at the end of the table.

"Please, have a seat," Santiago Jackson indicated chairs across from himself and Shirley Dresden. Yarbrough extracted a yellow legal pad and pen from her briefcase and laid them on the table.

After several minutes of relaxed, chatty, informal conversation, the prosecutor said, "Mr. Martin, Ms. Yarbrough indicated last week you are open to a guilty plea. Is that correct?"

"It is," Will answered. "Assuming we can agree on a deal."

"I'm curious, now that you've agreed to confess your guilt," Shirley Dresden, the FBI agent said. "What made you think you'd get away with it? I mean, with all of those investors lined up, something had to seem fishy to at least one or two of them. And your partner, Harman Tucker, was bound to catch up with it one day."

Will's smile appeared to be one almost of pride. His voice was calm and deliberate. "I was making everyone money—the investors, Harman, everyone working in the office. If my clients were getting a nice return on their investment, why would they think anything was wrong? The truth is, I didn't believe anyone would ever notice. And they didn't until I mishandled one of their checks."

"Okay, so down to business," said Santiago Jackson. "Ms. Yarbrough, you said on the phone you want to discuss a plea deal. What about restitution? We've identified $8.7 million converted to his own use from the excessive funds."

Will answered, "I don't have anything close to so much money, Mr. Jackson."

"Well, I have to tell you, you're not going to get away with only a fine. If you can't make restitution, it becomes a much harder bargain. There has to be some prison time."

Adrienne Yarbrough interjected, "Mr. Martin has mentioned another possibility. As he says, the funds aren't there to make all of those people whole at the same time. What if you were to permit him to stay on at Kaycee and help these people make back the money he took?"

Astonished, Jackson jerked his head back as if he had been shot. "Are you serious?"

"Look at it this way," Will said. "I'm highly skilled at making people profits. I've been doing it my entire career. I know I did wrong, and I'm sorry. But I can help them recover their losses under supervision, I swear."

The prosecutor laughed in disbelief. "There's no way in hell I would let you do something so crazy. No way."

Will's lawyer glanced at her client briefly, then pulled the yellow pad closer and picked up the pen. "All right then, let's talk about dropping the state charges and reducing the federal to two counts of wire fraud. Assume for a moment you'd be willing to accept such a plea, then what would we be talking about?"

When the meeting was over and Will and his defender gone, Dresden started packing up her briefcase. She stopped and cast an incredulous look at Santiago. "Can you believe it? The investigators told me Martin is always trying to make some grand gesture to save his butt. They said he did the same thing when the government was getting ready to kick him out of banking—wanted them to let him stay on at his savings and loan and salvage it for everyone. He was apparently incensed when they said 'no'."

She rose and led the prosecutor out of the room. "This one takes first prize."

CHAPTER FORTY-FIVE

I didn't have much time for golf when I was laboring in the savings and loan vineyard. I couldn't risk any of my customers saying, "There's Monty Johnson over there on the first tee. Who is looking after my savings?" I played, on average, twice a year, when we were off at one of the association conferences in some nice resort and there was leisure time built into the agenda on one of the days.

So, my game was never very good. During my career, I didn't even keep a handicap because I completed so few rounds.

After we moved to Topeka, I found myself with more time on my hands. My one-year consulting agreement with Topeka National Savings required whatever days and hours were needed. At first, I spent several days a week meeting with management, discussing issues and sorting through personnel matters from our merger. But after several months, they called me in less frequently. I attended board meetings and sometimes offered observations about the operation. But they had a tightly run ship, and my contributions were minimal after we got the two systems working well together.

"I still have months left on my contract," I told Sarah one Saturday morning as we ate breakfast. We were on the patio, watching our golden retriever Ella look for chipmunks in the yard as we had coffee and eggs. "But honey, unless and until I move on to something more demanding, I think I'll start playing more golf."

"You've always enjoyed the game," she observed. "But that was when you played so little, you didn't take it seriously. Promise me you won't become one of those husbands who gets obsessed and cranky if you don't shoot—what's it called—par?"

I laughed. "Yes, honey, it's called par. And don't worry. I have no illusions about being Arnold Palmer. It would be fun to get out there once or twice a week and see how I like it as a steady diet."

"Where would you play?" she asked. "And with whom?"

I felt my eyes light up. "Aha," I said. "I thought you'd never ask. We could join the Topeka Town Club if you wanted to, of course. I checked into it, and right now there's no waiting list for new members. But it's very expensive."

"How expensive?"

"Very. But honey, you've seen the club over on Eighty-Eighth Street Court, right? Strawberry Creek Club. We drive by it on the way to the mall. I stopped in there the other day and talked to their general manager. They would love to have us as members, and he said the club pro could evaluate my game and pair me up with some other comparable players."

"It sounds ideal," Sarah said, finishing off her orange juice. "What does it cost?"

"It's half what we would pay at the Town Club. And, they have a nice, cozy dining room where we could have dinner once in a while."

"Oh, Monty," Sarah said, "you know how much I love to cook. I don't want to eat out all the time like so many people we know."

I laid my hand on her arm. "Sarah, honey, you are the greatest cook in the world. I love your dinners. But it wouldn't hurt us to go out on a Saturday and give you a well-earned night off."

It was settled. We joined. The head pro took me out for eighteen holes one afternoon, and after watching me duff around to a ninety-six, said he would find me some members to play with. Within weeks, I was invited to play with three retired corporate executives whose fourth moved to Florida. They played every Tuesday and Friday. I found them to be congenial and, like me, high handicappers. Each round we put five dollars apiece in the pot, and it amazed me how people who made lucrative salaries in their heyday could carry on such heated arguments over fifteen dollars.

* * *

I can't describe my delight when my oldest son, Dwight, called to say he was coming to Topeka to celebrate my sixtieth birthday. "I have a rare day off, Pop, and I thought we could get a round of golf in," he said.

Dwight was a doctor. At least, he'd finished medical school and his residency and now had a fellowship at University of Kansas Medical School—a total of nine years toward becoming an oncologist. He lived in Kansas City with his wife and four children. Between family demands and work, about the only time we saw him was when we drove up and wedged our way into their lives for a day.

"Is your brother coming?" I asked eagerly. "You know he loves the game." Truman was a financial consultant and we rarely got to see him, as well.

"He wanted to, Pop. But his firm has some major clients coming in that day. You know how hard it is for us to coordinate any time off."

"What about Kathy?" I persisted. "She should come and bring the kids. Sarah can entertain them while you and I play."

"Too many obligations," he answered. "Soccer practice, ballet rehearsal, piano lessons, you name it. So, I guess you would be stuck with me. What do you say?"

"I think it would be great fun," I said, overjoyed. "I can introduce you to our new club, and if there's time after our game, Sarah can come out and join us for a bite. Will you be able to stay overnight?"

"No, Pop. I have obligations the next morning. It'll be Monty and Dwight Johnson for the afternoon."

"Son, I'm excited you're coming. We'll be a two-some, and I'll take your money."

He hoo-hawed at that. "We'll see."

* * *

My birthday fell on a Friday in April, and we had an early afternoon tee time. Sarah planned to join us at the club at six, and we would have dinner before Dwight had to go back. He met me at the club parking lot and surprised me with a new set of clubs, a big red bow tied around the bag.

"I'm overwhelmed," I said, transferring them from his car trunk to mine. "I'll play one more round with my old, worn-out cast-offs and break these babies in on the range next week. Are you sure they're good for four strokes less a round?" I gave him a hug. "Thank you, son."

"They're from Truman and me both," Dwight said. "He knows more about golf, so he picked them out."

I signed us up in the pro shop while Dwight perused the racks of golf clothes. I turned to watch him for a moment, and it struck me how much he was maturing. The slender frame I remembered from his teen years had filled out solidly, and his hair was beginning to show some gray. He looked more like my father than

I ever had.

Let the cajoling begin. Dwight had always been as competitive as I, and even better with the jibes and side bets. It was one of the best times I'd had in years. After our game, we went to the men's grill for a post-round beer. "I appreciate your coming down here to let me take your money," I started the inevitable joshing. "Son, if you could keep those three-hundred-yard drives on the fairway instead of the woods, maybe you would be a little more successful, financially speaking."

Dwight shot back, "Well, Pop, if you hadn't demanded five strokes a side, it wouldn't have been a contest."

The back-and-forth went on for five or ten minutes, until I turned serious and addressed a subject I had thought about ever since Dwight's call.

"Being a med school grad," I said, "I assume you studied some psychiatry."

"A little," Dwight confirmed.

"I'd like to ask you about something. There's a man who used to work for me, quite a few years ago. He was a super employee with a great future. But he moved on, and since then his life has been on a downhill slide. He has been in and out of trouble in his profession, and a week ago I learned he's pled guilty to cheating his customers out of millions of dollars. He's going to be sentenced, and the speculation is he'll get anywhere from five to ten years in prison."

"Pop, for God's sake," Dwight exclaimed. "Who is it?"

"It doesn't matter," I answered. "He was long-gone when you were pretty young. But he grew up in Wichita and had a bright future. Now, not so much. So, here's my question How can that happen? What makes someone brought up in a good household, in small town Kansas, go out into the world and become an entirely different person who cheats, steals and becomes consumed by material things?"

Dwight took a long swallow of his beer, thinking. "There's a tough question. You might be surprised at how little attention is paid in psychiatry to the very human trait of greed. From what I remember, people who studied it—big names like Freud—don't agree about the cause. Some believe we come into the world self-centered and greedy and have to be tempered by the rules of society. Others say we're born good but are changed by something in our environment, like a deprived childhood. Still others blame it on DNA. They believe it's in our genes to reach for high social status, so we'll become more attractive to others."

"It all sounds pretty esoteric to me," I said. "What do you think?"

"It's hard to say which of those theories is correct. But there's a lot of evidence greed is an addiction, regardless of the cause, and I buy into that. Addicts—of anything, drugs, sex, fame, riches—can never get enough. They reach one high, and they need to get higher. They make a lot of money, and they need more. Otherwise, they'd have to deal with the idea someone might be superior to them.

"When they reach so extreme a level, it doesn't matter who they hurt or what they contribute to society. What matters is the accumulation of wealth and material things. At some point, they have no concept of obligation to others—what they call *noblesse oblige*. The thing they can't realize, because they are addicted, is none of it really brings them happiness. It only sustains their ego."

Dwight took his last sip of beer. "I remember going to New York with some med school friends. There was a country and western restaurant there, in Greenwich Village I think, with a sign on the front saying, 'Where Too Much Ain't Enough.' That pretty much says it all."

He exhaled. "Whew. I'm worn out from simply talking about it." He turned and asked, "Does it sound anything like your former colleague, Pop?"

"I'm not sure," I answered, "but I think so. It seems to me, he's had a lot of chances to stop and say, 'I have enough.' Yet he didn't ever seem to do it. I know one thing. Tomorrow I'm going right out and giving away all of my hard-earned riches."

Dwight laughed. "Not so fast there, grandpa. You have offspring to put in your will. And a crowd of needy grandchildren to help put through college. Maybe medical school."

"All right," I said. "I have a better idea. Let's go into the dining room. It's about time for your mom to arrive, and we're going to treat her to a very, very expensive dinner. If I recall how much you eat, that should pretty much drain all of my savings."

CHAPTER FORTY-SIX

We were all scared as sin when Dad got sick.

Mom called to say he was in the hospital and he had been in constant abdominal agony for several days. "He couldn't sleep, couldn't eat," she said.

I could hear the pain in her voice.

"They're running tests as we speak," she added.

I was in my spanking new office when she called. It was eighteen stories high in an all-glass structure near downtown Topeka. The building's brilliant gleam in the rising sunlight as I drove toward it each morning seemed to call out, "Come work here, Monty Johnson. I'll provide comforts and joys you never experienced in those stuffy old bank buildings." Everything inside was pristine and modern. My furniture looked and smelled as if it had just come off the showroom floor. The interior designer even plopped a wonderful, silk ficus tree in a corner. Such a setting can give you a false sense of importance, but at my advancing age, I didn't mind.

Semi-retirement hadn't lasted long, not even the length of my one-year consulting contract with Topeka National Savings. They were gracious enough to let me out of it when the offer came in—CEO of Midwest Financial, an investment advisory firm. In fact, I think they were happy to see me move on, since the merger was complete, and they didn't need me looking over their shoulder anymore.

My new employer offered me a different perspective on the profession I had toiled in my entire career. Except instead of lending mortgage money and taking deposits, I was now knee-deep in the business of helping people invest in the kinds of securities that made my savings and loan business so miserable in its later years.

And then there were my new golfing companions to be considered. These retired corporate execs welcomed me with open arms—and pockets—when I decided to give regular golf a spin. I enjoyed the heck out of the experience, didn't lose too much money and associated with some of the finest men I'd ever want to meet. I was happy to call them friends.

But still a mere sixty, I wasn't quite ready to jump on the retirement train.

"I have a nice opportunity," I said to Sarah as we shopped on a Saturday morning in Jayhawk Supermarket. She was sniffing the cantaloupe while I stood dutifully behind with the cart it was my privilege to push as she made our grocery decisions. "Their top man is retiring, and they want me to come run the show. I think I'd like to do it."

Without looking back at me, she continued to thump the melons and asked, "We wouldn't have to move, would we?"

"No, in fact, the office is closer to where we live than Topeka National's."

She made her choice, laid it in the basket and led me toward the meat counter. "What about your golf game? You were so excited to get to play more."

"I'm not ready for full-time sports," I said. "I enjoy the devil out of it, but I can probably get away occasionally on a Friday if they need a fourth. Or some Saturday afternoon, you might even ride around with me while I play nine holes before we have dinner at the club. What do you think?"

She pointed so the counter man could wrap up a nice piece of salmon and turned toward me. "I think you've been itching to get back in the game for months now. If you like this company, go for it."

And so, I was ensconced in my fancy CEO's office, reviewing a report on new accounts our advisers had acquired in the past month, when Mother voiced her concern about my dad's health crisis.

"I'm so worried, Monty. He never gets sick. This could be something really bad."

"Mom, I'm going to call Sarah right now," I said. "We'll be down there this afternoon."

"Maybe you should wait until we get the tests back," she said. "If it's not serious, you won't want to drive clear to Wichita." I could hear in her voice it wasn't her true sentiment. My mother always worked so hard to present the practical side of an argument, but her emotions betrayed her.

"We'll meet you at the hospital," I promised.

The drive to Wichita took about two hours. It was a straight shot down the Kansas Turnpike. I set it on seventy-five the entire one hundred forty miles. Getting to the hospital was also no problem; I laid my eyes on the place the first day of my life, and we had been there often ever since—the maladies of our children, Sarah's run-in with pneumonia, my appendix operation, you name it.

Mother rose to meet us in the OR waiting room. Her forehead was drawn with worry lines, and her hair and clothes told us she had been there many hours.

"They came back a few minutes ago," she said as she hugged Sarah. "It's not nearly as bad as I thought." She turned to give me a kiss and continued, "Monty, it's his old gall bladder. They're going to remove it in about two hours." Her eyes went to mine and began to tear up.

"But Mom, this is really good news. They don't

even cut you open for that anymore. Just punch a little hole in your belly button and yank the sucker out."

"I know," she acknowledged, "but I was so worried it might be cancer or something. I'm a wreck." Then the tears began to flow. "What would I do if…" her voice trailed off.

We both hugged her and sat her down.

After a few minutes, she gathered herself. "Now, there's no reason for you two to stay. Who knows when he'll feel chipper enough to have anyone in? Go on back to Topeka, and I'll call you when he feels well enough to talk on the phone. I'm so sorry I made you drive on down here, but I didn't know what in the world to think."

She batted down every argument we used about staying. Finally, we agreed to go back home and wait for her call.

* * *

"Monty, what do you think about stopping by the old school for a few minutes? It's not far out of the way from the turnpike entrance," Sarah said.

"I think it's a great idea," I replied. "They built quite an addition to the place, and we haven't ever seen it."

We swung a dozen blocks south and west, and there we were, the scene of the crime, where a young girl named Sarah Madigan allowed herself to be charmed by one Monty Johnson. As we parked in the visitor's lot and walked toward the building, a flood of memories swept through me. I imagine through Sarah, as well. I remembered parking my old Ford in the lot with several basketball buddies in tow. Joining a stream of teens on a winding, red-brick walkway between rows of massive cottonwood trees, deep green in summer and harvest gold in the fall. I remembered how they sent cascades of billowing white fluff, like a flotilla of cotton candy, into the breeze every spring. Just as they did now, on this early day in May.

As I did each day when I attended there, I fist-pumped, for luck, the brass Cougar emblem embedded in a small brick wall in front of the building. Sarah and I climbed the wide concrete steps flanked by cast-stone *balustrades,* and I was momentarily caught off-guard by the entrance. I recalled the front doors were once massive, carved-oak slabs. At some point they had been replaced by steel-and-plexiglass entries equipped with heavy security bars.

A uniformed guard approached and let us in. Back in our day, there had been no such thing.

"Folks, can I help you?" He was tall, silver-headed, about my age, with a deep and authoritative voice.

I glanced momentarily at his holstered sidearm and hoped he didn't ever have to use it.

"We're two old alumni in town for a few hours and wondered if we could look around. We've never seen the new addition."

"We're about twenty minutes until bell," he said. "Is there anything in particular you'd like to see?"

"I heard they have a big trophy exhibit in the new wing," I said. "I played a little ball here, three hundred years ago, and I wouldn't mind taking a look at it."

"Tell you what," he said. "Let me have a peek at your ID, and I'll walk you down there."

"That's very kind," Sarah offered.

The case was much larger than I would have imagined, the entire length and height of one wall, but then it had to chronicle some fifty years of exploits of the South Wichita Cougars. We marveled at the dozens of trophies, game balls, team photos and other memorabilia they'd been able to cram into it. And then, I spotted our niche—the Fifties. I found the cheerleading squad first, and there was young Sarah in her cute outfit. They were all in mid-leap, hair flying, mouths open in some kind of cheer. The caption read, "Second Place, State Cheerleading Clinic, 1959," and a broad red ribbon with gold lettering was draped across it.

"There you are, Miss Madigan. You haven't changed one bit," I joshed.

"I hope that's not true," she said. "Did I ever look so puny?"

We both laughed.

Then she said, "There's my hero." It was the team photo, 1959 Regional Champions, me in the center holding the ball. "Look, there's Sumner Davidson," Sarah went on. "He looks too big and strapping to have such a little-boy face."

I said, "Sumner told me at the high school reunion he teaches humanities at a small college in Washington state. And plays cello in some big civic orchestra."

"Cello? For goodness sakes."

"Sumner was a good basketball player, but he was also one of the most talented people I've ever known. I always admired him for being someone who could do just about anything he set out to do."

I looked below the photo and there was the real ball I held, signed by Paul Sarkesian. Next to it was a framed picture of our coach in a suit and tie.

The guard was still there, peering over our shoulders. "So, this is you in the photo, Mr. Johnson, with the ball?"

I chuckled. "You don't recognize me with the gray

hair?" We turned to go, and I said, "Thank you for putting up with two old geezers."

"It was my pleasure," he said. "Now I have to get upstairs before the bell rings. Can you two find your way out okay?"

As we made our way toward the exit, I said to Sarah, "It was nice to see ourselves frozen in time for a few minutes. Now, back to reality."

We'd almost reached the doors when Sarah grasped my arm. "Monty, let's go in here for a minute." She veered to the left.

I learned years ago never to ask, "Why?" Just go with it, and you'll find out. We entered a brightly lit, bookcase-filled room.

"I didn't spend much time in the library, so I didn't recognize it," I wise-cracked.

Sarah approached a young female, a student, and asked, "Do you keep all the old yearbooks in here?"

The girl, thin, frizzy-haired, flashed a wide grin full of braces and answered, "Yes, ma'am. On the far wall there. They go way back, for many years."

"They'll have to," I said and watched the braces sparkle again.

Sarah found our senior years' books, mine 1959, hers 1960. I took mine and sat down at a table, thumbing through it, letting the scenes from a bygone era engulf me. So many teachers and classmates forgotten in the wake of life. So much activity not given credit for the formation of young souls. I was astounded at how much I remembered, and how much I had forgotten.

And then, my lovely wife stunned me, as she is wont to do. Having stayed standing at the wall of yearbooks while I drowned myself in my own past, she laid in front of me a different book, from 1962, open to a single page. It was mostly photos, and I could tell it chronicled the queen competition of the annual carnival night, a fund-raiser for the band.

My heart nearly stopped at the largest picture. It depicted a young man impeccably dressed in a navy suit and tie, his white shirt showing French cuffs. He was walking down the aisle of the gymnasium between rows of chairs and a wall of on-lookers. The young girl on his arm wore the long dress of a queen candidate. She was movie star pretty, looking nervous, no doubt wondering if a crown was waiting for her.

Beneath the photo read the caption, "William Martin escorts Belinda Patterson in the presentation of Carnival Queen candidates." The description further directed my eyes to the gaping spectators as the couple passed. It read, "Looking on are Mary Phyllis Gunderson in the green top, and Leslie Dickerson in the pink sweater."

Will and Leslie. I stared at the images for what seemed like an hour, then looked up at Sarah.

She said, "So young. Think what might have been."

* * *

Driving home, Sarah fell asleep. We were both dog-tired, but I couldn't have slept if I had wanted to. The darkened, overcast sky reflected our headlights back to the highway, the signposts and center stripes glinting and fading, glinting and fading, as our bright beams approached and passed.

Yet all I could think about was the photo.

A young man, no more than seventeen, erect and fresh-faced, his arm extended for his queen candidate, his bright, dark eyes focused straight ahead toward an unknown future. And as he passed, a young girl in a ponytail and pink top, straining forward to watch him from her sideline chair, her shining green eyes glued on him like an adoring teen idol.

If only I could have been there to warn them at that moment. I would have said, "You hold your fate in your hands. For God's sake, choose wisely."

I knew it would take a long, long time to erase the image from my memory.

CHAPTER FORTY-SEVEN

Coach Ron Slay handed his credit card to the attendant at the convenience station.

"Hey, Coach," said the bearded, tattooed, wrinkled man behind the cash register. He flashed a gap-toothed smile. It was a common occurrence for people around town to recognize the leader of the Topeka University Eagles basketball squad.

"How are you doing?" Slay replied.

"Just gas today? Nothin' else?" Ron shook his head no, and the man ran the card.

As Slay turned and walked toward the exit, the man called out from behind, "Coach Slay, you headin' out to practice?"

Ron said over his shoulder, "Nope. Going to prison."

The man's raspy laugh rattled loudly behind the coach as he left the building and climbed into his three-year-old SUV. He drove several blocks to the Interstate 70 entrance and headed east through a light mist. He was due at his destination at nine o'clock.

After forty minutes, with the precipitation lifting and morning sun trying to break through, Slay took Exit 212 and drove north on Tonganoxie Road. He turned onto South 20th, passing a church, fraternal lodge building and bar and grill—one of thousands of streets just like it on the outskirts of Anywhere, U.S.A.

He made the final turn onto Highway 73 which locally was known as Metropolitan Street, a four-lane thoroughfare every bit as disagreeable as the visually polluted road he had just exited. He passed a steakhouse on the left, its lot half-full at breakfast time, and an auto repair shop on the right where a mechanic was rolling out a tire display.

And then, rising out of nowhere, the enormous Leavenworth Federal Penitentiary emerged, an edifice so imposing it seemed to blot out the rising sun. Ron pulled the car off the street into a supermarket parking lot and stared, awestruck, as if he had seen the Sphinx on the surface of the moon. The prison loomed forty feet above street level and more than ten football fields end-to-end. Its presence, encompassing nearly 23 acres, dominated the surrounding area. With its enormity and grand design, topped by a magnificent dome, the facility in any other setting might be mistaken for a center of government— the *Palais Royal*, for example, or the *Kremlin*. One of United States' first federal penitentiaries, the "Big Top," as it was often called, was a breath-taking sight.

The minimum-security satellite camp was far less impressive. It was lower in height and scope. Whereas some 1,700 prisoners populated the bigger building, the adjacent facility's capacity was fewer than 450. It had no external fencing and slept its inmates in dormitory arrangements as opposed to cell blocks.

As Coach Slay entered the reception area to check in as a visitor, everything appeared gray—the walls, the floors, even the furniture borrowed the drabness of its environment. The inmates' pants and shirts, though kha-ki, seemed to replicate the dust-like tone of their surroundings.

* * *

Visiting prison was a learning experience for the coach. "I'm going to see a former student there, but I didn't know it would be such an involved process," Ron said to a fellow physical education faculty member on a Friday in the gym office. "You don't walk in the door and say, 'I'd like to visit my friend, please.' I wrote him asking if it would be okay to come. He called to say you have to get on the visitation register. The prisoner has to request you be added, and everyone on the list has to have a previous relationship—a family member, or someone else connected to the person's past. He asked to put me on the list, and they approved me as his high school coach. He mailed me a form to fill out and return to the prison staff. Then they did a background check, to make sure I wasn't going to smuggle in a saw, I guess." He grinned. "I got a letter from him three days ago saying I was approved."

"When are you going?" asked the colleague.

"They only permit visits on Saturdays, Sundays, Mondays and federal holidays," he responded, "So it's all set for tomorrow. I have to admit, I'm a bit nervous, not knowing what to expect."

She cackled. "You're kind of suspicious looking. Watch out. Maybe they'll lock you up."

Slay joined her laughter.

* * *

A guard escorted the coach into the camp courtyard, a large, open area with seating scattered throughout for visits. The earlier shower had ushered in a chilly early October breeze, but Slay was required to stow his coat in a locker when he checked in. He shivered as he entered the visiting space, but the rising sun bathed the area and promised higher temperatures later in the morning.

Ron glanced around and spotted his former student. Will sat unsmiling at a table near the far end of the yard. His physique clearly displayed a loss of ten pounds since being incarcerated. Otherwise, there was little change in his appearance.

As Ron approached, Will stood, extended a hand and greeted him solemnly, "Coach, it was good of you to come. It has been a long time."

"It has. But you were in the senior class when I got my first head coaching job. When I heard about your troubles, it seemed right to reach out." He paused. "I didn't think to ask if you needed anything."

Will waved it away as they sat down. "It's not permitted, Coach. I work for pay at the textile factory, and there's a good commissary and drug store available."

"They give you a job here?" Ron asked, surprised.

"We provide supplies for the bigger prison," Will explained. He paused, then smiled for the first time. "It looks like college coaching agrees with you."

Ron Slay ran his hand over his head. "You didn't notice all the new gray hairs. High school players hang onto every word and buy into your philosophy. The college guys are eager to learn, but they don't hesitate to challenge your assumptions. And sometimes they ignore you and do it their way."

He paused, "Are you doing okay in here, Will? Do they treat you all right?"

Will replied, "There's no violence in the minimum-security part, so that's good. There isn't even a fence, and we don't live in cells. They trust us to stay put, not fight and avoid trouble. I'm in a partition of one of the dormitories—sleeps four, like a fraternity house. We have a good library, and I spend a lot of time reading business magazines. When I get out of here, I'll need to be up-to-speed if I'm going to resurrect my career."

"That's a great attitude, Will. You were a lot like that on the basketball court, many moons ago. A positive outlook, I mean. What do you think you will do? I heard banks are out."

Will's upper neck and ear lobes glowed slightly crimson. "That's true, Coach. But there are other avenues for someone with a business background. I've met a fellow here whose friend on the outside might be able to use me in his company. Helping people overcome their pasts is apparently a mission for him."

They made small talk for another fifteen minutes, followed by an awkward silence.

Finally, "I hope you don't mind my asking," Slay said. "Have your children been here to visit?"

Will waited a full minute before responding. "I don't want them to come. Chip is going to college in California. My first wife is looking after Haley."

Again, he hesitated. "I don't get many visitors. I appreciate your coming, Coach. I realize it's a hassle."

The coach shrugged his shoulders, as if to say, "It's no problem."

Will clasped his hands together, elbows on the table. "The man I mentioned, the one who might give me a job, wants to come talk. I don't know if I can get him in. But if so, I'll meet with him. I'm chomping at the bit to plan my future."

CHAPTER FORTY-EIGHT

"Will, I'm Leon Christiansen." The man sliding into the seat opposite Will in the visitors' courtyard was middle-aged, solidly heavy-set with short, salt-and-pepper hair and a van dyke beard. His deep voice had a Midwestern accent, a subtle but distinct set of pronunciations characterized by such sounds as "warsh" for "wash," and "aigg" for "egg." It was early April, six months to the day since Ron Slay's visit.

"I don't know how you managed to get me in," Leon said. "I've had closer relationships with several others here who had a devil of a time adding me to the list. You must have the magic touch."

Will smiled. "Some say I have an art of persuasion. It wasn't that difficult."

"So, Will, less than a year to go. Are you interested in getting back to work?"

Will answered, "Absolutely. I asked you to come because I met your friend Ted while he was here."

"Yup," Leon said. "As you know, he was released two weeks ago. I own a company, United Holdings, which manages mortgage firms. I'm going to help him get into one of my regional offices. He's a good accountant and financial analyst. Didn't deserve to be here."

"Ted said your holding company manages over 500 mortgage brokerages. That's a heavy burden, if you're running it all yourself."

"I have a lot of help," Christiansen said. "Each region headquarters oversees a hundred or so branches. The thing is, the past several years, we've grown like a hog in the sty. I could use some help if the right man came along." A faint grin crossed his lips. "Will, I probably know nearly as much of your background as you do. After Ted told me about you, I did some research. I already knew about Quivira, but I didn't connect it with the guy in here, this Will Martin fellow. Being based in Kansas City, I was well aware of the Kaycee Holdings situation." Leon sat back and squinted at Will, as if sizing him up. "What made you do it? The Kaycee thing?" he asked bluntly.

"Like I told the FBI, it was easy, and I thought undetectable. I was making everyone money, and I reasoned, 'Why not pay myself a bonus?' Leon, I meant what I said in the courtroom. I have real remorse for my behavior. I slid down a slope I would never ski on again."

He hesitated and looked his visitor squarely in the face. "My parents raised me in the church, and I got away from that. In here, I found my faith again. I go to Mass every Sunday. I pray God will forgive my actions." He paused. "That's about it."

Leon smiled widely for the first time. "Will Martin, that sounds great to me. Let's keep in touch. When it's time for you to walk free again, maybe I can help you get back on your feet."

* * *

Transition House was one of the many non-profit locations where prisoners lived out the final months of their incarceration. It was part of the prison system, overseen by a staff answerable to the penitentiary director. Inmates released to their care were required to stay sober, drug-free and to search for employment. They surrendered a portion of their pay to help defray the cost of confinement.

A Leavenworth director's order cut Will's forty-two-month sentence short for good behavior. However, he was confined to several months in the transitional housing facility, "…to afford an opportunity to adjust to and prepare for the re-entry into the community…" the decision read.

Will's new home was near the Kansas-Missouri state line in Metropolitan Kansas City. Many of the forty temporary residents were dealing with substance abuse problems. Others displayed emotional difficulties from their prison experience. While he stayed there, two people checked out and failed to return, were apprehended and re-sentenced to prison.

His assignment to that location, rather than in the town of Leavenworth, was due to Will's new job. Leon Christiansen hired him upon transfer from prison to a position in one of his Homeland Mortgage Corporation's branch offices.

"I vouched for you, Will," Christiansen said during his final visit to the Leavenworth camp, "so don't let me down. The place where you'll live is a couple blocks from work, so you can walk to and from. We'll get you through this interim step at Transition House, secure your full release and talk about where you go from there."

"Leon," Will said, "I can do a few more months standing on my head. Especially since you're giving me this opportunity to exercise my brain again. I look forward to suiting up and working every day."

"You won't need to dress up in this place," Christiansen replied. "You can show up in casual clothes. I realize you're accustomed to running the show, but this is a menial job. You'll do clerical work in support of the personnel. It's not ideal, but it will mean a paycheck and a path to opportunity. I'll have something great lined up for you when you get your full release."

Will walked from the half-way facility carrying a bag with his personal items. He climbed into the over-sized luxury SUV and nodded at his boss. "Thanks for picking me up, Leon."

Christiansen shook his hand. "I imagine these past six months have seemed like years." He nodded toward Transition House. "That couldn't have been a pleasant place to live."

"To the contrary," Will responded. "The Leaven-worth Camp wasn't dreamland, but it wasn't nearly as bad as the Big Top would have been. Yet this place was a step closer to civilization, so I didn't mind it. In fact, in some ways it reminded me of my childhood in Wichita, growing up in a humble, no-frills home."

As Leon pulled the vehicle out of the parking lot, Will said. "This is some set of wheels, Leon. There's something I've never understood. Not being critical, you understand, just curious. Ever since I started making real money, I have always driven nice cars—expensive, but not as big as a freight train." They both laughed. "Seriously, I don't get the attraction of driving such a mon-ster."

Leon said, "My business takes me out on the high-way quite a bit, especially between the Kansas City of-fice and St. Louis. When I'm tooling down Interstate 70, I don't want to feel like a little weenie up against those eighteen-wheelers."

He turned onto State Line Road. "For the next two or three days, you can stay at our house. We'll have you in your own place soon."

As they pulled onto Ward Parkway, Will said, "This route brings back some memories, not all pleasant. We're a rock's throw from where I got into trouble."

"That's all behind you, Will. You paid your dues."

Leon pulled the car into a parking lot and stopped in a space fronting a men's clothing store.

"What are we doing here?" Will asked.

"It's time to get you dressed up," Leon said, smiling widely.

"Leon, I have suits in storage," Will argued.

"It's been over three years, Will," Leon said emphatically. "You're probably a different size. We're going to give you a fresh start."

The shop was upscale, selling only tailor-made clothing. Will scanned the fabric samples fanned out by a sales clerk.

"Here's a great-looking gray pinstripe," the man said. "And I really think this pale blue window-pane would look good on you.'

Will shook his head no. "It has to be navy blue, with only a hint of stripe." He pointed at a sample. "This one. This is what I wear. Neckties to match. Oh, and I like white shirts, French-cuffed and monogrammed."

The salesman took Will's measurements and wrote up the order. "We'll have four suits and all the trimmings ready to pick up in three days," he said.

As they left the shop, Will said to Leon, "You're aware I can't possibly pay for this, right?"

Leon chuckled and laid a hand on Will's shoulder as they walked toward the car. "We'll take it out of your paycheck."

"Not with what I'm making, clerking in the Homeland branch."

Leon paused as they reached his SUV. "You're through with that office," he said. "I'm setting you up with a substantial position. You should get out of Kansas

City. One of my regions, with about one hundred HMC branches, lacks leadership. I want you to oversee the operation."

"Where?"

"Have you ever been to Orlando?"

As they drove toward his house, Leon said, "Will, I've been thinking about you a lot. You say you returned to your faith. And you want a decent, honest life. There's a woman, a family friend, I want you to meet. Her husband passed away several years ago, and she's still trying to get past it. She is attractive, smart and a ball of fun. I'm not trying to marry you off or anything, but I want to introduce you. Maybe a new friendship could help you both move on with your lives."

CHAPTER FORTY-NINE

I've always considered myself a realist. You can pay the mortgage, or you can't. When stocks go up, bonds usually go down. If you step on a nail, it's going to hurt. But I realize there are people who live in a different universe—who understand how string theory can tell us what goes on inside black holes, who talk to plants and watch them react, who have seen unicorns. I can't recall anything quite so abstruse ever entering my left-brained consciousness. Who you see is who I am.

It follows, then, when an event occurs that seems surreal, I react as if I had seen aliens.

One such moment came on a hot summer morning when I'd barely started my workday. It was 2003, and we would commemorate the second anniversary of the horrific World Trade Center attack in a few more months. We had just run Saddam Hussein out of Kuwait. Those of us trying to help steer clients through economic uncertainties were hoping predictions of a strong third quarter would work in our favor.

I was starting to read a report when the face poking into my office doorway caught me off guard, stunned me, as if my morning coffee hadn't yet hit its mark.

"Hello, Monty. Are you busy?"

"Oh, my Lord, Will Martin," I exclaimed. "Of course not. Come in, please."

He was decked out in his customary navy suit and tie, and only a trace of a smile crossed his lips. Will was thinner, paler than I remembered him, but given his recent history, it shouldn't have surprised me.

"It's good to see you again," Will said in the polite and deferential manner I'd always associated with him.

I leapt out of my chair and went around the desk to shake his hand. "Please, sit down." I motioned to the little grouping of chairs around a small conference table in the corner. It was where I held most of my one-on-one conferences. When I sat down across from him, I'm sure I gaped at him like a tourist. It was an eerie sensation, considering how long it had been, knowing where he'd spent the past few years.

"When did you get out?" I asked, trying not to stammer.

He squirmed uncomfortably at the question. "About a month ago, Monty. Six months early for good behavior, they told me. It seemed important to look you up—you and your family were always so good to me. I would have come sooner, but first of all I wasn't aware you'd left Wichita. And then, I've been busy trying to shift my gears again, do you understand?"

"Absolutely," I said, still feeling fully immersed in a hallucination. "Will, I'm truly sorry I haven't been in touch since you—you know…" I stammered.

He shook his head, cutting me off. "No, Monty, it's all right. I didn't expect to hear from you. I was pretty embarrassed to be in there. You did me a favor, really. But that's over now, and I have to put my life back together."

"What are your plans?" I asked.

"I have something in the works," he said. "Someone I met in Leavenworth introduced me to a guy who believes in giving people a second chance. I found my religion again when I was there. And I want to be a productive member of society as long as I live, to make amends for all the pain I caused people. I got what I deserved, but it's over now and I'm simply not going to dwell on the past. Plus, he introduced me to a woman, a friend of his family's, and we have been talking about getting together."

"What? Do you mean marriage?"

He smiled. "We'll see."

"Can you tell me more about this new job?"

"I'm not at liberty yet. Let me have your card. I'll be in touch after it's all settled."

"I have to ask, Will. You don't have to talk about it if you don't want to. But knowing what I do about your lifestyle, your penchant for nice things, houses, cars and the like, how did you survive in such an oppressive atmosphere?"

Again, the squirming. I regretted having asked, but I admit the question had dogged me since he was convicted. I didn't expect the person who emerged to be anything like the old Will Martin. Yet here he was, suited up and ready to go.

"I was pretty worried. Even though I thought the sentence was fair," he said, "going to Leavenworth weighed on me a lot. It's a medium security penitentiary and my lawyer told me the gangs are pretty bad. Black toughs, white supremists, Latinos, they all run their own little drug scams and stick together. He said anyone coming in there who thinks he wants to get along with everybody is in for a tough time. So, I thought this was not going to be good.

"But I caught a break. My attorney got me assigned to this minimum-security satellite facility adjacent to the main prison. It's not a hotel by any means, especially for someone who's accustomed to the finer things in life. But they aren't in cells over there, it's more like a fraternity house bunk-bed arrangement. There's a visitors' lounge where we could sit in the courtyard and interact, not like in the movies where you have to look at each other through a glass window and talk on the phone. It was not a pleasant experience, but I kept thinking, 'Will, you came from humble beginnings, shared a bedroom with a sibling, ate simple meals. If you grew up in such an austere environment, you can survive this for three years.'"

He continued, "I've always told people I mentored in the business, 'Life is a long, dark, unknown road, a trip much farther than your headlights can shine. Just concentrate on what's in front of you the first few miles, and you'll make it.' The philosophy helped me a lot the past few years."

"And now you're a free man."

"Ron Slay came to see me," he said. "He told me he wanted to reach out, since I was one of his South Wichita boys. I was a senior on his first Cougars team."

"I remember," I said. "I talked to you guys after a game one night."

He looked down, as if trying to remember. Then his eyebrows went up and he pointed over at me, nodding in recollection. "How long ago was that?" he said. He looked around the room. "You look like you landed in a good place."

"The thrift business is a different animal these days, as you well know." I took a quick look at his expression, realizing I might have touched a nerve. If I did, he didn't show it. "So, after we merged with Topeka National, and I left, I was fortunate to find this firm. They're terrific people, and I'm happy to be in the driver's seat."

"Consorting with the enemy," Will showed a bit of the grin that so endeared him to people in the old days.

"The very people we used to compete with tooth and toe-nail."

"I guess enemy's the right word. Or maybe I got re-ligion." Again, I watched for a trace of negative reaction in Will but saw none.

We chatted for ten or fifteen more minutes. He told me again he'd found his forgotten faith in the peniten-tiary, expressed hope this new career opportunity would turn his life around, felt he might have found someone to love again. And then, as quickly as he descended on my usually ordered existence, he said goodbye and was gone. I was left to ponder the things I should have said, should have asked. But being submerged in the bizarre appearance of an old friend who became a different per-son, I could not.

I sat at my little conference table, lost in memory and thought, not only awestruck at what had just trans-pired, but also thinking back on the incredibly calami-tous events of past years. I rarely dwelled on those days, except Will's return forced them on me.

And I wondered, was he now what he appeared to be—a changed and better man? Or was he, as many of his detractors claimed, a smooth and seductive salesman forever?

* * *

In the evening, I called Lawson Jeffries. He told me he'd left the public television station and was about to embark on a new position with a commercial TV outlet there. "I'll be going from begging for quarters with my hat in my hand to selling advertising and sweating out the ratings."

I wished him luck. Then, "Will Martin came to see me this morning."

"Yes, I heard he was out," he said. "I hoped he would come down to Wichita. Maybe sell insurance or go back and see if he can get his old position running Dave Carlson's office supply business."

I laughed at the thought. "That'd go over like sin on Sunday. Prudence would love it."

"I'm saying he should live out the rest of his days in dignity and make an honest life for himself. He was so successful then, when everything was simpler than the path he chose. People liked him, admired him really, and he made a positive contribution here. If he returned, we would all help him recover from a nasty past."

"Lawson, I don't know if it's in him to do such a thing," I said. "Once you've been to the top of the mountain. Know what I mean?"

"Yes, I do." He answered. "I heard your father was in the hospital."

"He's all right now," I said.

"Someone said you came down. You should have stopped to see me," he scolded.

"It was only a couple of hours, Lawson. I swear, next time I will look you up. And you remember where Topeka is, right? You also have a phone, correct old pal?"

"I do. And I will."

CHAPTER FIFTY

Will's marriage to Rosemary Gray was his third. The first, to Prudence, ended in divorce. Leslie's unusual accidental death abruptly ended his second. Rosemary had been widowed for five years when Leon Christiansen introduced her to Will. They were married within months.

The couple lived in an upscale Florida city named Windsor, a quiet, suburban-feel neighborhood less than ten miles from Orlando's theme parks. Much of the neighborhood was surrounded by Windsor Lake. The majority of homes were one-story ranch style, and prices ranged from $400,000 to more than $3 million for those on lakefront property. Will and Rosemary bought a five-year-old stucco-and-tile house several blocks from the lake for less than one million. It was not as luxurious as other abodes Will had lived in. But it was stylish and comfortable, with five bedrooms and a large lanai in the back. Middle upper-class, would be an apt description.

Will's workspace in Orlando was in the office park building where Homeland Mortgage Corporation's regional staff was headquartered. By 2007, he had worked for Leon Christenson and his extensive mortgage operation over four years. Will toiled long hours, often traveling to branch offices in Florida and adjoining states to review their operation. When he was in Orlando, he regularly put in twelve-hour days.

He was surprised on a Wednesday evening, shortly before seven in the evening, by a visit from Rosemary. The building had essentially emptied sometime after six, and he glanced up from his computer to see her pulling into the near-empty parking lot. Rosemary was fifty-eight, olive-complexioned and thin. Her hairdresser touched up the auburn tone in her hair weekly to cover encroaching gray.

As she entered and flashed a warm smile at Will, he jumped to his feet.

"Rose. What are you doing here?" He seemed flustered.

She kissed him lightly. "You've been going at it way too hard. I came to take you to dinner."

He looked down at the unfinished work on his desk. "I can't, Rose," he said. "I'm flying to Atlanta in the morning, and there's much to do before I leave."

Rosemary shook her head and took his hand. "We're going. I made reservations at Barrett's Steakhouse less than a mile away. We'll have a nice meal, and you can return and finish if you have to. I'm having dinner with my husband."

"All right," he conceded. "We'll take separate cars, because I need to come back."

* * *

Barrett's was in a stand-alone, sand-colored stucco building with no particular architectural significance. Inside, the lighting was amber and muted. A circle of large, leather-seated booths ringed the horseshoe-shaped bar, nearly always crowded with the after-work set. What the establishment lacked in ambience, it made up for with excellent food. Without reservations, diners often waited an hour for a table.

Will ordered a ribeye, and Rosemary chose the salmon. As they waited for their meals and nursed glasses of wine, Rosemary fidgeted.

"There's something I want to propose," she said.

"Sure," he responded.

"I'd like us to take a trip. We've been married nearly

four years, and we never go anywhere. Will, have you ever been to the Caribbean?"

"Only Saint Martin, several times," he replied.

She grew animated, her dark brown eyes brimming with excitement. "I love St. Thomas. My late husband and I went there often, Will, and its loads of fun. The beaches are gorgeous. You can take catamaran cruises to snorkel and then watch the sunset. There are historic old buildings to explore. I remember this one castle called…"

Will held up a hand and cut her off. "Rose, wait. First of all, I'm from Kansas. I don't snorkel. But more to the point, I can't take a vacation. I manage over a hundred branches for Leon, and every one of them is a headache. Sorry, but it's out of the question."

"I knew you'd be stubborn about it, you work so hard," she said. "But I came prepared. I'll pay for everything. Plane fares, luxury hotel, the whole trip. I want this, Will. I need this."

Will shook his head no as the food arrived. He cut into his steak, took a bite and paired it with a sip of cabernet. He glanced up momentarily, then stopped chewing as tears flowed freely down his wife's cheeks.

"Rose. What in hell's the matter?"

She pushed her plate away and took a long, slow drink of pinot grigio. Choking back tears, she said, "I'm making an effort, Will, for God's sake. I want to make the marriage work. But I can't do it alone. I try my best at all times to look pretty, not for myself, but for you. Yet you never compliment my appearance. I rarely even rate a kind word from you."

Rosemary paused, looked him dead aim in the eyes and lowered her voice. "We haven't made love in months and months." She watched for a reaction, but his face was expressionless. She went on, "And now this outright refusal to consider a vacation."

He started to speak, but she reached across and put a hand on his lips. "No, let me talk. My husband and I traveled a lot, and it brought us closer together. I thought a trip might help you and me. When Leon introduced us, he said you found religion in prison. You haven't been to church, that I know of, since our wedding in that little chapel. I'm doing all I can. But slowly and surely, I find myself giving up. Let me gift you this trip."

"I have too much at stake with this job, Rose." His voice became hard-edged and agitated. "I had everything when I was in Houston, and they took it away. Then, when I tried to climb my way back, I ended up in prison. That was my fault, and I paid for it. But now I have another chance to do something big, to make my life a huge success."

"Your life?" she wept. "Don't you mean our life?"

Will's voice jumped several decibels. "I don't need this, Rose. You need to get off my case."

The woman whose disposition was usually pleasant hissed, "Don't you dare raise your voice." She gathered her handbag, tossed her napkin on the table and slid out of the booth. "You can have my salmon. And pay the damned check."

She turned and hurried toward the exit, sobbing.

CHAPTER FIFTY-ONE

A man and woman sat having coffee together in an Orlando pancake restaurant. It was no casual Monday morning break. Rather, the conversation was intense and serious. Taylor Bradford was a former vice president of Homeland Mortgage Corporation, owned by Leon Christiansen's United Holdings in Kansas City. With him was Sally Garrison, an HMC broker who ran her own branch office.

"Last week, I notified Leon I was going to terminate my affiliation with HMC," she said with acerbic bitterness in her tone. "I went to the office this morning and couldn't get access to my bank account. Apparently, on Friday afternoon the son-of-a-bitch froze me out of the funds I use to run my business."

Bradford shook his head no. "It wasn't Leon Christiansen," he said. "I hear that kind of shit is happening all over the HMC network. I'll bet a hundred dollars it was Will Martin's doing. Will is Leon's attack dog"

"Martin? He doesn't work for United Holdings anymore," she said.

The former VP's laugh had a sarcastic edge. "Who says?"

"Leon Christiansen says. He told a reporter for the *Orlando Post*. Or at least, it's what they wrote."

"Sally, listen to me. Martin has been running the show for United Holdings for almost five years. I know, I was at HMC headquarters where Will keeps his office. He isn't officially on anyone's payroll. Leon calls him a consultant. Smoke and mirrors. Make no mistake about it, Martin is in charge of every move HMC makes. Everyone thought Christiansen sent him down here to do marketing and help us get customers. Bull. You don't buy a pencil without his approval. And if you cross him on anything, or argue with him, you're out on your ass. He's the boss, period, end of paragraph."

"Then why would the owner tell the press he let him go?" she asked.

"Will Martin is an ex-con. Did some time in Leavenworth for embezzlement. Leon hires former convicts because he's a good guy and wants to help rehabilitate them. But a couple of the states where HMC does business found out about United's hiring practices and took exception. One of my former VP colleagues told me last week two states fined Leon a total of a million dollars for ignoring their regulations and putting ex-cons like Will Martin on his payroll."

Two people slid into the booth next to them.

Bradford glanced at them and then lowered his voice. "So, does Will Martin still work for United Holdings and run HMC? Leon Christiansen says no, and you won't find the man's name anywhere on the executive payroll. But trust me, he's still calling all the shots. Who knows? Given his history, he might have his hand in the till."

Sally took a gulp of coffee and bristled, setting her jaw defiantly. "I'm trying to run a damned mortgage office, and I can't do it without operating funds. If Martin made the decision to deny me access to my bank account, I'll find some way to make him pay. I processed loans last week and banked tens of thousands in fees. That's my damned money."

"I wish I could still be there to help you," Bradford said, motioning to the waitress for a check. "But Leon's thinning the ranks, and I was a casualty. He brought in a guy a month or so ago to help sort out some of the firm's compliance problems, but he lasted about three weeks. Pfffft, he was gone. Now rumor has it Leon is shopping around trying to find someone who'll take the branches off his hands. He wants out. He's already lost about two hundred offices, down from five hundred a year ago. It's going from bad to worse."

"Count me in the two hundred," Sally lamented. "Frozen bank funds or not, I'm getting out while I can." She reached for her purse.

Bradford waved her away and put a ten on the table. "This couldn't come at a worse time for you," he said. "It looks to me like everything in real estate is getting ready to take a nose-dive. You know better than I do what kind of problems are emerging. Over-built housing. Scrambling to sell mortgages and get people into those houses. Easy loans to people not qualified to pay them back. You heard New Century Financial declared Chapter 11, right?"

"Sure, but Taylor, they're a sub-prime lending outfit. Their mortgages are the riskiest in the market. I make my living in a different space."

"What's happening to all of those risky mortgages, Sally? They're getting bundled into securities with good mortgages and sold to the highest bidder. I'm no investment expert, just a corporate head-hunter. But I know what I see, and I say it doesn't look good. We're about to plunge into real estate hell."

"You're depressing me, Taylor," she said. "We're talking about my future."

"Sorry, but I don't envy you. At least, being in personnel, I can switch industries."

Sally responded, "If the bottom falls out of the real

estate market, nobody in business will be safe. Not even a personnel expert looking for a career change."

"I hope to God you're wrong," Bradford said.

CHAPTER FIFTY-TWO

Will Martin's attempt to raise his career once again from the ashes was going well. His strong relationship with Leon Christiansen, chief executive officer of United Holdings in Kansas City, was solid. The company, founded by Christiansen ten years earlier, was making money through its mortgage loan branches under the Homeland Mortgage Corporation brand name. But as 2007 wore on, the business started getting shaky. HMC was losing offices. Mortgage terms became more liberal to get buyers into housing. What would in time become a massive waterfall of foreclosures was just beginning.

As for the overall economy, former HMC vice president Taylor Bradford's prediction was turning out to be true. Despite the U.S. stock market hitting an all-time high in October 2007, the slide began. After two consecutive quarters of declining economic growth, the economic downturn, later to be dubbed The Great Recession, picked up steam as the calendar turned the page to 2008.

By March, after losing billions in unwise mortgage investments, the renowned brokerage firm Bear Stearns collapsed. IndyMac, a huge mortgage lender, fell in July. In September, the U.S. Treasury took over management of the two companies that guaranteed eighty percent of home mortgages, Freddie Mac and Fannie Mae.

Against this background of bad economic news, Christiansen flew to Orlando to see Will. They met for dinner in Celebration, the charming little planned community south of the big tourist attractions. They eschewed a well-known Spanish restaurant in the center of town for a quieter, less crowded café on a little side street dotted with art galleries. The weather was warm with a soft breeze blowing. They sat outside. An occasional person meandered by as the two men talked.

"You and Rosemary doing okay?" asked Leon.

"Yes, fine," Will lied.

"She's a great lady."

"I agree," Will answered.

"Will, I came down to talk business," Leon said. "You've done everything I asked you to do and then some. I can't thank you enough. But we had to give up our license in Georgia and we're being fined big-time by South Carolina for hiring you. It's damned unfair, and I argued with them, told them how I believe in people who have turned their lives around. But I lost. Plus, Will, I have to move on. Baltimore Insurance is getting out of the bonding industry, making it nearly impossible to operate several hundred offices. This business is falling at my feet, and I've convinced another firm to take over a lot of our branches. As I told you months ago, you need to get your own thing up and running as fast as you can."

Will nodded. "I'm working on it, Leon, but it's a lot harder now than it used to be. In the past, I could schmooze people and bring in the business by the truckload. But my past has caught up with me. It's harder getting people to talk to me now, and even more difficult for them to trust me with their investment."

"You're a survivor, Will. I have no doubt you'll make it."

"Maybe," Will said. "I can't help thinking this is *déjà vu* two decades later. Everything that's happening feels like the savings and loan crisis all over again."

* * *

Much later, Will arrived home, walking unsteadily into the house after spending several hours at Barrett's bar. Rosemary met him in the great room. She was dressed ready to travel, and two packed bags sat by her chair. Though her face showed no emotion, her eyes were red from crying.

"I've called a taxi to take me to the airport," Rosemary said, her normally cheerful, musical voice a monotone. "I've told you for weeks I don't believe you really care about me. I can't do this anymore."

"I've said I love you," Will answered impassively.

"You never act like it," she argued.

"It's my work, Rosemary," he said. "The economy and real estate are in the toilet. It's all getting so much harder and more demanding. It drains your energy."

She shook her head. "I know what's going on. Leon called to say 'hello' and told me you're out of a job. But it doesn't matter. Will, face it. You married me because I'm a well-off widow you thought could help you get what you wanted. This house is in my name because you couldn't qualify for a mortgage, with your record."

"I got us a one hundred percent mortgage through HMC. It didn't cost you a thing," he protested quietly.

"Half the monthly payments," she said. "And I'll give you credit, you pay your share of the expenses. Now that Leon has let you go, you won't be able to do that."

She stiffened against tears beginning to emerge. "I would gladly handle the finances until you get something else. But Will, I want more than you're equipped to give. I want affection. Special moments. Fun, for God's sake. I thought you were ready to give those things, but it's obvious we made a mistake. You're married to your work, and I'm merely a convenience. Whatever happens, that's not going to change."

The cab's horn honked out front.

"Goodbye, Will. Good luck." She picked up the suitcases and moved toward the door.

Without protest, he held it for her.

* * *

Barely a month later, after a full day of working on setting up a new investment business, Will heard a devastating message from his sister while listening to his voicemails. He hadn't spoken to her since long before being incarcerated.

"Will, I wanted you to know our brother Terry has passed away at his home in Belgium. He's been sick from some kind of rare blood disease. I got word two days ago he was gone. He is being cremated, and there won't be any service. I thought you should know. 'Bye."

That was all she said. She left no contact information, nor any other message of a personal nature.

Will walked slowly to the front window, his shoulders sagging. He pulled back the drape and stared out into the moonless night.

He lingered there for a long time, unmoving. Finally, he turned, wandered back into the living room and slumped heavily onto the sofa.

He had not talked to his younger brother in nine years, not since Terry moved to Europe.

CHAPTER FIFTY-THREE

"Hello, Mr. Strausburg. My name is Will Martin. I understand Enterprise Lending is assuming responsibility for most of United Holdings' HMC branches. I don't know if Leon Christiansen told you about me, but I did considerable work for him on that business, actually running it for him the past several years. I also have a lot of experience in savings and loans and other real estate investment ventures, so I believe I could be a substantial help to you. I'd be happy to meet and discuss an arrangement, either as an employee or a consultant. Again, my name is Will Martin. When you get this message, please call me back at the following number…"

After Will left the information and hung up, he sat back and sipped on the scotch he had poured. Leon had not notified him of the completed transfer of the HMC offices. Instead, Will had seen a brief report on the six o'clock news' "Business Today" feature. Given his experience and history with United, he might well be able to resurrect his career with this new company.

He finished the drink, poured another and began to make other calls.

"Hello, Walker Bannister, old friend. Will Martin here. I guess we've both been through a lot since our old days of making money at Quivira. Which is why I'm calling. I've completed a successful engagement with a real estate investment firm in Orlando, so I'm in between jobs. I've put together a mortgage investment company and am starting to raise funds. Walker, I'd love to get you in on the ground floor of this venture. I'm asking you if you'll throw in with me, send some investment my way and I'll make you a good profit. Please call me back at…"

"Greg, this is your old friend, Will Martin. I hope you have recovered nicely from the savings and loan debacle. It was a tough time for all of us, but you've never let anything like that get Greg Jacobson down. With your skills, I imagine you're sitting on a pile of development cash by now, which is why I'm calling. My new mortgage investment company is looking for a few people who'd like to make some insane amounts of money. You know I'm good at scoring profits. Give me a call back and let's arrange to meet somewhere and discuss the opportunity…"

"Bernie, this is Will Martin, a voice from the past. I thought about you the other day when I saw your father being interviewed about a bill he's sponsoring in the Senate. I've lost track of what you're up to these days, but I imagine you're mining for gold or diamonds someplace. Anyway, I have a terrific investment opportunity I'd like to present to you at your convenience, a way to make some easy money. Please call me back…"

After making the last call, he poured another scotch and leaned back in the chair, his eyes closed. Within minutes, he dozed off.

* * *

Will awoke with a start at the car horn blaring outside. He was still fully clothed in his big chair by the phone. He looked at his watch; it was seven-thirty in the morning. Shaking off the grogginess from a night of sleep sitting up, he walked unsteadily to the front window. Pulling the drape back and peering out, he saw a teenager across the street hurry out to a waiting car in the driveway.

Will rubbed his head and eyes and walked slowly

into the kitchen. Finding no coffee or breakfast food, he drove three blocks to the Taco Boy drive-through.

"I'll have a breakfast burrito and large black coffee," he murmured.

He pulled the lid off of the coffee and sipped at it while he drove across the street to a convenience store. He put coins in the machine and retrieved a copy of the morning paper.

Arriving back home, he sat down at the kitchen table and drank half of the coffee before unwrapping the burrito and taking a bite. He unfolded the *Orlando Post* and thumbed through it to the business section.

Will scanned the articles, flipped the page and spotted a brief story about Leon's arrangement with Enterprise Mortgage:

> *Local Firm to Take Over Mortgage Offices*
> *Harris Strausburg, president of Enterprise Lending headquartered in Orlando, said his firm has acquired all of the Florida and Georgia branches of Homeland Mortgage Corporation. The Homeland offices have been operated by United Holdings in Kansas City, Missouri, for the past ten years.*
>
> *United, owned by Leon Christiansen, has been a troubled firm recently and finally closed its doors earlier this year.*
>
> *"The company where we got bonding for our offices, Baltimore Insurance, decided to get out of that business," Christiansen told the Post. "It was pretty much the final straw, so we are transferring the business to Enterprise in fairness to our customers and employees."*

*Christiansen's company has been repri-
manded by several states' regulators for its
policy of hiring felons, including the former
CEO of Houston-based Quivira Savings Bank,
Will Martin. He served a three-year sentence in
prison for taking millions of dollars from an investment firm in Kansas City. Martin reportedly
was running the HMC offices for Christiansen.*

*"I want to make one thing clear," Straus-
burg told the Post. "Will Martin is not, and will
not be, part of my company as I take responsibility for these offices. Mr. Martin has no association with Enterprise Lending whatsoever."*

Will flung the paper across the room. He finished the
burrito and carried his coffee to the chair where he had
slept. He punched the message button and listened.

"Mr. Martin, this is Greg Jacobson's office manager.
I listened to your message this morning and am sorry to
say he is in Australia and New Zealand for the next two
months. I'll be happy to relay your message to him, but
his access is very limited, and it will probably be some
time before he can get back to you. Thank you, sir."

Beep.

"Hey, Will, Bernie Franklin. How'ya doing, old
buddy? Hope all right. Listen, I'm in Chile working on
a deal. Don't have anything good to tell you about funds
for investment. We're hoping to strike something rich
down here, and if I do, I might get in touch. Until then,
take care."

Beep.

"Will, this is Walker Bannister. Long time. Listen, I
wish you well in your new venture. This damned reces-

sion is killing all of the development deals. I have friends who are having to sell their own residences to stay afloat. As for me and my wife, we're hunkered down out here in California blowing through our reserves and hoping things will turn around soon. Hope you can find somebody with some cash, but for right now, I'm not your man. Good luck."

Beep.

It was nearly ten o'clock. Will finished his coffee and sat for long minutes, staring into space. Finally, he went to the couch, found the remote and turned on the twenty-four-hour news channel. The anchor said:

> *"Good morning. It's Saturday, March 10, and here's the latest news. More than two months into 2009, the economic news continues to be devastating. Yesterday the Dow Jones Industrial Average fell to its lowest point yet in this so-called Great Recession. At 6,547 points, it has now dropped more than fifty percent from its all-time high set in October 2007.*
>
> *"Some investment experts and economists believe the slump might turn around anytime now, but there are still many who have the pessimistic view the recession could continue for the rest of the year.*
>
> *"Whichever happens, the consensus is that digging out of this hole and regaining what has been lost will take a long time."*

CHAPTER FIFTY-FOUR

The taxi pulled up in front of the rental car build-ing near a famous Orlando tourist attraction. Will Martin paid the driver and stepped out. He looked around at the swarms of shorts-clad visitors streaming into and out of the area like an army of ants searching for water.

Inside, after waiting in a short line, Will stepped up and laid his driver's license and credit card on the count-er. "I have a car reserved," he said, pointing at his name on the cards.

The attendant *tap-tapped* and pulled the record up on her computer. "Yes, sir, Mr. Martin. I see you have a compact car rented for two days. Sir, would you like to consider an upgrade to a standard car for only ten dollars more per day?"

"No thank you," he answered softly, smiling polite-ly.

"Okay, I simply thought, you're a pretty tall man and look like you might be more accustomed to a larger, nicer car than this."

"Well, I had to sell my Mercedes. For now, this will do nicely. Thanks."

"All right then," she went on, "do you want to ac-cept or waive the collision insurance?"

"Waive it, please."

"All right, initial here. And you understand by sign-ing this waiver you'll accept full responsibility for any damage occurring to the vehicle?"

"Yes, I do," he answered.

"One final thing, Mr. Martin. Would you like the gasoline agreement? You let us refill it at the per gallon rate written on this document. Or do you plan to fill it up before you turn it in?"

"I'll return it full."

She *tap-tap-tapped* a final time on the computer. "This shows you plan to drop the vehicle at the Orlando airport, is that correct?"

"Yes, it is."

She looked up and smiled at him. "Then you're good to go, Mr. Martin. Here's your copy of the contract, the keys, and your car will be waiting in the parking lot outside in space number eighteen."

* * *

Will steered the little car onto Interstate 4 East, then onto Highway 528 and finally the turn-off to Orlando International. He followed the signs to the parking garage and drove inside. As usual, the lower levels were jam-packed. Will steered the vehicle around and around, eventually ending up on the top level, more than one hundred feet up. He sat there for a long time before climbing out.

Staying next to the car, Will sent out a message on his smartphone device.

Hello George, he tapped out on the tiny keyboard. *It has been a while since we've communicated. I wanted to reach out and say I'll look forward to getting together soon. Will Martin.*

Next he dialed a call, only to get a voicemail recording. "It's me. I just wanted to say hi," he spoke to the recorder. "We'll talk later."

He walked to the three-foot high barrier and paced back and forth several times. Worry lines appeared in his forehead, and his normally calm and inexpressive face looked panicked.

He removed his glasses and put them in his suitcoat

breast pocket. Then he took two steps and slipped over the wall.

The full weight of Will's body ripped through the fronds of an Areca palm tree and continued on down through some low-growing shrubbery, hitting solid ground full-force with a resounding thud.

Two travelers pulling their luggage behind them stood in horror for a moment, staring across the grounds at the unmoving body, then reactively sprinted toward it. One, a man wearing a Hawaiian shirt, shorts and sandals, stopped, retrieved his cellphone and dialed 9-1-1.

Within minutes, two patrol cars screeched to a stop at the scene. Officers dashed toward the site. In another few minutes, an ambulance arrived. Two EMTs scrambled out to retrieve a gurney from the back, while a third raced toward Will. A police officer who had been attempting CPR stepped away, shouting breathlessly, "I was getting a pulse."

An EMT retrieved Will's billfold and handed it to the officer. Then he and his partner slowly and carefully hoisted Will onto the gurney. The policeman riffled through the cards in Will's wallet.

After the ambulance drove off, its siren blaring, one of the police cruisers pulled away. The two remaining officers talked to the witnesses.

"It was no accident," the flowered-shirt traveler said. "I saw him pacing back and forth up there," he pointed. "I kept watching, because I couldn't figure out what the hell he was doing. Then he simply stepped over. The man was trying to kill himself."

"I saw it too," said the other witness. "It happened just like he said."

"Let me get your names and contact information,"

the policeman said. "In case we need to be in touch with you later. This area has surveillance cameras, so I imagine the tape will confirm what you're telling me." He turned toward his partner and handed him Will's billfold. "Phil, check out the guy's ID card and find out who to notify, okay?"

* * *

Inside the ambulance, the paramedic riding in the back strapped Will to a trauma board and placed him in a cervical collar to keep his neck and head in place.

He put his stethoscope to his ears and listened. "I'm still getting a weak pulse," he shouted to the two in front over the wail of the siren. "But he's not breathing." He hooked Will up to a ventilator. "Guys, I don't think he's going to make it."

At the hospital, the EMTs rushed the gurney into the emergency room entrance where hospital personnel took over.

Within minutes, the emergency room doctor pronounced Will Martin dead on arrival.

CHAPTER FIFTY-FIVE

I didn't get to play golf much anymore, only on a rare Saturday when someone from the club would call, needing to fill out a foursome. Or on the few occasions when my boys came to visit together. That's what I called my double-dip treat, in honor of my days as a kid when we would stop by Mr. Graham's ice cream factory to get a free cone.

But on this soft early spring day, when I got a call to join some friends, I was delighted. It was perfect weather, seventy and sunny, and we had a 12:30 tee time. After a quick lunch, we spent a delightful time hacking around the Strawberry Creek course. We finished at five, had a beer, and I went home a happy man.

Little did I know how dramatically my upbeat mood would change the minute I listened to my messages.

"Monty, this is Lawson Jeffries. I'm calling with some bad news. Please give me a call."

I returned his call immediately. "Lawson, it's Monty."

"Hello, Monty, how are you?"

"Sorry not to return your call sooner. I've been on the golf course. What's the bad news?"

"I imagine you've heard by now," he answered. "Will Martin is dead."

I sat there stunned. "No, Lawson, I hadn't heard. What happened?"

"He committed suicide, Monty."

He might as well have punched me in the gut, because the words knocked the breath right out of me. I sat down abruptly, unable to answer. Will was only sixty-four.

"Monty?"

"Yes," I said finally, "I'm still here. It's just so hard to believe. Do you know the details?"

"He jumped from the top of the Orlando airport parking garage. At first, they thought it was some kind of bizarre accident. But there were witnesses. They said he got out of a car up there, paced around a little and stepped over the wall. One of our newsroom guys brought me the news service dispatch. It said he was DOA."

"My Lord, I'm absolutely shell-shocked," I uttered. "And sorry for you. I know you guys were friends."

"I hadn't seen him since before Leavenworth," he said. "I don't know how you explain it. Will got on a roller coaster that climbed higher and higher, and when he ran out of options, I guess he decided there was only one way to get off."

"I don't think it's that simple," I said.

"He wasn't an evil person, Monty. Not the Will Martin I knew and worked with. He might have caused problems for a lot of people, but—and you're going to think this is crazy—I don't think he meant to. I think he couldn't help himself. When he went to prison, they say he signed a confession about how sorry he was he hurt people, and he would gladly work the rest of his life to make it up." He went on, "I saw a news story quoting the prosecutor, saying Will was a man of many talents who surrendered not to his intelligence but to greed. Do you think it's true, Monty?"

"Yes, I think that's it exactly."

.We promised to look each other up, stay in touch. I was pretty sure we wouldn't. People say, "Let's have lunch." They mean it, but life gets in the way.

I went out on the screened porch with a glass of

wine to wait for Sarah. She had been playing her regular weekly *mah-jongg* game at a neighbor's house. It was getting chilly. I pulled on my old sweater and watched the sun fading rapidly into dusk. A deer was helping itself to my recently planted vincas in the backyard until our golden retriever, Sparky, spotted it and chased it off. He stood watching proudly as it leapt the fence and disappeared into the woods.

Sparky then commenced his patrol of the backyard. He was a big boy. We had gotten him as a pup when Ella went over the rainbow bridge. We loved her to pieces and grieved miserably when she left us, she had brought us so much joy. But we accepted death is part of life, and this clumsy galoot helped us recover from our loss. Over the years, he grew into his big paws and took his place as her rightful successor.

When Sarah got home, she found me on the porch and put her hands on her hips. "Thank you, Mr. Johnson, for waiting for me."

I tried to grin but couldn't. "Go pour yourself one, honey. I have bad news."

When she returned and I told her, both hands went up to her mouth in horror, and then she cried.

"That poor man," she said finally, her head on my shoulder. "He had such a tragic life. Three siblings dying at birth when he was growing up. Two failed marriages and another ending in a bizarre death. A son killed in an auto accident. Scandals, lawsuits, three years in prison. The sheer weight of all of those tragedies…" Her voice trailed off.

Sparky was now romping around the edge of the tree line on the back of our property. "Look at the big old clod-hopper. What's he up to?" I asked.

"There are critters out there in the trees. He's starting to age, but his nose is still young. It's like you old men at the mall who look at young girls with your twenty-five-year-old brains."

"Who does that?"

"I didn't mean you. It's those other men."

We sat and smiled together. Finally, I said, "I don't know, honey. Who can say what makes someone like Will tick, let alone what makes him give up? You could be right, all the tragedies in his life became too much to bear. Maybe this stock market crash wiped him out. Or, there could have been some new scandal or another crushing lawsuit brewing nobody knows about.

"But I think he simply became someone else from the nice, innocent kid I knew in the neighborhood, or the admirable young man who worked for Dad and me. It's like Dwight said the day he came and played golf on my birthday. He told me about a restaurant in New York with a sign saying, 'Where Too Much Ain't Enough.'" I took a sip of wine, remembering, then said, "It's a sin, you know."

"What is?" Sarah asked.

"Greed."

"If it is, Will Martin paid dearly for it," she said with true sadness in her voice. She stood up. "Do you think you should call Coach Slay?"

I replied, "Yes, I will in the morning."

Sarah stretched and said, "I'd better go in and get dinner on the table or you'll divorce me."

That brought a small chortle out of me. "You say it every day. Maybe sometime I'll do it."

"What? Divorce me?"

"No, not come in for dinner."

"Ha. Not a chance." She bent over, kissed me and disappeared into the house.

"Sparky."

He stopped hunting, raised his head, listened.

"Dinner," I called out. It was one of the eighty or ninety words in his vocabulary. And his favorite. The big boy came galloping, shoulders rippling, tongue hanging, oozing respect, love and hunger all in one happy expression.

As I watched him lumber toward the house, I whispered a quiet prayer of thanks for everything I had.

The End

Acknowledgements

My sincere gratitude to advance readers Pamela Sammons, John Staton, Sammy Kirkendoll and Nicole Valek, for your valuable input and candor; to the afore-mentioned Pamela Sanders for being there to listen, for your encouragement, unending support and intelligent ideas; to Valerie Clark, writing coach extraordinaire, film-maker and author, for your wise counsel; to Coach Ron Slaymaker for your contributions to the story; to Monica for your tenacious proof-reading, and to my new friends at Waldorf Publishing LLC for working so hard to bring this book to the public. And special thanks to the late Dr. Green Wyrick and author Ann Arensberg, who encouraged me to write when I needed it most.

About the Author

Donald Reichardt is co-author of The Grace Gleason Files, a trilogy of crime thrillers inspired by true events: *Justice On Hold*, *The Blue Wall* (a 2016 finalist in the Next Generation Indie Book Awards), and *Unholy Mind Games*. Donald is also author of an anthology of short fiction, *Corporate Lies and Other Stories*. Three of the stories were finalists in Byline magazine's national competition.

Donald is a graduate of Emporia (Kansas) State University. While completing an English education degree with a journalism specialty, he was sports editor, associate editor and editor of the campus newspaper, *The Bulletin*. During college, he was a part-time sportswriter for the city's daily, *The Emporia Gazette*. While a graduate student, he was assistant to the publisher and columnist for the weekly *Emporia Times*.

After several years of teaching and writing for newspapers, he launched a public relations and marketing career with the Southwestern Bell Company, where he edited two employee newspapers and later created and directed the company's news management department. He moved to AT&T in New York as a member of the executive speechwriting team.

Later he was named director of corporate communications for South Central Bell and then head of public relations, public affairs and advertising for Southern Bell. In 1988 he created the BellSouth Corporation's first companywide advertising department, was named executive director-advertising and brand management and then executive director for BellSouth's 1996 Olympic Games marketing and sponsorship programs.

Donald has written speeches and policy correspondence for Fortune Fifty CEOs and many other senior officers. While at BellSouth, Donald served on the National Advertising Review Board, was a member of the Association of National Advertisers management committee and served on the board of the American Advertising Federation Foundation.

An accredited (APR) member of the Public Relations Society of America (PRSA), Donald was president of the Alabama and Georgia chapters and was the Southeast District chair. He was elected to the national PRSA College of Fellows and to the Georgia Public Relations Hall of Fame.

He left corporate life to consult and write, counseling clients in strategic planning, marketing and public relations and writing more than 60 by-lined articles for business newspapers and magazines, most frequently for the American City Business Journal network (more than 40 publications) and the *Atlanta Business Chronicle*.

For four years he represented the Advertising Council as its outreach partner in the major Southeast television and radio markets. He wrote strategic plans pro bono for four non-profits. He lectured on screenwriting at the American Intercontinental University's English classes in Atlanta.

In 2011, Reichardt received Emporia State University's Distinguished Alumni Award, the highest honor given to ESU graduates. The Donald Reichardt Center for Publishing and Literary Arts was opened in 2014 at the university and is the center for its creative writing activities.

CPSIA information can be obtained
at www.ICGtesting.com
Printed in the USA
LVHW090136180921
698069LV00001B/2

9 781636 848402